T0246260

Wuhan

WUHAN
A Documentary Novel

Liao Yiwu

Translated by Michael Martin Day

polity

Originally published as 當武漢病毒來臨 *Dāng Wǔhàn bìngdú láilín* (When the Wuhan Virus Comes) by 允晨文化 Yunchen Wenhua/Asian Culture, Taiwan. Copyright © 廖亦武 (Liao Yiwu) 2020, 2021. All rights reserved by S. Fischer Verlag GmbH, Frankfurt am Main.

This English edition © Polity Press, 2024

Polity Press
65 Bridge Street
Cambridge CB2 1UR, UK

Polity Press
111 River Street
Hoboken, NJ 07030, USA

ISBN-13: 978-1-5095-6299-2 – hardback

A catalogue record for this book is available from the British Library.

Library of Congress Control Number: 2023947106

Typeset in 11.5 on 14pt Bell MT
by Cheshire Typesetting Ltd, Cuddington, Cheshire
Printed and bound in Great Britain by CPI Group (UK) Ltd, Croydon

The publisher has used its best endeavours to ensure that the URLs for external websites referred to in this book are correct and active at the time of going to press. However, the publisher has no responsibility for the websites and can make no guarantee that a site will remain live or that the content is or will remain appropriate.

Every effort has been made to trace all copyright holders, but if any have been overlooked the publisher will be pleased to include any necessary credits in any subsequent reprint or edition.

For further information on Polity, visit our website:
politybooks.com

Contents

Contents

To the Reader

"Wuhan virus" is not a political term, but rather an objective description of the truth: Wuhan is the birthplace of the powerful virus that is harming the world today; or one could say: this virus was first discovered in Wuhan, and "Wuhan virus" is of the same nature as terms such as "Chernobyl nuclear leak," "Fukushima nuclear disaster," and "Ebola virus" (after the Ebola River in West Africa). The World Health Organization (WHO) designation of "Coronavirus disease 2019" (abbreviation: COVID-19) is an ambiguous one, a product of compromise. It deliberately avoids naming the origin of the virus, just as the SARS outbreak in China in 2003 also avoided naming the origin of the virus, and as a result most Chinese later forgot that the first SARS patient was discovered in Foshan, Guangdong Province.

For a time, the term "Wuhan pneumonia" was used by the local authorities in Wuhan, but this was later strictly banned by the Central Committee of the Communist Party of China (CCP), which then took advantage of the pandemic to set off a wave of nationalism and xenophobia. The CCP also pushed countries all over the world to follow the WHO and refer to the "Wuhan virus" as "COVID-19," which will also facilitate the falsification of history in the coming years. (This is what the Communist Party does best.) Maybe, after several years of ideological propaganda, the vast majority of Chinese people will only know that COVID-19 came to China from the United States, and that Wuhan was the first Chinese city to be infected – just as when describing the 1959–62 Great Famine in China, in which nearly forty million people starved to death, the official textbooks declare: "Under the leadership of Chairman Mao and the Communist Party, we defeated the three years of natural disasters caused by Soviet revisionism." This also corroborates the brainwashing dictum of Oceania in Orwell's 1984: "Who controls the past controls the future: who controls the present controls the past."*

* An asterisk indicates an explanatory note at the end of the volume.

Prelude

The Intruder

On February 26, 2020, twenty-five-year-old Kcriss* wakes up very early. As usual, he wraps himself in armor-like protective clothing, puts on his face mask and goggles, and looks off into the distance, like an astronaut on the moon.

He creeps downstairs, maneuvers into his car, and drives away. Taking a deep breath, he tells himself to be very careful, because today he'll penetrate Wuhan's super-sensitive P4 laboratory to attempt to solve the mystery of the Wuhan virus leak.

Kcriss wants to do it, so he's doing it, regardless of the dangers involved. The city of Wuhan has been sealed off for more than a month. The sun shines along the way, the air is fresh, but there's no life, nothing – the traffic lights are still working but the traffic police aren't. After a fast drive, he arrives at Zhengdian Park, Wuhan Institute of Virology, Chinese Academy of Sciences. The P4 laboratory is in here and, as expected, it's become a restricted military area, a large zone sealed as tight as an iron drum. He's ordered to stop for inspection by two blue-clad figures carrying guns. Fortunately, all his documents are in order and his temperature is normal. Kcriss tells them he's just passing by, and immediately reverses his car as ordered, not daring to utter the term "P4."

Kcriss is frustrated, but unwilling to give up, he drives around the periphery of the giant iron drum. He looks around from time to time, pretending to be lost, but actually looking for a way in.

No luck. The weather's excellent, visibility is good, but the area is awfully desolate, there are no signs of life. Winter is not quite done. Several patches of man-made forest, appearing like psoriasis scabs on earth scratched by fingernails, show only brittle branches and dead leaves, and no trace of people, dogs, cats, or birds.

Kcriss parks his car in an alley, a short distance from a three-way junction leading to the highway behind him. In front, all the buildings are no more than three floors high, only the P4 laboratory – a cylinder attached to a larger rectangle – towers aloft into the sky, reminding him of the outer shell of the Chernobyl nuclear power plant. The nuclear radiation from Chernobyl was thought to be enough to kill off the entire European subcontinent within a few months. Tens of thousands of workers immediately descended upon the site when it began to melt down in April 1986, casting an incomparably huge shield to seal the ruins of the plant forever, as if closing Pandora's box. But now, with what is, potentially, an opening of a similar box, the Wuhan virus has rushed out into China and spread beyond to every corner of the world, where every day the numbers of the dead rise. Can this Pandora's box be closed again?

Kcriss has nothing to do but stay in the car and go online to watch Chai Jing's scathing documentary about air pollution, *Under the Dome*, on YouTube. He's seen it many times but still feels euphoric whenever he watches it. Time passes, and, oblivious, he gradually forgets where he is, also forgetting he lives in a police state.

A few dozen yards away at a third-floor window, several Domestic Security officers have been staring at his car. Initially, they think this is a contact point, and that a hidden agent will furtively appear, handing Kcriss a pile of information, but the plot they hope for does not unfold. Security Team leader Zhao murmurs, "Two going on three hours watching you in your car. You planning to spend the night here?" He beckons and asks his assistant Li to fiddle on the computer. Engrossed in Kcriss's every move in the car as if it were a movie, Zhao says, "Zoom in closer. Hey, he's pretty much acting the part of an operative of some sort. You can watch that long film about smog anywhere, instead he's sitting in his car watching it here near the P4 lab. Something's definitely up with this."

The Skynet surveillance system has been in place across China for a few years already, so all Li has to do is click on the mouse and the hidden cameras on either side of the alley scan up and down, left and right. Two, then four split screens appear on the computer monitor. Eyes, nose, mouth, close-ups one after another. Kcriss's pores are enlarged. "The corners of his mouth are foaming," Li says, "he must be really lit. Such a handsome guy and he's not out chasing girls – he must be gay."

"You don't know shit," Zhao says. Then he signals everyone else in the room to gather round. Seven heads come together, zeroing in on the computer screen. One fat guy, Zhou, pipes up: "Team Leader Zhao, it's been long enough. Bring him in."

"Yes, take him back to the bureau and deal with him there," Li agrees.

"Still more shit," Zhao frowns. "You think he's a local undercover filmmaker, like Fang Bin? That it doesn't matter if we grab him and release him and a little footage ends up on the Internet?"

"What are you saying?" Li responds.

"Look at this guy's equipment: off-road Volkswagen, top-grade protective clothing, large-screen mobile phone with a high-definition camera, his gestures and movements. How does this compare to mere undercover filmmakers? Sure, they're all working against the Party Central Committee, but Fang Bin pedaled a broken bicycle, and Chen Qiushi rode an old motorbike, the video they shot had no outdoor scenes . . . But this is outdoors. That guy Fang Bin filmed in a hospital, and the camerawork was straight and horizontal, like a corpse. He repeated the line 'eight more dead' at least eight times.

"With all this gear, it seems this Kcriss has some support. He's been a moderator on both Phoenix TV and China Central TV [CCTV], and then he had the balls to resign! With that temperament he's definitely a second-, third-, or some other generation descendant of Communist Party leadership. Just in case . . . in case he's come down from above, from one power clique or another. I don't know. Too many people are dead this time, there's never been so many, nobody can take on that responsibility . . . Enough bullshitting. We're Domestic Security here. It stands to reason that to ensure the restricted access to P4, any intruder can be picked up. But this handsome guy, let the National Security Bureau handle it."

Zhao dials the phone of the local director of the National Security Bureau and exchanges a few words. The director says there's not enough manpower, and National Security is a "hidden battlefront" anyway, always staying behind the scenes. They'd try their best to provide a thorough background on Kcriss and his hazard level. However, according to standard cooperating procedures, it'll still be necessary for Domestic Security to act on the matter. Zhao declares that won't do, that he's a person within their purview. It's time for the "hidden battlefront" to surface.

Domestic Security are experts at catching people, moving faster than lightning when necessary. Before the discovery of Kcriss, there were the two previous "citizen reporters," Chen Qiushi and Fang Bin, who both managed to broadcast the Wuhan epidemic through social media. The first didn't have time to leave evidence of his arrest, it simply evaporated, causing Chen's mother to jump the Great Chinese Firewall, posting a "missing-person" notice every day; while the latter simply shouted "I've no fever, I don't need you to isolate me," repeatedly, from behind an iron grille and door, until they smashed them in and he was quickly pushed to the ground – the usual rough stuff at which National Security agents, with their higher education, are naturally inferior. As everyone knows, their strengths are in the high-tech field or "infiltrating the enemy" – so today, with a potential intrusion at P4, when the director of the local branch of the National Security Bureau commands agent Ding Jian to take two others with him to perform official duties, he also instructs them not to use a police car with the National Security emblem on it.

After a slight hesitation, Ding Jian takes his people down to the garage, finds a white off-road vehicle, and drives it out himself. By this time, Kcriss has been settled in his car for a few hours, his bottled water already finished. Still thirsty, with nothing around, he decides to go buy some water outside the P4 area. To his surprise, as his car exits the alley, Ding Jian's vehicle is backing up towards him on the one-way street. Kcriss thinks it's violating traffic laws, trying to cut corners by turning into the alley. But then the unmarked car skids to a stop, blocking the road.

With both feet, Kcriss smashes down on the brakes and two plumes of green smoke spew from his tires, his car screeching to a halt inches from the other vehicle. He reacts quickly, crunching the gears into reverse, back into the alley, speeding the wrong direction toward the other end. Terrified, and clocking about 200 kilometers per hour, Kcriss continues for quite a long while before finally exploding into the correct lane of a proper road. That his path is clear is pure negligence on the National Security agents' part. Had it been Domestic Security, another car would have been blocking the other end of the alley. But still, Kcriss hasn't been able to shake the vehicle chasing him, the National Security car's loudspeaker blaring "Stop immediately! We order you to stop immediately!" all the while.

Apart from this frenzied pursuit, the road that seems to lead to freedom is endless and features no signs of life. The drooping red sun slowly sets on the endless procession of lifeless buildings. Once upon a time, the hundreds of square miles of the Jianghan Plain were full of vehicles and people, boats and goods. Wuhan, famous historically, has been the largest and most important water and land transportation hub in China since ancient times. On the map, it's at the center of the heartland of China, with transportation routes extending in all directions like capillaries, intertwined, pulsating, flowing, like the blood in God's palm. The Beijing–Canton Railway and the Yangtze River are like two major arteries, enabling the societal operations of this authoritarian empire. In 1966, the seventy-three-year-old monster Mao Zedong orchestrated the death of Liu Shaoqi, then the president of the country, and unleased the catastrophic Cultural Revolution upon hundreds of millions of Chinese people. He chose Wuhan as its launchpad and had himself drifted a few miles in the water of the Yangtze before coming ashore here, where ten years earlier, in 1956, he'd written these lines of poetry: "I have just drunk the waters of Changsha/ And come to eat the fish of Wuchang" . . . and two lines he'd written as a boy in 1917: "Confident of a life for two hundred years, I'll swim for three thousand miles." The swim caused a sensation, and the local *Red Guards Battle News* erroneously reported that the latest scientific test results showed that the physical health of Mao, the reddest of the reddest red suns among the world's people, could be maintained for at least a hundred and fifty to two hundred years . . .

Today, this and a number of similar Wuhan myths have blown away with the wind; instead, the opposite, myths of truth, like the underground "grapevine news" of the Cultural Revolution, spread among the people. One such example: the P4 team extracted the SARS virus from a bat, and after cooling treatment and by way of an "intermediary host," this new coronavirus was spawned using "artificial intelligence." Infected patients have no fever and no cough at the start, then there is a slight fever and cough, and it's not until later that breathlessness rises and falls suddenly like the crest of a wave, before falling to the bottom of the valley of death in the blink of an eye. Another myth of truth that has arisen on Chinese-language websites overseas is that the "Wuhan virus" is the "ultimate biochemical weapon" for dictatorship to defeat democracy. Originally, it's said the first target was a recalcitrant Hong Kong, but like the Chernobyl nuclear disaster in the former Soviet Union, there was an accidental leak and uncontrolled proliferation due to loopholes in the bureaucratic system. This was followed by suppression of "rumors" about the disease in the name of national interests, deceiving the public, and losing the opportunity to quickly close the Pandora's box, so that the initial plan to seal off Hong Kong and put it under martial law instead became the fate of Wuhan.

Wide-eyed Kcriss has also heard all kinds of P4 rumors. Because Wuhan is sealed off, the P4 within its borders has become a politically taboo topic many Wuhan people suspect in their hearts but dare not voice out loud. Kcriss truly cares little about life and death, just as on the early morning of June 4 over thirty years before, a poet named Liao Yiwu wrote "Massacre"* with the gunfire and screams of the Tiananmen massacre still echoing in his ears ... the subsequent pursuit and imprisonment were inevitable, but, fuck it, how could he repress the righteous recklessness of his youth! So now, in an SOS distress video lasting just over thirty seconds, with a car nearly taking flight and white-knuckled hands about to lose control of the steering wheel, Kcriss testifies: "I'm on the road, I'm now being chased by National Security in a car that isn't a police car . . . I'm in Wuhan, I'm driving fast, very fast, they're chasing me, they must want to isolate me . . ."

Then he speeds up onto an overpass, slows a bit, and the vehicle behind comes upon him, scraping his car as it does. He flicks the steering wheel to the left, like in a spy movie, as the other car falls back. He steps on the gas, desperate.

Kcriss finally escapes into a parking garage beneath his apartment building, the electronic barrier coming down just behind his car as he speeds in and as the National Security car arrives. If it had been Domestic Security, they'd have smashed through the barrier. But National Security, who are slightly better educated, brake and call a security guard. This is a high-end residential area, the garage is very large, but due to the strict closure of the city, the power has been shut off for several days. Kcriss doesn't dare turn on his car lights even though he can't see his fingers in front of his face. Relying on his memory of the garage, he spends a while cruising around for a parking space in what is now a dormant beehive of vehicles. At the moment he shuts off his engine, the National Security vehicle drives by with its head lights on high beam. He lies down on the front seat and holds his breath. The National Security vehicle slows down, its headlights sweeping from left to right over his car, across his windows. It passes by and, like a weasel, Kcriss slips out of his car and lithely moves toward the elevator door, opening it with the induction card on his key. The elevator lights up and the National Security agents rush over.

Kcriss is now a couple of minutes ahead of the security agents as he sprints upstairs into his apartment and locks its very solid door behind him. Like a mouse forced into a hole by a cat's claws, he dare not turn on the lights or take off his protective clothing, even though he's soaked through with sweat. Instinctively, he turns on his computer, aims its camera at the door, and in the pitch-black darkness where there might be an explosion at any moment, the livestream begins . . .

Boom boom, boom, boom boom boom – incessant pounding on the door. Kcriss stands for a while by the door, then creeps to the other end of the room. *Boom boom, boom, boom boom boom* – the pounding continues unabated. Kcriss moves into an inner room, like a ghost, shrinking into a corner. At that moment, there are over eight hundred domestic netizens, also known as "the melon-eating masses," who've jumped the Great Chinese Firewall and are now peering back into Kcriss's apartment in Wuhan, commenting on his dark screen on YouTube:

– *Open the door, I'm here to check the water meter.*
– *What's happening in there? Even if you don't turn on the lights, we know you're there.*
– *It makes no sense to keep the lights off. With so many surveillance cameras, where can you hide?*
– *Everyone can see your bravery!!! You'll encourage more of the 80s and 90s generations to come forward!*
– *Turn on the lights, it makes no sense to have the lights off like this. They know you're at home, whether you turn the lights on or not, so it'd be better to turn them on and say something.*
– *This broadcaster is a post-90s guy who works in the media and used to be an entertainment program host on CCTV. He would have had a promising future but spreading the truth about Wuhan's heavily infected areas is truly commendable! Please everybody, follow him and help him!*
– *Turn on the monitor and hide the camera a little further away – if they catch you, you'll get it all on camera. Eat some bread or something first, so you'll have strength to resist.*
– *This is how it is in the celestial empire.*

– *CCTV? Damn.*

– *Are the cockroaches still outside the door? You won't fall into this trap again if you throw yourself down into the street.*

– *Seriously, you should be prepared for anything, but it's not a big deal. If you escape, you'll be on fire on YouTube, and if you can't escape, you'll be on fire in the foreign media. Today I saw Chen Qiushi's video in the Japanese news. Part of the reason why this is happening to you is because of him. He'll support you tomorrow, or else he'll regret not mentioning you! He has 270,000 followers all over the world, and they can certainly do more than the few thousand of us here. First, get a good night's sleep and prepare for the fire. I personally hope you only catch fire on YouTube.*

– *Dress up as a god and play the devil, mobilize public opinion, really make a public figure of yourself! And if National Security catches someone like you? What do you care about security agents! Yesterday you're chased by them, today your apartment searched, tomorrow who knows where the story leads?*

– *Isn't it exciting? What are you afraid of? Take it all on! You used to be cocky and all full of yourself, but a coward all along? What're you doing wearing a mask?? What are you truly afraid of??*

– *Go home, don't cause trouble. Who knows how a mental retard like you will die.*

– *Get out of the waters you've stirred up, quick!*

– *Please don't worry, at most all they want is to talk with you. Don't be so suspicious, okay?*

– *Think about whether it's worth it, there are so many scumbags here.*

– *Safety is what matters most, so stop broadcasting.*

– *I also work in the media. If I didn't have a wife and child, maybe I'd be with you. #Ashamed.*

– *Stop being silly . . . think about how to get out of this wolf's den.*

– *Don't be afraid, they won't do anything to you.*

– *Brother, cheer up, stay strong, express what you want to express.*

– *Safety first, brother, stop broadcasting.*

– *Don't frighten yourself, your video has nothing sensitive in it, at most they'll just ask you to tea to warn you that you're illegally over the firewall.*

– *Don't be discouraged, lad.*

– *Get a move on and leave China forever.*

– *If you can't escape, just sit down and talk. Or are you angling for political asylum, acting in a play you're directing yourself?*

– *Enough of the sarcasm here everybody! Hurry up and contact all the bigwigs you know.*

– *You must stay calm, otherwise you'll be dragged to some pop-up hospital, and it'll be tragic if you get infected. The people there will not save you . . .*

– *The security agents aren't so insistent at the door now, maybe awaiting instructions from superiors, and they are almost certainly watching the live broadcast. But they'll definitely cut the power and Internet when they attack again. So, you've got to make a plan ahead of time, think about countermeasures. Otherwise, take advantage of the time lag between now and when they receive exact orders, wipe all the information they might be looking for and take the initiative to open the door and ask them why they've come? Anyway, it'll be contained, all out in the open, better than the silence once the power and the Internet are cut . . .*

– *Chen Qiushi, Fang Bin, Kcriss . . . nobody knows who the next to be "isolated" will be. If sharp criticism were to completely disappear, mild criticism would seem harsh; if mild criticism were also not allowed, silence would be seen as having ulterior motives; and if even silence is no longer allowed, it will become a crime if it were not praised enough; and if only one voice is allowed to exist, then that sole voice must be a lie.*

Distracted, Kcriss quickly scrolls down through the messages. His mobile phone is also vibrating constantly. He picks it up and puts it to his ear. It's a local friend who's helped him and has already fallen into the hands of National Security. "They know you're inside and can't escape. Open the door, okay?"

He cuts off the call, but his friend phones again. "Please, Kcriss, I've a wife and child . . ."

He sighs and stays on the line but puts the phone aside. He takes off his mask, strips off his protective clothing, lies down for a few moments, and then sits in front of the dark screen of the computer. As memories of the past flood over him, he can't help crying.

At this moment in Berlin, thousands of miles away, an exiled writer named Zhuangzi Gui is also staring at Kcriss's live dark screen, unbeknownst to him, and, like all the "melon-eating masses," he can't resist writing a message:

> *The story of Kcriss is tragic and inspiring. This land of our ancestors, this hometown that has been mentioned countless times in our ancient texts, is the dream of my father's generation and not the Communist Party's, nor that of atheistic boors like Mao Zedong and Xi Jinping.*
>
> *If twenty-five-year-old Kcriss still has the courage to create and smash an egg against the stubborn stone of dictatorship, what reason have we to despair?*
>
> *We want to seize back the homelands and hometowns deep in everyone's heart, regain our normal everyday anger, compassion, and love, reclaim our ordinary human nature and temperament, and recapture the appreciation of beauty that has left our hearts beating in anticipation countless times, like the hermit-poet Tao Yuanming over 1,500 years ago sighing in a poem over Jing Ke, the would-be assassin of the first emperor of the Qin Dynasty six hundred years earlier: "A gentleman will die for one who knows his worth;/ With sword in hand I leave the capital of Yan," . . .*
>
> *I say thank you to this Kcriss, born in 1995, the hope of China's future is in you.*

After sending his message, Zhuangzi Gui does an Internet search on "Kcriss" and is startled by what he finds: it turns out that this handsome twenty-five-year-old graduated from the Communication University of China and was promptly hired as the host of CCTV's *Fashion Carousel*, where he became a big star with millions of social media followers. He often traveled to various parts of the country, setting trends in food and tourism. He could be seen squatting in the desert eating grilled meat, or standing on a boat fishing: "Wow, this is the first time I've held such a big fish." "Wow, chicken grilled with watermelon, I'll eat the soup first . . ."

Zhuangzi Gui feels this doesn't sit right with Kcriss's role as an "intruder," so he switches over and watches the young man's "Disobedience TV," a personal channel he founded on YouTube after he resigned from CCTV in 2018. The essence of the title was that he refused to comply with CCTV, as evident in his opening remarks for his first vlog: "Yo! Hello everyone, my name is Kcriss, just call me Kcriss. . . .The most important title I seek is to become the number one vlogger in China." Next, he performed some rap, hip-hop, and backflips, and showed some film of himself traveling around the world on a motorcycle. He also put on sunglasses and imitated his idol, the American vlogger and filmmaker Casey Neistat. On the wall behind him were posters of the American singer Bruno Mars and Apple founder Steve Jobs.

A WeChat message changed Kcriss's life.

On New Year's Eve 2020, like hundreds of millions of other Chinese, he is watching the Chinese New Year Gala on CCTV. This year's theme is "Coming Together to Fight Pneumonia." Then Kcriss's phone vibrates:

> *The doctors at Jinyintan Hospital haven't eaten a thing all day, and now have solicited food donations from our association. Can you believe this? I really can't believe it, but I have to believe it. I only know that at this moment doctors don't have any new protective clothing, so they don't eat all day because they don't dare take off their protective clothes as they won't have clean ones to put back on. Now our association is contacting the hospital and preparing to send over convenience foods – how is this a suitable atmosphere for watching the Spring Festival Gala! Outsiders have absolutely no way of understanding the despair in Wuhan at this moment. Patients are dying on the floor without being treated because all the supplies are running out. Watching the shouting of those slogans on TV news feels ridiculous. What's next? Everyone will have to rely on themselves! Only themselves! The only thing this great nation is capable of mobilizing effectively is a variety show . . .*

A sense of shame wells up in Kcriss and he immediately decides to go to Wuhan to get to the bottom of things.

First he calls his father, seeking support, but to no avail. So, he goes online and invites some former classmates from the

Communication University to join him, proposing to organize an epidemic investigation team, but few respond. Eventually two decide to participate. Confucius says: "If one travels in threes, one will surely teach me something," so Kcriss is secretly pleased with this.

However, a few days before his departure from Beijing, one of his prospective teammates is locked into his twentieth-story bedroom by his ever-vigilant parents, who take shifts guarding him, refusing all negotiations; while the other sends a message saying that upon his return from a vacation in Indonesia, it was discovered he'd had contact with people from Wuhan while abroad and he was immediately isolated. And, so, in two days, Kcriss suffers two setbacks. Feeling frustrated, he decides to soldier on and shoulder the risk alone.

The atmosphere in Beijing is also quite tense, with the government banning all gatherings and closing all meeting places, and access to residential areas is based on an "entry pass" system that limits the time and the people one can see. Despite this, Kcriss manages to visit with one Wuhan native who'd arrived in Beijing a generation before him. The two meet at the entrance gate to his apartment complex. Kcriss has his temperature taken and is sprayed with disinfectant before they are escorted to an elevator by a security guard. They go up to the twenty-fourth floor, enter the apartment, take off their masks, and wash their hands with disinfectant. His acquaintance's wife makes tea, and they sit down. The older Wuhan native cuts straight to the point: "I think it's dangerous for you to go now, and it doesn't make much sense."

"Why?"

"It won't be long before Beijing becomes Wuhan, before all cities in China become Wuhan, all following the same path to lockdown. You might as well stay here, as you can do the same thing in Beijing as you would in Wuhan."

"But Beijing is not the source, Wuhan is."

"Wuhan is also not the source. It's like the Yangtze River with its origin in the vicinity of Geladaindong Peak on the Tibetan Plateau. But the real source is just a small puddle. Can you find that puddle?"

"I'll go and I'll try. Current information indicates the earliest patient came from the wildlife trade stall area of the South China Seafood Wholesale Market."

"It's sealed off. No clues to be found there."

"I'll try."

"Don't try!" the older man flatly says. "If you must go, act as an ordinary volunteer, try to help others as much as possible, and then take some not-too-sensitive videos along the way, so you can protect yourself and not cause trouble for others."

Kcriss is silent, but his heart is on fire. He thinks of the Czech writer Milan Kundera in *The Unbearable Lightness of Being* describing the decisive moment for the protagonist Thomas, when after the Prague Spring of 1968 is suppressed by Soviet tanks and he goes into exile in France, with his lover Trisha remaining in Prague, he ignores his friends' dissuasion, returning from Paris to her side and loses his freedom forever. No matter the age of the novel, Kcriss feels he's in exactly the same situation, and at this moment, the truth is his Trisha and the city of Wuhan is his Prague.

The older man seemingly reads his mind and sighs: "Wuhan is much more terrifying than you can imagine. The officially publicized numbers of the diagnosed and dead are only a small part of the actual number. Many people have been infected but cannot get a diagnosis – even those with symptoms – let alone treatment. The hospitals are overcrowded, people can't get a bed. Even if there is one, there's no effective medicine, so how can a doctor treat the disease? There's an acute shortage of materials, so what is there to treat it with? As a result, neither the officials nor ordinary people are sure of what's going on. Every person you walk past might be asymptomatic or symptomatic, it's just too dangerous! So, if you want to go, you must try to keep a distance from everyone. You'll need a contingency plan in case you're infected or suddenly have respiratory problems. You must bring enough of your own supplies: protective clothing, goggles, and even a helmet, things you'll definitely find are not available in Wuhan. In addition, ethyl alcohol, disinfectant, and masks are all basics you'll need to take. Also, how are you going to get into Wuhan?

Someone will have to meet you, otherwise you'll be in the dark, without transportation, no idea where to live . . ."

When Kcriss leaves the home of the older Wuhan man, it's getting late and fire-red clouds cover most of the sky. Kcriss never returns to his own home in Beijing. Instead, he drives straight to the expressway to the south, traveling across half of China to Changsha in a day and a night. There, while waiting for a local friend by the side of a road, he crosses over the Internet wall to an overseas website and the first thing he sees is: "Why hasn't Big Xi gone to Wuhan?" The answer is that his confidant, Cai Qi, secretary of the Beijing Municipal Committee, had the misfortune of contracting the Wuhan pneumonia while inspecting Beijing's Xicheng District Health Department. And as the slightly feverish Cai Qi reported to Big Xi, even China's Emperor of the Moment became a suspected carrier and had to be isolated in his residence in Beijing's Zhongnanhai District. Kcriss has a good laugh about this and the weariness of his long journey suddenly vanishes.

His Changsha friend meets him carrying the news that all roads to Wuhan have been closed. And on midnight that day, February 12, the railway will also be shut down. The last high-speed train through Wuhan that will pass through Changsha that afternoon is all that is left. So, Kcriss immediately rushes to the Changsha South Station, where his friend advises him to buy a ticket for the stop after Wuhan, to avoid attracting attention.

Kcriss entrusts his car to his friend and, shouldering a large bag and dragging a suitcase, climbs up into a lightly populated carriage. He pulls out his smartphone and starts to make his first video. In it, he states he's been to North Korea, a place haunted by ghosts in broad daylight, where he took a lot of film openly as well as some sneak shots. He guessed that working for CCTV offered him cover as the subjects of Fat Kim the Third* didn't take any action against him . . . but this time it's different.

He arrives at Wuhan Railway Station after dark, passing through a passageway and the great hall, usually bustling with activity, but empty today. Kcriss walks behind two local travelers, teasing their children in the Wuhan dialect as he does so. He's met by a friend outside the station, where they get in a van and his friend's wife gives him some masks and disinfectant, despite their scarcity. Kcriss is very moved, and asks offhandedly if there have been deliveries of materials donated from various places in China. His friend responds: "What donations? During this epidemic, prices have soared, there's been nothing that hasn't cost money." Kcriss says, "That doesn't sound right. The Chinese Red Cross receives large amounts of medical and other critical supplies every day, and they should be distributing them to residents of various communities for free, according to the regulations." His friend replies, "From SARS in 2003 to the Sichuan earthquakes in 2008 until now, official agencies have never failed to collect money. Whatever's given to the Red Cross is flipped and the price doubles. Grab feathers off a flying goose as it passes, if you know what I mean." Kcriss responds, "I understand. But even migrating geese should be stopped in flight, confronted, and made to pay for their passage. If the geese disagree, bring them down, pluck them, and make them into soup." His friend laughs and says, "Your explanation's very graphic. So, why," he asks, "is the transliterated name of the WHO Director-General Tedros Adhanom Ghebreyesus '*Tan Desai*'?" Kcriss tells him, "'*Tan*' is a homonym for wine jar, '*dé*' means 'morality,' '*sai*' means 'plug' or 'clogged,' so the full meaning of the name is 'soaked in a wine jar all day, sense of morality blocked.'" His friend laughs loudly and says, "This African wino really has no sense of morality, just like the organization he heads. Together with the Chinese Red Cross, both institutions are drunk, like the Communist Party branch secretary who Big Xi dispatched to Wuhan, every day bragging about the great power of the government's efforts to control the epidemic, especially the miraculous Chinese medicine antiviral drug Double Goldthread (*Coptis Chinensis*). I think it was the day before yesterday that Director-General Tedros was summoned by Big Xi, and his wallet and his balls were suddenly bulging afterwards. So much so that he's learned to use Old Mao's motto 'a single spark can ignite a prairie fire' to describe the spread of the Wuhan virus outside of China, duping everyone into continuing donations to Beijing . . ."

Everybody knows this type of humor is born out of bitterness, a characteristic of many cultures. Just like the the German joke in which a man asks for a song from an Iraqi refugee singer who's lost his family, and after the Iraqi has sung his heart out, the German's face goes blank and he says: "I asked you to sing, so why are you crying all the time?"

———

His friends take Kcriss to the check-in desk at a building that claims to be a guesthouse and say their goodbyes. He feels the building is too empty; he walks a few feet in the corridor and hears the echo of his footsteps in the distance. His predecessor Chen Qiushi had also come to Wuhan as a "citizen reporter" and had lived in a different building nearby. Chen was still broadcasting live from his room the night before he was arrested. At the end, he had croaked, "I am not even afraid of death. You think I'm afraid of your Communist Party??" – It was destiny.

Kcriss's first live program features the high-speed rail and the sealed city, both inside and out, a sky alternating between light and darkness, and the Software Engineering Vocational College school building where school bags and textbooks are piled up after the district government aggressively requisitioned it for the Wuhan Pneumonia Mild Case Isolation Zone. But his anchor room is the same type as Chen Qiushi's: a bedroom from where he broadcasts sitting on a bed. However, Kcriss's camera shots, depth of field, and sound processing are all quite professional. He starts to record:

In the Internet era, the dissemination of information is no longer restricted by spatial distance. But with the outbreak of the epidemic, information has also broken out, though much is difficult to verify. Official reports about Wuhan leave us increasingly further from the truth.

I would like to use my eyes and ears to gather information and make judgments. Before coming here, a friend in the mainstream media told me that the government had made arrangements for all official media reporters to stay in a hotel next to Wuchang Railway Station so as to oversee their work and assign reporting tasks. If one has no official media credentials, it's very difficult to engage in media work in this besieged city, it's even a bit dangerous, as all the epidemic's bad news is submitted to and reported by the central government . . .

Just as Kcriss is starting to feel confident, a phone call cuts in. It's the building manager, who, in an anxious voice, asks him to come down immediately. Kcriss keeps shooting video on his mobile phone as he goes down, and the manager's sister-in-law leads him outside to meet a mask-wearing policewoman sent from the local police station. Kcriss immediately takes advantage of his good looks, calling her respectfully "little elder sister." The policewoman seems a bit embarrassed and softly says, "This is a notice from the higher ups, you can't stay here." He says, "Little elder sister, I've only just arrived, you can see it's dark everywhere, where would you have me go?" The policewoman says: "It's not that I won't let you stay." He says: "So what should I do?" and turns to look piteously at the manager's sister-in-law, who says, "I just look after the keys, so I'm no use to you." After a while, another police officer comes, whom Kcriss similarly calls "little elder brother." In a flash, the eyes of the younger elder brother and the younger elder sister meet, and they agree he can stay for one night but must leave the next day.

Kcriss gets a little emotional after he goes upstairs to continue the live broadcast. He says Chen Qiushi had lived in Wuhan for more than a week until he went missing, but he can only stay one night. Then he presses the button on his smartphone, and all the audience hears the manager's sister-in-law say: "Brother, there is really no way. I've phoned around for you, and sent a WeChat message, but no one dares take you in. Now, the government's authority is delegated from the city to the districts, and from the districts to the residential areas, divided up into small pieces. Everything is closed and sealed off, only one person in each household is allowed to go out with a 'pass' to buy daily necessities just once every three days. I've heard that in some neighborhoods, people are not allowed even to enter or leave the main gate. The neighborhood property managers register what's to be purchased and set the prices, so you eat what you eat, as if everyone's in a jail together . . . So, where's an outsider like you to go?" Then the police officer says, "If you don't move out tomorrow, they'll go through each room searching for you. I can't possibly hide you . . ."

As the folk saying goes: when the legendary Eight Immortals crossed the sea, each displayed their supernatural abilities. Kcriss dared to resign from CCTV and come here, and in the final analysis, he has magical powers too. With the help of an unnamed friend, first, he moves into a residential area under the ruse of being a volunteer, and a few days later he moves again. He also gets hold of a Volkswagen off-road vehicle, and this, in addition to his pure Beijing accent, regulation protective clothing, and look of a pampered son of a family of influence, leads the police who check his ID to be more courteous than they might otherwise be.

To Kcriss, having just arrived in the city, the sunshine, air, and quiet streets and alleys feel both beautiful and deceptive. At first, he contacts those he wants to interview through information he found on microblogging services like WeChat and Weibo, and many agree to talk, but later change their tune when he can't enter any local people's homes. He visits the location of the "Ten Thousand Family Banquet," which had occurred before Spring Festival on February 15 in the Baibu Pavilion area of Jianghan District. It has been the most notable source of infection after the South China Seafood Wholesale Market. A girl breaks the news that many people who attended contracted the virus, and due to a shortage of nucleic acid testing they hadn't been able to get diagnosed. Moreover, she said the local government concealed the number of deaths, out of fear of reporting them to the higher authorities.

So Kcriss hurries to see for himself. It's a huge residential area of over two hundred apartment buildings and home to more than a hundred thousand residents. The surrounding shops are all closed, but he discovers an official media reporter from elsewhere in China wandering outside the #2 Building Gate. The two begin a loud conversation and are intercepted by the guards. Then they go around to another gate, trying to hide each other, but just as they're about to slip in, the security guards of several gates come rushing over to them. Kcriss has some experience with this and shouts repeatedly: "Don't come near me! Keep your distance! It's dangerous, understand? I'm not going with you, alright?" The security guards are somewhat subdued by this, but tenants on the upper floors hear the commotion and immediately open their windows and voice their support: "Why do you have to drive away reporters? We've been in here for nearly two months and there's been no sanitation or disinfection . . ." Kcriss turns to ask if this is true, and a minor bureaucrat type says it's nonsense, we've records of cleaning and disinfection.

Suddenly, several women come rushing downstairs to confront the guards. One woman scolds him, saying, "Your cleaning and disinfection is just to put a checkmark in the logbook outside the corridor door every day. In fact, absolutely nothing's ever done, there's no smell of disinfectant, and the elevator buttons are all covered by spiderwebs. In the past, we'd go to the supermarket at the main gate every three days to buy necessities. Later, after somebody fell dead there, we haven't dared go." Kcriss asks her if she knows of any fever patients in the neighborhood. The women say they don't know as they can only communicate with each other through WeChat to find out which buildings post a "fever building" notice. As to which household in the "fever building" is suspected of infection, diagnosed, dead, or taken away or not, whether sent to an isolation shelter, a hospital, or a crematorium, nobody can be sure. The government never announces such things – but the number of security guards is always increasing.

Finally, the property management boss arrives on a bicycle and confirms that nucleic acid testing resources are limited, and even if there were more fever, you'd still have to wait for notice from higher authorities. For example, a place like this with several dozen to a hundred households is only allocated two testing slots today, maybe just one tomorrow, and maybe none the day after.

What can you do? Just stay isolated at home, rely on yourself. Didn't Chairman Mao say we should rely on the masses?

So, Kcriss walks the streets of the besieged city unhindered. On Twitter, a mix of short videos of tragedies and absurdities is streaming out every day: a security guard sitting in front of a computer suddenly keeling over, twitching on the ground for a few seconds, then not moving anymore; a virus victim with a confirmed diagnosis, rejected by a hospital, going nuts in an elevator, smearing saliva and spitting, shouting he's taking revenge and wants to infect others; an elderly person in a wheelchair, waiting in line at a hospital for three days and three nights before finally giving up in despair; a little girl pursuing a corpse cart in a hospital; a ninety-year-old who tearfully complains about the situation to everyone before jumping off a building . . . The final result of isolation at home is often a confirmed diagnosis of one person, which the others in the family can also not escape, leading to a succession of reports of entire dead families. It's as if black vultures are hovering over the city. People can't stand it. Over the Internet, some of them reach an agreement that at midnight one day the residents of dozens of buildings will simultaneously turn off their lights, open their windows, and howl into the night sky like wolves.

The family of Chang Kai, film director and head of the television department of Hubei Film Studio, contracted the disease one after another, all exterminated within seventeen days. He left a final testament of his ordeal:

> On Chinese New Year's Eve, in compliance with government orders, I canceled my reservation for a banquet at a luxury hotel. To make up for this I took on the role of chef and brought the members of our family together in our home for a joyful evening.
>
> As everyone knows, a nightmare has befallen us. On New Year's Day, my father came down with a fever and a cough, had difficulty breathing, and I went with him to several hospitals for treatment. But they all reported there were no beds available. I sought help wherever I could, and still no bed.

Extremely disappointed, we came home to attempt to save our-selves, me doing my utmost filial duty by his bedside. A few days later, unable to save the situation, my old father left this world with recriminations in his heart. After such a heavy blow, my mother was exhausted both physically and mentally, her immune system failed, and she too became severely infected and died.

After serving my parents at their deathbeds for several days, the ruthless coronavirus also devoured my wife and me. I went from hospital to hospital begging for help, but my words counted for nothing, I could find no bed, and then fell gravely ill, thereby missing out on all hope of treatment. With my dying breath, I hereby attest to all my relatives and friends as far away as my son in England: all my life I have honored my parents, and fulfilled my responsibilities as a father. As a husband, I have been devoted to my wife and have been an honest man in all things.

To the people I love and who love me, I bid you farewell forever!

On the evening of February 19, an online ad for "Register to Carry Corpses" pops up on Kcriss's smartphone:

> *The Wuchang Funeral Home urgently seeks to recruit 20 people to trans-port corpses tonight.*
> *Job requirements: Male or female, 16–50 years old, unafraid of ghosts, bold and strong.*
> *Working hours: 0–4, with minimal breaks.*
> *Salary: 4,000 Yuan for 4 hours, plus a snack.*
> *Where to meet: Tonight at 23:00 at Yangjiawan Subway Station on Line 2.*

A good lead to follow! Kcriss is immediately excited, hurriedly wolfs down some bread, turns his car around, and drives off to check out what's happening. Night falls imperceptibly, and it's still a long way to Wuchang, so he speeds to the nearby Qingshan Funeral Home. Like the ghost stories in the Qing Dynasty book *Strange Tales from a Chinese Studio*, the road leading to this gate to hell is dark and an eerie wind is howling. He sees the lights atop the gate from a distance, and approaches slowly, stops, gets out, and is about to enter when a woman's voice drifts out from the darkness: "What're you doing?"

"There's news on the Internet that corpse carriers are being recruited here, 4,000 Yuan for four hours."

"What?"

"Online recruitment . . ."

"There isn't."

While this stalemate continues, a car suddenly drives up right behind Kcriss's. The man in the car doesn't get out, instead poking his head out of the window and asking: "I'm recruiting the corpse carriers, are you up for it?"

"I've just come by to ask about it."

"Will you do it?"

"Some in our WeChat group want to."

"Are you a volunteer?"

"I help friends in my group find work."

"Then write down my phone number: 13437282."

"A Qingshan or Hankou number?"

"Qingshan. And take my WeChat address, too."

"Okay, got it all."

"Are your friends young? Any older ones?"

"Yes."

"How old?"

"About thirty."

"From the countryside?"

"Of course."

"Are they afraid?"

"If there's money . . . Hey, how much are you actually paying?"

"It's like this: if you don't carry any bodies today, you don't get paid; if you do, the price starts at 500 Yuan. The first body 500, the second an added 200, and the third another added 200. There's no cap, so you'll be encouraged to carry ten or a hundred, as long as you can do it."

"Are people already working?"

"Right now I've only two left, there was a bunch before."

"How much can you earn in a day?"

"More than 1,000 Yuan. It starts at 500, plus 200 and another 200 on top, that's the limit."

"How many do you want?"

"Two people per squad, no limit on how many."

"When will the work start?"

"Wait for my call. There's quick money in this."

"I think it's still a little short. It's carrying corpses."

"It's a lot, regular workers are paid just 3,000 a month."

"I saw a corpse carrier ad offering 4,000 Yuan. There's great demand now."

"It's dropped recently. There's no longer a short supply. 4,000 Yuan, impossible. Can't pay it. All the dead bodies in Qingshan District are contracted to me, and I only get 3,500 Yuan from a family. How can I give you 4,000? Generally speaking, if you go with me, you can earn over a 1,000 Yuan a day. "

"Pneumonia patients or ordinary people?"

"All. It's a bit dangerous, but I provide full PPE."

"Okay. Understood."

A verbal agreement is reached, and the corpse carrier foreman drives away. Kcriss looks up and gazes at the crescent moon slipping in and out of the dark clouds, imagining it to be a ferry full of dead souls from the epidemic zone. He holds his breath for two minutes, takes deep breaths for five more, thereby confirming that he isn't infected before crossing the dark open ground as he follows a booming sound and approaches the crematorium. At the top of two flights of stairs is a glass double-door with the words "Important workplace, off limits to unauthorized personnel," and in smaller print next to this: "One family member may enter for verification and signature." Kcriss keeps to the dark inside the building, his camera lens hidden like himself, as he goes down a long, gray corridor, until banging up against the innermost wall. On the left side of the corridor there's a succession of tightly closed doors with incinerators behind them. But as he slips into the corridor, he's hit by sterilization fumes and the deafening cacophony of corpse-burning. He hurriedly shrinks back into the dark, like a frightened cat.

He records the following:

Started shooting at 10 p.m., left at 11, the furnaces still at work, very loud.

As of February 19, the official number of deaths in the Wuhan area from the new coronavirus pneumonia is 1,497. In the 38 days since January 12, when the first case was diagnosed and died, there has been an average of 40 deaths per day;

According to public data on the website of the Wuhan Municipal Government, in 2018, the city had a registered population of 8.873 million, with 47,900 deaths, a death rate of 5.51 per thousand, and an average of 137 deaths per day;

There are a total of 7 funeral parlors in the Wuhan urban area, with 74 cremation furnaces: Hankou 30, Wuchang 15, Qingshan 5, Caidian 10, Jiangxia 7, Huangpi 7, Xinzhou 5, and one cremation furnace processes one body every 60 minutes. If the 137 bodies were evenly distributed, each furnace would process 1.74 bodies each day.

Therefore, taking as an example the Hankou funeral parlor dedicated to cremating the remains of new coronavirus victims, if the 30 ovens work for 8 hours a day, the cremation capacity would be about 240. The official figure for deaths due to the new coronavirus is only 40 per day, and when the conventionally dead sum of 52 people is added to this number, the total is 92.

Doesn't it stand to reason that they shouldn't have to work overtime like this?

This sort of simple arithmetic in addition to field investigation effortlessly discredits the lies hatched by powerful authorities. Just like the door that separates the cremation furnace from the outside world, all that's needed is a slight push. However, for thousands of years, human beings have paid a painful price for this "slight push." Kcriss unconsciously inherited his method of pursuing the truth, now known as "common-sense reasoning," from thinkers such as Socrates, Confucius, and Laozi. Socrates reasoned with common sense in demonstrating the immortality of the soul, but the authorities charged him with deluding the

youth of Athens and sentenced him to death by drinking poisoned wine. Socrates, undaunted, used his last hours in his cell to
continue to discuss with people why the soul was immortal. He
calmly and incisively responded to their doubts and questioning,
so that his opponents felt deep goodwill toward him and pangs
of conscience, ultimately and inescapably submitting to his logic.
Over time, this scene became the cornerstone of the proper form
of democratic rule. It is also a superlative elucidation of the idea
"God is everywhere," consistent in spirit with the daily question-
and-answer sessions the wandering Confucius conducted with his
students as set down by the Han Dynasty historian Sima Qian. It
is reminiscent as well of Confucius's purported visit with Laozi,
who held contradictory political views to his. After the meeting,
Confucius praised Laozi by saying, "I have seen a dragon in my
lifetime," to which Laozi immediately replied: "One day when you
and I have become decaying bones, this dialogue between us today
will still echo in people's ears."

And so, Kcriss exhorts himself to exercise restraint, since that is
the only way he can stay in Wuhan long enough to unearth more
of the truth, bit by bit. Consequently, that is why at the end of his
live broadcast, he gently asks the question: "Doesn't it stand to
reason that they shouldn't have to work overtime like this?"

He wants to continue to be discreet. Over the next few days, on
several occasions, he drives past the widely acknowledged starting point of the Wuhan virus, the South China Seafood Wholesale
Market, even though it has already been entirely cleaned up.
He wants to continue his "slight push" and get closer to the P4
laboratory, 32 kilometers away from the market. According to
a report on Radio France Internationale, on January 25, 2020,
two days after the Chinese government announced the closure
of Wuhan, Major General Chen Wei, China's chief biological and
chemical defense expert, was sent to take over command of this,
the nation's top virus laboratory, built with the help of France,
and now also listed as a military restricted area.

At midnight on February 26, 2020, Kcriss, who'd earlier escaped from the P4 laboratory area to his residence, makes an indistinct appearance on the darkened screen of his live broadcast. The silhouette of his head wearing goggles looks like a skull with empty eye sockets. He pants raspily, and then attempts to hold his breath as the security agents knock on the door. He's motionless, but the sound of rustling clothes still emanates from the dark screen as he subconsciously shudders. The melon-eating masses at home and abroad are leaning over the Great Firewall, constantly supplying him with ideas by way of their comments. He twice points the phone screen at the YouTube comments, where it shows: "They're prying open the door!" Suddenly, the phone beeps twice. He hurriedly mutes it, and then he cries – people can't see it, but they can sense his tears falling in the dark:

> I don't know what I've done wrong. Everything was sealed up there, I couldn't get in. Then they chased and I fled, all the way back here . . . Now, I've slowed down, I'm not afraid. What's the use of being afraid now? I've watched Chen Qiushi's videos and I thought he was awesome. Hospitals, isolation shelters, residential buildings – he went to them all. And the people he interviewed were more interesting; he even produced a show with the family members of victims of the Wuhan pneumonia. He also went to a hospital to verify the video of "Three Bodies Lying in a Corridor" that circulated on the Internet at the time. In the end, a nurse told him: "Yes, it's true, but you can't blame us. We, too, have to wait for the undertakers, and that day they were extremely busy . . ."
>
> I don't know what state Chen Qiushi was in when he was taken away, or whether there was any physical conflict. Or what's going to happen now. Before I came to Wuhan, I'd expected this to happen, but I didn't expect it to happen so soon . . .

He's becoming a bit incoherent, so he turns off the computer and stands up, his shadow swaying on the dark screen: "Now I'm on an adrenaline high and I'm feeling confused. I've taken my temperature and it's quite high, but not in the 'suspect' range; it's excitement."

Sporadic movements can be heard throughout, and many of the melon-eating masses can't bring themselves to leave. Afterwards a Taiwanese girl says: "I followed for a while and thought the signal was bad or the picture had failed. I didn't know he was fighting with the deepest darkness." Zhuangzi Gui, an exile in Berlin, continues following Kcriss for 2 hours and 25 minutes of torment in what feels like an airtight barrel of explosives, before he finally sees Kcriss turn on a light, take off his mask, and in a lowered voice say: "I just moved from the living room to here [bedroom], what I'm wearing [a protective suit] is too loud. I don't know what they're up to, just guarding the door all this time."

Kcriss stands up and walks to the end of the bed, takes off his rustling protective clothing, and tiptoes over to turn off the lights. He then doesn't appear onscreen until the 3 hours and 8 minutes mark, but a series of phone calls come in. They are from a local friend who's being held by the Security Bureau. Over the length of this 3 hour, 54 minute, and 22 second period of being trapped like a beast, Kcriss only occasionally turns on the lights to make appearances, commenting briefly about this "darkest time."

Zhuangzi Gui remembers his many arrests several years ago – in a bewildering rush, there'd been no live recording, only memories and the passage of time. On one occasion, they'd come to his door for interviewing a Falun Gong member who'd escaped from a mental hospital, and Zhuangzi Gui climbed to the seventh-floor roof and escaped down the stairway of an adjoining apartment unit. Another time, in deep winter, he was awakened from a dream by someone knocking on his door. He jumped from his bed and put his pants on backwards, but still they caught him and took him away.

He also recalls the arrest of his friend Liu Xiaobo. To date, aside from a few scattered memories, nothing written or filmed has surfaced addressing what happened during that lethal arrest in midwinter 2008. Later, the Nobel Peace Prize laureate died a death that was completely controlled by the state, and then a suspicious prison fire wiped away all the unanswered questions about what had actually occurred.

He also remembers a line from a recording made by Wang Yi, a fellow native of Chengdu: "After a while, I didn't know who'd knocked on the door and come in, whether it was friend or foe." He searched for the video of Wang Yi being arrested at home on the eve of the tenth anniversary of the May 12, 2008 earthquake in Sichuan – probably filmed by his wife, Jiang Rong. But no video or text has yet appeared about Wang's latest arrest on December 9, 2018, for which he's been sentenced to nine years in prison.

And he recalls many other arrest scenes. The opening chapter of *The Gulag Archipelago* describes dozens of arrests. Solzhenitsyn wrote there, "How do people get to this clandestine archipelago? Hour by hour planes fly there, ships steer their course there, and trains thunder off to it – but all with nary a mark on them to tell of their destination. . . . [T]hose who, like you and me, dear reader, go there to die, must get there solely and compulsorily by arrest."*

In the Internet age, Kcriss has been able to leave a record of his arrest. There are many unanswered questions, but it's relatively complete. Since the film was uploaded to YouTube in real time, it's been forwarded and copied countless times, and the Communist Party has been unable to destroy it. This is unique in the history of such arrests in China and other totalitarian regimes.

People are destined to disappear, but the truth will remain, and this is precisely what Kcriss desires. So, he walks out from behind his airtight iron curtain, puts his hand on the doorknob, faces the camera, and issues his own "Arrest Manifesto":

I'm ready to open the door. May I say a few words?

First, I really admire everyone who has come to hunt me down. I admire that in broad daylight, by various means, you've so easily discovered my precise location and have also detained my friends. Second, since I've come to Wuhan, all that I've done till now conforms to the contents of the Constitution and the laws and regulations of the People's Republic of China. I've been to all the places identified as dangerous always wearing a full set of protective clothing, with goggles, disposable gloves, and disinfectant.

I've got lots and lots of it. Ample supplies. 3M masks that were bought for me by a supporter-friend. So, I'm in good health now, and I'm in great shape physically. If I have a so-called fever, it can only be because I wear a protective suit that's too close-fitting, and my soaring adrenaline levels make my temperature rise as well.

Naturally, third, to this point it's not very likely I won't be taken away, isolated. What I want to make clear is I've brought no shame on myself, my parents, my family, nor on my Alma Mater, the Communication University of China, and the media I studied there. I've also brought no shame on this country; I haven't done anything detrimental to the country! I, Kcriss, am twenty-five years old this year. Like Chai Jing, I also want to be able to go to the frontlines as she did in 2004 when she made a film like *Beijing Fights SARS*, or when she released *Under the Dome* in 2016, which was blocked everywhere on the nation's Internet. I think this sort of work is valuable!

You big men outside the door, if you went to middle school – of course you did – if your memory is good enough, you'll definitely remember a middle school reading text of Lu Xun's: "Has China Lost Self-Confidence?" There's one passage I've always taken as a standard: "Since ancient times, there have been those who have pled for the lives of the people, those who devote themselves to hard work, and those who abandon themselves to the search for truth . . . these are the true backbone of China."

I don't want to muffle my voice, and also I don't want to close my eyes and block my ears. It's not that I'm not able to keep a wife, children, and a warm house. Of course, I've that ability. So, why did I resign from CCTV? I did it so China can have more young people, more young people like me who will stand up!

This is not because I want to do something, not because I want an uprising, not for that. It's not as if whenever we say two words, we oppose the Party. I know idealism was destroyed at the turn of spring to summer in that year [1989], but sitting quietly minding one's own business has no effect. Young people today go to gaming sites, online video sites, switching between various social media every day. They probably don't even know what's happened in the past and probably think the historical results they live with today are what they deserve.

Do you remember Truman in *The Truman Show*? I think everyone is like this. When we discover a strange signal on a radio station, when we find an exit, we'll go out and never come back. Anyone who's seen the anime series *Naruto* knows . . . I'm finished speaking. Sorry, a final word . . .

To put it simply, I very much understand you out there. I understand you are carrying out orders. And I also sympathize with you, because when you unconditionally, irrationally support such cruel commands and then execute them, there'll come a day when such brutal orders will come down on you!

OK, at this point, I'm ready to open the door.

Kcriss opens the door, and the headless silhouetted torsos of two men float in. He utters: "These are my friends . . ." and then the scene abruptly ends. But the subtitles are frozen forever: "I'm being searched!!! I'm being searched!!!"

There is no film of the search. But anyone who's been arrested knows the next step must be a comprehensive search, of the body, of all devices, and then of the entire apartment, including the toilet and the windows, just as army engineers would go about detecting mines, repeatedly screening everything inch by inch. First, computers and mobile phones are seized, the Internet is cut off, and anti-spyware experts swiftly set to work. In less than half an hour, they find everything there is to find on every computer and mobile phone, with all deletions restored. Then there's the personal search, with all clothes stripped off. On March 16, 1990, Zhuangzi Gui was arrested for making and distributing the audio tape of his long poem "Massacre." Not only were all his clothes removed, he was also shaken and pinched repeatedly, and his anus was jabbed and stirred with a chopstick. In this empire, a large number of criminal cases have proven this to be a necessary step – as the anus is the only place in the body where criminal evidence might be hidden. Drugs or a USB flash drive containing several gigabytes of top-rated ideological poison can be inserted into the rectum above the sphincter.

No one knows how they treated Kcriss. When it comes to destroying a person's will, the National Security Bureau are the connoisseurs. The NSB are on the "covert battlefront." Generally speaking, they do not surface in public, only analyze and rate the objects of their monitoring, giving them such ratings as "ordinary," "striving," "dangerous," and "especially dangerous," before submitting proposals for security agents to implement.

But this time, they themselves make an appearance.

Ding Jian, the National Security team leader in charge of spreading and tightening the net, comes through the door, presents his badge, and announces: "In accordance with Article 75 of the Criminal Procedure Law and Article 108 of the 'Provisions on Procedures of Public Security Organs in Handling Criminal Cases,' the regulations stipulate that Kcriss, a non-resident Chinese national temporarily living in a certain community in the city of Wuhan, will be appointed to a monitored residence in a designated place for a period of six months. If the investigation of the case requires, this term may be extended as appropriate with the approval of the prosecuting authority."

Kcriss is stuffed into a police car and taken away. Handcuffed, wearing a black hood, and not knowing where the residence they've "designated" for him will be, or for how long he'll be isolated. His family will not be notified, of course. Several days later, somebody reveals that Chen Qiushi has also been "appointed to a monitored residence in a designated place." Maybe they are in the same place, separated by a wall, but never to meet . . .

Everything is quiet on the dark screen, and the melon-eaters on both sides of the Great Firewall have all scattered, but Zhuangzi Gui remains in place. Time passes imperceptibly while he sits motionless like a woodcarving, until the window brightens. His wife gets out of bed, followed by their five-year-old daughter, Ant, who runs to him shouting: "Baba!"

He nods, his eyes still not leaving the computer, which has already shut down automatically. His wife comes to urge him to get some sleep. He lies down fully clothed, Kcriss's "Arrest Manifesto" still echoing in his mind, especially his mention of Lu Xun. If it were the 1920s and 1930s, it's likely he'd have been his student, like Liu Hezhen and Rou Shi, who were both killed by warlords of that time. "In Memory of Miss Liu Hezhen" and "Remembrance for the Sake of Forgetting" are two of Lu Xun's most famous eulogies. They commemorate these two passionate youths, both of whom were as young as Kcriss when they died. Kcriss seemed to be a reincarnation of them nearly ninety years later.

A famous passage from "In Memory of Miss Liu Hezhen" goes: "I understand the reason why this decadent nation is silent. Silence, silence! If it doesn't erupt in the silence, it perishes in silence." And in "Remembrance for the Sake of Forgetting," Lu Xun wrote: "Late one night, I was standing in the courtyard of an inn surrounded by piles of tattered things; the people were all asleep, including my woman and child. I had a heavy sense of the good friend I'd lost, of the brilliant youth China had lost . . ."

Zhuangzi Gui and Lu Xun were in similar situations; he, too, feels he should write something for "the brilliant youth China had lost." However, when it comes time to write, he realizes that writing about Kcriss is more difficult. Liu Hezhen and Rou Shi, the two youths resurrected in Lu Xun's texts – one shot down by the troops of warlords during a street demonstration, and the other jailed for publishing underground publications and later executed – their cases were clear and simple and had nothing to do with state secrets; but Kcriss had been merely in the vicinity of the P4 laboratory, had done nothing, but was chased and arrested. Zhuangzi Gui goes on the Internet to search and finds an overwhelming amount of news and speculation surrounding the P4. "Kcriss drove to the periphery of P4 and was intercepted by gun-wielding soldiers wearing biochemical protective clothing from head to foot. About to be detained, he had no other choice but to abandon his plan . . ." Zhuangzi Gui returns to his desk working through the evening of the next day on into another late night before the manuscript is finally finished. He then emails it to *International Focus*, a magazine in Houston. Two days later, his landline rings, and it is the magazine's editor, John.

"Hello, Mr. Zhuang, I've read your manuscript, can you talk about it?"

"No problem."

"The second line of the fourth paragraph: a patient who'd suddenly fallen to the ground shouts: 'Direct hit!' That almost sounds like 'A bullet hit me!' Did you invent this term?"

"Not me. Many people in Wuhan call a diagnosis the direct hit."

"Understood, thank you. Next is the penultimate paragraph: 'Kcriss, this rash "intruder," brings to mind Valery Legasov and others who made the truth about Chernobyl public. In April 1988, Legasov was overwhelmed by the pressure on him and committed suicide – and Kcriss issued his final call for help after the crazy pursuit of him by the National Security Agency . . .' Do you think this analogy . . ."

"It's quite appropriate."

"What about evidence?"

"I've already reported it."

"I called our reporter in Beijing and he said, although there are many rumors about the P4 making or leaking viruses, they cannot be confirmed. Experts from the WHO have also been there and found nothing."

"But Kcriss was arrested because he got close to the P4."

"Our reporter said that he might also have been arrested for going to the Qingshan Crematorium to investigate the number of deaths. Before him, there were two other journalists, Fang Bin and Chen Qiushi, who'd also disappeared because they'd investigated the true number of deaths. Concealing the epidemic, deceiving the people and the international community is the norm for all dictatorships."

"He went to the crematorium on February 19 and had no problem. I've a record of it. A week later, on February 26, when he went to P4 it became a major event."

"Do you mean there are more terrible things being concealed, like the Chernobyl nuclear leak? But there's a lack of evidence. Our magazine will not publish conjecture about what happened as regards the 'P4 virus–Kcriss–the National Security Agency,' we don't publish literary fiction."

"I know."

"But we will publish 'citizen reporters missing in the Wuhan epidemic.' One after the other, Fang Bin, Chen Qiushi, and Kcriss ignored their own personal safety and revealed the truth of deaths deliberately concealed by the government. These names are still very new in the West . . ."

"That's not bad," Zhuangzi Gui said indulgently, "I'll modify it."

And so, this all passed and was forgotten.

———————

Today's news becomes old news in the blink of an eye. Within two or three weeks, the name "Kcriss" is mentioned by few outlets as he is buried beneath all the new information online. As if on schedule, the Wuhan virus rushes out of the country and runs rampant all over the world. Reading the newspaper at home on March 22, Zhuangzi Gui learns that the number of confirmed cases in Germany has already exceeded twenty-five thousand, including Angela Merkel's personal physician. So, the German Chancellor announces she'll isolate herself at home for fourteen days . . . Then, British Prime Minister Boris Johnson, who once vigorously promoted "herd immunity," also announces he'll isolate at home. Soon after, feeling worse, he is moved to an intensive care unit . . . Zhuangzi Gui suddenly looks up and wonders out loud to his wife what's happened to Kcriss. She looks at him in surprise, as if he were asking after a person long deceased.

Just as Zhuangzi Gui sighs with regret, the landline rings. He answers it. It's the seventy-four-year-old composer Wang Xilin, who currently lives in the east of Berlin. Zhuangzi Gui is just about to say hello when he's subdued by a thunderous roar. Wang's as deaf as Beethoven, so he speaks very loudly: "Zhuangzi! Remember Ai Ding? You met the historian at my place on the eve of the closure of Wuhan! We drank together, worried about the virus together, until late at night! You and he both inspired me to use Wuhan as the setting for the ending of my opera 'Forging the Swords,' based on the Lu Xun short story –"

Wang Xilin keeps on speaking, without regard to anything and anyone. Several times Zhuangzi Gui shouts: "Could you put in your hearing aid?," but is ignored. Finally, he roars: "Wang! Put in your hearing aid! I remember Ai Ding!!!"

Thank goodness, Wang Xilin hears him: "Okay! Wait a minute! Now I'm telling you that Ai Ding is officially missing!! Since we last saw him, he's returned to China. We were in contact through WeChat. Later, because of the transmission of the epidemic, our WeChat accounts were blocked. Still later, I learned he was being watched by the police . . . can we meet and talk? I have a letter for you from him here."

Zhuangzi Gui's first instinct is to decline, as the German government is gradually implementing lockdown orders. Except for supermarkets, almost all businesses are closed and even groups of more than three people are not allowed, let alone casual visits to the homes of friends. But Wang Xilin is accustomed to breaking all social norms, so what could he do?

Regardless of his wife's attempts to dissuade him, Zhuangzi Gui rides his bicycle from the west to the east of Berlin to see Wang Xilin. Everything is closed along the way and people are few, like in wartime movies. Even Friedrichstrasse, usually the busiest spot in the center of Berlin, is deserted. A train sighs loudly on the top of an arched bridge that had been the central border crossing between East and West Berlin before the Wall fell.

Zhuangzi Gui has to cycle for a few hours to Wang Xilin's home and is stopped by a police patrol along the way. They check his passport and give him some advice before letting him go. By the time he reaches Höhenschönhausen, the former East German National Security Agency prison, it's already dark. Dr. Cai, Wang Xilin's wife, is waiting to meet him by a nearby prison gate. They walk alongside the high walls and electrified fences for ten minutes before coming to a building where Wang Xilin's new residence is located on the fourth floor.

The pandemic is at its peak, so handshakes and hugs are taboo. Instead people touch elbows or the tips of their shoes. But Wang Xilin can't help embracing Zhuangzi Gui before leading him into the kitchen, where they proceed to eat and drink. Wang's wife and daughter, one to the left, one to the right, like door gods, protect the seventy-four-year-old reprobate. His eating and drinking is strictly limited; they take cups and plates from him at every turn. Zhuangzi Gui can't help laughing. At which point Wang Xilin thunders: "Drink more, Zhuangzi, and I'll talk about the business at hand. Do you remember how Ai Ding ate and drank for a few hours and got totally plastered last time we met? Well, then he got on a plane and went back to China, all dizzy and confused . . ."

1

A City Forced to Close

At ten in the morning on January 23, 2020, government officials in China announced the implementation of the "Wuhan City Closure Order." The subway and all buses, trains, planes, and ships ceased to operate, and nearly nine million residents were told they would not be allowed to leave. By ten o'clock the next morning, other cities in Hubei Province, such as Ezhou, Huanggang, Red Cliff,* Xiantao, Zhijiang, Qianjiang, Xianning, Jingmen, Dangyang, Huangshi, Enshi, and Xiaogan, had also announced the implementation of similar closure orders. It was precisely at this historical juncture that the unlucky Ai Ding boarded a Hainan Airlines flight from Berlin Tegel Airport and began his long trip home to Wuhan. However, as soon as he landed at Beijing Airport, he was informed his previously booked flight to Wuhan had been canceled.

He instantly called his wife at home in Wuhan, who exclaimed, "What?! You could have come back sooner or come back later, but instead you come back precisely at this time!" He said, "It's the same as I've done during Spring Festival in previous years; the ticket's booked half a year beforehand." She asked, "You can't change it?" He replied, "This type of special-price ticket can't be changed, unless it's voided; moreover, I'd have had to extend my visa in Germany. Getting this done at the Foreign Affairs Bureau is a real pain." Now what was he to do? Surely Wuhan, well known as "the main thoroughfare of nine provinces," its dozens of roads extending in all directions, couldn't really be closed? But his wife assured him it was.

While the competence of the communist army in serving the people is extremely low, its effectiveness at closing a city to the people is very high, and if they still can't get it done, they bring in a field army. Ai Ding continued, "I'll first get a feel for what's going on around Wuhan and take my chances when I find a way in. I know the terrain. If I can't get in by water, I'll do it by land. If the roads are blocked, I'll attempt it overland at night. It'll be no problem as I'm part-coyote and part-weasel anyway." His wife said, "No, please, don't cause trouble. If you're caught and isolated, your dad is sick in bed again, so I'll not be able to come and help you. It'd be better if you flew to Changsha and stayed at my parents' house for a while." He replied, "But your parents have gone to Shanghai to find your younger brother." She shot back, "Exactly, and they wouldn't dare take you in if they were there either."

Ai Ding still wanted to talk, but his wife made a show of her steely will and simply hung up on him. He'd not expected when he returned to his homeland, even before his feet had touched the ground, that he'd be forced to find his way home cross-country. Fortunately, Beijing had not yet declared an emergency. Contrary to what happened later, he wasn't required to quarantine for fourteen days as soon as he got off the plane, nor was he forced to stay in a hotel with a guard outside his door at a daily cost of 1,000 Yuan.

After a few hours' wait, Ai Ding boarded a plane with a long line of other passengers and took a window seat. The crimson clouds at sunset looked quite spectacular, like mountains made up of tens of thousands of tons of blood oranges. On an impulse, he took a few photos and sent them to his wife on WeChat, expressing his thoughts: "A beautiful night, a lengthy road, Wuhan people have a hard time returning home." In the blink of an eye, his wife replied: "Wuhan people have a hard time leaving home too, eh. Hey, have you got a mask, hand sanitizer, and mouthwash with you?"

The entire cabin was filled with pristine white masks and flight attendants shuttled back and forth spraying disinfectant.

Next to Ai Ding was a middle-aged couple. The wife had a baby in her arms, so a stewardess leaned over expressly to check her seat-belt – night fell as they lifted off. In a flash they were over 10,000 meters in the night air. A flight attendant handed out small snacks and small bottles of water. Soon after, Ai Ding had been slapped and blood was streaming down from two scratch marks on his left cheek. As the woman with the child was drinking water, she'd casually asked him where he was from, and he'd answered Hubei. Without another word, she then attacked him with a flurry of blows. Ai Ding warded her off, but he's an intellectual and couldn't give as good as he got. And the couple wouldn't let up, unfastening their seat-belts, standing up, and yelling for a flight attendant. When one hurried over, the woman revealed Ai Ding's identity: "There's somebody from Hubei sitting here! We won't sit with a Hubei person! We're afraid of the virus!" The flight attendant replied, "I'm so sorry, but there are no empty seats."

The man said, "That won't do, a small child is the most susceptible to infection." The flight attendant responded: "Every passenger had their temperature taken before boarding the plane, and this gentleman was normal. How about if I get my forehead gun and take it again. Would that be okay?" The couple yelled in unison, "No it would not!"

The attendant was overwhelmed and called for the cabin manager. Now many other passengers were standing up and scolding Ai Ding: "Why didn't you let us know you were from Hubei before boarding? Have you no sense of public morality?" "You're supposed to self-isolate if you get sick, don't act all innocent, you've boarded this plane to harm us all." "You're a sly one, underground Hubei guy." "We Chinese want to revoke the citizenship of Hubei people!"

Seeing the situation was getting out of hand, Ai Ding stood up too and loudly explained: "I'm an overseas scholar just returned from Germany. I haven't been in Wuhan for a year." But the situation was out of control. Someone shouted: "Liar!" and somebody else: "We demand compensation from the airline! A diagnosed coronavirus patient is on the plane!" Ai Ding anxiously yelled in response: "I've not been diagnosed!" The crowd roared back: "But you could be infected! Where are the air marshals? Hurry up and deal with him! Hey, any of you people here, if you're from Wuhan or Hubei, please come forward and confess immediately, self-isolate, don't act against reason and nature."

Befuddled by all this, Ai Ding had to go to the rear of the plane with an air marshal and was locked into a bathroom for isolation. After the plane landed in Changsha and all other passengers had left, he was taken to the Huanghua International Airport police station. He showed them his passport and boarding passes for international flights, proving he was a Wuhan native who had nothing to do with the Wuhan virus. "Even so, even if you have never had a fever," a police officer said, "you'll still have to stay in a hotel near the airport for two weeks. You'll be responsible for your own expenses during the quarantine observation period, which is necessary as we've no way of investigating those with whom you have been in contact in Germany."

"But there is no novel coronavirus in Germany."

"We can't guarantee they won't find it in the future. This virus is like a spy, with a long incubation period and no warning signs."

The Changsha police were surprisingly reasonable, and Ai Ding was released after only one week of isolation. Before leaving, he was also given ten pricey N95 masks, but, of course, that cost was included in the invoice for his lodging. Due to the high-speed rail restrictions, he took a sterilized airport bus to Zuanshi Ling Street in Yuelu District, north of the Xiangjiang River. After getting off the bus, he used his smartphone map to locate his wife's family home behind a branch of the Industrial and Commercial Bank of China. Once he got the key from a neighbor, he entered, collapsed on a sofa, took out his phone, and sent a WeChat message that all was well to his wife and his old friend Wang Xilin, far away in Berlin. His wife replied: "Our daughter and I know you're like an insatiable cat circling the cauldron of Wuhan, but under no circumstances can you come back now! We've over a dozen dead in this building! Four entire families are dead! Originally it didn't seem so many would die, but the hospital couldn't squeeze them all in and told them all to isolate at home. What the hell?! Stay home and infect others. Right now, a crematorium collection truck is still parked below. It was driven over here from a neighboring community. I'm using our daughter's telescope to see inside and it's stuffed full of bodies. The workers are struggling to cram still more inside. And this leads to a landslide of bodies falling all over the place, and now they're being lifted and restacked like pieces of wood. The body bags are all yellow, indistinguishable. Resources here are tight, there're no spare vehicles for corpse transport . . . We've not been downstairs for over a week now. We don't dare go out! We've still got rice, flour, noodles, and frozen meat, but no vegetables."

Ai Ding was flabbergasted. At the time, he still didn't understand what his wife was describing would also eventually become the daily epidemic situation throughout the country. Over twenty days before the closure of Wuhan, the peak of the traditional surge of people traveling throughout the country prior to Spring Festival was underway. More than five million people fanned out like bees across China from Wuhan, and the number of other fish that slipped the net from other cities in Hubei was countless. According to the official response of Zhong Nanshan, the leader of the top-level expert group at Epidemic Central, on January 20 over five million suspected virus carriers were traveling outside Wuhan, and there was no way to test them, much less diagnose and isolate them. Hundreds of thousands of people who were fine today, without a fever or cough, might tomorrow suddenly fall to the ground, twitch a few times and die, unexplained and unnamed on a roadside, on a corner, indoors, under a bridge, or in the wild. Of course, they would have identity documents, but no one would dare rummage about for them. Witnesses could only keep well clear, call 110 or 120, who would then tell an overworked funeral parlor to rush over a vehicle, which would directly haul the body off to be burned without delay. The ability to follow normal procedure, to enter a hospital, line up, take a number, be tested, diagnosed, hospitalized, die, be cremated, and have the death registered for inclusion on a list of deaths officially recognized by the great fatherland was no longer possible without extraordinary connections and social status.

With bad news from the closed city of Wuhan pouring in, death became the norm, nothing to fret over. Effectively under house arrest, the citizens of Wuhan scrambled to upload their selfie videos to WeChat and Weibo. As the epidemic was so ferocious, there was no need to worry about the police admonishing or arresting anybody. However, the cyber police were still incessantly deleting posts, issuing warnings, and closing accounts, so the game of "deleting posts, reposting posts" was never ending. Moreover, the nimble reposters often got a step ahead, taking a text or video that hadn't yet been deleted over the Internet firewall and then bringing it back again. One of these was of a ninety-year-old man who'd somehow climbed out of a fourth-floor window and was shown hanging onto a guardrail and complaining tearfully in the bright sunshine. His elderly son and daughter-in-law had long been "suspected" of infection. The community had sent them to two hospitals, but they were never "diagnosed" with the virus, meaning they could only be isolated at home. Now the entire family of seven was "suspected" and they were all laid up in their beds waiting to die. The old man felt it was his fault for having lived too long. And then he jumped . . . There was also a six-year-old child whose parents were working elsewhere and couldn't return home because of the closure of the city. The child had only a grandfather in his seventies to look after him. Late one night, the child woke up and reached out, but Grandpa wasn't there. So, he rushed to the bathroom and found Grandpa asleep there. Only he'd suffered a sudden heart attack and would sleep forever. The child couldn't move him, and was worried Grandpa was freezing, so he dragged over a quilt to cover him. The child continued living there, eating biscuits to tide over his hunger, until fortunately he was discovered by neighbors . . . And there was also the story of the crematorium where the funeral workers used large shovels to fill garbage bag after garbage bag with hundreds of the deceased's cell phones. Suddenly, one of the phones rang, and a funeral worker murmured: "Even now they get no peace . . ."

According to the research and statistics of Bloomberg News, during the first two months or so of the epidemic, of the named mobile phone users of China's three major telecommunications companies – Mobile, Unicom, and Telecom – more than 8 million, 7.8 million, and 5.6 million respectively were "unaccounted for." These twenty million or so users, who all personally registered onsite with an identity card, were preserved as state secrets for a short time and then destroyed forever.

"No one can see the novel coronavirus, so people from Wuhan and Hubei Province are treated as if they themselves are the novel coronavirus," Ai Ding complained to his WeChat circle of friends. He briefly described his experience on the plane, and just ten minutes later it was deleted by the Internet police. He was angry, but there was nothing he could do about it. He got up and went to the bathroom to wash, but there was no water. He knocked on the water pipes and checked all the taps. No problems. So he opened the front door, planning to make inquiries. To his surprise, he found a "Friendly Tips about the Water Cut" notice that had seemingly just been posted on his door:

Resident friends:

In view of the current novel coronavirus epidemic, to protect the public and your health, we are suspending water usage for all Hubei Province residents. All people from Hubei, or people in our district who have contacted Hubei residents or traveled to and/or from Hubei, are required to register at the community workstation as soon as you see this notice, to cooperate with the community's "Trinity" epidemic prevention team there and undertake a health assessment, after which water will be restored. Please inform each other of this matter. We apologize for any inconvenience caused.

Zuanshi Ling Street Office Party Committee,
Yuelu District, Changsha
January 31, 2020

Ai Ding sighed, grabbed his passport, and hurried to the place designated by the Party committee to register. Unexpectedly, it was too late, they'd already left work. All the shops on the street were closed, so he bought bottled water and bread at a small supermarket nearby, and planned to make do for the night with what he had.

Just at this moment, Wang Xilin in Berlin responded to an earlier message, and they began a video chat while thousands of miles apart.

"Finally you've a place to stay! Good. Zhuangzi Gui, the writer, called me looking for you."

"Give him my WeChat address. I'll video with him too."

"He doesn't use WeChat."

"There are no Chinese people at home or abroad who don't use WeChat, even the pro-democracy elements do."

"Zhuangzi said that Sina, Sohu, Tencent, Alibaba, Microsoft, Yahoo, etc., are all not safe if they're used on domestic technology, or have anything to do with it."

"So sneaky. What secrets does he have?"

"None."

"Then give him my postal address: 163 Sina."

"Domestic again? Then no."

"What about Hotmail?"

"Also no. Is there a landline there? I'll have him call you."

A while after they ended their video chat, the landline rang; it was Zhuangzi Gui, who immediately asked, "Do you have Skype?"

Ai Ding hesitated: "Yes. But I rarely use it, it's not very convenient."

"Why?"

"I am currently in China and can't use it directly. I have to find software for getting over the Internet wall."

"Then find it, I'm waiting."

"Can't you speak on the phone?"

"No."

Zhuangzi Gui hung up the phone. Ai Ding felt his chest tighten, but he'd had drinks with Zhuangzi Gui and knew the story of the old fox's escape across the Chinese border. At the time, Zhuangzi Gui carried four Motorola cell phones the size of playing cards. One was for public use, specially for comrade police to eavesdrop on, and two were for specific use: one to contact criminal syndicates and one for overseas human rights workers. The other was a spare.

So he did as he was told and fiddled about on his laptop, and in a while he got what he wanted and was using Skype video. He said with a wry smile: "Zhuangzi, after so much trouble, what do you have to say to me?"

"Domestic Internet and telephones are monitored, even in the Arctic and the Antarctic. As long as you use 'Made in China,' it's controllable."

"But we're not saying or doing anything to subvert the country."

"Hard to say. If nothing happens that's fine, but when anything happens, everything on the Internet becomes evidence of a crime. Do you know the Early Rain Covenant Church case? On the evening of December 10, 2018, simultaneously at different locations, the Chengdu police arrested nearly two hundred house church members relying on surveillance and tracking of their WeChat friend group. Pastor Wang Yi was sentenced to nine years in prison."

"What've I got to do with Pastor Wang Yi? I'm not even a Christian."

"You're so interested in bats, and bats are inseparable from the P4. You're running back to Wuhan at this time, what're you thinking?"

"Nothing."

"You've studied history and you're an impulsive person. How can you not be interested in that? If you're not careful, you'll end up in a bigger hole than Wang Yi. If you use WeChat, Weibo, or any other domestic platforms to debate whether the Wuhan virus leak is intentional or unintentional, it'll be too sensitive . . ."

Suddenly, Ai Ding's scalp felt numb. Zhuangzi Gui continued: "I've checked into it. Wu Xiaohua,* who claims he wants to confront the scientist Shi Zhengli, may be a pseudonym. Shi Zhengli knows who he is, so she dares not respond directly. And yours is a real name, citing lots of materials on these matters from official websites, including the Wuhan Institute of Virology. You're wise to use the faults found by others to urge reform. But what the Communist Party hates is you catching them off-guard with this.

"Shi Zhengli thinks it was all a result of diet. Doesn't that go against common sense? If you want to lie, first eliminate all the evidence, and then wipe your ass! And there's so much great evidence on official websites, on 'immunity,' 'epidemic prevention,' 'human health,' and the like. Shi Zhengli traveled all over the world to collect bat specimens, and then worked hard on counteracting viruses with viruses. She's had success, adventure, published papers, made reports everywhere, won awards ... What about an antidote? And a strong virus with no antidote seems to have leaked out, it's the same as the Chernobyl nuclear leak ..."

Midnight had crept up on them and there was not a sound to be heard. But just as they were about to end their conversation, there was a sudden loud knocking at Ai Ding's door. He immediately turned off his computer, jumped up, and rushed to the peephole to see who it was. Those outside said they were from Epidemic Prevention Headquarters. He asked what they wanted. They replied, "For the safety of you and others, we've decided to impose compulsory isolation on you, as someone from Hubei. If your body temperature is normal for two weeks, without any wheezing or coughing, you'll find you won't have missed anything when you reappear."

Ai Ding was shocked and hurried to open the door to argue, but the door was locked from the outside. He heaved it open a crack and roared like a caged lion: "Is this reasonable?!"

Those outside scattered like rabbits: "Quick, shut your mouth! Do you understand what droplet infection is? People can be reasonable, but viruses can't!"

Ai Ding was shaking with anger. The door was pushed closed again by outside force. Then there were crashing and banging noises as the whole door was nailed shut with wooden planks.

"Hubei guy, listen, hold your horses," those outside tried to appease him. "Whatever you need to eat and drink, write it on a note, and push it under the door with money inside. Of course, you can also use Alipay on WeChat to pay. The QR code of the Epidemic Prevention Headquarters is public, you can do it by scanning. We will purchase what you want for you and then drop it into the kitchen through the skylight. Thank you for your cooperation."

"There's no water."

"It's been turned on now."

Boiling with anger, Ai Ding turned away to send a WeChat message to his wife. She replied: "The whole country is a prison, how is any isolation different?" He said he wanted to go home. She sighed: "It's hard to explain all that's going on at home in a few words! Your dad's over ninety, I'm afraid he won't see out the end of this epidemic."

Ai Ding held his head, stunned, trying to suppress the madness. To divert his thoughts, he called Zhuangzi Gui in Berlin again. Zhuangzi Gui appeared, with his big bald head and a wide grin. As Ai Ding vented about everything, Zhuangzi Gui said: "Do you have any booze over there? Take a few sips and then speak more slowly." Then, with wine glasses raised thousands of miles apart, Zhuangzi Gui continued: "Mine is red wine. Chinese spirits are very expensive here, I can't afford to drink them."

Ai Ding immediately went to a cupboard to get a bottle of Xiangjiang Daqu spirits, poured a glass, and drained it in one gulp. Zhuangzi Gui chastised him: "You can't do that. Drinking is not for numbing yourself, but for adjusting your emotions. People these days run away from their feelings. Drink a few sips while you're low and you'll be fine."

"What can I do?"

"What can't be done? It's just a sealed door, not prison or anything. If you're really thinking of escaping, climbing out of a window should do . . . you've committed no crimes."

"I've a home I can't return to, and no place to go. Even if I did, I'd be grabbed and isolated on the way there. This is the state of our fucking fatherland."

"You've returned from Germany, that's very clear. You've no connection to the Wuhan virus."

"I'm from Hubei and have a home in Wuhan."

"So?"

"Hubei people now are like the Jews under Hitler, this is already the third time I've been isolated by the 'Waffen SS.'"

Zhuangzi Gui was silent. The two of them sadly drank over the video feed. Ai Ding felt his stomach churning and swallowed some bread to suppress the sensation, but only felt sadder and couldn't help crying. Zhuangzi Gui tried but failed to console him, finally pulling out a bamboo flute and softly playing a song called "Yangzhou Andante: Famous Town on the Left Bank of the Huai River," composed by Jiang Kui during the Southern Song Dynasty:

Ever since the Turkish [cavalry] spied across the river, then left,
its ruined pools and towering trees
seem weary of telling of war.
Dusk comes on gradually
with clear bugles blowing the cold
all here in this deserted city.*

This was nearly a thousand years ago, when a poet of antiquity returned to his trampled hometown after the iron hooves of an army of alien invaders had swept past. The bleak devastation of that time must be similar to the streets of Wuhan emptied by the raging virus now. But people of this country now seem much more vulgar, indifferent, and cruel. Kang Zhengguo, a scholar of classical Chinese literature at Yale University, after being twice arrested when returning home to visit relatives, changed the title of Tang Dynasty poet Wei Zhuang's lyric poem from "Don't Return Home Until Old, Homecoming Will Break your Heart" to "Don't Return Home if You Leave the Country, Homecoming Will Break your Heart," which was widely recited among overseas students for a time. Sadly, our country mistreats its own kind more than anyone else.

After a long while, Zhuangzi Gui put his flute aside and tried to comfort Ai Ding: "As it's the same everywhere, you should follow the example of the writer Fang Fang and write a *Diary of a Closed City.*"

"Good idea. However, the city is too big, and my vision is not so great. But as I've nothing else to do, I'll write a *Diary of Closed Gates.*"

It was almost noon when Ai Ding woke up the next day. As was his habit, he opened a window to ventilate the room but was seen doing so by an anti-epidemic patrol. They immediately stormed towards him, waving sticks and shouting, so he quickly closed the window again. He then bathed, cooked, read a book, and paced the apartment. From the kitchen to the living room to the bedroom, he walked slowly, taking about two minutes a turn. He walked around thirty times and then did thirty pushups. Afterwards he turned on the computer and thought about how he should write. He pondered and meditated on it, thinking to himself that this wasn't the material for any kind of literary work, so it would just have to be a true record of real events.

2

A Viral Prison
Made in France

Sunlight entered the house through a window and brightened half the living room, but the trees outside were barren and the tall buildings silent, even though Ai Ding knew there were people in every room. And so he began to write . . .

My name is Ai Ding and I was born in 1970, in the year of the dog. My hometown is Shennongjia Ravine in Hubei Province. In the early 1990s, I was admitted to the History Department at Wuhan University, where I went on to complete my Bachelor's, Master's, and Doctoral degrees, and then remained to teach. Two years ago, the government allowed me to apply for a scholarship at a university in Germany as part of an exchange program.

Returning home for Spring Festival is a Chinese ritual, so I always book a specially priced round-trip ticket half a year in advance. Unpredictably, the situation suddenly changed this year, and now, in dire straits, I am taking the advice of the exiled writer Zhuangzi Gui and am writing a diary to pass the time . . .

Far away, in Berlin, Zhuangzi Gui recorded his own thoughts: "For a writer who has been a political prisoner of the Chinese empire, my choices nine years ago were exile or death (including brain death). It is a sad fact that most of the writers who stayed in China later became almost vegetative. During this Wuhan plague, it seems only my old acquaintance Fang Fang is writing a diary . . . Whether it's good or bad, right or wrong, a diary is the best means to counteract amnesia, especially after the passage of many years. There are too many distressing memories in China at the moment, so the time has come once more for people – including writers – to become vegetative (or even brain dead)."

I don't have the talent of a writer, so let me go back to the origins of all this amid the tremendous clamor of speculation and truth jumbled together on the Internet, and take a look at these lethal SARS viruses, both the current incarnation, COVID-19, and its predecessors . . .

Let's go back to the 2003 Severe Acute Respiratory Syndrome epidemic. China calls SARS "atypical pneumonia," or just "atypical" for short. In fact, SARS was first discovered by the Italian doctor Carlo Urbani. On February 26, 2003, he treated a "bird flu patient" from Guangdong, China, at the Hanoi French Hospital in Vietnam. The patient's breathing was weak, and his life was in danger. After repeated comparisons of X-rays and based on his many years of clinical experience, Urbani diagnosed this initial patient, Johnny Chen (Chen Qiangni), with a new type of infectious disease he had never seen before. He immediately informed the WHO in Geneva, "This is SARS," he pronounced, "a type of 'Acute Respiratory Syndrome', which is extremely contagious. Please prepare to prevent epidemic spread."

Then, through diplomatic channels, Dr. Urbani met with officials of the Ministry of Health in Vietnam and informed them of the danger of an epidemic, thereby getting the government's attention. As a result, the borders were closed, the news of a serious public health threat was announced, national epidemic prevention was initiated, and all movements of "Patient Zero" from when he crossed into Vietnam from China were immediately investigated: only seven people, the medical personnel who saved the life of Patient Zero, had been infected and required immediate isolation. Ultimately, Vietnam had contained the spread of SARS by April 8, 2003. From the discovery of Patient Zero to the end of the epidemic, only sixty-three people were infected, five of whom died.

Because of his unceasing efforts to save SARS patients, Dr. Urbani was also eventually stricken by the disease. On March 29, 2003, he flew to Bangkok, Thailand, but felt ill after landing there. He went into quarantine and soon died, all efforts to save him having failed. A little over half a month later, the WHO announced the adoption of Urbani's name for this coronavirus variant of SARS, in honor of this martyr to his profession.

At the time, China was also experiencing the devastation of SARS, but most people in China had never heard of Carlo Urbani, nor did they know of the epidemic prevention situation in Vietnam, as the Chinese government has long been accustomed to concealing the truth and deceiving its people. At a press conference held by the State Council on April 3, 2003, Minister of Health Zhang Wenkang answered a reporter's question on SARS as follows: "There have been only twelve SARS cases and three deaths in Beijing. SARS has been effectively contained in China. . . . All are welcome to come to China to travel and negotiate business. I guarantee everyone's safety. It is safe with or without face masks."

The military doctor Jiang Yanyong, who was on the medical front line, learned of these lies from the TV news and was furious. At that time, at just the three military hospitals of the 301, 302, and 309 army divisions, there were over a hundred infected patients and nine had died. He immediately emailed CCTV and Phoenix TV but received no responses; so he granted interviews to *Time* magazine and *The Wall Street Journal* in the United States. A well-intentioned reporter suggested: "You may do this anonymously." But he replied: "No, not using my name would make it not credible. All I've said is true and I will take full responsibility for it. I'm protected by the Constitution, but I've also prepared for the worst-case scenario."

Being courageous just that one time in his life was enough to go down in history. As a result, a little later, the Central Committee of the CCP was forced to announce the truth of the epidemic situation and initiate national epidemic prevention. All of us who lived in China then remember that at the time all freeway exits featured checkpoints and temporary isolation rooms.

Aged rice vinegar and the Chinese medicine isatis root were sold out everywhere. In Guangzhou, a bottle of white vinegar rose in price to 1,000 Yuan, as it was said to have special anti-epidemic efficacy. Ultimately, however, SARS was fully contained. Party General Secretary at the time, Hu Jintao issued instructions that nobody should conceal or lie about the epidemic. Subsequently, the Minister of Health, Zhang Wenkang, and the Beijing Mayor, Meng Xuenong, were removed from office.

But how about seventeen years later? Dr. Jiang Yanyong is now old and the person who inherited his "whistle-blower" status was Dr. Li Wenliang. Li was reprimanded by the police after he merely forwarded information to his WeChat circle of friends. And eight other doctors who spread "rumors" of the same nature were forced to confess to the crime of "rumor-mongering" and were silenced. And if they all had been interviewed by foreign media like Jiang Yanyong, it's very likely they'd have been accused of being a counter-revolutionary group, as it is no longer the Minister of Health doing the concealing and deceiving but the Emperor himself.

In 2003, SARS came without a shadow, and left without a trace. Vietnam had a Patient Zero, but China did not, and nobody cared much about it. When all was said and done, compared to the millions of dead victims of myriad political campaigns since 1949 in China, SARS was nothing. Even compared to the June 4 massacre of 1989, where it is estimated by some that at least ten thousand people were slaughtered, only a few thousand died from SARS.

In the same vein, no one imagined that the P4 laboratory of the Wuhan Institute of Virology had any connection to SARS. Yet seventeen years later, it would become the "suspected cradle" for a new coronavirus that has changed the world.

On January 8, 2018, the China Science Network published a long report, "A Record of the Construction of the P4 Laboratory and of the Research Team of the Wuhan Institute of Virology, Chinese Academy of Sciences," which revisited an old matter:

In February 2003, then Director of the Wuhan Institute of Virology of the Chinese Academy of Sciences Hu Zhihong unexpectedly received a phone call from Chen Zhu, Vice President of the Chinese Academy of Sciences, who asked if Hu could undertake the task of constructing a P4 laboratory in Wuhan. . . . Then from April 5 to 11, Yuan Zhiming, who later succeeded Hu as the Director of the Institute of Virology, visited France with Chen Zhu to negotiate with the French side on cooperation in the construction of the P4 laboratory. . . . The internationally top-level P4 laboratory in Lyon, privately operated by the Mérieux family foundation, was later handed over to France's National Institute of Health and Medicine. . . . Substantial progress was made in the talks between China and France. That evening, Ambassador Wang Shaoqi of China allowed Yuan Zhiming into the embassy's Confidential Room, where he wrote an internal-use feasibility report of nearly ten thousand words which was then sent to China.

The content replaced by ellipses above was removed by the cyber police in China. Jiang Zemin's son Jiang Mianheng, who was President of the Chinese Academy of Sciences, must have approved the lengthy report. In accordance with traditions handed down from the Mao Zedong era, it would also have become an "internal reference" document for the Central Political Bureau of the CCP and the surviving veteran Party leaders of the time. Only after consensus had been reached among these readers could the following item from *China Science and Technology News* have been released on May 28, 2018:

> Vice President Chen Zhu met with French virologists Jean-Claude Manuguerra and Ralf Altmeyer of the Pasteur Institute in Wuhan, and discussed the current SARS virus research situation, virus mutation, and pathogenesis with the French experts, and both parties hope to strengthen cooperation as regards the new challenges facing humankind.

Subsequent reports were of only a few words in length, until December 31, 2019, when a news report on the China Business Network summarized the project as follows:

This project helped China build a P4 laboratory modeled on the "box-in-box" construction template of France's P4 laboratory in Lyon. After the outbreak of the SARS epidemic in 2004, when French President Chirac visited China, he projected that it would be completed and delivered in early 2015 and would ultimately officially enter operation in early 2018. The laboratory represents the most technologically advanced P4 laboratory today, [achieved despite] the enormous opposition of other developed countries [against approval of the project]. For this reason, Alain Mérieux, a third-generation descendant of the French Mérieux family, used almost all his French political connections to finally convince France to cooperate with China ... the P4 laboratory is also a model of the "Belt and Road" Initiative, from Lyon to Wuhan.*

The Wuhan P4 biosafety facility is known as the "Supervirus Prison." It's said there are ten protective doors that restrict each entrant in phases; if one is not tightly closed, the next will not open, and security is also automatically alerted. The prisoners here are the most dangerous "prisoners" on the planet, and if they escape, it will result in an enormous, and possibly irreparable, catastrophe. But even so, it should not have taken fifteen years to build the P4. Why did Alain Mérieux have to use "almost all his French political connections" to complete this "model of the 'Belt and Road' Initiative"?

On January 25, 2020, Radio France Internationale (China) released a report, "Why the Sino-French Wuhan Virus Laboratory P4 Cooperation Project Has Caused Controversy," filling in a previous news gap:

China's demands had caused differences between the French government and virus experts, as although the Chinese Virus Center can combat sudden infectious diseases, some French experts worried that China would use the technology provided by France to develop bio-chemical weapons. At that time, the French intelligence service issued a stern warning to the government. . . . But with the support of then Prime Minister Raffarin, China and

France signed a cooperation agreement during Chirac's visit to China in 2004. France would assist China in the construction of the P4 virus center, but the agreement stipulates that Beijing cannot use this technology for aggressive activities. When the agreement was signed, it caused controversy. Raffarin stated that the heads of government of the two countries signed a cooperation agreement, but then the executive branches blocked everything in every way possible. . . . The French General Directorate of Foreign Security pointed out that RTV, an architectural design firm in Lyon, was originally responsible for the engineering of the laboratory, but in 2005 China officially chose the Wuhan local design office IPPR [China IPPR International Engineering Company Limited] to be responsible for the project. However, according to the French security department's investigation, the IPPR Design Institute was closely related to subdivisions of China's military that had long been surveillance targets of the US Central Intelligence Agency. Due to the above security concerns and repeated delays in the implementation of the agreement, in addition to a diplomatic crisis between the two countries in 2008, the Wuhan P4 Virus Center was not officially operational until 2017. The French Prime Minister, Bernard Cazeneuve, attended the launch ceremony of the laboratory.*

The "Supervirus Prison" was finally completed and is a state-of-the-art crystallization of the official friendship between China and France. The most terrifying "prisoners" from Nature are collected as specimens and held in custody within it. Yes, it can develop vaccines for the benefit of humankind, just in case . . . French post-impressionist painter Paul Gauguin once said that "aside from poisons, there are also antidotes," the implication being "don't make poisons without antidotes." Moreover, if the antidote is in the hands of delusional dictators, the entire planet may become a prison controlled by viruses, and the dreams of the late tyrants Hitler, Stalin, and Mao Zedong will finally be realized: their successors will become the prison wardens of all sentient creatures.

The streetlights were on, the brittle branches outside the window were swaying, and now a few snowflakes were drifting down, a rare sight in Changsha. Ai Ding turned up the heat but still felt cold, so he wrapped himself in a quilt and leaned back on the sofa. Suddenly he heard a loud crash outside and he jumped up and stretched his neck to look out the window. A man had fallen headfirst and was lying on the public green, still twitching, but, of course, his head was broken open like a watermelon with pink gobbets of fruit blossoming under the streetlight.

The soundproofing of the window glass was good, so Ai Ding on the ground floor could only vaguely hear the wailing from above. After a while, a corpse truck arrived, and the person who fell was packed into a body bag. Snowflakes were still flying. Everything was as silent as it was at the beginning, as the Polish poet Wisława Szymborska has written. Over the next few days, the corpse truck visited three or four times, all during the day-time.

Ai Ding felt a bit apprehensive, so he poured himself a glass of wine and picked out a book by the Song Dynasty poet Li Qingzhao to console himself. He leafed through to a lyric poem, set to the tune "Note after Note," which matched his mood of the moment:

> Searching and searching, seeking and seeking,
> so chill, so clear,
> dreary,
>   and dismal,
>   and forlorn.
> That time of year
>   when it's suddenly warm,
>   then cold again,
> now it's hardest of all to take care.
> Two or three cups of weak wine –
> how can they resist the biting wind
>   that comes with evening?
> The wild geese pass by –
> that's what hurts the most –
> and yet they're old acquaintances.

. . . .

I stay by the window,
how can I wait alone until blackness comes?*

Ai Ding whispered: "How can this be Li Qingzhao, when it's clearly me, Ai Ding. The ancient writers have said it all before." So, he drained his glass and called up Zhuangzi Gui on Skype.

Zhuangzi Gui immediately appeared from thousands of miles away, still smiling and bald. Ai Ding was a little tipsy and shouted: "Where's your glass? A drink?"

"It's just past noon here, a bit early for drinking."

"Killjoy."

"Okay, fine, I'll pour a glass now. Hey, have you enough reserves over there?"

"My father-in-law's a wino, so there's plenty here. What're you doing?"

"I was reading *Prisoner of Mao.*** The author was a Sino-French man of mixed parentage named Bao Ruo-wang, born in 1926 on the eve of the Anti-Japanese War, who understood four languages. Because he was translating for Americans, he wasn't able to escape from China before 1949 and was labeled a 'historical counter-revolutionary' during the Campaign to Suppress Counter-Revolutionaries in the early 1950s. In late 1957, he was sentenced to twelve years in prison. In 1964, when China and France established diplomatic relations, he was pardoned and sent back to France. I'll read you the beginning:

On the afternoon of Friday, 13 November 1964, a political prisoner was released at the Chinese border checkpoint of Shumchun, the principal land entrance to Hong Kong. He was hardly important enough for any consideration. . . . That prisoner was myself.***

Ai Ding said: "I remember France was the first of the Western democracies to establish diplomatic relations with the CCP."

"True. And as this *Prisoner of Mao* was also very popular in the West, it stands to reason that anyone who read it should have

understood what a communist dictatorship with Chinese characteristics is. For example, the following paragraph:

> [T]his ... is the simple and powerful gist of what is known as
> brainwashing: submission of your will to that of another. Once the
> act of submission has been obtained, it is not difficult to increase
> it from begrudging to enthusiastic – or even to fanatic. It is only
> a question of how powerful the authority is. I hadn't yet had any
> contact with the total pervasiveness of that authority, but I would
> very soon. It didn't take me long to submit, either.*

"Thank you, Zhuangzi. I'm wondering, if they'd read the paragraph you just read out to me before deciding to go ahead with
cooperating on building a virus prison, would they have continued to pursue it?"

"This is just one book. Global capitalism will not be inter-
rupted by a book. Over a hundred million people in China have
died of starvation, beatings, and political campaigns, all of which
has been noted and published in the West. But what has this
changed? During the June 4 massacre of 1989, so many Western
journalists were present and recorded so many bloody scenes, but
within just a few years it was forgotten as circumstances changed.
The Chinese market is too big and costs too low, so everyone
wants in . . ."

"Russia is also very big and cheap."

"The West is very wary of Putin; France wouldn't help Russia
build a P4."

"And China's okay? Is Xi Jinping less despotic and less dangerous than Putin? When in truth . . ."

"In truth, this virus, fuck, let's not mention it. I'll read you
another paragraph:

> During my fifteen months in the interrogation centre, I ate rice
> only once and meat never. Six months after my arrest my stom-
> ach was entirely caved in and I began to have the characteristic
> bruised joints that came from simple body contact with the com-
> munal bed. The skin on my ass hung loose like the dugs of an old

woman. Vision became unclear and I lost my power of concentration. I reached a sort of record point of vitamin deficiency when I was finally able to snap off my toenails without even using the clipper. My skin rubbed off in a dusty film. My hair began falling out. It was miserable. . . . Food obsessed us so completely that we were insane, in a way. We were ready for anything. It was the perfect climate for interrogations.*

3

Who's Eating the Bats?

A i Ding continued to write . . .

All over Wuhan, there were countless dead people, and most of those still alive were not permitted to enter the overcrowded hospitals. Of those who were allowed in, many lay on their sides in the corridors, and those were the lucky ones.

The medical staff were also afraid of becoming infected. There's a video of a nurse in a hospital in Wuhan who collapsed and cried so hard that another nurse put her arms around her while crying and shaking herself. At the desk, their shift leader was making a phone call and screaming: "There's absolutely nothing! Three days and three nights, we've been afraid to take off our PPE once it's on. If we take it off, we can't put it on again as it's coming apart at the seams. Several doctors and nurses are using raincoats as PPE . . . What the hell is going on? The reagent test kits have been used up – what are we supposed to use to make diagnoses and save people? Cut the crap and get us supplies now, or get people in here ASAP to replace us . . ."

The most popular article on the Internet was "A Funeral Worker's Statement" under the name of "Lu Wen," which read:

After January 10, 2020, the crematorium held no more farewell meetings or memorial services, the monks and priests no longer chanted the sutras for the dead, and no mourners were seen.

Worried about the spread of the novel coronavirus, the higher-
ups informed us these activities had to stop. . . . The corpses from
undertakers' vehicles were unloaded and simply piled haphazardly
in front of incinerator doors. We were too busy to take breaks, and
those doing the corpse handovers weren't able to help cremation
staff register the deceased's names, ID numbers, or sort out items
on the bodies, like money, mobile phones, etc. . . . One day, our
four vehicles transported 127 bodies, the incinerators were at full
capacity, cremating 116, with 11 left to burn the next day. Body
bags were in short supply. . . . When we rested, we knew there
were two bodies waiting for us in Sanyuan District on Hebin Road,
and three more in the Siwei Apartments also. We were planning
on waiting for a phone call, not wanting to get halfway there, then
getting a call sending us back to the riverside Cuiye community to
pull out one who'd just died. At the time, people often jumped into
the river, but the water was shallow. Instead of floating down the
river, the corpses kept sinking and resurfacing, getting stranded
on the riverbanks, and the police would call us to pull them out.

On the surface, the three towns of Wuhan – Wuchang, Hankou,
and Hanyang – were empty, but beneath the surface they seethed
like a bubbling pot of porridge. Shut up in their cages, the nine million "prisoners" all rushed online to vent. "Why is this happening?"
The crowd was furious, "Exactly who should be held responsible?"
At the start, the spearheads were pointed at Wuhan Mayor
Zhou Xianwang. He'd known early on that the virus was powerful, so why did he conceal it? In an interview with CCTV on
January 27, Zhou shirked any responsibility: "As the local government, I can only disclose the information I obtain after authorization to do so. This was not understood by many at the time. . . .
Later, especially on January 20 when the State Council executive
session convened . . . they demanded local areas take responsibility. Since then, our work has been more proactive."
What this meant was that they reported the epidemic to the
imperial court but didn't dare disclose anything publicly without
instructions from the highest levels until January 20, when the
Emperor gave the word. "Our work has been more proactive."

The subtext here was: "If you want to settle accounts, go find the Emperor." This Zhou guy was a rabbit in a rush to bite people. So as not to be framed as a scapegoat in future, he'd appease the populace by killing off one to warn off a hundred others.

With this warning, everyone naturally turned their spearheads on the Emperor. Although they dared not express it openly, the rumors of infighting at court were surging like a raucous rising tide. Xu Zhangrun, a professor at Tsinghua University, composed a call to arms, "Angry People No Longer Fear," that was everywhere on the Internet. The Internet police couldn't delete it fast enough and closing hundreds of thousands of WeChat and Weibo accounts didn't do the trick either. Then, Dr. Xu Zhiyong sent the Emperor "An Exhortation for Dismissal," triggering another upsurge in Internet activity. There was even a "news picture" of the Emperor being "diagnosed" in bed, with a caption stating: "Fuck, still haven't issued an 'Edict of Self-Blame.' Can't you even copy the work of an ancient emperor?"

With this, the Emperor couldn't control his temper anymore, and he had Xu Zhangrun and Xu Zhiyong arrested, claiming that instructions from on high had been issued many times, such as: "On January 7, when I chaired the Politburo Central Committee meeting, I proposed requirements for novel coronavirus epidemic prevention and control work." As to what the requirements were, he didn't clearly name them, and nobody can find a record of them. What *can* be found is the Emperor's New Year's Day speech:

> 2020 is a year of landmark significance, as the comprehensive goal of broad-based wealth in our society will be fully realized – which has been our number one priority for the past one hundred years. 2020 is also the year we will decisively battle against poverty; we are resolved to win the difficult battle to eradicate it, alleviating poverty in rural areas on schedule and removing the stigma currently endured by poverty-stricken counties.

The Emperor's speech made no mention of the Wuhan virus, and the initial source of the virus, the South China Seafood

Wholesale Market, was also closed on New Year's Day. However, at 1:30 a.m. on New Year's Eve, Li Wenliang, an ophthalmologist at Wuhan Central Hospital, was summoned to the Municipal Health Commission to answer to the rumor that "Wuhan is about to see a breakout of a SARS coronavirus pneumonia." Until he had to go on his shift at dawn that day, Li was interrogated by the Hospital Surveillance Section and forced to write "Reflections and Self-Criticism on the Dissemination of Untruthful Rumors." On January 3, he was summoned to the police station and signed a "Letter of Reprimand."

Besides him, there were as many as eight other "rumor-mongering" doctors, perhaps more, and they, too, were publicly warned on CCTV without being named. They had simply forwarded the fatal truth to their peers, relatives, and friends through a WeChat group – because as early as December 15, Wuhan Central Hospital had already admitted a patient with "unexplained pneumonia," with the number increasing to twenty-seven people in the next two weeks. In another four days, it had increased to fifty-nine people, and all were closely connected in some way to the nearby South China Seafood Wholesale Market.

As to the "rumor" that SARS had made a comeback after seventeen years, following the closure of the South China Seafood Wholesale Market and the Emperor's "landmark significance" speech on New Year's Day in 2020, it was passed down the streets and alleys of Wuhan until finally everybody had heard it. But no one was willing to admit they were "spreading rumors," as spreading rumors is a crime, and the police will come to arrest you as soon as you're reported. According to domestic media reports, on the evening of December 30, 2019, a completely unaware Gao Fu, Director of the Chinese Center for Disease Control and Prevention, who after the SARS experience had established a reporting system for hospital infectious diseases covering the whole country, only accidentally saw the "Emergency Notice":

According to an emergency notice from higher authorities, a succession of pneumonia patients have inexplicably occurred at the

South China Seafood Wholesale Market in our city. In order to better respond to the situation, all units are requested to immediately take inventory and count unexplained pneumonia patients with similar characteristics who have been seen in the past week. A stamped statistical report should be submitted to the Medical Administration Management Office of the Municipal Health and Sanitation Commission by 4 o'clock today.

Gao was shocked and immediately made a phone call to verify that the news was correct, and then immediately reported the matter to the State Council in Beijing. The next morning, the first group of epidemiologists was sent to Wuhan. But their final verdict: no clear human-to-human transmission phenomenon was observed; no infection of medical personnel was discovered. They declared the epidemic "preventable and controllable."

From his perspective, the poorly informed Emperor had been bamboozled by experts who'd lied about the situation on the ground, and so he couldn't remember what instructions he'd given during the meeting on January 7. And so, due to the poor handling of the situation, the opposite instructions became the ones that were followed. Over the next two weeks, Wuhan would convene the Provincial People's Congress and the representative assembly of the People's Political Consultative Conference, as well as the "Ten Thousand Family Banquet" gathering, the traditional high point of Wuhan's Spring Festival. And more than five million migrant workers would leave Wuhan to return home for the Chinese New Year . . .

Doomsday madness. Like a high-speed train rushing toward the edge of a deep abyss, once the serious threat of "human-to-human" transmission of the SARS COVID-19 virus was declared by the medical expert Zhong Nanshan on January 20, suddenly the brakes were pulled, stunning everybody.

But the city was closed too late.

———————————

Today, the South China Seafood Wholesale Market has been officially designated as the source of the Wuhan pneumonia. Government records show that the earliest patients were the merchants and customers there. There were wild animal stalls in the market, and it's said there were civet cats, pangolins, monkeys, deer, hares, and so on. The original vector bat of the new coronavirus was included in the mix.

As we know, the people of Wuhan tried to find out who or what had responsibility for all this, but it ultimately was blamed on the bad habits of "Wuhan people who like eating wild game"! Even a fake advertising video about "Braised Bats" came into being to meet the historic moment, circulating on various Internet platforms. In the medical chamber of an imperial palace, sounds of the ancient long zither floated among the beams, while a costumed beauty used chopsticks to pick a bat skeleton out of a small bowl of soup and placed it in her mouth, chewing with obvious relish. The caption running along the bottom of the video says: "*The Yellow Emperor's Classic of Internal Medicine* states: This soup has the wonderful effects of nourishing the skin, moistening the lungs, promoting yin, supplementing yang, prolonging life, and so on."

This and similar fabrications were really too sinister, as people were dying every day in Wuhan. The authorities concealed the truth and hoodwinked the people there, announcing only hundreds of deaths. And all this was actually brought about by Wuhan people's eating habits?! This is reminiscent of the old 2003 story of Cantonese people eating civets infected with SARS. Even Shi Zhengli, the "Batwoman of the P4 Lab," stepped forward to tell people to "watch and listen fairmindedly" to what the authorities had to say in a WeChat message:

You're welcome to forward this. The new type of coronavirus pneumonia of 2019 is nature's punishment for the uncivilized living habits of human beings. I, Shi Zhengli, guarantee on my life this has nothing to do with a laboratory. I advise those who believe and spread harmful rumors on social media, those who believe the unreliable so-called "academic analysis" of Indian scholars, to shut your stinking mouths, and at the same time forward this humiliating message, that the Indian scholars have already withdrawn their as-yet-unpublished paper.

Rumors are never sufficiently believable, yet high-level experts like Shi Zhengli evade guilt by affirming some rumors while they attempt to persuade everyone to shut up. Isn't this even more despotic than the reigning Emperor himself? Moreover, you Shi Zhengli are not yet the Emperor. So, many residents familiar with the South China Seafood Wholesale Market came forward to confirm that there are absolutely no bats in Wuhan. Even if they were imported from other places, just a look at a bat's appearance would be enough to see that no one would dare eat them. As for other wild game, the prices are high and the great majority of Wuhan people can't afford to eat any of it – and this has nothing at all to do with Indian scholars withdrawing their *Lancet* paper* exploring the source of the virus in Wuhan.

I've just found a very popular domestic video. Though the setting is unclear, this person speaks Mandarin, but with a Wuhan accent. I've transcribed it as follows:

I'm the chair of the Conference of Chinese Thought, Xiang Qianjing. Today, let's talk about whether the new coronavirus in Wuhan originated from a natural mutation or artificial manufacture in a laboratory.

The Lancet, an international medical journal, indicates that the first confirmed infection in Wuhan actually had nothing to do with the South China Seafood Wholesale Market. On January 27, a related scientific magazine [*Science*] also published a report entitled "Wuhan Seafood Market May Not be Source of Novel Virus Spreading Globally."** Tong Yigang, a professor at Beijing University of Chemical Technology, confirmed that the seafood market is only a collecting and distributing center for viruses, and that it cannot be said that it was the original transmission point of the virus from wild animals to humans.

Did the virus truly originate in wild animals, such as bats? In fact, how can we know in how many countries, in how many remote places, how many people are eating wild animals every day on this planet? Before humans learned to domesticate animals, didn't everyone eat wild animals? In Indonesia, there is a market called Tomohon that is well known for selling wild animals such as bats, mice, and pythons, and that attracts many tourists. Chinese tourists have named it the "Market of Terror." If viruses originate from wild animals, why didn't the government shut it down? This is a matter of common sense.

Even now, experts have found no evidence that bats directly make people sick. And since this is the case, who is misdirecting everybody's view on this matter? The aim of misguiding people is to cover up something, but what is there to cover up? ... An old saying goes: when Heaven does evil, it is forgivable; but when you bring it on yourself, you're done for. So, I hope everyone will stop wrongly blaming bats and other wild animals.

On January 24, a paper collectively written by thirty doctors, including Huang Chaolin, Deputy Director of Wuhan Jinyintan Hospital, was also published in *The Lancet*,* and indirectly corroborates the above statements. The "first confirmed patient" specified in the paper was over seventy years old and had an illness onset date of December 1. "Because of Alzheimer's disease, he hardly went out," his family said, "let alone go to the South China Seafood Wholesale Market." Following this, the Jinyintan Hospital treated three patients with the same symptoms who also had nothing to do with the South China Seafood Wholesale Market.

And so, as everybody engaged in chasing down the date of the discovery of Patient Zero, the date of the virus's onset grew ever earlier. Unconfirmed rumors had it that on November 17, a fifty-five-year-old man was diagnosed with the virus and died. An even more potent rumor was that a man named Huang Yaling was Patient Zero. He became infected as the result of an accidental leak of the virus at the Wuhan Institute of Virology and died.

Due to improper handling, however, when his corpse was sent to a crematorium for incineration, it infected funeral workers. In response, the Institute of Virology issued a statement refuting this rumor. Shi Zhengli, who oversaw the P4 lab, stated in an interview: "Not one person at the institute has been infected by the virus, our institute has zero infections."

The people of Wuhan had been online pursuing those responsible for the virus from the time the city was closed on January 20, and with this it all finally reached a climax. And so, over time, the blame gradually shifted from the Wuhan Mayor Zhou Xianwang, to the current Emperor, to the Wuhan Health Commission, to the first group of epidemic experts, to the South China Seafood Wholesale Market, to bats, to natural or artificial viruses, to the Institute of Virology, to the P4, and now to Shi Zhengli. According to her Chinese Wikipedia page, her primary scientific contributions are "the discovery and identification of new viruses such as adenovirus and circovirus in bats, further confirming that bats are natural hosts of multiple viruses . . . and [she] has also participated in infectious human coronavirus research."

4

Li Wenliang is Gone –
The Truth is Dead

Today, the thirty-five-year-old doctor Li Wenliang passed away. A hundred million people were mourning on the Internet. Images of silk flowers, candles like snowflakes and hail swept over every social platform in China. The Internet police and government-hired hands did their best to remove them, but couldn't keep up and ultimately gave up. If Chinese officials had allowed this virtual space to reflect reality, the brigade mourning the "whistle-blower" would have been even more powerful than that mourning Mao Zedong in 1976. The death of old Mao was the death of a remote, godlike figure. Little Li succumbing to the virus himself was a further death blow to those sympathetic hearts who were witnessing the terrible suffering caused by the epidemic.

I once said that my opposition to the Communist Party was not political but aesthetic. As long as a person speaks important truths in public, that person has the possibility of becoming a hero in an aesthetic sense, just as Li Wenliang saying "a normal society cannot have only one voice" is tantamount to his paying the price with his tragic death. These inadvertent words of his just happened to hit all the vulnerable points of this authoritarian society.

On the afternoon of December 30, 2019, Li issued a warning in a WeChat group: "Seven cases of SARS have been confirmed at the South China Seafood Wholesale Market and they have been isolated in the emergency department of the Houhu Campus of our hospital." At the same time, he attached a MapMi test* diagnosis to the message. An hour later, he again stated: "The latest news is that coronavirus infection is confirmed, and virus typing is in progress. . . . Please don't transmit this news, have family and relatives take preventative measures."

Eight doctors that we know of forwarded the same message, and in the blink of an eye all became "rumor-mongers" violating national laws. They were officially warned and forced to shut up. A few days later, CCTV publicly refuted the rumors. On January 3, the police summoned Li Wenliang to the police station. After a hearing, they announced he had been reprimanded according to law:

Wuhan Public Security Bureau. Zhongnan Branch. Zhongnan Road Police Station
Letter of Reprimand

Person admonished: Li Wenliang, male, Date of birth: October 12, 1985, ID number: 210********,

Current address [location of household registration]: No. 648, Minzhu Road, Wuchang District, Wuhan City, Work Unit: Wuhan Central Hospital.

Illegal behavior: December 30, 2019, WeChat group "Wuhan University Clinical Level 04" published untrue statements about seven SARS cases diagnosed at the South China Seafood Wholesale Market.

In accordance with the law, you are now warned and reprimanded about illegalities related to the expression of untruths you made on the Internet. Your behavior seriously disrupted social order. Your behavior has exceeded the scope allowed by law and violated the relevant provisions of the "Public Security Administration Punishment Law of the People's Republic of China," which is an illegal act! The Public Security Bureau hopes that you will actively cooperate with their work, follow the counsel of the police, and cease illegal behavior. Are you capable of doing this?

Answer: Yes [with fingerprints].

We hope you will calm down, reflect on this, and we must warn
you: if you persist in your views, do not repent, and continue to
carry out illegal activities, you will be punished by the law. Do
you understand?

Answer: Understood [with fingerprints].

Reprimanded: Li Wenliang [with fingerprints]
Reprimanders: Hu Guifang, Xu Jinhang
    January 3, 2020 [stamp of the law enforcement agency]

Li Wenliang took the official document and returned to the
hospital in shame, thinking he'd redeem himself through good
work, while feeling very depressed. A little later, on January 8,
while examining an eighty-two-year-old glaucoma patient, he
was accidentally infected. "She didn't have a fever at the time. But
she had a fever the next day," Li Wenliang said. "The CT showed
viral pneumonia. But our hospital still didn't have test-kits to
diagnose patients, so she wasn't diagnosed. Many people didn't
care and there were no special protective measures, and I also
was careless when in contact with the patient. Later, I had a fever
and cough, and was hospitalized on January 12, from suspected to
confirmed. . . . My parents were also infected."

Then he was moved into the intensive care unit and put on a
ventilator. He died within a month of being reprimanded.

Right now, there are dozens of closed cities in the country. No,
if you count the medium-sized cities, it's in the hundreds, and if
counties are included, it's in the thousands. The initial symptoms
of the vast majority of the deceased, such as the old woman who
infected Li Wenliang, were not diagnosed in time, so the "number
of deaths from new-type coronary pneumonia" will be a mystery forever. Li Wenliang's nickame was "Truth." When he died,
the "Truth" died with him – but that other "Truth," the SARS
whistle-blower of 2003, the military doctor Jiang Yanyong, is
still alive, almost ninety, and he declared: "History is taking giant
steps backwards."

Li Wenliang's source had been Ai Fen, the Director of the Emergency Department at Wuhan Central Hospital. When a reporter interviewed her, she immediately said, "I am not a whistle-blower; I hand out the whistles." The MapMi test diagnosis form forwarded by Li Wenliang to the WeChat doctor group and disseminated by them had first been in her possession, and was photographed with the words "SARS coronavirus" circled in red.

At the time she had carefully read the test notes: "SARS coronavirus is a unistrand positive-strand RNA virus. The virus's main mode of transmission is close-range droplet transmission or contact with the respiratory secretions of patients, which can induce a kind of obvious infectivity that may involve multiple organ systems in a unique pneumonia, also known as atypical pneumonia [or SARS]." She'd immediately broken out in a cold sweat. Her original intention had been the same as that of Li Wenliang, to warn everyone to take precautions; and her experience was also similar to his. However, she was punished by the hospital's CCP Disciplinary Committee, which is to say, the Party's supervisory department tasked with purging dissidents, as Ai Fen's rank and qualifications were much higher than Li Wenliang's.

She was severely reprimanded as never before: "Director XX has criticized our hospital doctor, Ai Fen. As the Director of the Emergency Department of Wuhan City Central Hospital, you are a professional, so how could you have been so unprincipled and lacking in organizational discipline as to manufacture rumors?" Then they ordered her to go back to "refute the rumors" and eliminate their adverse effects: "There are more than two hundred people in the department who must be communicated with verbally, one by one. Do not send them WeChat or text messages. You must talk or call each person, but you are not permitted to say anything about this pneumonia, even to your husband."

Ai Fen was stunned but stood up to their bullying, saying: "I did this alone, it has nothing to do with anyone else. Just take me to jail . . ."

She didn't go to jail, but just like Li Wenliang, she had been seriously wounded, both physically and mentally, and had no choice but to shut up. According to what she said later, as early as December 16 and 27, 2019, the Emergency Department of the Wuhan Central Hospital, Nanjing Road Branch, had received two cases of "unknown pneumonia." Due to great pressure as a result of a directive issued from the central government to localities calling for a crackdown on "rumors," the more forbidden the issue, the less control there was over it. Ai Fen's hospital also housed over two hundred infected patients, and several had died, including Jiang Xueqing, the Director of Thyroid and Breast Medicine. On January 21, the Emergency Department received 1,523 patients, three times the daily peak average, and 655 of them had a fever. Later, Ai Fen recalled, when the city was closed and all was dark, "People would stand in long lines, and suddenly a person would fall down and die. There were others who couldn't make it to the line-up and died in their cars." She continued speaking to the reporters, "Before, if you made a mistake – for example, if an injection was not made in time – patients would make a stink about it. Now no one was arguing with you. Everyone has been crushed and stunned . . . when a patient dies, it's rare to see the family crying, as there are too many, too many. Some families do not beg doctors to save their family member, instead saying to them: 'Oh, let them be free of it quickly, it's already at that stage.' Because at the time everybody was afraid they'd be infected . . ."

None of this had to happen! As a Communist Party member, knowing it was too late for regrets, Ai Fen said: "We knew this day would come."

And so, Dr. Ai Fen's humanity trumped her Party loyalty as she stood there being interviewed by China's *People Weekly*. Her testimony was the most sensational of any in the whole country during the epidemic, and it echoed and extended Li Wenliang's tragedy. Therefore, when its online version surfaced, it was immediately deleted by the cyber police, and a warning was issued about the paper journal's cover. Unfortunately, these actions were a bit too slow and the article "The Person Handing Out the Whistles" survived for a few minutes – and in those few minutes, the web worms proved themselves quicker than the cyber police, copying it, and not only sending it out from multiple WeChat numbers at the same time, but also posting it to overseas platforms on the other side of the Internet wall. The cyber police went into action again, this time with their numbers increased tenfold, reporting to the National Network Management Office and the National Security Bureau, preparing for multiple simultaneous arrests in various parts of the country as they had in 2011 when crushing the "Jasmine Revolution." But more worms lurked throughout the land, emerging in droves, and their speed of transmission was a hundred times faster than the Wuhan virus. The cyber police's strength was increased by a multiple of a thousand, and hired hands of a thousand times a thousand were added. This was too crazy, too exciting, and was a fitting response to the famous saying of Tsinghua University professor Xu Zhangrun, "Angry people no longer fear." The thousands upon thousands of "criminal" webworms copied and distributed the article almost at the speed of light. It was translated into English, French, German, Spanish, Portuguese, Japanese, Korean, Italian, Czech, Polish, Hebrew, Vietnamese, and another forty languages within a few hours. The variant versions of written Chinese included Oracle script, Classical Chinese, Seal script, the vertical type of premodern texts, inscription script, Western Xia, Braille, Cantonese, Sichuan dialect, ancient calligraphy, faux-Mao Zedong calligraphy, QR code, garbled code, barcode, mabinogi, elven runes, alien languages, and so on. The imperial censorship system, which originated in Western technology, had finally been tormented into paralysis. During this tragic global disaster, this was the only thing to raise a laugh. In a torrential flood like the Wuhan virus, the people of China had finally found their freedom of speech.

This scene brings to mind one in Gabriel García Márquez's *One Hundred Years of Solitude*: one sunny morning, the old grandmother Úrsula looks up and finds the vast horizon draped with glittering dewdrops; in the blink of an eye, the dewdrops grow larger, becoming ever-wriggling beetles; in another blink of an eye, the beetles become a dense crowd of heads. This is the fruit that was hurriedly planted by Colonel Buendía while on a camp bed during the civil war, and which now extends through the wilderness to the town of Macondo; the fruits have a red scar on their necks from when they were beheaded – it is the mark of the endless fecundity of the Buendía family.

5

Daily Life in Isolation

I was still curled up in bed at nine in the morning when I heard someone banging at the door. I got up and rushed out of the bedroom, pulling at the door out of habit, only then remembering it had been nailed shut. So I asked who it was through the door.

"We're from Epidemic Prevention Headquarters. Three days ago, you used WeChat Alipay to order pork and vegetables through us. We're delivering it now. Please open the kitchen skylight."

I was really excited. I hadn't eaten fresh meat and vegetables for over a week! Luckily, my parents-in-law had stocked up with some canned braised pork, rice noodles, oil, salt, and booze. However, without vegetables and fruit, I'd come down with severe constipation. I used the toilet at set times every day, but still couldn't shift my bowels. I went through all the boxes and bags in the house and eventually dug out a big package of *coptis bolus*, and quickly swallowed two packets of it. But the load still wouldn't drop. After I gulped down another packet, the landslide finally cracked loose and it all gushed out. Afterwards, when I stood up, my vision went black and there was a roaring noise in my ears, as if a train was passing. One of the symptoms of Wuhan pneumonia is diarrhea, followed by convulsing on the ground – and this scared me from taking any more of the medicine. So, my constipation picked up again from where it had left off.

I'd ordered three pounds of pork, five pounds of white radishes, three pounds of carrots, five pounds of Chinese cabbage, five pounds of potatoes, one pound of red chilis, one pound of ginger root, all for a total of 400 Yuan. But I could understand prices skyrocketing in extraordinary times, as punctual delivery was all that really mattered.

I went to the kitchen, climbed onto the stovetop, and cracked open the grease- and grime-covered skylight. A cold wind gusted inwards. The people outside were still far off, but using a 10-meter-long pole, they hoisted up a plastic bag as big as a basketball at the end of it, took careful aim, and dropped it straight in. I wasn't able to catch it, and the plastic bag slammed down to the floor together with the kitchen's overhead light.

I jumped to the ground and yelled: "What the hell?!" But the two delivery people had already shouldered their long pole and walked off. I looked closely at the goods scattered over the floor, and except for a piece of pork belly with two rows of teats, shiitake mushrooms, potatoes, and some broken glass, there was nothing else.

Changsha's considered a prosperous place, there's never been a shortage of daily vegetables. But shiitake mushrooms, did I buy shiitake mushrooms? 400 Yuan buys only this much? The price was extortionate. So I asked about it on WeChat, to no response. As I was endeavoring to bite my tongue, I saw a piece of news: convoys of trucks carrying supplies for Wuhan from the southeastern provinces have been passing through Changsha day and night, and two trucks loaded with mushrooms were intercepted by the epidemic prevention department. This sort of blatant "highway robbery" committed by local governments first occurred in Dali, Yunnan Province, where it turned out that several truckloads of medical supplies on their way to Sichuan were intercepted. The central government issued a critical public circular, but the medical supplies had already been divvied up and couldn't be recovered.

I stewed the pig teats with the mushrooms and potatoes in a large pot. Over the next few days, I savored the main ingredient, mushrooms stolen and sold at high prices. The sow belly was the hardest to cook, and after simmering it for three hours, the nipples were still erect as if inflated, creating an indecent association in my mind. I tried to bite into it, but it was like rubber. This sow must have been at least a great-grandmother. Just look at those two rows of uniform buttons, fit for a general. It reminded me of the first time I was in Germany, when I bought some pork and returned to my rented room to stew it. The smell was strange compared to the pork I was used to eating in China. It came as a great shock when I realized that what I was eating in Germany was what pork is actually supposed to taste like. Naturally raised pigs and pork had been virtually eradicated in China. The pork at home must have been all been pumped full of water, or clenobuterol hydrochloride, or else the pigs were raised on feed laced with hormones so that they fattened up within three months.

In the evening, I complained to my wife on WeChat video about all these infuriating incidents. She comforted me, saying over and over again that she'd already submitted an application on my behalf to the community epidemic prevention center, vehemently demanding her husband be reunited with her at home in Wuhan. The reasons: I'd returned from faraway Germany, where the virus had not yet reached, to China, where there was an epidemic. I should not have been quarantined for even one day, but when I couldn't enter Wuhan, I'd flown to Changsha and had been quarantined twice there without explanation. Of course, in extraordinary times, safety comes first, and we didn't blame our disaster-laden birthplace. However, in our own country, not being able to return home was not reasonable under the circumstances.

I couldn't but instantly feel sorry for myself. My wife said, "What's the matter? Cheer up. Your dad just departed this world, so there's lots of empty space in the house and in our hearts. When the old man was sick in bed, I was busy with this and that every day. After a while, I grew exhausted, even fed up with it all. But now he's really left, I can't get to sleep at night, dream about him even. Then I dream of you, standing at the head of the bed in a mask. I call out, 'You're back, what're you standing there for, go wash your hands and disinfect and change your clothes.' And you laugh. When you do that, I understand what it is you want to do and quickly tell you to get into bed. We kiss through masks and fumble around with our gloves, and it's actually quite exciting. Are you laughing yet?"

I said, "I haven't been in your arms for a year, so it will take more than masks and gloves to keep us apart. Not even cowhide, rhino hide, or the hide of the Bull Demon King himself can stand in the way of my lust! If you want to get the virus, we'll do it together. We'll get up to romantic mischief, creating an epidemic version of Liang Shanbo and Zhu Yingtai,* be transformed into two novel coronavirus butterflies, flapping away while coughing and spitting . . . Of course, we don't want to infect our daughter . . ."

My wife laughed, called me a "hooligan," and turned off the video.

My dad died of old age today. I was his only son. When my mom gave birth to me, she was in her thirties and he was well over forty. It was very rare to have a child at that age in the country-side in the 1970s. I loved my dad and feel very sad I couldn't fulfill my filial duty and be by his side at the end. But as a historian I know that since 1949, so many people have died terrible deaths in numerous natural and manmade calamities. So his peaceful depar-ture has given me some solace.

On WeChat video, my wife had asked him to raise his hand and wave to me just before he passed. With his sunken cheeks and toothless mouth, the old man attempted to laugh, but I cried. My wife asked me what I was crying about when many diagnosed novel coronavirus patients were dying much more abruptly than this, and even family members had to keep a distance of over 2 meters, hoping only that the undertakers would quickly carry them away before they infected others. "Your dad is actually lucky." But when the word "lucky" came out, she couldn't help crying too.

Dad was ninety-three years old, and when mom died at eighty-five, he'd been left to his own devices in the countryside at

Shennongjia. At the time, his legs and feet were strong, and he had no problem taking care of himself, but I was still uneasy about him being alone. Five years ago, we brought him to Wuhan to live with us in a high-rise apartment building. He said he'd never lived so high and wanted to get back to the earth. We refused his request, not expecting that simply saying no would be the end of it. Just before I went to Germany as an exchange student, he'd fallen badly coming out of the elevator and had been paralyzed. So my wife felt it necessary to resign from her job as a hospital nurse and since then has been specializing in the care of the old and the young at home.

I told my wife, "I owe you too much." She said, "What are you on about? If I'd not quit my job three years ago, I might have been the one you'd be saying goodbye to today, as there are a lot of serious infections and inadvertent deaths among medical staff now. At the start of the epidemic, nobody knew how to deal with it, so they handled it like SARS in 2003, thinking it was enough to wear masks and gloves and ordinary protective clothing. But it's turned out to be several times more infectious than SARS, and they have to be tightly wrapped in PPE from head to toe. Droplet infection from sneezing and saliva, infection by nasal mucus, even infection from blinking and tears. I've been blessed by your father's misfortune."

After having been awake and alert for twenty minutes, dad's head fell back, and he died. My wife closed his eyelids, put in his dentures, wiped his face with hot water, and then put on a little make-up for him. Our ten-year-old daughter didn't understand the sorrow of death. She ran back and forth, helping her mom get out new clothes and getting her grandpa into them. He lay in his coffin until 11 p.m., when the undertakers arrived. In our unusual times, all dead are treated as if they've died of novel coronavirus, all similarly zipped into a yellow body bag. The workers received 5,000 Yuan in cash, made out a receipt, left a phone number and a WeChat address, while saying, "All funeral parlors in Wuhan are working overtime. The body is cremated the day it's received, never the next day. We guarantee to store the ashes immediately, while still hot, and the name and address of the deceased will be put on the urn. Please be assured there won't be any mistakes made. So as to avoid community infection, during the epidemic, customers without authorization to collect ashes will not be admitted. When the epidemic has passed, the government will of course notify all family members to go to line up to collect the ashes in an orderly and disciplined manner. The cost of the urn is not included in the 5,000 Yuan funeral expenses."

My wife asked: "How long must I wait? Also, when the time comes, everyone will go to the crematorium at once. Won't that lead to community infection? How long will the line be? Besides, your dad wasn't diagnosed with the novel coronavirus. Will he be counted as a victim?" The undertaker said, "It's not possible. If a corpse hasn't gone through a formal nucleic acid test in a hospital, it won't be counted. People are going out like lights, and nobody knows for sure what's wrong with them. This government worries about losing face, so try to keep your voice as low as possible, since groundless arguments won't get you anywhere." My wife said, "You're too damn kind! Have you become numb after cremating all those people?" The undertaker nodded. She also wanted to open the zipper for a last look at dad, but the undertaker stopped her, saying it was unnecessary. My wife just kept on videoing it all, and so our family of three watched the old man go out the door one last time.

My wife, she's Hunan born and bred, so when darkness falls, she shows what she's made of. Usually she's shrewish with a fiery temper, swearing like nobody's business, and it's more than this educated country bumpkin can take. When I'm being scolded by her, in my heart I'm shouting "Divorce" over and over again. When she notices that, it's "What're you grumbling about? What's that coming out of your cakehole? If you've got it in you, spit it out.." Fortunately, I refrain. As a result, I can still say today, "If there's a next life, I'll still want to marry you, my Hunan wife."

Dad had gone forever. My wife closed the door and said she was exhausted and needed to sleep. She turned the camera on our daughter, who, I realized, had curled up at the end of the bed like a puppy and fallen asleep. My wife turned off the video-feed, but my mood was still all over the place, so I opened a new bottle of spirits and took a deep swig . . .

Having written this much, Ai Ding remembered there was a seven-hour time difference between China and Germany in winter. It was still evening over there with Zhuangzi Gui, so he called him on Skype.

Zhuangzi appeared holding a glass with the same old line: "It's still early, but . . ."

Ai Ding cut him off: "My dad just passed."

"How old?"

"Ninety-three."

"He did well."

"Nothing good ever comes from your cakehole."

"Zhuang Zhou* sang songs when his wife died; Ruan Ji** brayed like a donkey to mourn the death of his friend and everyone said he was crazy, but it's a fitting, eternal acknowledgment of life: he was born here, grew up here, perished here, like the leaves of a tree, like the tides, like the clouds rolling by."

Ai Ding couldn't help but smile. And they carried on drinking and chatting as if there were nothing but a pane of glass between them . . .

I'm no scientist, and I am exhausting my brain investigating the origin of the Wuhan virus. Maybe it's all in vain, but my door has been sealed shut, and the TV is broken. Aside from drinking and reading, I've only this to while the time away.

When communicating on WeChat today, my wife said, "The Grim Reaper is roaming the neighborhood. You can't see him, but he always has his eyes on you. He took a whole family of four from the building opposite ours. The reason was, again, that there were too few places allocated to the community for admission to the local hospitals. A car was sent to pick them up, but they were sent back by the hospital. As a result, a 'suspected' can't become 'diagnosed' and has to isolate at home, and a week later, three more are taken away in body bags." My wife's tone was calm, like she was chatting about household matters.

"Death is a family routine in Wuhan," she continued, "Jumping off buildings and bridges is too commonplace, nothing new, not worth mentioning. There was a migrant worker who couldn't get back to his hometown in Xiangyang. He slept in the underground garage at night and eventually finished all his food. So he tried to beg, squatting at the overpass. But as there were no people or cars all day long, who could he ask?! That evening, an old man finally appeared, which pleased the worker, but as the old man approached, he realized the oldster had been diagnosed and, fearing he'd infect others, had sneaked out of his family home, ready to end his life at the bridge. The old man was penniless too, and the migrant worker cried in disappointment. The old man also cried, saying, 'You're still young, not sick, you've a life to live.' The worker said, 'It's taken so long for anybody to come along, but you've got nothing to share! I'm cold and hungry but dare not take your cotton-padded jacket because I'm afraid of contracting the virus.' The old man said, 'It seems you still want to live, I'll write a suicide note for you to take to my home according to the address on the letter; after you deliver it, my children will give you a little money.' The worker asked, 'How far is it?' The old man replied, 'You'll need two to three hours to get there.' The worker said, 'I can't walk for even ten minutes, so just let me jump first. Could you film it with my mobile phone? I'll say a few words and you can post it on the Internet, maybe people in my hometown will see it.' The old man said, 'Okay, I guess I could do that.' Then the two climbed up to the middle of the bridge arch as a cold wind howled angrily. The old man raised the mobile phone, but after thinking it over for a while, the migrant worker couldn't come up with anything remarkable to say. The old man said, 'If you don't speak now, the phone'll run out of power.' So, the worker shouted, 'Everybody's dead!' and jumped. With that the old man finished filming, noted the location, and pressed send. Then he shouted, 'Those who deserve to die die, those who don't must be very careful,' and he jumped too."

It made me think of a poem written by the renowned scholar Ai Xiaoming, called "They're All Gone." Ai has made many excellent documentaries and her poetry is also documentary-like:

Mister Tian of Wuhan says
third from left in the photo, a neighbor from the community
gone the day before yesterday, both old and young
Fourth from left his wife
his daughter the same age as my grandson

Mister Wang of Wuhan says
my high school headteacher's gone
Visited him last summer
he invited us to dinner
then walked me to the intersection
I remember him saying
such a hot day
you shouldn't have come
The woman howling behind the hearse says
Qinqin, your baba's going this way
you've no baba anymore

Doctor Liu Wenxiong of Xiantao's gone
January 21, he saw 180 patients
3,181 consultations in a month
every night consulting by phone
Only two days off that month
on the third, to hospital with pains in his chest

Doctor Xia Sisi is gone, a two-year-old remains
Her full-moon face reminds me of childhood
29 at the end, why 29
An unresolved number and eternal sorrow

Far far away a beekeeper
also casts away his colony and goes
Bees hover among the flowers

honey already sealed into jars
An empty road, he just can't wait
When mama goes, she says
Sorry, girl
I'm going first
You should find a good person to marry
I don't want to hold you back

When gramps went
he left no will
A high fever burned out the virus in him
Parkinson's given as cause of death

A dad goes quietly
a series of pleas for help recorded on his phone
I've a fever, I've a fever
and the Community reply: No way
No hospital will receive you

When baba left
he went without a key
Some don't want to go
dragged out and down the stairs
I heard a man yelling all the way
Let me turn off the TV
Let me lock the door
Let me take my phone

Aaaiii, how can you beat him?
A man is hitting him and pressing down on his head
wanting him to squat and wear a mask

A wardmate in the mobile hospital says
I've had seven
all've died

A doctor tells a relative, you can't fall
his situation already very acute

The relative tells a patient
listen to the doctor, don't worry about a thing
The patient says, I'll donate my body to the nation
but my wife?

Every day I hear someone's gone
I pray, don't be someone I know
be a better friend than this
say you're going and just go, leaving me this spring
a Parrot Cay of lush fragrant grass*

There's also the sensible child
covering up a grandpa suddenly dead
I hope someone takes him away
far far away
to the beautiful country**

When Chinese orphans arrive
parents gather at airports to receive them
Spring hangs about here
The virus strolls leisurely here

Some spread news of receiving money
Some burn paper money by the road
burned for those gone
also for the novel coronavirus

If you must die, it's best to go quickly
Those who shouldn't go will return
Rising wisps of blue smoke are wishes
Those who've left hear all

You want to come back for wine when flowers blossom
to remember giving out wedding candy
to tightly embrace relatives and friends who've not had time to
   say goodbye
to hug Wuhan, your thoughts of home

I unwittingly began to cry after reading this poem, perhaps touched off by the "thoughts of home" at the end. Even if it was thoughts of so many dying back home, I still wanted to embrace it all.

At this point, my wife broke in on WeChat, saying the application she'd submitted had been approved by the Jianghan District Epidemic Prevention Headquarters, and they'd already called Hunan to tell them. Both places agreed I could go after my fourteen-day quarantine period had expired. I asked, "What happens if I'm intercepted on the way there?" My wife said, "When you get out, they will give you a pass with a big red seal and send a special car to take you to Changsha Railway Station. The last high-speed train is at two o'clock in the afternoon, but the terminus is not Wuhan. You should get off at Wuchang Railway Station. There's no public transport in the city, but you're familiar with the roads, so you'll have to find your own way home. If you can't, call again."

In two days, the nightmare will be over. It's been eighteen days since I've returned to my homeland, and now I'm finally getting a "confirmed" diagnosis from the government: going home is easy. Thanks to you, my wife.

6

An Asymptotic Spreader

I woke at 5 a.m., got up and tidied the house, crammed all my stuff into a backpack, and hung the computer bag on my chest. Fortunately, I didn't listen to my wife, so I also had an oversized trolley-suitcase, otherwise I'd have been in trouble.

Over these two weeks, I had finished off five bottles of my father-in-law's Xiangjiang Daqu liquor, one bottle of Erguotou sorghum spirits, and one bottle of Luzhou Laojiao liquor, an average of half a kilo a day. Feeling somewhat giddy, I wrote a bit more in this diary, but there's nothing much else of note. As Wuliangye grain liquor and Maotai liquor are expensive, I didn't dare touch them, nor was there a need to. I remembered a few years ago, a domestic writer called Old Wei wrote a collection of stories about people on the bottom rungs of society, which included the drinker's heartfelt wish: "Letting a drunkard choose the booze is like letting a housewife into a supermarket, everything's beautiful, every type of booze is easy on the eye."

I made up the bed, covered it with a dustproof bedspread, mopped the floors, wiped the windows, cleaned the three rooms thoroughly, all in two hours; then I drank some more water, swallowed a pill of *coptis bolus*, and squatted on the toilet. After I dropped a load, I replenished my stomach with two bowls of instant noodles. At nine in the morning, my wife called and she sounded excited, saying she hadn't been downstairs for yet another week, but the small market by the apartment doorway had opened for two hours today, and no matter what, she was going to buy some meat and vegetables to make a decent welcome-home dinner for me.

We blew a few kisses at each other via video, and my daughter showed up to say, "Baba, the house is so deserted." Tears welled up and out of my eyes at that. I choked them back and said it's a blessing not to be sick. My daughter said, "What's the matter with you, Baba." But my wife quickly cut off the call.

Everything packed and ready, Ai Ding reclined on the sofa and waited. It was almost noon when he heard footsteps outside the door, so he jumped up and went to it. He heard crunching sounds as they removed the boards sealing the door. It seemed the nails were hammered in deep. After a quarter of an hour, those outside called out: "Hello? Hello? Are you there?" He replied, "Yes." A person outside said, "Open the door please."

He unlocked it from the inside, then opened the door, and a gust like a whirlwind suddenly burst in. Ai Ding swayed a couple of times as if drunk, and as he was about to step out, those outside screamed, "Slow down!" He saw two figures in blue protective clothing dodging away to the left and right, holding up rod-like insecticide sprinklers that they pointed at his head as they began spraying disinfectant at him. They sprayed him up and down, left and right, in his mouth, nostrils, and ears. Of the nine orifices,* the anus is the dirtiest and most toxic, and he considered asking them if they wanted to spray there too, but thought better of it.

Then they took his temperature, checked his ID card, and filled out sections of the non-resident isolation form. When the formalities were over, Director Wang, a middle-aged man who claimed to be the director of the community Epidemic Prevention Headquarters, handed him a "pass" with a big red official seal on it, waved his hand, and a small Jialing motorcycle drove over.

"This is the special car?" Ai Ding asked.

"In the emergency period, private cars are not allowed to leave the area, and our community has only been allocated two taxis.

They're busy every day transporting the sick. So please make allowances for us. Now get on, time's running out."

Ai Ding put on an N95 mask and rubbed his hands with disinfectant before shouldering his backpack and adjusting the computer bag position across his chest. He'd be riding on the back of a motorcycle but seemed unwilling to put his arms around the thick waist of the driver. Director Wang made the introductions: "This is Master Wang Erxiao. He came to Changsha to work on construction from the old revolutionary base at Taihang Mountain in Shanxi Province. When the virus came, he couldn't go home, so he has been working for us here, doing odd jobs."

"In the emergency period, isn't it just possible that two people sitting so closely together might lead to infection?" Ai Ding asked.

"Master Wang Erxiao is absolutely not ill," Director Wang assured him.

"So much nonsense!" the driver shouted suddenly. He immediately kicked the motorcycle into gear and made a few turns before firing off like a bullet. "The fare's 200 Yuan!" the driver shouted.

"You're blackmailing me!"

"What's the problem? The poor have to live too!"

Ai Ding was so angry he pulled hard on the driver's waist. The motorcycle swayed, and this beast of a driver yelled, "We're just about to cross an overpass. Do you want to die together here?"

"It's too criminal!"

"Listen, I'm also risking my life doing this. Just deal with it. And since there aren't any people or cars or any traffic police on this road, I'll sing you some 1930s anti-Japanese revolutionary songs in my hometown dialect to lighten the mood. Consider it an additional entertainment service."

"Go to hell!"

Ignoring Ai Ding, he started singing:

Brother Monkey wants to be in the Red Army, but the Red Army
    doesn't want Brother Monkey,
As a monkey's butt sticks up, it'll be easily exposed as a target;

Brother Monkey goes to the political commissar, the commissar's
 also a monkey,
As monkeys love monkeys, Brother Monkey can join the army;

Brother Monkey goes to scout the enemy, halfway up a mountain
 on the way,
As a monkey's butt sticks up, he's discovered by the Japanese
 devils;

Brother Monkey sets off running, and the devils chase him down
 with two bayonets,
For the revolution and the Party, Brother Monkey is gloriously
 sacrificed . . .

And so Wang Erxiao drove his motorcycle with Ai Ding sitting
behind him as they raced towards Changsha South Train Station.
Wang Xiao was elated at having successfully extorted money, so
he sang, over and over in his loudest voice, the old revolutionary
songs of his hometown in Shanxi. And before Ai Ding knew it,
they'd crossed the Xiangjiang Bridge. A wind was whipping up
whitecaps on the river; as they looked across the broad horizon
ahead, an auspicious-looking colorful cloud seemed to be wafting
toward them from afar, connecting Orange Isle in the middle of
the river with the riverbank opposite. Ai Ding remembered reading that when a young Mao Zedong was studying in Changsha
Normal School, he often came here to discuss the world's major
events with his classmates while they were all swimming. Mao
could not then have predicted he'd later become a dictator whose
name would forever carry a stench. When the money-mad Wang
Erxiao saw they'd reached this place, however, he abruptly stopped
singing and, with an affected air, opined that his middle school
textbook contained Mao's poem "Orange Isle." After pointing to
the colorful cloud on the horizon, he returned to Mao, saying:
"Wow, the head of the Chairman on a banknote is truly dearer
than one's own parents."

Ai Ding felt goosebumps hearing this, and said, "Let's go. Drive
on." Unexpectedly, just as he said this, the motorcycle began to

wobble. Then it zigzagged several times, like the side stroke of a sword, rushing onward at a tilt. Ai Ding hurriedly called on Wang Erxiao to stop, but he didn't seem to hear, his body suddenly stiffened, and his neck stretched straight out like that of a barking dog, but he didn't make a sound. Then, he began to shake as if he was being electrocuted, all while Ai Ding was still holding onto him. Ai Ding quickly let go of his waist, stood up on the back of the bike, and leaned past him to grab the handlebars. They sped into the heart of the garden at the intersection and crashed to the ground.

Ai Ding jumped up immediately and removed the motorcycle from on top of Wang Erxiao's right leg as he lay twitching on the ground. Wang Erxiao's mouth was wide open, but his nose and throat had something blocking them. His feet were desperately kicking out, and he seemed to be doing all he could to eject the blockage. His eyes looked like they were about to pop out. But finally, he took a sudden deep breath, held it for half a second, then spat it out, a long-lasting feculent jet that seemed to have expelled his entire life and smelt worse than shit. Then his shoulders shook, his head tilted to the side, and he was finished.

An asymptomatic Wuhan pneumonia patient had died like this. Everything had been fine a few minutes earlier, with Wang Erxiao singing loudly and dreaming of making a fortune as Ai Ding held tightly on to his thick waist. And now Ai Ding was stupefied, instinctively looking about, around the intersection's garden, up at the high-rise buildings rolling off into the distance, the roads extending in all directions, but spied no trace of anyone. He looked up at the sky and muttered as if in a dream, "Too high, too high." He was at the bottom of what seemed like a deep well. Why couldn't this higher world just raise him up?

He took out his mobile phone to call 110, and then 120, but no one answered either number. So he called Director Wang, who'd guaranteed that Wang Erxiao was okay. But when Ai Ding heard somebody at the other end of the call ask who was calling, he immediately hung up. As if just waking up, he suddenly realized he was in big trouble. As of this moment, he'd became a genuine "suspect," someone who'd had close contact with somebody who'd died of Wuhan pneumonia and he was now legally bound to be isolated.

"No, I can't take it anymore, I have to go home," he murmured to himself. "I've had contact with him, yes, but I wore a mask and gloves, and the clothes were thick. I should be fine."

So he squatted in the middle of the garden, pulled out the disinfectant from the backpack, rubbed it onto his hands and face, onto all exposed or possibly exposed parts of his body, took off his mask, gloves, coat, outer trousers, socks, and shoes, and threw them all away. Then he dressed again for battle, stood up the motorcycle and carefully wiped it down with alcohol and disinfectant from the handlebar and the bike's body to the front and rear seats. Finally, he inspected it from a distance of 5 meters, and, speaking to the dead body on the ground, brought his palms together and said: "I'm sorry, Master Wang Erxiao, I owe you 200 Yuan. I'll give it to you when we meet next time."

He tightened his belt and started the motorcycle, continuing on his way as if he were some sort of bandit. Before him was a long, straight avenue, which he traversed as quickly as the wind for Changsha South Train Station was located at its end. He'd be in Wuhan an hour and a half after he got on the high-speed train. "There's nothing I can do about all this," he muttered again, "I must go home."

However, after all this trouble, he was late. As it turned out, he'd arrived eight minutes early, but the ticket window closes ten minutes before the train departs. He dumped the motorcycle and went straight to the ticket-check gate, but there was no ticket for him there and they wouldn't let him in. "Will it be possible to get a ticket after I get on the train? Please!" He showed them his special pass and ID card, but they weren't interested. "I don't have a fever!" They shook their heads. This was followed by a long whistle; the train had left the station.

———

Now like a migrant worker who couldn't find a job, carrying a big bag, aimlessly pushing a motorcycle, covered in sweat, the hapless Ai Ding found himself sitting cross-legged on the street slapping himself in the face. His wife didn't answer his calls. But Director Wang called and roared: "What the fuck happened?!" before then unexpectedly saying, "Don't do anything. We're very sorry about this bad luck today."

At first, Ai Ding couldn't believe his ears. Then he began to suspect it was some sort of trap. But Director Wang went on to say: "The government has already seen what happened on the other side of the Xiangjiang Bridge through local surveillance video on the Skynet Electronic Eye. They know everything about your situation. It was an accident, nothing to do with you."

"Wang Erxiao's illness is related to you!" responded Ai Ding.

"Ai Ding, you shouldn't say such nonsense! I'm not a doctor, and even if I was one, he didn't exhibit any symptoms, I couldn't see a thing. Damn! . . . And I've also been exposed: I have to go into isolation for the next fourteen days starting now. But please rest assured, as far as you're concerned, this matter is over. The government will notify his family at an appropriate time."

"You'll have to take full responsibility if I've been infected."

"No. Sir, the government has seen all you did to disinfect and change your clothes in the intersection garden. After repeated observation and research, we all agree that your steps were reasonable and met the current national epidemic prevention standards. You can't possibly be infected! So, on behalf of our community Epidemic Prevention Headquarters, I'm informing you that the previous decision to lift your quarantine is still valid."

"That won't do. I'm coming back now."

"Coming back to do what?"

"I have now become someone 'suspected of infection' because of you . . ."

"Because of Wang Erxiao, not me."

"Who introduced me to Wang Erxiao?"

"Nobody. He came to you."

"He was the 'special car' you arranged for me."

"What a joke! Our community's special car can't have been a motorcycle. Our two special outbreak cars are fully sterilized, and the front and rear seats, drivers and guests, are separated by bulletproof glass."

"Have you no shame at all?"

"Be careful what you say. I won't be insulted. Wang Erxiao did come to you. Originally, I was going to stop him, but because you two hugged so warmly, the security risk was too great, too great . . ."

"Good God, you really have no shame."

"I've continually advised you to wait, but you've repeatedly emphasized that your wife and children are in Wuhan and your heart's set on a quick return. Putting myself in your shoes, I felt some compassion, I was afraid you'd not make the last high-speed train . . . Ah, as a Party cadre, this has been my greatest dereliction of duty . . ."

"Wang, you just wait, I'm coming back immediately."

"To do what?"

"I'll tell you when I'm back."

"I'm in isolation and can't see you."

"I'll be accompanying you for another fourteen days' quarantine."

"But our resources are limited. You don't want to further burden the community."

"I'll be at my in-laws' house. How's that a burden on the community?"

"Somebody has to be hired to seal the door."

"I'm going to report you!!"

"Report away . . . it's hard being a good person."

Director Wang hung up the phone. Seething, Ai Ding immediately turned the motorbike around and began traveling back the way he'd come. But just as he was about to cross the Xiangjiang Bridge, a police car headed him off. Two police officers wearing blue protective clothing got out and made a show of checking his ID and pass, then opened the trunk and forced him and the motorcycle into it. He yelled loudly all the way back, but the police officers remained silent.

At the entrance to the community's police station, Ai Ding was spray-disinfected again, his temperature was taken with a forehead gun, and his cell phone and computer were confiscated. He was then locked in a cell to cool off for the night. Early the next morning, he was arraigned by the station political instructor, and even through a glass partition, he couldn't wait to shout: "I want to bring a lawsuit!"

"This isn't a court, what lawsuit? You're sick, eh?"

"Of course I'm ill. I came into contact with Wang Erxiao, who died of Wuhan pneumonia after I was introduced to him by Director Wang, so I'm now 'suspected.' I must have a nucleic acid test. If it's positive, I request admission to hospital for treatment, and want Director Wang's legal liability investigated."

"Director Wang has isolated himself. He's also a victim."

"That's got nothing to do with me."

"Why's a fucker like you so cold-blooded? Director Wang has said good things about you all along, pleading your case, wanting us to let you go home as soon as possible."

"Without a test, I don't dare go home, in case I infect my wife and child . . ."

"You've no fever and your breathing's normal."

"Wang Erxiao didn't have a fever either and was breathing normally two minutes before he died. The virus has an incubation period, and there are as many asymptomatic cases as there are hairs on a cow."

"This is a police station, not a hospital."

"You can contact the hospital, no?"

"Are you a Party leader? The hospital's overcrowded right now and medical resources are in short supply. The medical staff are working round the clock and aren't even able to save the lives of locals. At least a few hundred are dying every day. As an outsider, especially one from the province of Hubei that has caused great pain to the people of the country, why should we use our resources on you? A nucleic acid test? That's one big demand . . . they cost hundreds of Yuan a kit; are you going to pay for it?"

"No problem, I'll pay. And whether or not there's a 'confirmed diagnosis,' I'll remain here to fight the lawsuit. If I win, Director Wang'll have to pay."

"And if you lose?"

"Then death also wins. If I die of illness, Director Wang will have committed murder indirectly."

"Fuck off!"

"No I won't!"

"What's the matter with you?"

"I've got a wife and a child. I don't dare leave without a test."

"Fine. If you won't leave, we'll arrest you for 'causing trouble.' Anyone who causes disorder for the Party and the government during this emergency will be punished as befits 'especially serious circumstances.' We'll have no problem keeping you here for five years of reform through labor."

Ai Ding began to howl angrily, and if he'd had a knife in hand, if there was no glass partition, he'd have rushed them. But even if he'd been a tiger, all he'd have been able to do was roar. The political instructor stood up, said, "We've done our best," then turned and left. A lunch box was pushed through a window in the partition, which he vehemently refused. The man behind the glass said, "Don't make life difficult for yourself."

It was almost afternoon when Ai Ding's cell phone was returned. He anxiously opened WeChat, where his wife had left a voice message: "They've spoken with me. We'll talk more when you're back, husband. Don't cause any more trouble. Your daughter and I miss you."

7

Passing through
No-Man's Land

At two o'clock in the afternoon, when Ai Ding was feeling completely defeated, Director Wang finally called. "Mr. Ai Ding, I have no choice either . . . who wants to put others at risk? I have a wife and a child too. What'll become of them if something bad happens to me? Think about it from my point of view, I have nothing against you. Why should we die together? Whatever you do, don't act like you're some sort of human bomb, because I'm not a bomb disposal expert."

"Stop talking nonsense. What can I do? Now the high-speed train's stopped running, there's no transport at all."

"The local government has decided that Wang Erxiao's effects, namely the Jialing motorcycle, will be loaned to you temporarily. After the epidemic, we can discuss a discount deal on it. Take the highway from Changsha to Yueyang, an ordinary car can do it in just over an hour. From Yueyang you can cross the provincial border, and then you'll be in Wuhan in a flash. Even if the motorcycle is half the speed of a car, you shouldn't have a problem getting home today."

"The freeway's closed."

"You've been specially authorized to use it and a police car will escort you to the entrance."

"The motorcycle's out of gas."

"There's a gas station beside the police station; you'll be allowed to refuel there for free. Please be aware, though, you're not allowed to stop anywhere for any reason, not at restaurants, not at hotels, and you're not allowed to have contact with any local residents."

"Can I stop at a kiosk?"

"The gas station has a shop where you're allowed to buy things while you refuel. You'd better make a list and get everything at once."

Ai Ding's mood gradually improved, but then he felt hungry. With his troubles behind him, he stuffed himself with the two lunch boxes given to him at the police station, before going with the police to refuel and get supplies; then he was driven by the police to the expressway toll booth, where they unloaded the motorcycle. He started the engine and set off, entering the freeway through a temporarily opened side gate. A few faceless police officers waved him on his way, wrapped up in their protective suits, like astronauts about to be elevated out of this empty country into an equally empty sky.

Ai Ding knew this road was monitored by the nationally integrated Skynet electronic eye, so he gunned his engine. The entirety of the city of Changsha seemed to be empty, and the expressway to Yueyang was empty as well – a great wonder of the world unfolding before him as he drove alone along the usually jam-packed high-speed corridor. If his motorcycle were replaced by a horse, he'd be an ancient emissary delivering the mail. The setting sun was sinking into the mountains and rivers, and the expressway was like a ghost ship gradually losing its shimmer, from whose deck you could see a crescent moon emerging from inverted waves. The stars were like mouths, pale, opening and closing, silently singing a dirge.

The speeding Ai Ding savored his reversal of fortune, enjoying the privileges of his "exit under guard," and arrived at the ancient city of Yueyang by Dongting Lake at five o'clock in the evening just as the sky was turning monochrome. There was a roadblock ahead and so he drove off the expressway on to an ordinary road.

Ai Ding passed by the world-famous Yueyang Tower. Of course, he couldn't casually stop and climb it like the writer Fan

Zhongyan did under the Northern Song Dynasty, and he also couldn't then face the billowing river and write ". . . be the first to bear the world's hardships and the last to enjoy its comforts. Alas! Without such a person who will keep me company," and so on, but he still couldn't help braking and admiring its towering silhouette. Inadvertently, he also noticed a sign on a wall:

Border Villages and Towns in Yueyang, Hunan, and Hubei Provinces Implement Centralized Checkpoint Control

Recently, many Yueyang WeChat groups have been spreading false information such as "Yueyang is closed, highways are closed, and Yueyang cannot be entered." In this regard, the government's Epidemic Prevention Department announces the following:

1. The prevention and control of the epidemic is the top priority, and it must be prevented from spreading internally and from being imported from outside. Starting from January 24, all counties, towns, and village groups under the jurisdiction of Yueyang City bordering on Hubei Province will be isolated from each other. Travel must be approved at the community or township level, all necessary travel must be done at speed, and no stopping over outside the area will be allowed without good reason.

2. All domestic public buses and passenger lines are suspended. The nine crossings into Hubei, including Hongqiao Town and Nanjiang Town under the jurisdiction of Pingjiang County, are fully closed. The four villages and towns in the area of Xiangling City and the Hubei border, near Wuhan, are key fortified areas in the province. Exit is permitted; entry is denied to all.

3. Our city is the passageway from Hubei into Hunan, and the Beijing–Guangzhou Railway and the Beijing–Hong Kong–Macao Expressway pass through the territory, so the city will not be closed for the time being. Instead, thirty-five check posts have been established at all intersections in the city, especially at the junctions leading into Hubei Province. The expressway has also not been closed yet. However, every vehicle entering Yueyang will be subject to mandatory security checks, disinfection of people and vehicles, and body temperature scans.

This was an old announcement promulgated over half a month beforehand, and now all parts of the country had regressed into the Spring and Autumn Period of the ancient Zhou Dynasty more than three thousand years ago. Thousands of "princes" under the name "the Zhou Son of Heaven" had divided the land into fiefdoms, each with guarded boundaries. So, wanting to leave Yueyang City, Ai Ding didn't know where to begin. He used his mobile phone to check a map of the area. It was only 42 kilometers from Yueyang to Xiangling, and Xiangling was located at the northernmost tip of Hunan, protruding deep into the hinterland of Hubei, nearly 200 kilometers away from Wuhan. If his motorcycle traveled at 50 kilometers an hour, he'd get home before midnight.

So he turned onto the 107 National Highway and sped onward, the cold wind piercing his clothes like a knife. There was nothing but red lights along the way and he ran them all. Finally, in the distance, he saw two trucks blocking the road, with a man standing on top of one of the truck cabs waving a five-star red flag. Ai Ding slowly came to a stop and the flag bearer jumped down with a somersault. He came to his feet 5 meters away and shouted, "Where have you come from?"

"Changsha."

"Where're you going?"

"Wuhan."

"Going to Wuhan at this time, are you sure?"

"I live in Wuhan."

"Holy cow! A Wuhan person!"

A dozen villagers lying in ambush in the truck suddenly stood up, all wearing raincoats and masks and holding red tasseled spears, like the Boxers encircling the foreign devils in old movies. They all climbed down and encircled Ai Ding. Then countless spray nozzles went to work on him, and he was swallowed up by a thick disinfectant fog for five minutes. Like the "Monkey King" Sun Wukong flying in the clouds, at first he could only hear the sound of bronze gongs in his ears, followed by a bugle playing charge, and finally someone yelling: "Elders and villagers in quarantine, all of you at home, listen carefully! Just now, we've intercepted a Wuhan native wandering around the area, one who's brought the catastrophic novel coronavirus to 1.4 billion Chinese people, and we're now disinfecting and interrogating him! It's very dangerous, comrades. If you're not careful, you'll die! But please rest assured, at this critical juncture for the Chinese people, our village Party branch will act as it's sung in the national anthem: 'With our flesh and blood, let us build a new Great Wall, and enfold the whole village, men, women, and children.' If the virus carriers dare to invade, the first group to go out to meet them will be us Communist Party members . . ."

The sound of applause seeped out through the cracks of the doors, windows, and tiles of the whole village, followed by slogans yelled straight up into the sky: "Down with the people of Hubei! Down with the people of Wuhan! Long live the Communist Party! Long live Big Daddy Xi! Support the Party branch! Win the People's War to bury the coronavirus disease!"

Like a rat crossing a street, Ai Ding had the misfortune of becoming teaching material by negative example in an epidemic prevention propaganda war. Further in that vein, he was also poked in the butt countless times by red tasseled spears. Afterward, he learned that several of the villagers had died of the illness not long before, but that some villagers, against regulations, still went out to the lake to cast nets for fish in the middle of the night. They'd been caught by patrolling militiamen, beaten soundly, and had their fish and nets confiscated.

After the initial commotion, these people hastily checked Ai Ding's pass and ID, finding them in order. The red flag was waved two more times, and he was allowed to pass through the space between the two trucks. He continued on his nighttime journey, but his mood had plummeted to new depths. At that moment, he could still hear an epidemic prevention jingle blaring from the loudspeakers attached to the front of the trucks:

Don't run around at home,
Go to bed, read the papers,
Use a spatula to stir the food.
Don't make rumors, don't spread rumors,
Everyone must bear this in mind.

Ai Ding drove on for a few kilometers and his mood gradually improved, so he squeezed the accelerator, increasing his speed, wanting to let everything out. Unexpectedly, two bright searchlights swept over him from a distance, instantly forcing him to shut his eyes and brake hastily. He saw a troop of men rush out carrying wooden swords and wearing monster masks, blocking his way: "Where've you come from?"

"Changsha."

"Where're you going?"

"Xiangling." Ai Ding hesitated slightly, not wanting to do anything rash.

"Pass?"

He handed it over.

"ID card?"

He handed that over too.

"From Wuhan?"

"Temporarily staying in Xiangling." He had an idea, "Going back to Wuhan now would be a death wish."

"The pass states you've been in isolation for fourteen days, you've been tested, and your health is normal. But you still have to be sterilized."

"But I've already been sterilized."

"Up ahead is Han Family Village, this is Miao Family Village – it's different."

So the monster mask took hold of canisters in both hands as if he were holding two large pistols, the jets of fine spray went from left to right, then head to toe. He then ordered Ai Ding to open his mouth and fired two squirts into it, after which he seemed to be greatly relieved. Following this, he actually patted Ai Ding on the shoulder and invited him to a meeting.

"It's too late," Ai Ding said.

"It's just past nine o'clock, not so late."

"I've something else to attend to."

"These days, the virus is the biggest thing."

Ai Ding grew anxious, but had no choice but to go to the village and do what he was told. The phone vibrated again. It was his wife, but he didn't dare answer.

The lead monster mask introduced himself: "My name's Shen Ding, almost the same as yours, but I've a lot of history in these parts. Our Miao Family Village migrated from Phoenix City in western Hunan during the Wanli reign period of the Ming Dynasty, though we've no idea why. In short, the great Phoenix City writer Shen Congwen is a relative of mine, and the village ancestral hall has a tablet dedicated to that old gentleman and a collection of his complete works." Then Shen Ding told someone to bring a mask for Ai Ding to wear: "This is a Nuo opera mask, did you know?"

"Shen Congwen's *Random Notes on Western Hunan* mentions it," Ai Ding replied. "Your customs here must be very different from the neighboring village ahead."

"The Miao people are more cultured than the Han people. The Miao people respect their ancestors and the Han people dig up their ancestral graves. They also beat people to death and bury them alive at every opportunity, in the cruelest possible fashion."

The meeting's venue was located on the national highway. Two searchlights illuminated two stools in the middle of the road. About twenty or so masked villagers were scattered about. Everyone applauded, and the village headman, Shen Ding, strode forward to speak: "The novel coronavirus is attacking us, and the Party and the government must take charge of the overall situation, so they've no time to look into local matters. Consequently, the authorities have informed us that villages must isolate from each other, manage themselves, and solve any problems by themselves. This is equivalent to the 'small country, few people' situation written of in the *Book of Changes*. Since our Miao nationality's 'small country' has been isolated, over twenty people have died in the village. All were 'suspected,' none 'confirmed,' as we've not been allocated a quota to go to the hospital. If we prematurely send patients to Yueyang, they'll definitely not be able to get past the neighboring Han village. Without instructions from above, there'll definitely be fights.

"If matters go on like this, the number of dead will increase. I learned from the village-to-village WeChat group that there are more dead people in the Han villages on either side of us than in our village. Closing villages is no problem. The problem is in each household, where there is no ability to isolate from each other. It's still a table full of people eating from one cooking pot. If there's just one infected person, a whole family can become ill. What should we do?"

The villagers whispered among themselves, then nominated one person to come out and say: "What should we do? Accept our fate. All we can do is take the body temperatures of each person at the same time every day and isolate if anybody has symptoms."

Shen Ding nodded and said, "We can't split up when eating, but how about sleeping?"

The villagers whispered together again, and then nominated a different person to come out and say: "We should split up."

"The old people have no problems with it, but are the young people for it?"

"Since three or four years ago, when family planning policy was relaxed, we Miao people have enjoyed preferential treatment. Now that a couple is allowed to have two to three children, the female comrades haven't been able to guard their bellies and the male comrades haven't been able to bag their cocks, which has led to a population explosion. Living standards have declined. Now there's an epidemic, everyone must resist doing it, which we might regard as 'refunding an overcharge or asking for a surcharge when prices change.'"

"That makes a lot of sense. Restrain yourself and build up energy. If you ejaculate too much, your immunity will be poor, and the virus will catch hold easily."

"As this is the case, I'll go door-to-door tonight, ringing gongs to inform everybody; after that, every night the militia will be sent round the houses, and if any illegal love-making is discovered, a fine of 200 Yuan will be imposed."

"Village representatives, please vote with a show of hands . . . All approve. Okay, bring me a pen and paper, I'll write a couple of posters with catchy two-liners and hang them at the entrance to the village."

So everyone asked for the 3-foot-long giant brushes, spread out two large sheets of paper on the road, and under the full beam of a searchlight, they watched Shen Ding remove his mask, roll up his sleeves, and set to work:

> Sleeping in separate rooms, will you die if you don't kiss? Never;
> Will you die if you share the same bed in the same room? Definitely.

The crowd applauded and cheered. Then, a stranger wearing sunglasses took the stage with a three-stringed zither. Shen Ding introduced him to Ai Ding: "His name is Zhang Naisong, an artist from Gansu. He'd been wandering to the south and into our village when the virus arrived, so he's stuck here for the time being."

Zhang Naisong clasped his hands in greeting while turning in a circle, took out a hip flask from his trouser pocket, gulped down a big mouthful, and then played the zither and sang in comic dialogue fashion:

> Wild animals are truly pitiful,
> A taste for wild game enters restaurants,
> Contracting the coronavirus and getting pneumonia,
> After washing brains, wash hands frequently, then wash faces,
> Call it the Lord Corona, and the brain loses a string.
>
> The novel coronavirus is spreading,
> Animals imprison humans in cages.
> Grandpa and grandma can't buy masks,
> Wearing an orange peel instead's no joke.
> As it passes through villages each becomes impassable,
> The provincial Party Secretary's also a stranger.
>
> The host's on the front line fighting the virus,
> The nanny buries the cat alive and incurs Imperial displeasure.
> A helicopter "breaches" the cordon,
> Avoiding charities to perform a charity.
> The Red Cross embezzles material and keeps out journalists,

The driver of an official car carries a mask, says it was booked for
a leader.

"Benzalkonium chloride" prevents SARS, "Shuanghuanglian oral
liquid" is anti-viral,
Just as smog is anti-missile, and kelp anti-submarine.
The search for isatis root keeps me awake; I can't get my head
around it,
The shuanghuang lotus seed mooncakes theory is even more con-
fusing; it gives me jaw ache.
I didn't want to talk about these things,
But that drink of booze just now,
has left me in a hot panic . . .

Ai Ding was fascinated. It was almost half past ten when it ended.
Shen Ding said: "Except for Miao Family Village, there's no place
that'll let you stay overnight on this road. Besides, our village is
sandwiched between two Han villages, wolves in front and tigers
behind you, who knows what sort of monsters you may still run
into."

Ai Ding felt apprehensive but nodded in agreement. It was
arranged he would stay with the village committee, next door to
Zhang Naisong. After all his activity, he was too tired, so he sent
a WeChat message to his wife explaining the situation and went
to lie down. Just as he was falling asleep, there was the sound of
gongs outside, and then a man and a woman yelling: "This is an
urgent notification from the village committee: starting tonight,
to prevent the spread of the epidemic, couples must sleep in separate rooms. Hugs and kisses are not allowed. Female comrades,
you must be more standoffish. Male comrades, you must be firm.
Don't let a moment's impulse cause an irreversible tragedy! The
darkness is temporary, the light will come. Once the epidemic's
over, everything will be fine . . ."

The next day, as dawn was just breaking, Ai Ding tiptoed out the
door onto the road. The entire Miao Family Village was quiet,

just a few dogs scampering about at the foot of walls. When they saw him, they didn't bark, instead wagging their tails, which unexpectedly greatly moved him. When people are moved like this, they feel good, thinking luck will follow. Out of fear of disturbing anyone, Ai Ding pushed his motorcycle along the road through the village. Even after reaching the national highway, he pushed it along for a while before starting the motor.

But just as he'd begun to pick up speed, after about 2,000 meters, when he raised his head he saw more than a dozen parachute-sized hydrogen balloons swaying in the dew-heavy air of daybreak, all with big red streamers attached. At first glance, he thought there was some sort of big celebration. But upon closer examination, he turned ashen-faced and suddenly felt involuntary shivers wrack his body. It turned out the balloons were carrying epidemic prevention slogans:

> Coronavirus is not terrible, as long as everyone obeys the Party
> Going out without a mask, such a bastard isn't human
> Be well behaved at home to prevent infection, even mothers-in-law must be driven away
> People who return from Hubei and don't report are time bombs
> Bringing illness home, unfilial people, infecting parents, totally lacking conscience
> Bringing illness home, disowned by relatives, if you dare come from Wuhan, we'll refuse to admit you
> Running around today, next year grass will be growing on your grave
> Those who don't report their fever are class enemies lurking among the people
> This New Year's Eve don't visit friends, the visitors are the enemy; if they come, don't open the door

There was also an extra-long slogan, the hem of the streamer almost dragging on the ground. Ai Ding had to stop the bike at the side of the road and stare at it for a while before he could make out all the words:

Everyone you meet on the road at this time is a lonely ghost demanding your life

This really spooked Ai Ding. And in front of him, a fence ran across the national highway, winding off left and right for miles, surrounding the East is Red Village that he wanted to pass through. He couldn't imagine what horrible things might happen once he crossed the boundary between the Miao and Han villages, now just a few hundred meters away. So he turned back.

The guards of Miao Family Village had already woken up and taken their posts. Two of them were the same ones he'd met the night before, and they allowed him back into the village.

He had nowhere to go except back to the village committee building, and it just so happened that the Gansu artist Zhang Naisong was opening his door at that point to let some air in. Ai Ding cupped a fist in his other hand, greeting him from a distance as if he were his savior. The two were 5 meters apart as Ai Ding parked the motorcycle, unloaded his backpack, and then took a big step forward. He stretched one of his legs forward in the air, and when Naisong saw him do this, he did the same, until the tips of their feet touched together, a position they held for one minute – this gesture being a plague-era substitute for shaking hands or hugging warmly.

Naisong said: "I understand your desire to return here, but leaving without saying goodbye was unkind."

Ai Ding asked his forgiveness. Naisong nodded, went into his room, brought back a fresh flat cake as wide as a washbasin, asked Ai Ding to catch it, and then threw it. He caught the frisbee-like food and took a big bite of it. Naisong then said: "The place there in front of us was originally called Shit Egg Village. A few decades ago, it was inspected by Chairman Mao, who'd returned to visit his hometown, Shaoshan. Suddenly it went all red, and the name was changed to East is Red Village, leftist as hell. When I first arrived in this area, I had the misfortune of being caught by them and was quarantined as 'suspected.' I had to pay 200 Yuan a night for a dog kennel and dog food. On the third night, I took advantage of the militia taking a nap and escaped over the wall."

Ai Ding wiped away some cold sweat, saying: "Sounds dangerous!"

Naisong said: "You're the one in danger. I'm not. I'm settled in Miao Family Village. If the virus doesn't go, neither will I."

"But I've no choice but to go."

"It's more difficult to get past East is Red Village than to cross a national border now that political power is decentralized and the villages are autonomous."

"I've a pass issued in Changsha to leave the province under protection."

"Oh, really? That's equivalent to a diplomatic visa granted by the State Council. They'll let you pass."

"What if I get stuck?"

Naisong thought it over for a bit, took out a pen and paper, then on his knees drew for a while, before he handed the paper over and said: "Go out of the village, drive 1,600 meters, then get off the national highway on the right, go 3 kilometers along a dirt road, and then another few hundred meters on the paths between the fields. That way you'll bypass the East is Red Village and cross the boundary between Miao Family Village and Majia River Village. Majia River is a Muslim village; they're simple people there. But, man, you've got a bit of a background, they'll want you on your way quickly."

Ai Ding took the hand-drawn map and couldn't help shedding a tear. He clasped his hands together and used them to bow three times to Naisong. Naisong quickly returned the same. Ai Ding then turned and left, and, following the plan closely, he successfully crossed the village border.

It was a bright midday as Ai Ding turned back onto the national highway at the fork in the road at Majia River Village, and he sped up. On the left before him was Dongting Lake. The sound of wind in his ears seemed to mingle with the sound of the waves. The field of vision was extremely broad as Ai Ding stopped to check an online map. After another village called Er Shao, he'd arrive at Xiangling on the border between the two provinces.

Er Shao is an abbreviation of "Second Shaoshan." The village was originally called Erhuang, *huang* meaning wasteland, and the reason for the name change was the same as the East is Red Village: an incidental inspection by Chairman Mao returning to his hometown of Shaoshan several decades ago. Mao even went into one of the villagers' homes, lifted the lid of a pot, and asked if there was enough food. The villager replied there was more than they could eat, that one-fifteenth of a hectare produced over 25,000 kilos of paddy rice, and even if an entire heavenly army descended, they couldn't eat it all. Smiling, the Chairman remained in the villagers' house and partook of the appallingly spicy chopped-pepper fish head and was inspired to write in calligraphy a new highest teaching: "Eat dry when busy, eat watery when idle."

The sentry at Ershao Village wasn't so hyperbolic – just official business done officiously: spray disinfectant, take the body temperature, check ID. When he saw the name of Wuhan in there, he wasn't taken aback in the least. He then checked the pass and carefully examined the official seals on the back of it. Changsha, Yueyang, Miao Family Village, Majia River Village: every time you cross a border, you had to have a stamp, as just like a visa for different countries, they're indispensable.

Ai Ding silently screamed to himself that things were looking bad, and as he expected, the sentry raised his head and said: "It's still missing East is Red Village."

Ai Ding argued: "I came from Majia River."

"Why go so far out of your way?"

"To look at the scenery."

"People are dead everywhere and you want to see the scenery?"

Ai Ding couldn't think of a response, but the sentry gestured for him to look at the slogans on red cloth banners in front of the roadblock. On the left was "If you go out, we'll break your legs; if you give us lip, we'll break your teeth." On the right, "Visit relatives and friends today, you'll be treated like a dog at home tomorrow."

Several burly men were now gathering around holding long shoulder poles pointing at him. Ai Ding hastily cried out: "How would I know my way around these villages!"

The sentry held back the other men: "All the villages along the national highway have to stamp border crossings. If you suddenly fall ill, the government needs to know where you've been. Understand?"

Ai Ding was trembling, at a loss for words. He had no choice but to waste another hour going back the way he'd come. Upon entering Miao Family Village for a third time, the same dogs were still at the foot of the walls, the doors were still tightly closed, but there was still the village committee. He knocked on the door, stepped back 5 meters, and Zhang Naisong, the local Avalokitesvara Bodhisattva who rescues the suffering, appeared.

"Haven't you left yet?"

This time, it was Naisong who took the big step forward and stretched out a leg, and Ai Ding followed suit, as they touched the tips of their feet together for a minute once more.

Ai Ding told him about his predicament, and Naisong said: "But your documents are okay."

"Yes, but what if there's a problem if I go to East is Red Village? Didn't they quarantine you?"

"Yes, of course."

"You've traveled a lot and know how to get around these formalities . . ."

"Well, okay, then give me your pass."

Naisong turned around and went into his room. After fiddling about for half an hour, he came back and told him, "Go quick, quick, and if you have to come back again, brother, I'll hang myself."

Ai Ding took a look and was stunned: "Naisong, brother, god, this fool salutes you!"

"I used soap to make a stamp for the pass, that should meet your needs."

8

On Two Sides of the Border

As dusk approached, Ai Ding was glad to see he'd finally arrived at the region of Xiangling, the "gateway to northern Hunan." Four of its towns border on Hubei Province, separated by the vast Yangtze River and by several of its tributaries in the area. Across the river in Hubei is Red Cliff, the site of a famous battle in the fourteenth-century historical novel *Romance of the Three Kingdoms*, which caused the dissolution of the Han Dynasty in around 220 CE. The poet Su Dongpo (1037–1101) of the Song Dynasty was once exiled to this place by the imperial court. One day he was drunk and went on a night cruise in a skiff, leaving behind the famous poem "Meditation on the Past at Red Cliff":

Eastward goes the great river,
its waves have swept away
a thousand years of gallant men.
And they say that west of the ancient castle here
is that Red Cliff of Zhou Yu and the Three Kingdoms.
A rocky tangle pierces sky,
leaping waves smash the shore,
surging snow in a thousand drifts.
Like a painting, these rivers and hills
Where once so many bold men were.*

Although Ai Ding was not much of a hero himself, the memory of that heroic battle prompted him to muse about the past. He remembered, too, that a few days ago he hadn't been able to stop himself from laughing when Zhuangzi Gui had imitated the military strategist Zhuge Liang, also known as "Crouching Dragon," debating with a group of Confucian sages. The inspector who was just then in the process of spraying and disinfecting him saw him grinning and, thinking it odd, asked him what was so funny? Ai Ding whimsically responded: "You will laugh at me being so sentimental, my hair streaked with white before my time."*

The inspector replied: "The novel coronavirus pneumonia has caused everyone to suffer terribly, and you're still caught up in that? Laughing at me too? You're really callous." Ai Ding told him, "They're lines from a poem by Su Dongpo." The inspector said, "To write poetry, you first have to be fully human. Does a paragon of passion like you who's so lusty even deserve to recite Su Dongpo's poems?" Turning red, Ai Ding choked back his fury and didn't utter another peep.

The border clearance procedures were completed, and the inspectors couldn't find any reason to detain him further, so they warned Ai Ding to depart Xiangling as soon as possible. He wiped the cold sweat off his brow and left as quickly as he could.

This inter-provincial port region was rich in black tea but had now become a heavily guarded city of death. Except for police cars and hearses, there was no sign of human activity in its streets and lanes. Ai Ding learned there were countless numbers of people from Wuhan and the rest of Hubei Province living in Xiangling due to geographical proximity and convenient transportation. After the closing of city after city in Wuhan and its surrounding area, a great mob of people came back to Xiangling to celebrate the New Year, and, as if each one of them had been a time bomb, all the people in the city were engulfed in the life-and-death turmoil that resulted.

Ai Ding hit the gas as he made good his escape from the city and arrived in the northernmost Hunan town of Bull** in a flash. Opposite this town, separated by a highway bridge, was the village of Bull under Hubei jurisdiction. There were checkpoints at the bridgeheads and under the bridges in each of the two provinces, and they were stricter than border checkpoints during World War II. Around each checkpoint were patrols of armed militia wearing red armbands, and they'd been expanded during the epidemic. The dozens of miles of traditionally complex, chaotic, and winding provincial borders had now also become distinct from each other. They'd dug out earthen trenches and stretched out barbed wire, and the villagers on both sides resembled border guards wandering about with leashed wolfhounds, taking shifts day and night, guarding against death. And it wasn't just humans, as even the cats, dogs, and mice that used to run around freely were now mercilessly slaughtered when they were caught crossing the border.

Ai Ding stopped his motorbike and underwent inspection. The border guard warned: "This is the inter-provincial end point, are you sure, comrade? You can't come back once you cross the bridge."

"What do you mean?"

"Prevention and control of the epidemic is currently at its most intense stage. 'Defense against external import, defense against internal export' is the top priority of our local Party organization. Our primary task in Xiangling is to strictly prohibit contacts between Hunan and Hubei people. You're from Hubei, but this is a special circumstance, and since Changsha has granted you permission to leave the region, we won't block you. But we must inform you that our Party's policy is to 'allow exit, not entry.'"

"What if the other side doesn't let me in?"

"You're all of the same province. Hubei is yours, and the virus is also yours. You've caused the deaths of so many people too. You're all of the same swarm of pests, how could they not let you in?"

"You ... you ... how can you say this? Could you please go to the middle of the bridge and communicate with those on the other side for me?"

"Are you asking me to go yell at them? Not happening. The virus can be transmitted by air-borne droplets and can survive for two hours in the air."

"Then stand a bit farther away. Besides, you're also wearing an N95 mask. It'll be okay."

"We Hunanese are all compadres of the great leader Chairman Mao. I'll not risk my life for a native of Hubei."

"Then . . . then . . . you can always phone the other side, yes?"

"No."

Ai Ding was furious, but he had to keep himself under control. He cast his gaze elsewhere. The sunset's glow on the clouds made them look like a pile of broken eggs dumped out on a mess of mountains, the darkening sky like an overturned bowl, and the faint starlight a patch on the bottom of the bowl. What could he do? His mind was spinning.

"I'll go to the middle of the bridge and communicate with them. If it's no go, can I come back?"

"That'll work. But if you're expressly rejected by the other side, it won't. Do you have any acquaintances in Xiangling?"

"No."

"If you can't cross the border, we'll arrange for you to stay at a government-designated hotel."

"Thank you."

Ai Ding parked the motorcycle at the checkpoint, walked the 30 or so meters alone with a large bag on his back, and noticed a conspicuous red line drawn across the bridge. He stood on the red line, formed his hands into a loudspeaker and shouted, "I'm from Hubei! I want to go back to Wuhan! Can you hear me?"

There was no response, so he shouted the same again and again, until finally his voice became hoarse. Then a loudhailer on the opposite side asked: "Coming back to do what?"

"I've come back from Germany, my home's in Wuhan, and my wife and daughter are waiting for me to return."

"Say that again: coming back for what? For the good of your family, of your hometown, please don't come back for a while longer."

"Comrades, fellow Hubei people, Communist Party members, please rest assured I'm very healthy. I've been quarantined and observed in Changsha for fourteen days. I've also gone through more than a dozen disinfections and tests along the way here. I've no fever or cough. I'm carrying a pass issued by Epidemic Prevention Headquarters, and on the back of the pass there are transit stamps from all the checkpoints I've been through. These are the same as the customs stamps for departure from Berlin and entry to Beijing, all of which clearly prove my activities have been harmless, and that I've also passed all physical and political checks . . ."

"What a load of nonsense! I've told you not to come, but if you must, then come on, I'll find out what you're really up to!"

Ai Ding thanked them repeatedly and couldn't help crying. But as he was about to turn around to get his motorcycle, he suddenly heard someone speaking to him in a lowered voice: "Hubei guy, careful not to be fooled!"

Ai Ding immediately looked around and saw a van parked by the bridge railing on the right and a hatchet-faced man poking his head out from the driver's seat. He hesitated, then moved closer. Hatchet-Face opened the van door, Ai Ding slipped into the back seat, and the two talked through a pane of glass. Hatchet-Face said: "I'm from Red Cliff on the other side, and my wife is from Xiangling on this side. We've been married ten years and have a ten-year-old daughter."

"Similar to my family."

"In past years, during Spring Festival, we'd run back and forth between both sides, at my mother-in-law's house for New Year's Eve, at my parents' house on New Year's Day, or the other way round. This year, because my mother-in-law had a bad cold, our family of three came over early from Red Cliff. I planned to show her filial respect and then return after New Year's Eve. But without warning, Wuhan was closed just before New Year's Eve, and then the whole province was closed, the world was in chaos and we were blocked everywhere. Before anybody could figure out what was going on, we'd already been delayed a few days . . ."

As he told it, on the fifth day of the Lunar New Year, during the peak of the epidemic, the Hatchet-Face family of three tried to drive home from Xiangling by way of Bull Town. Normally, the 107 National Highway would be unimpeded, with no checkpoints, but by this time, obstacles and outposts were set up at both ends of the bridge. The Hatchet-Face family had no problem getting out of Hunan, and, thinking they were all right, headed straight to Hubei, where they were then blocked.

"ID card?"

Hatchet-Face passed it over.

"Three people."

"My wife has one, and my daughter hasn't reached the age when she needs one yet."

"Household registration booklet?"

Hatchet-Face passed it over.

"Okay, please go back."

"I'm from Red Cliff. We want to go home."

"No way."

"What are you guys up to?"

"We're not up to anything. No way means no way."

"And the reason?"

"Everybody asks for the reason! If I explained, I'd have to repeat it a thousand times a day. Wouldn't that drive me nuts? Are you going to back up or not?"

As soon as Hatchet-Face said he wouldn't, a long iron rod was raised up toward his windshield. He was so scared, he immediately retreated, shouting, "I'm backing up, I'm backing up . . ."

A frustrated hatchet-face turned the van around and headed back to the other side of the bridge, as his wife sighed: "If we can't go back, we can't go back. We'll just be staying in a room no matter where we go, no?"

Hatchet-Face nodded and said yes, thinking this was just the way things were. Then, to their surprise, they were stopped again.

"ID card?"

Hatchet-face passed it over.

"Three people."

"My wife has one, and my daughter hasn't reached the age when she needs one yet."

"Household registration booklet?"

Hatchet-Face passed it over.

"Okay, you can go back."

"What are you doing?"

"You're from Hubei, and the Party organization has given us the task of preventing Hunanese from coming into contact with Hubei people."

"How's it possible not to come in contact? My wife and I have slept in the same bed for ten years, and my daughter is just as old."

"Your wife and daughter can go back to Xiangling, but you can't."

"I am a son-in-law of Xiangling."

"That doesn't fly."

"Then . . . then . . . then I can always drive them back to my in-laws' house, right?"

"No, your license plate is from Red Cliff. You can't cross between provinces."

"A little while back we could cross between provinces; the Party's policies can't just be changed at a moment's notice."

"Party policy is like the sun and will never change, but with the arrival of the novel coronavirus, everything has changed."

"And then?" Ai Ding asked.

"Since then I've been wandering on this 70-meter-long highway bridge. Cars and people can move about within 50 meters of that, but they can't get in anywhere."

"You're sleeping in the van?"

"It's the only place I can sleep."

"How about eating and drinking?"

"Once a week, my wife brings stuff to the checkpoint."

"Defecation and urination?"

"There're garbage bags in the back. Once a week, my wife takes them back and dumps them out."

"When do you think it'll end?"

"My wife says there's bound to be an end to it."

"If this goes on, if you're not sick yet you will be."

"Don't mention the sickness! If I really had it, I'd jump off the bridge."

"Please take care. I've got some German cold medicine in my bag. I'll give you two boxes of it."

"You're very kind."

"I should thank you. I almost ended up like you."

"If you were like me, I couldn't bear not taking you in. But if I took you in, it'd be difficult for the two of us to sleep in the van."

The streetlamps were lit and a crescent moon rose, shining brighter than the streetlights, but cold as ice. Ai Ding returned to Bull Town and stayed in a high-priced 500-Yuan-per-night hotel arranged by the government for "suspected" travelers during the epidemic. The beds were tidy, the Internet was free, and two meals a day were delivered to the room.

Ai Ding immediately called his wife and daughter on WeChat video, and summarized what had happened. All three of them were very anxious, realizing it was an impossible situation. His wife said: "This is not an accident. If you'd come home without a hitch, I'd have been surprised." Ai Ding said: "What happens next? My pass works in Hunan, but it'll become invalid once I cross the provincial boundary." She replied: "I'll call the community Epidemic Prevention Headquarters again and ask them to issue a pass for Hubei. I'll use WeChat to send it to you." He asked anxiously: "This won't be a problem, will it?" She answered: "Both government departments have already been in communication about this, so it should be okay."

Then she sighed and said: "Actually, I'm very conflicted. You're still outside and, although there're many dangers, there's always hope for what's ahead. Like your situation now, you're neither cold, nor hungry, nor sick, so it's not bad. Take the days as they come. The virus won't be here forever, right? But one day, when you're really standing in this room, maybe I'll be even more worried."

"Worried about what?"

"Some things have happened these past few days, so many I don't dare to even start talking about them. I'll just tell you about one thing: the small supermarket at the entrance to our community was closed the day before yesterday. The reason was that there's a female resident in the building behind, surnamed Luo, in her forties, and she went down to buy things there. As she was taking some instant noodles from the shelf, she suddenly fell to the ground in convulsions, her eyes glazed over like little bells. I was beside her at the time and rushed outside in a fright. Two rows of shelves were knocked over onto her. I didn't even stay to find out if she had died; I just rushed straight home, and I haven't slept the last two nights . . . I posted about what I saw online to remind everyone to be careful, but it was immediately deleted . . ."

Ai Ding wanted to say, "It'll be fine when I come back," but he shook his head and abandoned the thought, as he knew the situation wouldn't get better due to his return. His wife said, "Get to bed early tonight," and turned off the video feed.

Ai Ding took a shower and lay in bed, continuing to browse the Internet. An anonymous cadre of the Hubei Provincial Party Committee had surprisingly accepted an interview with *Halberd Weekly*, in which he reported that:

The number of hospital beds and medical staff in Wuhan ranks among the top three in the country. Yet, when the number of suspected cases first began to blow up, there weren't enough reagent kits, nor was there enough nucleic acid testing or CT scanners. On January 31, my mother developed a fever and went to line up at a clinic, where she almost collapsed.

Then we went to my work unit leaders. Frankly speaking, it was an attempt to take advantage of my relationship with them, but that method no longer had any effect. I went to see a top leader of a provincial agency, a departmental-level official. He looked around for me for a long time but still couldn't find a bed. At the time, I was still thinking that if even the leaders couldn't find a bed and such privileges were now useless, everyone had to be following the rules and going to hospital through regular channels. It was later discovered that this was not the case, that there was a real shortage of hospital beds. They were more precious than gold and scarcer than diamonds.

We were panicking at the time, wondering how it could possibly be like this. According to reports, there weren't even enough people to staff funeral homes. . . . The fear of this disease linked together with not being able to get into a hospital, in addition to a great number of messages on the daily Weibo pleading for help, made me feel the system had fallen apart. During that time, I became very depressed and couldn't sleep at night.

All I can say is that, faced with this test, Hubei Province and the city of Wuhan City failed to respond to nearly every problem they encountered. Normally that wouldn't be a big deal, but even if they'd done well under normal conditions, the real test is how things would turn out in a crisis.

Yesterday I read something that seemed like an aphorism and I felt very uncomfortable. It was, "No winter will never pass, and there's no spring that will never come." At the time, I was working overtime writing a report and I made use of this sentence. But when I think about it, so many people have lost their parents and children, and they'll be remaining in this winter forever.*

There was a very popular follow-up post below the interview, signed by the poet Wang Zang:

If you haven't been stabbed by a knife, you won't know the pain. Even the cadres of the provincial Party committee, with all their magical powers, are suffering. No wonder Professor Xu Zhangrun said, "Angry people no longer fear." So, the name of my poem is—

Terrified People are in a Rush to Kill Themselves

I'm afraid I'll lose this one remaining right
I must kill myself quickly
otherwise I'll be killed one day
and then deemed by a judge to be
a suicide
Isn't this what's called
to die dissatisfied?
What's more

only I can
kill myself completely
If someone else kills me
I'll still come alive in his dreams

Even though Ai Ding felt sleepy, he posted a short comment on the poem. He woke up the next morning and checked the Internet again, only to find that Wang Zang's suicide poem, his comment, and the rest of the thread had been deleted, and he'd been warned that he would be banned from the Internet if he wrote anything more like that. In these times, when there are so many indignities and grievances, you had to keep everything bottled up.

———————

At precisely twelve o'clock, someone knocked on the door, saying his food was ready. Ai Ding opened the door and dodged aside as a man pushed a dining cart into the room. Terrified, he stared at the man, saying: "You're Wang ... Wang ... Wang ..."

"Wang Erda, temporary cook at this hotel."

"Huh? Really?"

"Is there a problem?"

"You look exactly like someone I know."

"Who?"

"Wang Erxiao."

"He's my twin brother."

"Of course! Have you been sick?"

"You're the one who's been sick."

"I haven't. It was Wang Erxiao who got sick."

"He did?! How's he now?"

Ai Ding wanted to say "dead," but it came out as: "He's been isolated."

Wang Erda breathed a sigh of relief: "That's not unusual. These days, everyone's isolated."

"Have you been in touch with him?"

"His WeChat and mobile phone are no longer working."

"He's in the hospital."

"A pauper like him can be hospitalized?"

"When the virus came, he couldn't go back, so he stayed at the Diamond Ridge Street Epidemic Prevention Headquarters to do odd jobs. He got along well with people, but later he was suspected and hospitalized." Ai Ding didn't even blink as he spouted this nonsense, and Wang Erda believed him.

The more they talked, the more they got along. It turned out that the twin brothers had worked in a small enterprise producing ball-bearing steel in Liaocheng, Guanxian County, Shandong Province in 2017. Later, because of financial losses, the company had borrowed more than 1.3 million Yuan in loans from the local underworld with an annual interest rate of 12 percent. The owner, a woman, repaid more than 1.8 million in debt and had mortgaged her house, but still couldn't come up with the remaining 100,000 or more Yuan. So, the crime syndicate sent debt collectors to the company.

This sounded familiar to Ai Ding, who suddenly exclaimed: "Was this the Yu Huan murder case that shocked the whole country?"

"That's right. We were there when our boss killed the guy. On the first day, they came to the company and grabbed Yu Huan's hair and asked if she had the money, and our boss said no. One of them used the company's toilet to take a shit, and then they pushed the boss's head into the toilet to eat it. After they left, we called 110 and the mayor's hotline again and again, but nobody answered. The next day, eleven people came and forced Yu Huan and her son into the office and punched and kicked them. The gang leader, from the Du family, took off his pants, poked the boss in the face with his genitals, and slapped her with the soles of his shoes. He said, 'If you don't have the money, why don't you sell yourself for sex? Other people'll pay 80 Yuan, I'll pay 100.'

"I saw the situation was getting bad, so I quietly called the police. The 110 squad came and went into the office. After listening to both sides, they simply said, 'It's okay to ask for repayment of debts, but you can't beat people,' and left. I stopped them at the bottom of the stairs, and said if you leave, this mother and son will die. But they insisted on leaving, barging right past me. But at least a police car was dispatched.

"Now Yu Huan was really worried. She picked up a fruit knife from the table and asked the leader if he was leaving or not? Without saying a word in response, he rushed at her. Yu Huan was seeing red and stabbed him four times on the spot. The gang leader went off clutching his stomach and tried to drive himself to the hospital, but in the end his intestines spilled out everywhere and he died."

"I know everything about what happened later," Ai Ding said, "*Southern Weekend* reported that nearly two million netizens supported Yu Huan and her son. The authorities first sentenced Yu Huan to life imprisonment, and later, under all that pressure, they changed her sentence to five years."

"What you don't know is that because I'd called in the police, the mafia there were looking for us brothers, so we had to run away to our hometown in Shanxi that night, and then to Hunan a few days later. The construction company in Changsha only had a quota for one worker, so Erxiao stayed and I came to Xiangling to look for a job."

Ai Ding felt great respect for Erda. The two brothers might have looked exactly the same, but there was a difference in their level of intelligence.

———————

As night fell, when he was sure no one was watching, Wang Erda slipped into Ai Ding's room with some concealed wine and pork head meat. Ai Ding was overjoyed, and as it happened, his wife had just sent the new pass from Hubei. After half a bottle of wine, Erda happily agreed to help download and print it. He also said: "Being of help to somebody is uplifting; I'll be with the Buddha on my way to the Western Paradise. I'll go to Hubei for you to make inquiries. If all's good, you can go; if not, you'll be delayed temporarily. How about it?"

After feeling elated yet again, Ai Ding also felt a bit guilty. He didn't know how long he could wait, or even when he'd be able to confide the truth about Erxiao to Erda. And he still owed

200 Yuan for the fare. Before their final parting, he'd sworn to Erxiao, "I'll give it to you whenever we next meet." Was now that moment? No, it wasn't.

The next day, Erda got up early and went to the other side of the bridge to inquire for Ai Ding, but had the door slammed in his face. "Do you even know how to sing the national anthem? Do you realize our nation is in a very serious crisis?" shouted the border guard. The guy then added, "A strict order has been issued by the authorities: Even the Governor of Hunan wouldn't be allowed in."

"This isn't the Governor of Hunan. He's from Hubei, and he has a pass."

"If this pass was issued by some community in Wuhan, then it's only valid in that community; a pass for the entire territory of Hubei must be issued by the provincial-level Epidemic Prevention Agency."

"That's impossible."

"You think the threshold's too high? I'm declaring right now that we're stripping you of your Hubei residency."

"I'm from Shanxi."

"Oh, my mistake . . . We're striping Hubei residency from the holder of this pass."

"Are you a spokesperson for the Ministry of Foreign Affairs?"

"Of course not. A spokesperson for the Ministry of Foreign Affairs would be much tougher than me."

Erda was so mad he pulled off his mask, spat at the guy, then turned tail and ran. And the guy took off after him. Erda rushed to the red line on the bridge, where he suddenly stopped, raised up his ass, and let loose a horrible smelly fart right at the guy coming his way, who then choked and coughed a bit. Erda shouted: "Hubei people are so fucking evil, chasing me down to infect me!" which got a good laugh from the sentries on the Hunan side of the bridge.

Then a whistle sounded, as did a high-pitched tweeter, and on the two sides of the provincial red line people gathered quickly and launched into an entertaining war of words set on humiliating the ancestors of their opponents. Erda jumped around, swearing: "Sir, I just went over there, originally meaning to make peace and convince them to take back a Wuhan man from here. But instead, the guy starts blabbering about wanting to fuck up all the ancestors of the Hunanese! I say Chairman Mao's a forebear of us Hunanese, do you dare fuck him? He then says: 'I want to fuck all the ancestors of Hunan people except Chairman Mao.' He also says that even if the Governor came, he wouldn't let him in. The arrogance is just too much. You're just a fucking shit-eating farmer from Bull Village, an errand boy doing what he's told. Do you really think you've become a spokesperson for the Ministry of Foreign Affairs?"

The other side replied: "You donkey fart from Shanxi, don't act like a dog counting on its master's backing."

"I've the backing of Bull Town. You want a taste of it, donkey dick?"

"You can't write off two bulls with one stroke. We're all farmers. Tell us to eat shit, and you'll eat shit too."

"We're a town and you're a village: The level and quality's different. The higher level eats meat, the lower level eats shit. Since ancient times till now, your ancestors have been eating our ancestors' shit. And this epidemic also started with you. It's only coming to us after a load of your lot died. "

"You . . . you . . . you," the other side didn't have a comeback, just lots of yelling about male and female genitalia. In this regard, Chinese folk vocabulary is extremely rich, but not worth repeating here. In short, in the end, they all ended up like red-eyed bulls. All the young and strong men and women of Bull Village on the Hubei side came out from under the bridge holding poles, sticks, and spears, and resolutely marched onto the bridge. Their heads were black, their masks were white, and with an earth-shaking roar they shouted in unison, "You'll die with no descendants – Bull Town! Thieves and prostitutes – Bull Town! All wiped out by the virus – Bull Town!" There was nothing to match that on the other side, so they called the police. And police cars arrived on both sides at the same time. The police parked and watched for a while, irritated, before yelling through their bullhorns: "During the epidemic, it's forbidden to gather in groups, and all forms of provocative cursing and other rural entertainment is also banned. Please disperse and go home immediately. Otherwise, you will be punished according to the law."

Erda then rushed back to the hotel. On hearing all that had occurred, Ai Ding could only smile wryly. The road back to his hometown had been blocked, and the epidemic was far from being at an end. What could he do next? He couldn't stay in high-priced hotels forever. Erda could see what he was thinking and suggested Ai Ding move into his rented apartment: "There's one bedroom, a living room, and a kitchen. You can sleep in the living room and I'll sleep in the bedroom. You'll be at home when I'm at work in the hotel, so that'll take care of distancing."

"Does Epidemic Prevention Headquarters agree?"

"I'll work to get round the regulations, guarantee everything'll be alright. It shouldn't be a problem."

"Why are you so good to me?"

"You're an acquaintance of Erxiao. Most importantly, it's easier for two people to get through days like these."

"I'll pay the rent."

"One half each."

"I'll pay the daily expenses."

"One half each too."

"Thanks for taking in this old homeless dog. It's a great kindness that I'll never be able to repay in this lifetime. When the epidemic's over, I'll take you around my hometown as a small token of my gratitude."

"No problem."

Just at that moment, Ai Ding's wife appeared on WeChat and he introduced her to Erda over video. When she first heard about the "emergency situation," she was so sad she cried, and Ai Ding was rendered speechless. Seeing the situation, Erda cupped his hands and took his leave. The couple had nothing to say for a while, then their daughter appeared and called out to her father. Ai Ding responded but burst into tears. His daughter was a little shocked, so she said, "Baba, come closer and let me touch you." He agreed and buried his head in the phone, listening to his daughter say: "Baba's getting closer and closer, closer and closer every day." Ai Ding nodded quickly and then the video cut out.

After reconnecting, Ai Ding said: "Our daughter's not wrong. A little over a month ago, I was in Germany 10,000 miles away, and now I've finally reached the provincial border 100 miles away. If things were normal, it'd take a bit over an hour to get home by high-speed rail."

His wife said, "I'm guessing it'd take you over a month to walk that hour-long journey."

"Probably not that long."

"It's hard to say."

"Yes, it is hard to say. In ancient times, scholars who went to Beijing to take imperial exams would be gone for half a year or so. If you weren't on the pass list, you'd have to spend another half year going to Beijing a second time. Someone wrote:

You asked when I was coming back:
no date fixed yet;
in Ba's hills the rain by night
spills over autumn ponds.
When will we trim the candle's wick
together beside west window,
and speak back about this moment
of night rain in hills of Ba?*"

"My nerdy husband, I love you." And his daughter shouted: "We all love you!"

And so, the days and moods passed slowly. Ai Ding moved into Erda's rented apartment, each occupying a room of his own. Each morning, Erda went to work in an almost empty hotel as the chef and the cleaner for the entire building. His interpersonal contacts were limited to two security guards and one female front desk clerk. All four of them wore masks and goggles, kept their distance, and primarily communicated by sign language. Erda only removed the epidemic prevention equipment and clothes when he returned home in the evenings, where he chatted and drank with Ai Ding across a table. When they were in a good mood, the two of them would stay up past midnight, and sometimes on such nights they'd suit up and ride the motorcycle through the deserted streets. In these extraordinary times, with the city closed, only at this hour did the numerous checkpoints relax somewhat. Erda was familiar with the terrain and took on the role of Ai Ding's driver. Each time Ai Ding gripped Erda's thick waist, he'd think of Erxiao singing "Brother Monkey wants to be in the Red Army, but the Red Army doesn't want Brother Monkey," and of his sudden illness and tragic death. And again, goosebumps would rise on his skin. But fortunately, they'd been drinking and so the difference between people and ghosts didn't feel so great.

The corpse trucks also worked through the night, stopping from time to time in front of a building or on a side street. The corpses were collected like mail parcels: no one cried, and no one accompanied them out, as if this was all some weird silent film. Sometimes, the two of them would hide in the dark and watch. Ai Ding once asked Erda whether these people were all dead of Wuhan pneumonia and why they didn't go to a hospital, and Erda said, "There's a hospital in the city center that specializes in isolating fever patients, but almost no one goes there because there aren't any nucleic acid test kits, so it's impossible to get a diagnosis and there's even less likelihood of medical treatment. So all of Xiangling's been infected."

One time, they went out of Bull Town to Black Cloud Town by the Pantao River. On the bank opposite is Red Cliff in Hubei. There was a bright moon high in the sky, and from a distance, the confluence of the Pantao and Yangtze rivers sparkled in the moonlight, the waves looking like fish scales, diamonds, feathers, like micro-lithographs of skiffs. The battle of Red Cliff in which over a million warriors took part has been silenced by the years. A drunken Su Dongpo wrote poems to commemorate the warriors, and also the heroic beauties with lines such as "feather fans and silk kerchiefs" and "just wedded to the younger Qiao." Ai Ding sighed: "A thousand years pass in a flash, and no other Su Dongpo in the world."

Erda praised him: "Good poetry."

Ai Ding replied: "Good, my ass."

9

The Virus Leaves
the Country

The wind was whipping off the river, so they quickly turned back. It was 3 a.m. when they got home, and Erda hurriedly closed his door and went to bed as he had to go to work later that morning. Ai Ding wasn't ready for sleep yet, so he turned on his computer, climbed over the Internet Wall, and used Skype to call Zhuangzi Gui in Berlin. He heard Zhuangzi Gui's voice, but the video wasn't working: "Long time no see! Ai Ding, are you home yet?"

"Not yet," he said, clearly at the end of his patience. Then he briefly went through the frustrations of the past few days with his friend.

Zhuangzi Gui was surprised: "Still so much infection?"

"Yeah, it's everywhere. What about Germany?"

"I've heard it's in the south. Berlin is still free of it. If I wear a mask here, people will think I'm sick."

"How do you know you aren't? Have you been tested?"

"I had my temperature checked at Tegel Airport. It's normal. I'm in Brussels right now, attending a book fair."

"At this time? Still participating in a book fair?!"

"The organizer wasn't sure about it for a few days but decided to hold it as scheduled. Tens of thousands come to this book fair and it was organized long ago. Canceling it would be quite costly."

"It'll be even more costly now. It's been several months since the Wuhan pneumonia was discovered, and only a little over a month since Wuhan was shut down. The number of tourists who've passed through customs in China traveling to other now-affected areas around the world must be at least a few hundred thousand."

"Fuck. I remember, when China closed dozens of large cities, all the international airports were deliberately kept open for all the people escaping China . . . it was so dangerous . . ."

"Aren't you in danger, attending the book fair?"

"Just yesterday I attended the opening ceremony of the fair. There were more than fifteen thousand people, hundreds of book stalls, all in one huge building that looks like a flying saucer. No one was wearing a mask. I brought a mask but was embarrassed to take it out."

"You're done."

"What do you mean done? I'm still talking to you, aren't I?"

"After you go home, you'd better stay away from your wife and daughter, self-quarantine for fourteen days."

"Don't be crazy, Ai Ding. You're in much more danger than me."

"I'm like a frightened rabbit whose ears prick up at the slightest thing, so I'm fine for the time being."

The video suddenly started working. Zhuangzi Gui took a close look at Ai Ding: "Did you finish your glass?"

"Finished it a while ago."

"I'm in my hotel room now, so I'll drink with you for a bit. There are so many types of children's books at the Brussels book fair, more than anywhere else in the world, so there are loads of children who come. Because of my Chinese face, one child asked me whether the novel coronavirus is a flu. I said no, the novel coronavirus can kill people. The child shook his head and said that's not right, and his dad said, you know the flu kills people too, every year."

"What pathetic and misguided people. With these idiotic views, all Europe's going to fall . . . I hope you'll be all right, Zhuangzi."

"Chinese people here all wear masks and stock up on all kinds of disinfectants as they all know China's in dire straits. So I also brought a variety of disinfectants with me, and every hour or so, I go to the bathroom to spray my mouth, nose, and eyes . . ."

"You should warn the Europeans. You've had so many of your books translated, you should at least warn your readers."

"I'm not a medical professional, so I have no credibility. A report on the epidemic declared that there were 191 confirmed cases of new coronavirus pneumonia in the world outside China, which is less than 1 percent of the number in China. Commenting on this, the Foreign Ministry spokesperson Hua Chunying said: 'More frightening than viruses are the rumors and panic.'"

"But the country's been in chaos for a while now, with countless more dead people every day!"

"She also said: 'The WHO does not approve and even opposes the adoption of a travel ban on China,' and has reiterated that China has taken firm measures against COVID-19 and that she is confident that the epidemic is now under control. 'Some developed countries with strong epidemic prevention capabilities and advanced epidemic prevention facilities have already taken excessively restrictive measures that are contrary to the recommendations of the WHO. Even some American media and experts agree that they are too restrictive and not in line with the WHO's recommendations . . .'"

"I'm going to throw up."

"The Westerners here won't vomit. They don't necessarily believe the Communist Party, but they think they can trust the WHO."

"The Ethiopian Tedros Adhanom Ghebreyesus? He's the equivalent of the Party Secretary of China's Mission to the United Nations."

"You're not making sense. If I follow you, others will think that Hua Chunying is right: 'More frightening than viruses are the rumors and panic.'"

"Who's really creating 'the rumors and panic'?"

"Trump, the American President, is just like you, also a bit hysterical. The Emperor of Steamed Buns* and Fat Kim the Third are much more stable."

Ai Ding snapped off the video in anger. He didn't hear the irony in what Zhuangzi Gui said. This is a characteristic of Sichuan people, just as when the seventeenth-century Ming writer Jin Shengtan, who was about to be beheaded after being imprisoned for his writing, was still able to yell out: "Slow down, I've got an ancestral secret, and it's a pity that I won't be leaving it to posterity." The executioner asked, "What's the secret?" Sheng exclaimed: "When peanuts and dried tofu are chewed together, it has the flavor of ham."

If there'd been no Mao Zedong, the CCP, which now has been around for ninety-nine years, would have been wiped out by the Nationalists during the long Civil War. Mao Zedong devised stealthy military tactics that went against common sense and are now glorified as "guerrilla warfare." More importantly, he continually strengthened the Party's grass-roots organizations, a practice known as "Party branches built into military companies, small Party groups built into squads." In an army squad, a Party group had a three-person core among only a dozen people, supervising other fighters at all times and urging everyone to actively draw closer to the organization. Don't even mention disobedience, if there were even vague suspicions about somebody, a Party-line struggle session would commence, sometimes leading to death and even stigmatization of that person's family. This organizational structure still functions even now. With the arrival of the Wuhan virus, at the order of Party Central Committee Chairman Xi, the millions of Party members in village and street Party organizations in China were immediately mobilized to fortify defenses against the virus. Red slogans flooded the land as the Party vowed to drown the virus and the sick in an immense ocean as part of the People's War:

To eliminate the virus, follow the Party; One Belt One Road, do not look back
Remember you'll die quick if you get sick; couples in the same room often make love

If you dare to go out, [we'll] break your legs; if you dare talk back, [we'll] break your teeth

Mask or ventilator, you choose which you want

Knowingly conceal it, or don't isolate yourself, you'll die without offspring

It's shameless to go out to a party, and only desperados play mahjong together

If you want to continue to eat, don't go out for dinner, by not seeing family, you save them

Visit their homes this year, visit their graves the next

Visit everywhere today, you'll be visited by pneumonia tomorrow

To visit is to kill each other, to meet socially is to commit suicide

All dinner parties these days are banquets of death

But dealing with the Western devils is different. Let's just say there's a difference between the inside and the outside, that the Party's tight on the inside and loose on the outside. Zhuangzi Gui forwarded a video link to Ai Ding that was sweeping across Europe and told him: "Xinhua News Agency has reproduced it as the highlight of its big foreign propaganda campaign. The Shanghai-based website *The Paper* added fuel and vinegar to it and produced an extended version. There are dozens of edited versions, and I don't know which one of these damn things I've reposted."

Ai Ding immediately began watching it.

A fashionable young man with a Chinese face walks wearily toward the downtown area of Florence. He comes to a halt before a brick wall, along which Michelangelo had surely wandered centuries ago, then thrusts out his chest and stares into the distance. (*Voiceover: His thoughts grow wings, and in an instant he's returned to his homeland rising in the east. Ah, mother's instructions echo in his ears.*) – Ai Ding wondered whether he wasn't a second-generation Chinese born in Italy, and not the "Chinese overseas student" in the film – Then, the young man puts on an N95 mask and covers his eyes with a long strip of black cloth, after which he stands silently like a statue. A striking sign stands beside him, on which is written in English, Chinese, and Italian: "I am not a virus, I am a human being. Please don't discriminate against me!"

There's a constant stream of tourists. Every year, a multitude of artists come to make pilgrimages or perform in this world-famous Renaissance city-state. At first, no one notices him. (*Voiceover: His silent, powerful behavior counters the prejudice and racial discrimination brought against all Chinese people because of the pandemic.*) Eventually, people stop and gather around him, some take pictures and some whisper to each other.

Suddenly, a beautiful girl dressed in white approaches and hugs him. Her friends follow, hugging him tightly, touching him, rubbing his shoulders and hair, and finally everyone hugs in a group. Of course, given the emotional way of Italians, tearful kisses are inevitable. (*Voiceover: China has friends all over the world! Last year, Chairman Xi Jinping visited Italy for the first time and received the warmest welcome from this great country. The government and people fully accept the One Belt One Road initiative. Although there's a temporary setback at the moment, once the fog has lifted, the 2020 China–Italy Cultural Tourism Exchange Year will surely reach a great climax.*)

More and more Florentine citizens are embracing this sensational masterpiece of "I am not a virus, I'm a human being." Some even remove his mask and the strip of black cloth and kiss him even more passionately. (*Voiceover: This is them giving him the greatest support, and also giving the greatest support to China.*) . . .

After this video, another featured the protagonist of the "Hugging" activity in an exclusive interview with the China News Network, saying that about thirty to forty people had come up to hug him, far beyond his expectations. "After all, too many people have recently been saying that 'Chinese people have the virus.' We made this video in the hope that everyone will understand that not all Chinese people carry the virus. At the same time, we hope that Italians will no longer be afraid of us and prejudiced against us. Racial discrimination spreads faster than a virus."

After this, the video, "Pursuing Hugs," spread throughout Europe. Many Chinese overseas students in Spain took to the streets wearing masks and holding up placards with "#No Soy

Virus (#我不病毒)" printed on them, and were greeted with countless hugs; a smiling Chinese girl among tourists on the Piazza del Duomo in Milan, Italy, held up a placard saying "Please hug me, I am Chinese, but I am not a virus," attracting crowds of people of different skin colors to come forward and hug her; near the Eiffel Tower in Paris, another Chinese girl held up a paper sign on which was written: "Free hugs, please don't panic, I am not a virus!" which earned her many smiles, tears and hugs . . .

Of course, as everyone knows, about three weeks after this fad of "serial hugging," Italy, Spain, and France became the areas hit hardest by the Wuhan virus, with the number of confirmed infections and deaths ranking first, second, and third in Europe. Italy had not experienced such a rush on coffins in such a short period of time since World War II. Hu Xijin, Editor-in-Chief of *The Global Times*, a subsidiary of *The People's Daily*, commented on this:

> Italy has already been completely "Hubei-ized" and "Wuhan-ized" by the spreading virus. What's even more unfortunate is that it couldn't get the kind of medical aid that Wuhan and Hubei received from all over China. Italy is woefully lacking in specialized hospitals like those in Wuhan, and a batch of pop-up hospitals could not be created overnight. Many mildly ill patients had no option but to heal themselves at home. Although there have been city lockdowns in Italy, the community spread of the epidemic has been difficult to stop. The severity of the epidemic in other European countries has now surpassed the peak of the epidemic in other regions outside Hubei, China. They are now debating whether they should fully mobilize to fight the epidemic. This sort of hesitation is painful to watch. The United States is the furthest away from the epidemic, but the current situation there is already very bad on the east and west coasts, and will become worse. In addition, the US is embroiled in disputes over "public concealment" [of the true numbers from countries such as China] by some countries, and the future is unpredictable. . . .

Italy is in an embarrassing state, having added 427 new deaths in the past day and a total of 3,405 deaths, surpassing China's reported total of 3,250, thus becoming the country with the largest official number of deaths due to the novel coronavirus epidemic. . . .

Be strong, everyone. Don't think you're the most unfortunate. If you're a bit more optimistic, you may inspire more people.*

In another Internet call, Zhuangzi Gui told Ai Ding that, as Editor-in-Chief Hu had said, the heads of state of the European nations and the US were full of goodwill and optimism toward China. German Chancellor Angela Merkel made a public speech emphasizing that China should not be excluded from the 5G network, but shortly afterward, her personal doctor was diagnosed with COVID-19 and she had to isolate herself. Then British Prime Minister Boris Johnson was diagnosed and hospitalized. Meanwhile, after congratulating itself on the illusory "phase one victory of the trade war," the United States neglected to take sufficient precautions, and the number of deaths from the novel coronavirus soared, rapidly surpassing the number of US soldiers killed in Europe during World War II . . .

And so, under the leadership of the Party Central Committee and Chairman Xi, the hundreds of millions of people who had progressively defeated the virus had once again "stood up," as Mao Zedong had announced on October 1, 1949, at the Tiananmen Gate in Beijing, this time to save an anguished world. As the United States was the biggest stumbling block to "China saving the world," anti-Americanism had once again become the "strongest voice of the times." With more than eighteen million active fans and ranking first among domestic WeChat public accounts in terms of page views and click-through rates, the "Learning Place of the Way" forum was delighted when it learned the number of deaths from the novel coronavirus in the United States had exceeded 140,000. A quick commentary, "Impending Death: The US Sinks," was immediately published in which the 140,000 corpses were enlarged to one million, then stating that the one million corpses were all "whereabouts unknown." Combining this with the country's pork shortage, it concluded as follows:

> If they've been neither burned nor buried in mass graves, how do you deal with so many dead bodies? Where are they? It is highly probable that the United States froze these corpses and then passed them off as beef, pork, or other meat, processed into luncheon meat, hamburgers, or hot dogs, and gave them to unsuspecting Americans to eat. Many pork processing plants and dairies in the United States are now bankrupt. Cannibalism can not only solve the problem of food shortages in an economic crisis, but also solve the problem of corpse disposal. One could call it killing two birds with one stone.

10

Scientists against "Conspiracy Theories"

Out of pure boredom, Ai Ding's Skype conversations with Zhuangzi Gui increased in frequency. One day, Zhuangzi Gui said to Ai Ding: "I just watched the 2008 Nobel Prize winner Luc Montagnier on French TV, talking about how the virus was man-made: 'We came to the conclusion that there was manipulation around this virus. . . . To a part, but I do not say the total . . . of the coronavirus from a bat, someone added sequences, in particular of HIV, the virus of AIDS. . . . It is not natural. It's the work of professionals, of molecular biologists. . . . A very meticulous work. . . . After that, it may have accidentally leaked out of the laboratory. The so-called theory that it's from a seafood market is just a legend.' He also says: 'We're not the first to discover the HIV gene sequence in the novel coronavirus. Indian scholars had already discovered that the novel coronavirus's genome contains the sequences of other viruses . . . but they were pressured to withdraw their article before official publication. . . .'"*

"What pressure?"

"I don't know. I think Shi Zhengli also has been under a lot of pressure. It's human nature to rush to deny and divert attention. Who wants to take responsibility for such a terrible crime? I also saw Professor Simon Wain-Hobson of the Pasteur Institute in Paris being interviewed by Radio France International. He disagrees with Luc Montagnier's theory, and believes the Wuhan virus is a natural virus, but he also said: "The goal of the study of the so-called gain-of-function (GOF) is to add new functions to viral genes so that viruses can directly infect human cells, or enable viruses to spread directly through the air. At the time, I was practically the only expert who questioned this sort of research. . . . I think the above-mentioned research by Shi Zhengli's team is totally crazy research, bringing unnecessary risks to humanity."*

"To us laymen," Ai Ding said, it seems there's little difference between 'adding new functions to viral genes so that the virus can directly infect human cells' and 'detecting HIV in bat-derived coronavirus.' It's all terrifying news."

"To scientists," Zhuangzi Gui responded, "the two pieces of terrible news are very different, like that between the death of a cat and that of a dog, with bats and monkeys the methods of additions and insertions are completely different in specific experiments. But for all living things, from 2003 to 2020, from SARS to an upgraded version of SARS, it's all an indistinguishable bad deal leaving everything subject to abuse. Anyway, Simon Wain-Hobson says in the interview: 'China is a pivotal country and should have a high-standard virus laboratory, but the problem is that this is an authoritarian government.'"

"This all started with the official press release in May 2003," Ai Ding said, "when Chen Zhu, Vice President of the Chinese Academy of Sciences, visited France and announced that China had reached a consensual understanding with the French on the joint construction of a P4 laboratory (a microbiology laboratory with the highest level of safety) . . . The Mérieux family pulled all the strings they could to convince France to cooperate with China . . . Did they remember that they were collaborating with an authoritarian government?"

Zhuangzi Gui snickered and then deliberately took a contrarian position: "I feel Luc Montagnier is not reliable. Most Western experts are attacking his 'artificial synthesis' theory, and consider it a joke."

"Their basis?"

"They've tested the DNA/RNA and believe it's natural. The virus chromosomes didn't change when jumping from bats to human species. The insertion of four fragments of HIV, the rewriting, the unintentional leak from the laboratory, it's all nonsense."

"And so?"

"So the conclusion is: natural transmission. Shi Zhengli didn't lie. This is nature's punishment for humans' uncivilized living habits: yummy wild game! Eating civets in 2003 and bats in 2019, even if there were no bats in the South China Seafood Wholesale Market, there were other wild animals infected by bats. Recently, the Hong Kong expert Yuen Kwok-yung, one of six members of Zhong Nanshan's high-level group of advisors on the COVID crisis, published an article in the Hong Kong Chinese-language newspaper *Ming Pao*, and withdrew it shortly after. His thesis was that 'Wild game markets are the source of ten thousand toxins.' 'Wuhan's novel coronavirus is a product of our primitive culture in China, one where wild animals are captured indiscriminately, and the animals are treated inhumanely, so that people can satisfy their particular appetites by continuing to eat wild game; these deep-rooted bad habits are the source of this virus.'"

"Is this a 'Notice of Redress' issued to the CCP?"

"Ai Ding, we can't oppose the Party by losing our reason: science is science. Take a look at the Voice of America report* about scientists' condemnation of the 'conspiracy theories' that the novel coronavirus does not have a natural origin. It said that many authoritative scientists have opposed the theory that the novel coronavirus is an artificial synthesis, including twenty-seven prominent public health scientists from outside China. They issued a statement in the medical journal *The Lancet* on February 19: 'Scientists from multiple countries have published and analysed genomes of the causative agent, severe acute respiratory syndrome coronavirus 2 (SARS-CoV-2), and they overwhelmingly conclude that this coronavirus originated in wildlife.' ... These scientists have also been in contact with Chinese scientists, public health and medical staff who are fighting the epidemic. They express their support and 'strongly condemn conspiracy theories suggesting that COVID-19 does not have a natural origin.'"** Angela Rasmussen, a virologist at Columbia University's School of Public Health, holds the same view. She told the BBC* that, historically, all new viruses, including H5N1/ H7N7/H7N9 influenza viruses, MERS, Ebola virus, and Zika virus, are naturally occurring, and that at the moment, an example of a new virus appearing as a result of a laboratory accident has yet to occur."

"And the official Chinese response?"

"First. The Wuhan Institute of Virology fiercely denied the claim that the novel coronavirus originated at their laboratory. 'A Letter to All Staff and Graduate Students of the Institute' read: 'These rumors have caused great injury to the reputation of researchers at the institute who conduct their scientific research on the frontlines. These rumors have also seriously interfered with the work currently being done by the Institute in emergency response to the "plague."' Then, Foreign Ministry spokesman Geng Shuang spoke out in response to a related question, saying: 'At present, the WHO and the vast majority of the world scientists and professionals in the public health field generally agree there is no evidence that the new coronavirus originated in a laboratory.'"

"I'm sick of looking at your parrot face," Ai Ding snapped. He was getting so angry he wanted to turn off the video.

"Calm down. You need to understand what the experts are actually saying. There's also a long report from the BBC called 'Amid Political Disputes, How Do Global Scientists view the Wuhan Origin Theory and Virus Tracing?'** There, experts explain why it's not likely the virus leaked from a laboratory. Would you like to hear what it says?"

"I'm all ears."

Zhuangzi Gui read: "John S. Mackenzie is a professor of infectious diseases at Curtin University in Australia with nearly 50 years of research experience. In 2003, he was the leader of the first technical mission to China to investigate the origin of the SARS epidemic. He believes that the probability of the virus leaking from the laboratory is extremely low, because all P4 laboratories around the world must undergo strict inspections with the same standards to avoid accidental leaks. 'We call this kind of laboratory a box within a box within a box,' he told the BBC.

Such laboratories often have multiple safety procedures that are difficult to fail at the same time."

"Yes, a P4 laboratory is known as a Supervirus Prison," Ai Ding replied. "Under normal circumstances, the 'prisoners' cannot escape the prison – but what's not very normal is this: since January 2018, the US Embassy in Beijing has sent personnel to visit the Wuhan Institute of Virology many times, including once in March 2018 the US Embassy Counselor of the Environment, Science, and Technology Section, Rich Switzer. Shortly after one of these visits, in two diplomatic telegrams, US personnel warned of the security and management weaknesses of the Institute, noting that it lacked technical personnel with safety training. In addition, the external website of the Wuhan P4 Laboratory originally featured many photos related to bat virus research, which showed the staff capturing and sampling bats, as well as the laboratory dissection analysis process, all of which featured no security protection. These photos have recently been taken off the website."

Ai Ding went on: "There was also no precedent for the Chernobyl nuclear leak in Ukraine, but it happened, due to a mixture of human error and design flaws, exposing all of Europe to nuclear radiation; similarly the Wuhan virus has been disseminated to more than 180 countries, killing nearly two million people and counting, and there is also no precedent for that – and the CCP has been responsible for countless 'unprecedented' but terrible 'accidents' in science and other fields over the years."

"Ai Ding, you are simply wrong. Sharon Lewin, Director of the Peter Doherty Institute for Infection and Immunity in Melbourne, Australia, told the BBC that 'despite the similarities between the new coronavirus and RaTG13, . . . the pathway into the human body (i.e., on the receptor ACE2) has unique characteristics, so RaTG13 does not infect human cells.'"*

"You are simply off the mark, old man. Shi Zhengli has been engaged in research on the 'cross-species transmission' of bats through intermediate hosts and humans for many years, and her academic achievements have all been published in Chinese and foreign scientific journals. Many reports of her work have appeared in China's official media. Clearly, Sharon Lewin does not understand Shi Zhengli and her work.

"Angela Rasmussen, the virologist at Columbia University you mentioned before, believes that while this genetic strain in bats is naturally occurring, it has the potential to mutate into one that can infect humans: 'Although RaTG13 is the closest relative to the new coronavirus, it is still separated from it by evolution that took decades to complete. . . . Genetic evidence suggests this virus originated from a naturally occurring bat coronavirus, many of which come from wild bats in China.'*

"However, even if '[g]enetic evidence suggests this virus originated from a naturally occurring bat coronavirus,' this does not mean that the Wuhan P4 does not possess this type of virus; and it also does not mean the virus has not been processed. Just as the raw materials of alcoholic beverages are all natural, they become alcoholic beverages after processing.

"Professor Dale Fisher, Chair of the Global Outbreak Alert and Response Network under the WHO, told the BBC that within just a few months, the novel coronavirus has undergone over a hundred mutations. This level of activity further proves that the evolution of this virus can only be completed in nature. 'The coronavirus is clearly mutating more easily in the throats of millions of bats flying around than in a safe laboratory.'**

"Bats have an evolutionary history of fifty million years. Although they carry a variety of viruses, we've never heard of the direct infection of humans over the many years of their existence. Bat feces have been and still are a precious Chinese medicine from ancient times to the present, called *'faeces vespertilionis.'* Therefore, there is no scientific basis for 'The coronavirus is clearly mutating more easily in the throats of millions of bats flying around than in a safe laboratory.' Furthermore, are laboratories in autocratic states safe?

"Gerald Keusch is a Professor of Medicine and International Health at Boston University. He told the BBC*** that in the Nipah virus (NiV) outbreak in Bangladesh in 2019, records show that when humans drank fruit juice contaminated with fruit bat urine or saliva, they were probably directly infected, which means that bats could have directly spread the virus to humans.

"Experiments by Shi Zhengli and many experts have confirmed that the statement 'bats spread viruses directly to humans' is a commonsense error. The bat Shi Zhengli researched and named the 'Chinese rufous horseshoe bat (*Rhinolophus sinicus*)' has different characteristics to that of the tropical fruit bat in Bangladesh.

"Alexander Gorbalenya, a virus expert from Leiden University in the Netherlands, told the BBC* that because different people have different physiques, it may have been that before the virus became 'aggressive,' it had already spread in crowds for weeks, even months. He believes that due to the huge population of Wuhan, the difficulty in tracing the original source of infection is increased.

"I agree with the first part of his statement. As to the latter, I disagree with blaming the greater difficulty in tracing the virus's source on Wuhan's huge population. I suppose this person doesn't know the stories of the whistle-blowers Li Wenliang and Ai Fen.

"According to a study published in the medical journal *Infection, Genetics and Evolution*, the latest genetic analysis of the novel coronavirus carried by more than 7,600 patients worldwide shows that the virus has rapidly spread around the globe, which eliminates the hypothesis that the virus has spread around the world before it was discovered – 'Everything has to be based on a professional international survey,' Professor Gerald Keusch said. 'Conspiracy only breeds in darkness, and truth is the light that dispels conspiracy.'**

"Empty talk of 'conspiracy' and 'truth' is meaningless. Does it need to be repeated over and over again that dictators are capable of anything? How many people must die before even a little has been learned? How many people must die before the great multitude of Western high-tech projects exclude the CCP? These experts cannot even enter China, let alone Wuhan, let alone personally survey the P4 site. There the PLA's chief chemical weapons defense experts lead a large number of troops in guarding the laboratory. The P4 and the Wuhan Center for Disease Control (WHCDC), next to the South China Seafood Wholesale Market, possesses countless bats and countless other wild specific-pathogen-free animals that can be used in unscrupulously absurd experiments. At present, like the Zhongnanhai HQs of the CCP and central government in Beijing, the Wuhan P4 is a core state secret. No one supervises it, even less are investigations allowed. The evil is forever unknowable. How does anyone dare to say that everything has been 'based on a professional international survey'?"

Ai Ding continued his narrative . . .

SARS in 2003 was the first epidemic in this century to have a real impact on public health in China. The numerous diseases that had plagued China in the decades beforehand may have caused more deaths and more damage, because of the widespread and complete disregard for human life, but they were hidden behind layers and layers of secrecy and, therefore, never gained global attention. SARS was the sole exception. The mobilization of the entire population after the alarm was raised by the military doctor Jiang Yanyong, and the shock caused by cross-border infection from Guangdong Province to twenty-seven other provinces in China and twenty-nine other countries, shook the WHO and became a famous case in the history of global public health. And because of this, Shi Zhengli, who's currently caught in the vortex of the novel coronavirus, has said, in reference to herself and other public health experts: "We are the SARS generation."

According to official information and Shi Zhengli's own public account, when SARS was raging in 2003, causing over 10,000 infections at home and abroad and 1,459 deaths, it had a decisive impact on her. The first case of SARS appeared in the city of Foshan before spreading across the whole province of Guangdong and beyond. Shi Zhengli's colleagues detected the SARS virus in farmed civet cats in Guangdong wild game markets. After continued investigation, it was discovered that civet cats were only the "intermediate host" transmitting SARS to humans, and that the actual source was bats. Among virus experts, bats have a special status due to their long evolutionary history. They are the only mammals remaining on the planet that are able to fly and are a "natural host," also known as a "virus reservoir," to over one hundred potent viruses such as rabies, the Marburg virus, and the Nipah virus.

So, beginning in 2004, Shi Zhengli led her team on a journey to trace the source of the SARS coronavirus with the full support of the Wuhan Institute of Virology. No matter whether it was in the south or north, central or west, they went to twenty-eight provinces and cities in China, wherever they heard there were bats, just as if they were looking for a needle in a haystack. It took them over ten years to find the source of the virus.

In 2005, Shi Zhengli's team published their first paper, saying that the virus they had extracted from a bat was not a direct relative of SARS and could not directly infect people. In 2011, they found bat colonies of dozens of species in a cliff cave complex in Yunnan, equivalent to a natural gene pool of viruses. Ultimately, they isolated a new coronavirus which was nearly identical genetically to SARS. Twice a year each year since then, they've gone to these caves to take periodic samplings, and have repeatedly tested whether the bats have the ability to cross-infect between species.

Finally, on November 9, 2015 (corrected on April 6, 2016), Shi Zhengli and others published a paper, "A SARS-Like Cluster of Circulating Bat Coronaviruses Shows Potential for Human Emergence" in the international electronic journal *Nature Medicine*, the abstract of which follows:

The emergence of severe acute respiratory syndrome coronavirus (SARS-CoV) and Middle East respiratory syndrome (MERS)-CoV underscores the threat of cross-species transmission events leading to outbreaks in humans. Here we examine the disease potential of a SARS-like virus, SHC014-CoV, which is currently circulating in Chinese horseshoe bat populations. Using the SARS-CoV reverse genetics system, we generated and characterized a chimeric virus expressing the spike of bat coronavirus SHC014 in a mouse-adapted SARS-CoV backbone. The results indicate that group 2b viruses encoding the SHC014 spike in a wild-type backbone can efficiently use multiple orthologs of the SARS receptor human angiotensin converting enzyme II (ACE2), replicate efficiently in primary human airway cells and achieve *in vitro* titers equivalent to epidemic strains of SARS-CoV. Additionally, *in vivo* experiments demonstrate replication of the chimeric virus in mouse lung with notable pathogenesis. Evaluation of available SARS-based immune-therapeutic and prophylactic modalities revealed poor efficacy; both monoclonal antibody and vaccine approaches failed to neutralize and protect from infection with CoVs using the novel spike protein. On the basis of these findings, we synthetically re-derived an infectious full-length SHC014 recombinant virus and demonstrate robust viral replication both *in vitro* and *in vivo*. Our work suggests a potential risk of SARS-CoV re-emergence from viruses currently circulating in bat populations.*

Other papers in *Nature* have featured other virologists questioning the necessity of this study, believing it to be pointless but also of great risk. As Professor Wain-Hobson said, "If the virus escaped, nobody could predict the trajectory."**

Despite considerable controversy, Shi Zhengli's scientific career reached a peak at this point. She has since served as the Director of the Key Laboratory of Pathogeny and Biosafety of New and Virulent Infectious Diseases of the Chinese Academy of Sciences, the Director of the Research Center for Emerging Infectious Diseases of the Wuhan Institute of Virology, and the leader of the emergency research expert group of the "2019 New Pneumonia Emergency Science and Technology Project" of the Science and Technology Department of Hubei Province. She has been the recipient of a variety of honors and has attended various conferences; in a speech on the Beijing TV Station program *BUICK – One Speech* in 2019, she answered those who questioned the value of her research:

How did the viruses of these wild animals reach human society? There weren't so many infectious diseases in the past, so why are there so many now? . . . I've also had relatives asking, if SARS is gone, what's the point in you doing this? It's possible this disease will never return. But I feel all this work we've done, if we can prevent a disease outbreak, it'll make sense.*

While she was being battered by the storm of negative public opinion over a possible P4 leak, that month the *China Science Journal* interviewed the researcher Xiao Gengfu, the Party Committee Secretary and Deputy Director of the Wuhan Institute of Virology, as well as Deputy Director of the National Key Laboratory of Virology. He added some significant new details about the early stages of the pandemic:

Our institute initially received unexplained pneumonia samples sent from Wuhan's Jinyintan Hospital on December 30, 2019 and immediately organized a team to analyze them, and over the next seventy-two hours, on January 2, 2020, we were able to determine the entire genome sequence of the 2019 novel coronavirus. The virus strain was isolated on January 5, all of which provided an important basis for determining the pathogen, carrying out virus detection, drug screening, and research and development. Prior to this, our institute did not possess this virus.**

Aside from the lie "our institute did not possess this virus," everything else is factual. If the above work and assessments were made public on January 5 and the alarm was sounded, it would have been as Shi Zhengli stated: "all this work we've done, if we can prevent a disease outbreak, it'll make sense." It's a pity, then, that at the time, this was all classified as a state secret − when the virus was spreading, when the "rumors" were banned, when hundreds of thousands of people inside and outside the government gathered and cross-infected each other, Shi Zhengli and her boss consistently maintained a consistently high degree of acquiescence to the Communist Party Central Committee.

Regarding the "artificial virus leak" rumor that was spreading wildly in China, the *China Science Journal* asked Xiao Gengfu: "In 2015, the journal *Nature Medicine* published a paper entitled 'A SARS-Like Cluster of Circulating Bat Coronaviruses Shows

Potential for Human Emergence.'* This paper found that a virus called SHC014 was potentially pathogenic, and the researchers further constructed a chimeric virus. Shi Zhengli of the Wuhan Institute of Virology was one of the authors. What work did Shi Zhengli do in this research?"

Secretary Xiao responded:

> In this study, Researcher Shi Zhengli only provided the gene sequence of the spike envelope protein of the SHC014 coronavirus and did not participate in the specific experimental operation of using it to construct the chimeric virus. These virus materials have not been introduced into China. The animal experiments of this work were all done in the United States, and the US team only carried out mouse infection experiments, and no non-human primate infection experiments. In addition, the SHC014 and the 2019 novel coronavirus genome sequence similarity is 79.6 percent. They are not close relatives, and there is no live SHC014 virus in the Wuhan Institute of Virology. This is to say, the Wuhan Institute of Virology has never synthesized nor stockpiled the chimeric virus constructed by the US team, nor has it followed up on the research of the chimeric virus published in this 2015 paper.

Party member Shi Zhengli was forced to agree with Party Secretary Xiao's response to the question, because the CCP, like the Soviet Communist Party and the Nazis, enforces strict "democratic centralism within the Party": the individual is subordinated to the organization, the minority is subordinated to the majority, subordinates obey their superiors, and the whole Party is subordinated to the Party Central Committee – even if this means that almost a whole lifetime of scientific achievements are rejected.

Secretary Xiao's authoritative disavowal of responsibility was then creatively taken one step further by the "War Wolf" spokesman of the Ministry of Foreign Affairs, Zhao Lijian, becoming the first of the epidemic conspiracy theories: "Patient Zero of COVID-19 is in the US Army! The first symptoms of infection of the virus leaked by the US P4 are influenza-like. They brought the disease into China by participating in the 7th World Military Games in Wuhan, and then, voilà . . . it spread! Their biochemical weapons test was a success!" Zhong Nanshan of the China Engineering Academy also indicated that while COVID-19 broke out in China, its source was not necessarily inside China. President Trump responded: "We all know where it came from," and then directly called it the "Chinese virus." White House trade advisor Peter Navarro subsequently made the point that the outbreak could have been controlled in Wuhan, but the CCP concealed the outbreak for six weeks, and hundreds of thousands of tourists in the epidemic area took flights from there to Milan, New York, and other places, thereby spreading the Wuhan virus to the world.

It was late at night. Ai Ding, completely drunk by then, was about to collapse when he received four additional pieces of evidence from Zhuangzi Gui:

(A) Xiao Botao, a professor at the School of Biological Science and Engineering at the South China University of Technology, published an English-language report entitled "The Possible Origins of 2019-nCoV Coronavirus"* on researchgate.net, a global academic social networking site. Xiao certified that the "South China Seafood Wholesale Market" was only 280 meters away from the "Wuhan Center for Disease Control and Prevention (WHCDC)," where more than six hundred wild bats were kept for a period of time, and that in 2017 and 2019, bat blood and urine leakage accidents had occurred there. While researchers were extracting blood samples, some of them had been attacked by bats and contaminated by bat urine, after which they self-isolated for fourteen days.

Xiao Botao also pointed out that 96 percent and 89 percent of the novel coronavirus gene sequence was found to be similar to the coronavirus (CoV ZC45) of the "Chinese rufous horseshoe bat" found and named by Shi Zhengli in the cliff caves of Yunnan. However, the question of whether the pathogen can infect humans had still to be studied. The report indicated that thirty-three samples of the Wuhan virus were detected among the 585 samples collected at the South China Seafood Wholefood Market.

(B) *Le Monde* of France published an investigative report by Raphaëlle Bacqué and Brice Pedroletti* describing Shi Zhengli's panic when the COVID-19 infection began to spread in 2019:

"When Wuhan pneumonia broke out in December last year, Shi Zhengli, the head of the Wuhan P4 laboratory, was anxious and afraid. She said that she went over all her research and every movement she'd made, repeatedly. She was extremely worried that the genetic sequence showed that the killer [virus] had been leaked from her department. She told Jane Qiu, a reporter for *Scientific American*, 'It's really messing with my mind and keeping me up at night.'"

Many people at the Institute of Virology study coronaviruses. Shi Zhengli and her team did "function acquisition," which is to say "virus remodeling" experiments to make them more infectious and then identifying weaknesses to test treatments. In addition, Shi Zhengli published a report on the new viral genome results on January 20 this year, claiming to have found a virus that had not yet been recognized, and that was 96 percent similar to the bat coronavirus RaTG13.

(C) Around this time, Xi Jinping gave an important speech advocating the incorporation of biosecurity into the national security system and pushing for the introduction of a Biosecurity Law as soon as possible. Xi also made the point that because of the shortcomings and deficiencies exposed by this epidemic, the government would have to pay close attention to these problems in order to solve them, and to plug any loopholes ... perfecting major epidemic prevention and control systems and mechanisms, and strengthening the national public health emergency management system ...

(D) Before "Phase One" of the Sino-US trade agreement was signed and went into effect on January 15, the Chinese side specifically requested "a clause that calls on parties to enter consultations if 'a natural disaster or other unforeseeable event outside the control of the parties delays a party from timely complying with its obligations.'"*

This was followed by the closure of Wuhan on January 23, and the subsequent closure of dozens of other major cities in China. However, all other borders remained open for many days after that, allowing hundreds of thousands of passengers from epidemic areas to fly to all parts of the world . . . This seems to indicate that before China signed the trade agreement they knew a catastrophe was coming.

At the moment Trump signed the agreement, he thought he'd won the trade war, and abandoning Hong Kong was a price he was willing to pay. Little did he know that he had lost, big time. He had been deceived by one of those dictators he so admired, and was on the brink of "unrestricted biochemical warfare," with a scale and impact far beyond anything like a trade war . . .

11

Unrestricted Warfare

It was almost noon when Ai Ding got out of bed, brewed a pot of tea, and then reread the four pieces of information sent by Zhuangzi Gui the night before. The last one, on "unrestricted biochemical warfare," was very eye-catching. Yes, whether the Wuhan virus leaked from the laboratory or not, the results were in line with characteristics of "unrestricted warfare."

*Unrestricted Warfare** is a military book co-authored by Qiao Liang, who is Major General of the People's Liberation Army (PLA) Air Force, Deputy Secretary-General of the National Security Policy Research Committee, and a professor at the National Defense University, and Air Force Captain Wang Xiangsui. The term means "a war that transcends limits and battlefields," capable of being surprisingly effective and changing military dynamics. For example, on September 11, 2001, a small group of terrorists crashed into the Twin Towers in New York City, killing more than three thousand people. This is a typical "unrestricted war" strategy that changes the dynamics of a conflict. This globally shocking crime ignited patriotic anti-American carnivals in totalitarian China and caused waves of heated debate in the middle and higher levels of the army as well. The young hawks believed Mao Zedong's "People's War" theory was outdated, that there'll be no one battlefield in future wars, that the battlefields will multiply. There will be no fixed direction and form to them; instead, advances will be made in countless directions and forms, such as intelligence, biochemistry, technology, information, culture, propaganda, and so on, all of which must be regarded as matters of life-or-death importance in "unrestricted warfare." In short, bin Laden's al-Qaida and the Taliban's masterpiece of terror led to the book *Unrestricted Warfare* becoming the most popular reading matter in the military second only to Mao Zedong's 1938 classic series of lectures *On Protracted War.* There were even official rumors in China that *Unrestricted Warfare* alarmed the Pentagon and that it was considered "the most advanced military theory in the world, coinciding with the first strong military challenge since the disintegration of the former Soviet Union."

After a decade-long hunt, bin Laden was finally killed, but the CCP still maintains close contact with the Taliban. On June 20, 2019, after brainwashing camps holding more than one million Uighurs in Xinjiang had been reported by the media, a spokesperson for the Ministry of Foreign Affairs, Lu Kang, declared at a press conference that the Director of the Taliban Political Office in Doha, Mullah Abdul Ghani Baradar, and several aides were visiting China, where senior Chinese officials exchanged views with them on Afghanistan's "peaceful reconciliation process and combating terrorism."

There was an international uproar about the brainwashing camps, but this sort of disregard for basic human values is also part of "unrestricted warfare." The result: China prevailed, since the vast majority of Western countries remained silent for the sake of their economic self-interest, and Italy even went further, embracing the "Belt and Road" initiative in its entirety, embarking on a honeymoon with these Chinese thugs. Then, the United Kingdom, France, Germany, Spain, and the United Nations all began their own love affairs with these same brazen hoodlums. In accepting Huawei and 5G,* in acquiescing to the Hong Kong crisis and to the atrocities in Xinjiang and Tibet, as China becomes more and more outrageous in its human rights violations, as the use of facial recognition and other cutting-edge Internet technologies for monitoring entire populations are rolled out, "unrestricted warfare" is in its element, carrying all before it . . .

Fortunately, there are loads of online materials on "unrestricted warfare," so that it is possible to understand the mindset of the CCP. Of course, most of the people keen on this topic are militant IT generals warring on their laptops. The *People's Liberation Army Daily*, October 6, 2015 edition, includes the essay "Biotechnology Will Become the New Strategic Advantage of Future Military Revolution," which further expands on "unrestricted warfare," arguing that technological supremacy is vital to command of the battlefield. He Fuchu, one of the authors, is a biologist, an alternate member of the Central Committee of the CCP, a Deputy Director of the Science and Technology Commission of the Central Military Commission, and a Deputy President of the PLA Academy of Military Sciences. The article concludes as follows:

> Because the weaponization of living organisms will increasingly become reality in the future, non-traditional forms of combat will take the stage.... As the use and control of the human brain become possible, conceivable fields of operations will expand from the physical and information domains to the cognitive domain. The human brain may succeed land, sea, air, sky, electricity, and the Internet as the next field of combat. In future, "brain network-ing" may even help create a brand-new network as a successor to the Internet and the Internet of Things, by fully integrating bio-intelligence to levels above and beyond modern information technology.

Even now, there is a group of high-quality unrestricted warfare madmen among the Emperor's coterie today who are forcing more than one million Uyghurs in the concentration camps in Xinjiang to submit to the "Brain Network" test, and having successfully achieved information control nationwide, they've finally arrived at biotechnology – the threshold of "future biological weapons" – because, as has just been pointed out, the future of humankind is determined by those who have the most advanced technology. The 2019 Chinese movie *The Wandering Earth*, written by the well-known science fiction writer Liu Cixin, imagines that after five hundred thousand years, the sun is about to go out.

The surviving planet must re-start and goes deep into space in search of a new sun. And it is the CCP that will decide the destiny of all humankind! The United States and Europe have long since disappeared, and "the West" is completely finished. Only the CCP's empire remains, and due to its sophisticated technology and the loyalty of the people, it dictates the future of the planet five hundred thousand years from now. Fuck it, the sun is gone, but the police stations are still here, and the five-star red flag and other imperial logos are everywhere. So it was no small wonder that, at a press conference, even Foreign Ministry spokesperson Hua Chunying strongly recommended this "hugely pro-Chinese" film, which broke the weekly box office record with revenues of 2.8 billion Yuan in China.

As for how the Western powers led by the US imperialists will disappear, please see yet another military monograph: *The War for the Right to Control Life: A Reconfiguration of Military Strategy in the New Era*, from the New China Publishing House. The author, Guo Jiwei, is an army colonel, chief physician, and professor at the Third Military Medical University. An incident in the war for "the right to control life" envisaged by Colonel Guo is as follows:

There was a military doctor by the name of Dockett on one of the support ships in the carrier battle group. The aircraft carrier combat group was on an overseas mission to guard oil platforms. The sea was calm, and Dockett was bored. He was walking on the rear deck when by chance he saw a frigatebird with a golden underbelly perched high on top of the flagpole above the American flag. Dockett didn't pay it any mind. A few days later, the director of nursing reported at a routine briefing that the number of patients requiring infusions had suddenly increased. A thought flashed through Dockett's mind. He suddenly stood up and yelled, "That frigatebird!" In all his years of sailing in every one of the world oceans, he had never seen a frigatebird on the high seas. It couldn't fly that far. He suddenly understood: "We may have just suffered a biological attack!"

In the ensuing days, over half of the fleet's personnel developed symptoms of respiratory infection, and over a hundred officers and sailors died. The Fleet Command prohibited the transfer of the sick to land for treatment to prevent the spread of the infection. Finally, one starlit night, a hospital ship equipped with biological protection arrived to support the fleet. It was later discovered that a fishing boat a hundred nautical miles away had released a flock of virus-infected birds. They'd flown off in search of somewhere to land, and found this carrier battle group. In this way, a bird easily disabled and even killed a large number of troops in an entire aircraft carrier battle group.

This representative work on "unrestricted biochemical warfare" was originally published in 2010. Unexpectedly, ten years later, actual versions of the above scene spookily appeared:

> More than 500 officers and sailors of the US nuclear-powered aircraft carrier *Roosevelt* were diagnosed with Wuhan pneumonia, and one of them died. The captain was removed from his post for writing a letter requesting assistance, and he, too, was later diagnosed.

> Taiwan's Dunmu Fleet Command Center recalled a total of 744 officers and sailors from three warships overnight. After examination and testing, it was announced that a total of 24 officers and sailors in the fleet, aged between 20 and 40 years old, were diagnosed with Wuhan pneumonia. . . . At present, all officers and sailors on the warship *Panshi* have been evacuated and disinfection is underway.

The next day, Ai Ding and Zhuangzi Gui continued their discussion about unrestricted warfare. Ai Ding suddenly had a whimsical thought, thinking Hong Kong was in danger of becoming an extended version of unrestricted biochemical warfare. Zhuangzi Gui said, "It's unlikely because, while the Wuhan virus is harming the whole world, the CCP itself has also suffered heavy losses. The objective effect is a bit like what Hong Kongers often say, 'stir fried' (they all go down together). Today's Emperor doesn't want to be 'stir fried' with anyone, as he's looking forward to becoming the world leader through the 'Belt and Road' initiative."

Ai Ding started to say, "If nothing goes wrong . . .," but Zhuangzi Gui cut him off: "If nothing goes wrong, the virus will be sent into Hong Kong – hasn't that story already been broken online by some media? I don't really believe it, because not long ago the Sino-US trade war finally resolved after two or three years. Trump personally signed the agreement and then handed the pen to Liu He, China's contemporary Li Hongzhang.* Trump was smug, thinking that he'd signed the largest single trade deal in history, and Liu He had a forced smile on his face . . . but, in fact, Liu He was acting. He understood the Emperor's goal in all this was to consolidate CCP control of Hong Kong."

"Fatten America, eat Hong Kong?"

"As the saying goes: 'If you can't bear to lose a child, you'll not trap a wolf.' Today's Hong Kong begins with the 2015 book *Xi Jinping and His Lovers*. This was a gossipy political book similar to histories of the love interests of Mao Zedong, Deng Xiaoping, Jiang Zemin, Hu Jintao, and so on. Over the past few decades, countless copies of such books have been published in Hong Kong, and if intellectuals aren't interested, the ordinary citizens and mainlanders buy them to read and chat about after a meal . . . nobody really takes them seriously. But this time, the Emperor did take it seriously, even sending spies to various countries, kidnapping several Hong Kong booksellers from Thailand, Macau, and Hong Kong, and secretly detaining them for several months for interrogation. Gui Minhai, a Swedish national, was twice forced to do a 'television confession' and was placed under residential surveillance several times. Once he was even forcibly abducted right in front of the Swedish diplomats who were escorting him. Finally, he 'voluntarily renounced Swedish citizenship' and was sentenced to nine years in prison – this was the 'Causeway Bay Bookstore kidnapping case' that shocked many in China and other countries."

"Also part of unrestricted warfare?"

"Blatant cross-border abductions hadn't been seen since the CCP founded the People's Republic of China. Even during the

Cold War, they were unheard of. But the goal of deterrence was achieved: Hong Kong's publishing industry was silenced, everyone felt threatened, and books on politics and political affairs vanished immediately. A little later, the Umbrella Revolution failed and several of the movement's leaders were arrested and sentenced. Then in June 2019, Hong Kong Chief Executive Carrie Lam pushed the 'Fugitive Offenders and Mutual Legal Assistance in Criminal Matters Legislation (Amendment) Bill 2019' to legalize 'cross-border kidnapping,' which aroused public outrage. More than two million people took to the streets to demonstrate. The pro-democracy groups merged with the pro-independence revolutionary Returning Valiant faction. One of the members, Lee Yee, a journalist in his eighties, offered some insight into why people were so determined to fight this bill: 'In the past, all Hong Kong people restrained themselves. But this Chinese extradition ordinance tells us Hong Kong people have no way to live unless they choose to be slaves. So the ultimate battle of freedom versus slavery is now unfolding.' As June 2019 was precisely the thirtieth anniversary of the Tiananmen Square massacre, everyone thought Hong Kong would also be placed under martial law and be occupied by the PLA. Indeed, over five hundred military vehicles assembled along the border with Hong Kong on standby, while the number of armed police inside the city tripled. They were stationed in the five most strategic zones of Hong Kong, and more than seven million Hong Kong citizens watched it all on rolling TV news."

"But the Tiananmen massacre wasn't repeated."

"The killing of thousands of protesters against tyranny on the night of June 3 and the morning of June 4, 1989, was not repeated. But hundreds of suicides occurred one after another. There were many corpses, many girls raped, and the eye of a girl administering first aid was blown out. People both in their teens and in their eighties were arrested and held at the San Uk Ling Detention Center. University campuses were attacked, and mysterious trains traveled inland late at night. Thousands were arrested and tens of thousands went missing . . . but the atrocities were scattered and sporadic. Since there was no 'big production' like *Schindler's List*, a repeat of the massacre of 1989 that everyone feared, and because, like all news in the Internet era, today's blink of an eye obliterates yesterday's, the international attention was haphazard and diluted . . . But there's still hope, because everyone in Hong Kong understands that this is the final opportunity to resist, and there will be no second chance if it fails . . ."

"That crisis will go on for some time . . . But look, the sky is getting brighter in Germany, it's time to sleep, Zhuangzi."

"Okay, Ai Ding. I wish you a pleasant journey."

After ending the call, I stood up, my thoughts still churning like waves in a storm. Repression and resistance in Hong Kong will continue for a long time. Amid the distractions of the epidemic, the police actually arrested fifteen more movement leaders. During these troubled times, a general assembly of the People's Congress was convened in the imperial capital and a "National Security Law" modeled on China's was produced for Hong Kong – just as the Nazis formulated the "Nuremberg Laws" for Jews in 1935 – thereby rapidly advancing "one country, one system" for Hong Kong and the rest of China.

No holds are barred in transcending battlefields, boundaries, bottom lines, humanity, and time in the quest for final victory. The following description is from a writer who personally experienced June 4:

June 4 has already begun in Hong Kong. The killing is spreading quietly. Are there any limits? Is there one crystallizing event that will make everybody realize June 4 is here? There won't be. In this era of armed repression, tanks will not be used. They are not so stupid. That moment will never come. But they will order armed police to fire tear gas and beanbag projectiles at close range, and will fight to the death just the same, regardless of where they may be. So the June 4 of this era will be fragmented from a single major event of repression into countless seemingly smaller events. In fact, if the June 4 model is conventional warfare, a meeting of force with force on one main battlefield, then the contemporary mode of repression is terrorism, which means gradual escalation and decentralization of force. It makes you feel as if real war is a continuous falling back, never quite arriving, but each escalation is actually an intrinsic part of the war. You will never find a "bottom line" because that "bottom line" simply does not exist. The mode of repression in Hong Kong is to break the whole into pieces, to gradually escalate, and bring in reinforcements from the mainland. It should also be noted that in utilizing the mainland's armed police and the People's Liberation Army, they are simply following the old way of imperial suppression. And they use people from different regions and different ethnic groups to suppress each other to ensure that their collaborators will show no mercy to their opponents. The suppression of Hong Kong reflects the strategy of the contemporary empire: decentralization, terrorism (indiscriminate assaults, street fighting, surprise attacks, etc., but mainly because so-called "war" and "confrontation" have been completely reshaped), the disappearance of the main battlefield, and provoking mutual hatred between different ethnic groups. Although these are old tricks, they come in new modes.

When it comes to pressure, everybody has limits of acceptance. In accordance with the "unrestricted war template" of the CCP, the endangered state of Hong Kong will ultimately submit to China's rule. On the other hand, the Sino-US trade war is at a stalemate. Trump was aggressive, but Xi Jinping began to ally himself with North Korea's Fat Kim the Third, leading to repeated delays. On January 15, the exhausted parties finally signed the first phase of an agreement – to sacrifice a locality to the benefit of a globalized whole, a situation often seen during the two world wars. At that time, in Europe, no one sought out the opinions of residents in Poland, Czechia, Serbia, and other lands before the agreements were signed, leading to a great deal of human suffering.

However, the Wuhan virus has come, and no matter whether it is natural or artificial, intentionally or unintentionally leaked, it has changed everything.

God can't bear to watch anymore? Is this his "unrestricted warfare" on us? If he doesn't hit the brakes soon, it'll be more than just a warning to all of humankind.

I hope that after the free world has experienced the massive influx of the Wuhan virus, experienced tens of millions of infections and hundreds of thousands of deaths, it will finally slowly awaken to this "unrestricted warfare." I hope this will trigger a deep reflection on the disaster that has been communism in China for over a hundred years now. Just yesterday, I saw the following statement on the Chinese-language websites of the US embassies in both Germany and China:

> We, the foreign ministers of the United States, Canada, France, Germany, Italy, Japan, the United Kingdom, and senior representatives of the European Union emphasize that we are seriously concerned about China's decision to impose its national security laws on Hong Kong.
>
> China's decision does not comply with the Hong Kong Basic Law and its international commitments based on the principles of the legally binding Sino-British Joint Declaration registered with the United Nations. The proposed national security law can seriously undermine the principle of "one country, two systems" and the high degree of autonomy of the territory. This will harm the system that has contributed to Hong Kong's prosperity and its success of many years. . . .
>
> We strongly urge the Chinese government to reconsider this decision.

As far as I can recall, this has been the first "intense prompting" of China by officials of the Western democratic camp since the Tiananmen massacre thirty-one years ago; I hope this will be followed by similar forceful statements at the head-of-state level.

To save Hong Kong is to save the West itself. Freedom, democracy, and human rights must continue to be supported in Hong Kong and confirmed yet again by all humankind.

This is a city shielded by God, the Jerusalem of the East. May glory be to thee, Hong Kong. In the words of the Hong Kong people's national anthem:

> We pledge: No more tears on our land,
> In wrath, doubts dispell'd we make our stand.

Arise! Ye who would not be slaves again:
For Hong Kong, may Freedom reign!

Though deep is the dread that lies ahead,
Yet still with our faith on we tread.
Let blood rage afield! Our voice grows evermore:
For Hong Kong, may Glory reign!

Stars may fade as darkness fills the air,
Through the mist a solitary trumpet flares.
Now, to arms! For Freedom we fight with all might we strike:
With valour, wisdom both we stride!

Break now the dawn, liberate our Hong Kong,
In common breath: Revolution of our times!
May people reign, proud and free, now and evermore,
Glory be to thee, Hong Kong!

12

His Imperial Majesty Arrives

Like a blind grain of sand being blown by the wind around his chaotic homeland, Ai Ding had been tossed about for a month and a half, and was still blocked from crossing the border into his home province. But his wife said his luck wasn't so bad: he hadn't contracted the virus, and in Erda, he had made a friend to share his troubles in a foreign region.

Today was an unusual day. As per usual, Ai Ding got out of bed at noon, but he then saw a notice his wife had forwarded to him from the WeChat group network manager:

Today, various district bureaus in Wuhan have arranged for police to enter your home for security inspections. They will be in your home for about an hour. The police will wear protective clothing and will disinfect beforehand. Please actively cooperate with the police, and they will communicate with you on related matters. Thank you, all.

Ai Ding felt there was something fishy about this. Aside from the funeral workers who picked up his dad, the first people to come to his family's door since the city had been closed were the police! So he called his wife, but she didn't answer. He had been concerned, worried something unexpected might occur – and now it had! A few hours later, his wife's WeChat video chat started up, and her first sentence to him was: "His Imperial Majesty has arrived!"

At first, Ai Ding was taken aback, but then the penny dropped, and he realized what was happening: the Emperor had finally come to Wuhan! Might it be a sign that the travel ban would be lifted?

His wife said, "Only ghosts can know that. If you're not careful, you'll end up like a monkey fishing for the moon, celebrating prematurely." On a previous occasion, when Vice Premier Sun Chunlan of the State Council had dropped in, a pack of Party leaders accompanied a few representatives of residents on the inspection tour. It was all just a big act, and when someone opened an upper-story window and shouted: "Fake! Fake! It's all fake!!!" the pack of them were so scared they immediately beat a retreat. Moreover, given the ubiquity of the novel coronavirus at the time, the police didn't dare climb the stairs to grab the active counter-revolutionary, but just let it go.

Ai Ding said, "How can you compare a Deputy Prime Minister with the Emperor? Even if nothing happened to the person who yelled 'Fake! Fake! It's all fake!!!' last time, when the Emperor travels, it's a big deal."

His wife responded, "Yes, yes. Last time, there were only a few hundred escorts, and this time there'll be at least ten thousand."

"That's a bit of an exaggeration."

"All the police in Wuhan will be on duty, and that might not be all. First off, everybody in our East Lake community received that notice from the WeChat webmaster, thousands of households, two police officers sent to each one. That alone is over ten thousand police, as well as ground troops, personal bodyguards, a guard post every three steps, a sentry every five, and so on. What's particularly remarkable is that there are snipers all over the roofs of buildings, at corridor windows, and in the connecting corridors between buildings . . ."

Ai Ding's wife told him that after she received the WeChat notification about the "security inspection," as soon as she'd replied with "There are no hidden dangers in our home," she heard the network administrator's voice say: "The police are already on their way to your home, thank you for your cooperation."

Twenty minutes later, the doorbell rang. "Who is it?" Ai Ding's wife asked.

A voice answered: "Police."

"What for?"

"Official duties."

As soon as Ai's wife opened the door, two white-clad figures flashed past her, wearing protective clothing from head to toe, plus masks and goggles, so she couldn't see who they actually were the whole time they were there. She asked if they wanted a drink of water. The police officers shook their heads. She asked if they'd like to sit down. The police didn't say a word, just looked around, and then asked: "Where's your daughter?"

"In her room."

"Call her out."

"She's only ten years old. She hasn't been out for so long, she's a little afraid of meeting strangers."

"There's nothing to be afraid of, Uncle Police are here to protect her."

"Children nowadays are afraid of Uncle Police."

"Call her out. We're doing our duty. Our superiors instructed us: Nobody is allowed to be at windows facing into the community."

Their daughter came out and clung tightly to her mother's arm. They heard the police chuckling through their protective clothing: "What's your name?" Exposed above her mask, their daughter's eyes suddenly looked panicked. The police continued: "Uncle knows your name is Dandan. Uncle will check the residency registration book."

Ai Ding's wife said: "Just tell us what your orders are."

The police said: "Okay. First, you can't go near the windows and balconies. Second, your activities are restricted to this living room. Every move you make must take place within view of us . . ."

"Going to the toilet?"

"Except for going to the toilet, but you can't lock the door from the inside. Third, our visit here is not expected to exceed an hour. If it lasts longer, please bear with us. Fourth, loud noises are forbidden, and please don't talk unless necessary. Fifth, when we two talk with each other, you're not allowed to interrupt. Sixth, we've both brought our own snacks, water, and other necessities, and will not touch anything in your house. Seventh, please turn off your mobile phones, computers, landlines, and other communication equipment; we will check and approve each and every one of them."

"We can't remember so many regulations."

"Then remember this one: remain quietly in the living room."

So the mother and daughter sat down on the sofa in the living room, and the two police officers opened the balcony door, went out on it, and looked down attentively. There were similar white figures moving about on the balconies on each floor of the front, rear, left, and right apartment buildings. After the two of them checked everything in the apartment, inside and out, they moved over two low stools and sat on them facing each other, whispering, looking like a conjoined alien monster. And in a roof bunker on top of a building opposite, they could see a sniper's gun muzzle trained on them – the defense of the Emperor is mutually restrictive, the so-called "Skynet is magnificent, distant but watertight."*

There was a faint sound of thunder, and mother and daughter jumped involuntarily. The police hurriedly waved for them to sit down, and then pulled down the balcony shutters. But Ai Ding's wife was still able to determine that it wasn't thunder they'd heard, but a flow of people and cars below. Then, all the noise suddenly stopped, and for two or three minutes, it was completely silent. It seemed the birds and mice outside didn't dare make a noise, and neither did the birds, cats, and dogs caged inside like their masters, because his Imperial Majesty who rules all things was about to open his mouth: "Comrade residents upstairs, I am Xi Jinping. I have come to see you."

Then all was silent again, the sun seemed to shudder and quickly hide behind a dark cloud, and the wind seemed too scared to blow. But a person's head suddenly appeared in a certain window, and his loud shouts echoed among the apartment buildings: "Hello, President Xi! Chairman Xi goes to great lengths for us!" Then the same boot-licking flattery resounded from several other windows. Ai Ding's wife immediately thought of the last time there was a state visit, and someone had yelled: "Fake! Fake! It's all fake!!!" And she, too, had the urge to yell this, but for the sake of her family, she resisted it.

The Emperor subsequently turned and left. Then the mother and daughter and the police all breathed a sigh of relief. Next, they all drank some water and ate a little something. After an hour had passed, the police received the order to pull out and were about to say goodbye when they teased the little girl: "Dandan, call me uncle."

"You're not my uncle!" the little girl suddenly said loudly. "Get out you motherfucking big bad wolves!"

The Emperor made a swift inspection tour of Wuhan, a little over ten hours. After going around the Donghu community and Huoshenshan Hospital, he patted a few butts and took off. Due to the secretive nature of his whereabouts, this triggered another Internet storm. First there was a nursery rhyme from an anonymous composer:

> Big Xi comes to inspect
> Two police in each household
> Wholeheartedly and for the good of the people
> The police tell me to shut my mouth
> Shut up, don't talk,
> Just speak to say the Party is great
> Greatness is never adulterated
> Big Xi laughs at this, hahaha . . .

Following this, in the official centralized broadcasts, the Emperor appeared wearing a mask, imitating the people-friendly shows of Western heads of state. Accompanied by a small number of local leaders, he walked across the street and among the high-rise buildings of the community without any security guards in evidence. With an upwards gaze, he raised his right palm – and the Internet worms, who always seize on the slightest thing, immediately took a screenshot of this right palm and compared it with the right palm raised by the Emperor in other news items . . . and they discovered that the length of his pinkie was different! Then they found that the shape of one of his ears was also different!

As a result, speculation about the "False Emperor" spread like wildfire on the Internet. The fearless Internet worms enlarged the right hand and left ear of His Majesty on various occasions and made comparison screenshots, marking up the differences with dotted lines and measurements, then circling it all in red. After posting this all over both inside and outside the Internet Wall, tens of thousands of Internet policemen and their hired hands were left disoriented and overworked yet again. Even Erda, after seeing what was going on, took to reposting it and had his WeChat account blocked almost immediately, scaring him into writing three self-criticism letters to his WeChat administrator and promising not to do anything like it again. His account was eventually restored a week later.

This unprovable case of the "False Emperor" was reminiscent of Gabriel García Márquez's novel *The Autumn of the Patriarch*. Márquez describes a dictator so afraid of assassination that he carefully trains a double whose appearance, body shape, walking, speaking, waving, hiccupping, and even farting are exactly the same as himself, the most perfect double the world has ever known. Not only government officials and generals, but even the relatives of the President and his personal guards can't make out any difference between them. But after working as a double for such a long time, the double also develops the habit of being a President – office work, processing files, going on tours of inspection, launching wars, messing about with women, all matters big and small – so much so that he often forgets to ask for instructions and becomes a fully functioning President in his own right. And so, in the whole country, there is only one person who can distinguish the true from the false President, and that is the nanny and cook who have raised him. Countless times she has seen the President conquer his enemies and rule their lands, gallop onto the battlefield, and ride women as if they are his warhorses, with no kissing, no untying of his saber, no taking off his riding boots, always mounting from the right, stabilizing his body, and then eagerly pumping away. However, when the fake President does the same thing, he is just like any ordinary man, removing his sword, taking off his riding boots, kissing, and cuddling . . .

It's said that after Márquez published this work, the real dictator who was seemingly described in his story flew into a rage and vowed to force this "rumor-mongering bastard" to be locked up with a lion who hadn't eaten in three days, scaring the author into crossing the border overnight and fleeing to another Latin American country.

Whether true or not, the arrival of His Majesty in Wuhan was a sign of recovery. The national economy had been shut down for a long time, and the availability of daily necessities had been becoming increasingly tight. Ai Ding's wife said by video that they'd soon be in desperate straits: "We've still got money, but I can't buy things. Everyone's living frugally. How about you?"

"Erda's a chef in a hotel, so I benefit from that and eat my fill."

"Is the provincial border open?"

"Not yet."

"Did you go ask?"

"Erda had someone ask for me. I don't dare go myself. The people over there hold grudges."

"Did you offend them?"

"It was Erda. They know he and I are together."

The two of them had little else to say, touching the video screen with their index fingers simultaneously, both sitting at their bedsides, the sun shining outside their windows while birds chirped. Ai Ding's wife suddenly said: "Our family is so lucky; your father was ninety-three and he left without any regrets. There are three of us left, and none of us has been in a hospital or an isolation shelter."

"None of us has been sick. It's a real miracle."

Their daughter was in the living room watching TV, and when her parents spoke of a "miracle," she came over: "I know why we haven't been sick."

"Why?" they asked in unison.

"We eat white radishes." Then she started singing the epidemic nursery rhyme she'd just learned:

White radishes, one by one,
packed in the car, cheerfully.
Where're they going? To do what?
Gone to Wuhan to fight a demon.
What skill do they have? What ability?
High in nutrition and quickly digested.
As long as my radishes are here,
they keep the virus far far away.

Ai Ding chuckled and said, "It used to be double *coptis* could cure the virus, and now it's white radishes."

His wife angrily retorted: "Whatever our daughter sings is what it is. What does it matter to you?"

Ai Ding immediately laughed, but laughing can be worse than crying, so he dropped the subject a bit resentfully. Not long after, his wife forwarded him "oral accounts of survivors":

You were lucky to get an injection. After one shot, I was itching to line up again right away to get the next one. It took ten hours in line every time. And every time I'd get up at three o'clock in the morning, I didn't dare drink even a sip of water nor take off my mask. I'd line up until three or four o'clock in the afternoon and come back to my place at five or six o'clock to eat and drink a bit, then lie down to sleep.

Every day people died without a scrap of dignity. At the worst, four died within two hours. I had an injection on the second floor that day. It started at six o'clock and it wasn't quite eight o'clock when the last one died. First, two were brought from the ward upstairs. They were both a confirmed diagnosis. Two more fell dead beside me, and two more had died on the first floor in the afternoon. Those people who died in the hospital without a nucleic acid test were not included in the novel coronavirus death list, not even the suspected cases were included.

The granny who passed away at eight o'clock in the morning was probably in her seventies. She'd started to line up sometime after midnight. After getting an injection, she walked a couple of steps, then fell down and couldn't be revived. That was 2 meters away from me. Her two sons were about the same age as me. They wrapped her up in a sheet and dragged her away at nine o'clock in the evening.

There aren't enough staff and cars, and there's only one person in charge of maintaining law and order. The funeral home's car turned out to be a car built to haul one body at a time, but it ended up taking eight. I went outside to smoke that day and saw what looked like a container truck taking seven or eight corpses away. Hell has to be better than what I have been seeing.

Next was a description of a whole family that had been infected:

Both my mother and I were diagnosed. She was old and also blind, and had pretty severe symptoms. She was able to deal with it until three o'clock in the morning and then I had no choice but to drive her to the fever clinic at No. 4 Hospital to get her an injection. We waited another whole day today and didn't get home until eight o'clock in the morning. My father had also been coughing all this time, and my wife had some symptoms. too. With so many people, it was impossible to isolate at home. . . .

After I got the certificate of diagnosis, the first thing I did was tell the community organization and the property managers. At the time, our neighborhood still had posters saying "Epidemic-Free Doorway." All I could do was tell the building manager to let everyone know and be careful. But even now the "Epidemic-Free Doorway" poster is still on the wall, and no one has come to disinfect our place. Two benches have been put outside the door at the neighborhood committee office to prevent people from entering.

On February 9, my mother was finally placed in the hospital, and I went to the isolation center at Dongxihu Lake. At eleven o'clock in the morning on February 17, mother passed away after treatment proved ineffective.

Comparing his situation with theirs, Ai Ding had a deeper understanding of the "luck" his wife had spoken about. But just as his spirits grew low, Erda came back from work and cheered him up. Ai Ding casually chatted with him about what his wife had said, and Erda had similar feelings as it brought to mind his wife and child in his hometown, as well as Erxiao in Changsha. He said, "Erxiao's WeChat and phone still don't work. Might he have been diagnosed?" Ai Ding secretly grieved at hearing this but couldn't bring himself to say anything. Erda said, once the ban on travel was lifted, he'd go straight to Changsha, and if Erxiao was there, he'd immediately drag him back to Shanxi Province.

Ai Ding was afraid to go on talking about this. The two drank for a while and then went to lie down in their rooms. Ai Ding couldn't sleep at all as he had a bad feeling but didn't know why. As dawn broke, he rang up his wife on WeChat, who was dumbfounded, saying, "Husband, what are you up to this early?" and then hung up.

It wasn't till two days later that his wife called back and said her head felt hot. Ai Ding said it was because she'd been locked in so long, "It's nothing, stick your head out of the window, get some air and you'll feel better." His wife nodded, then changed the subject, saying, "Our daughter is acting very sensibly in this epidemic. Today she made the porridge, set out the plates and helped me to the table." Ai Ding said, "In another twenty-one days, it'll be Dandan's eleventh birthday, and I'll definitely be there." Their daughter began crying at this, and said, "Come back soon, Baba. Mama's sick. I'm scared."

Another three days went by and his wife's fever hadn't gone down. Ai Ding felt flustered and couldn't help saying the community Epidemic Prevention Department should be notified. His wife said, "They've already been notified." Ai Ding now said they'd been cooped up at home for so long, how was it possible they could get infected. His wife said, "The last time I went shopping in the small supermarket at the gate of the community, a woman fell to the ground, and I was only 2 or 3 meters away from her." Ai Ding calculated the time, and the fourteen-day incubation period of the virus had passed a while ago, so he said, "Don't worry about it." His wife said, "My symptoms are getting worse. Last night I was sleeping alright until I felt like I was suffocating and woke up. What will happen to our daughter if something happens?" Through gritted teeth, Ai Ding said, "Okay, okay, I'll think of a way to get back there quickly."

Erda had the next day off and Ai Ding told him what was going on at home. Erda was very sympathetic. As it was still bright daylight, he didn't feel it was proper to start drinking, so he went into the kitchen and grabbed a bottle of vinegar and took a chug from it, saying: "Your business is my business. I'll go out now and scout around, find someone, and when it's arranged, I'll see you on your way."

Ai Ding was moved to tears. He knew that Shanxi is the hometown of malted vinegar, and people of Shanxi drink vinegar as others drink wine, so he also grabbed a bottle of vinegar from the kitchen and chugged it until it was empty. It was so sour he grimaced when he said: "Do you want to crash the border together with me, brother? It'll be difficult. Do you know the story of Wu Zixu,* who escaped through Shaoguan Pass and his hair turned white overnight?"

"Of course I know it. If you, my brother, are Wu Zixu, then having your hair go white crossing the provincial border will be worth it, eh?"

"It'll be hard to get through even if we have wings."

"If we can't get though by road, we'll go by water. Wait here at home for news from me, brother."

13

An Illegal Border Crosser Goes Home

For two straight days, Erda was out and about, leaving in the mornings and not returning until midnight, when he'd drink with Ai Ding, though still preoccupied, answering a string of messages on WeChat. In the afternoon of the third day, he came back early and claimed it was done. With that, the two of them went to bed to rest their bodies and calm their minds. Later, they rose as the sun set, throwing punches toward the ceiling in their excitement. They went to the kitchen to cook a four-course meal of two meat dishes and two vegetables dishes, as well as an electric rice cooker full of white rice. Afterwards, the two stared at each other wide-eyed, feeling the worst was now behind them, and poured out two glasses of 56-proof Xiangjiang Daqu, clinked them together, and drank them down in one gulp. Then they lay down on the spot and snored like thunder until midnight, when they awoke gazing up at the moon.

Ai Ding's backpack was on his shoulders, and Erda had already pushed out the motorcycle, striking a pose as if he were about to charge into battle. They locked the door and set off, bypassing Xiangling's city center, avoiding the national highway, following the farm roads as they headed straight for a certain organization in a certain village in Black Cloud Town on the west bank of the Pantao River. They met no obstacles along the way, but when they arrived at the village entrance, a man suddenly jumped out and, with a lowered voice, asked: "Password?"

Erda braked and responded: "Friends come from afar."

The man said: "Though from far away, you must be executed."

With this, the connection was confirmed. Without saying anything, Ai Ding pulled out 1,000 Yuan from an inner pocket and handed it to the man; Erda turned off the bike's motor and pushed it along, side by side with Ai Ding, as they followed the man from the village. A few hundred meters away was the Pantao River, and 2 or 3 kilometers further down the river it merged with the Yangtze. The confluence is the site of the great ancient battle of Red Cliff. The wind was blowing in its seasonal direction, from south to north. In *The Romance of the Three Kingdoms*, it's said that Zhuge Liang was well versed in both astronomy and geography. He burned incense and reckoned that at a certain time in a certain month and on a certain day there would be a counter-seasonal southerly wind. So he had Zhou Yu equip fire boats in preparation for this event. And when the time came, they mounted a direct assault on Cao Cao's 700-nautical-miles-long water-borne military encampment consisting of a flotilla interlocked by chains, leading to the annihilation of Cao's entire army.

In the here and now, the river wind was intermittent, varying between hard and mild. A crescent moon, as if afraid of the cold, seemed to shiver and hide in dark clouds, with only a faint light shining through like needles. At the boundary between villages, there was a newly dug trench full of water, with a barbed wire fence erected in the middle of it. When the epidemic was at its height, there were militia and wolfhounds patrolling both sides at night. However, since His Majesty's visit to Wuhan, the situation had eased, and the wolfhounds and militia had been withdrawn. "But you still have to be careful," the man said. "If we get caught, they'll beat us with sticks till we're unconscious and then put us in mandatory quarantine."

"No way," Erda said. "You've been at this business for a while, no?"

"Yes, I have. Before, the walls had ears, now there are ears in the wind. You've never tried anything like this before. If you're caught – and you two want to remember this – it's only ever your first offense. This way you won't be beaten until you're disabled."

Ai Ding shuddered. To prove what he said was true, the man turned around and shoved two flyers from a month ago at them. Ai Ding put his in a trouser pocket, reading it carefully later:

All people are united in the fight against the novel coronavirus epidemic. Reporting of people who have entered from Hubei (especially Wuhan) and those who have had a clear-cut history of contact with Hubei people is welcome. Once verified, the first informant will be awarded 1,000 Yuan and the names of all whistle-blowers will be kept confidential. Conversely, if a person from Hubei (especially Wuhan) is harbored, once reported and verified, a fine of 1,000 Yuan will be imposed. Reporting hotline: 12345.

The three of them came to a hiding place by the river. The man untied a rope from the root of an old willow dipping into the water, and dragged out a fishing boat. The middle of the boat was about 10 feet wide, it was shaped like a fully drawn bow; and the two ends were sharp, like arrows. It is said this boat's design hadn't changed since ancient times. Ospreys with twine tied around their necks are positioned at both ends, ready to plunge into the waves to fish at any time, while a fisherman stands in the middle, line fishing or casting a net. To Ai Ding's surprise, even at this dire juncture, he was still reminded of the story of the ancient poet Qu Yuan conversing with a fisherman as he cast his net on the Miluo River. Qu Yuan said: "The whole world is muddy, and I alone am clean /All are drunk and only I am sober." The fisherman said: "If everyone is drunk, why bother being sober alone?" And then the lyric has Qu Yuan saying: "When the long waves of the river are clear, I wash my hair / When the water is muddy, I wash my feet!"

The fisherman pulled out a rope to fasten the motorcycle in the boat, after which Ai Ding got in and clasped his hands together to express his respect. He had already tightly embraced Erda, both acting as if they wouldn't meet again, while completely ignoring the danger of such an act during an epidemic. As the boat gently moved away from the shore and the moonlight glimmered on the waves, the form of his friend slowly grew smaller, but remained there on the shore throughout . . .

Accompanied by the sound of the oars, the boat slowly reached the middle of the river. Unexpectedly, the wind and waves were calm, and the moon made everything as bright as day. The fisherman said he hoped that when they arrived on the other side, the cloud now to the side of the moon would have floated over, covering it a little, making it safer for them.

Ai Ding nodded in agreement. Then his phone beeped. He hurriedly checked it and couldn't help feeling sad when reading the message from his wife:

Tonight, besides me, there's just an old scavenger at the Simenkou intersection, there's no one else to be seen. The lights on the riverside no longer flicker, and the sky seems to be shrouded by bat wings, leaving people breathless . . .

Just now at 17:30, a man jumped off the overpass at the intersection. He'd been standing on the bridge crying before his death, very sad and desperate . . . he'd been crying and shouting hysterically on this quiet street, and each sound he made pierced the hearts of passers-by. The gist of his lament was that he'd been infected with the coronavirus and couldn't stay with his family for fear of infecting his wife and children; there were no beds in the hospital, and he was renting a house elsewhere for the time being. He wanted to see a doctor but there are no buses, and it was a very long walk, and he didn't have the strength for it. Now he didn't even have food to eat, and death seemed better than this kind of life . . .

With his jump he ended all his grievances with the world. His blood blurred his face and covered his eyes . . . I was going to call the police but could hear a police car coming from somewhere nearby. I bowed three times to honor this dead man.

As the police pulled up next to where I stood, they urged me repeatedly not to leak a word of this onto the Internet. I laughed through my tears . . .

Ai Ding raised his head, sensing something ominous. The oars continued to creak. It had taken a bit over an hour to travel the 2 or 3 kilometers as they slowly pulled up to the opposite bank. In the shadow of a withered tree, the fisherman tied up the boat and helped Ai Ding lift the motorcycle ashore. The fisherman clasped his hands together and was about to cast off again when a whistle sounded. A few big guys seemed to pop out of the earth, knocking Ai Ding to the ground before pouncing on the fisherman. The two of them had their hands tied behind their backs before they could gather their wits. The headman had a beautiful beard, wore black clothes, and was holding a big knife, as if he were the reincarnation of Guan Gong*, and he shouted at them: "Bold-faced blockade runners!"

The two of them were quickly pushed to the ground. The head guy then called out: "You know the epidemic is everywhere, so why have you broken the ban on crossing the river?"

Ai Ding stood up, bowed, and said: "I've an emergency at home, so I've no choice."

"An emergency? Is your house on fire?"

"It's more urgent than a house on fire. My wife's been diagnosed and is waiting for me to return home."

"As she's already been diagnosed, what's the use of going home?"

"Use doesn't come into it. It's a matter of life and death. Please let me go."

"Epidemic policy trumps everything. Nobody dares violate the rules for personal gain."

"Brave men . . . brothers . . . how much will it take to buy our way through? Just speak up. As long as I can afford it."

"Our Party refuses to be bribed."

"So . . . what . . . what do you want?"

"Not so much. Just that you go back where you came from."

"Thank you for this great kindness!" said the fisherman gratefully as he quickly got up from the ground.

Ai Ding also thanked him, but was downcast, and was about to go to get the motorcycle when he was stopped: "This was used to commit a crime. According to law, it must be confiscated."

"This was lent to me by the Changsha Epidemic Prevention Department and must be returned to them . . ."

"Any proof of this?"

Ai Ding hurriedly took out his Hunan travel pass.

"This is not proof."

Ai Ding scratched his head and emptied out his backpack.

"Even with proof, it'll have to be confiscated temporarily. You can negotiate a resolution when the epidemic's over."

"So . . . so . . . so . . . can you give me a receipt?"

"No."

"It's worth over 10,000 Yuan and you won't even give me a receipt . . ."

"What of it?"

"This is robbery!"

"What of it?"

"I want . . .

"Do you want this?" The leader of the thieves lifted his broad knife and waved it at Ai Ding's head. He jumped away but he was hit by a stick in his side. In the boat, the fisherman yelled urgently: "Are you coming? If not, I'm going!" Under the pressure of the situation, Ai Ding jumped into the prow of the boat. And at that moment, the motorcycle's engine sparked up. The highwaymen jumped about under the moon, cheering: "Great! We can sell it for a fortune in a few days. Everybody gets a piece of this!"

Once the boat was out in the middle of the river, Ai Ding, feeling overwhelmed and very angry about what had happened, could no longer restrain himself, so he grabbed the fisherman and punched him. The moon was a bright white, the waves shone like fish scales, and the boat was bobbing up and down. The fisherman let go of his oar and grabbed Ai Ding's wrist: "Are you crazy?"

"I'm not crazy!"

"Fighting on this river, you and I are going to die together."

"I want us to die together!"

"You're crazy!"

"You're in league with them!"

"No!"

"The same river, the two sides colluding to make money off the virus. It's a good way to make a living."

"You're mistaken."

"I've been robbed of my motorcycle."

"The real problem was the motorcycle."

"Nonsense."

"I've been doing this secret border-crossing business since the virus closed the border, serving the people and earning a bit of money on the side. But my previous customers were all local people from the riverside communities, and even if I couldn't name them, their faces were familiar. When they got onshore, they were able to get home very quickly and quietly. But you brought a motorcycle with you."

"There's still one or two hundred miles. Do you want me to fly back to Wuhan?"

"If you hadn't had a motorbike, if they'd run into us, they'd have only charged 500 Yuan at most to let us buy our way through; but with such an unexpected windfall, who wouldn't want to rob you?"

"Fuck you!" Ai Ding was so angry that he seized an oar and swung it at the fisherman's head. The fisherman wasn't able to dodge away, so he plunged into the water, using his skill at the bottom of the boat to make the flat boat spin like a gyro on the surface of the river. Just as Ai Ding was about to lose his balance and fall into the water, the fisherman jumped back on board like a shark from a whirlpool, pushing Ai Ding to the floor of the boat as he did so.

"You're a friend of Wang Erda's, and I understand how you feel," the fisherman panted. "I'm really sorry about this screw-up. I'll refund you your 500 Yuan when we get ashore."

———————

The fisherman escorted Ai Ding out of the village. In the bright moonlight, he sketched a map showing him how to get from Black Cloud Village back to Bull Town, marking out two or three hidden sentry posts: "If you go around like this, you'll get back before dawn."

Ai Ding rushed off, feeling stumped. On the way, he received a WeChat message from his wife, asking, "Where are you?" He didn't dare speak bluntly, saying instead that he'd been delayed and didn't know what to do. His wife said that yesterday she phoned the community Epidemic Prevention Headquarters five times and sent them three WeChat messages, asking them to send her to the hospital for testing. Their response was that resources were tight, and they didn't have a quota. Then, his wife asked them to contact Changsha again. Ai Ding asked, "What was the result?" His wife said, "It turned out that the two sides really did get in touch, and Director Wang, the chief culprit, promised to resolve the problem as soon as possible." Ai Ding asked, "How will he do that?" Hs wife said she didn't know yet.

Suddenly, Ai Ding slapped his forehead and cried out with exasperation, "Whoever started the trouble should end it. How could I have been so silly? I lived with Erda for over a month and didn't say a word to him about his brother's death." His wife said, "He's so loyal, you really weren't much of a friend." Ai Ding replied, "I didn't dare tell him." She said, "You're resourceful, figure it out," and she then recorded a brief passage and asked him to forward it to Director Wang. The message read: "My husband Ai Ding returned from Germany over forty days ago and has not yet returned home. Now, I'm in a desperate situation and he's so upset all he can do is prepare to return to Changsha from Xiangling to seek you out. He will be together with Wang Erda, the twin brother of Wang Erxiao, who was killed by you, Director Wang, to seek justice through the law and to make this case public by way of a live webcast."

"Wife, my wife, you . . . you're a more cunning strategist than Zhuge Liang!"

"If I weren't desperate, do you think I'd want to do this?"

"Are you really . . ."

"It's already past four in the morning. I woke up choking again, I'm very tired, but dare not sleep because it feels like drowning, hard to breathe. I struggled to wake up, worried that I'll be gone all of a sudden, and then what will become of our daughter? And then I sent you the WeChat message, desperately hoping to get you back here!"

At this, Ai Ding howled like a wolf and then immediately covered his mouth. His wife said: "I'm guessing it's pointless waiting for a diagnosis! In this big area, dozens of apartment buildings, people say thousands have died, but only a hundred or so were sent to hospital and diagnosed with the virus before they died. Even doctors and nurses have died without being tested."

"Don't worry, you'll be okay, I feel sure of it! Just be patient for a little longer . . . How do you think you got the virus?"

"It was in the elevator. The Epidemic Prevention Headquarters looked at a surveillance video during this period and discovered a strange woman with disheveled hair, patting and touching everything in the elevator, spitting and blowing her nose, constantly shouting: 'Spit's the only weapon I've got!' Just after she'd left, I happened to need to go downstairs to the gate to pick up the vegetables I'd ordered . . ."

Ai Ding was thunderstruck.

The sky had begun to brighten. As if in a dream, Ai Ding somehow found his way back to Erda's place. The sharp morning wind slashed at him so harshly he covered his face, and the door squeaked as he gently opened it. He then saw Erda dressed simply and looking as if he was suspended in midair, seemingly in a trance. Taking a closer look, Ai Ding saw he was actually sitting cross-legged on the table. In turn, seeing it was Ai Ding, Erda jumped straight up off the table and punched him.

Ai Ding fell onto his back, bleeding from the corners of his mouth, but repeatedly shouting: "Good punch! Good punch!" Erda lifted him up, dragged him to the bed, and said: "Your wife sent me a WeChat telling me about Erxiao's misfortune. I already know everything. Older brother, you've not been a good friend to me, so I punched you; but older sister has been a very good friend. She may not live, yet still cares what happens between you and me. This feeling, this brotherly bond, you and I can both understand."

"Whatever you need me to do, just ask."

"I've got all the information about Director Wang. Your better half wants him held accountable, seeking compensation on one, two, three, and four clauses. I've downloaded and saved the statement she recorded. When the epidemic is officially over, I'll go to Changsha. I'll ask you to come to testify for me at that time."

"Of course."

"You've had a difficult night. Get some sleep now."

Ai Ding was physically and mentally exhausted, but his mind was working full tilt. Erda handed him a cup of hot sugar water, and he drank it down in one go. Feeling a little better, Ai Ding lay down on the bed. After a while, in a daze, he heard Erda talking to himself in the next room: "Erxiao, you're gone without a trace. You didn't say goodbye to your brother or your parents, and there are no ashes, nothing of any kind left behind. You and I were twins for a time, but now, as in a dream, I wake up, or you wake up, and we're separated like the yin and the yang. We can't see one another.

"Grandpa gave us our names. He was a highly respected orderly of General Lu Zhengcao, but because he was illiterate, he never advanced beyond that. His children, of course, also didn't benefit from his status. The only thing we got from him was that old anti-Japanese ditty from the 1940s, 'The Song of Erxiao the Cowherd.'

"When our mother was pregnant, they thought she was having only one child. Grandpa got a bit drunk and was suddenly inspired to choose the name 'Second Youngest' (Erxiao). So, when two were unexpectedly born, to keep the name 'Second Youngest,' he had little choice but to name the other 'Second Eldest' (Erda).

"Now, Erxiao, you've gone ahead to see Grandpa, and you will now be able to sing him 'The Song of Erxiao the Cowherd' in heaven."

Then there was a pause of a few seconds before a raspy singing voice started up:

The cows are still grazing on the hillside, but who knows where the herder is,
it's not that he's lost the cows while playing, the cow-herding child is Wang Erxiao.

On the morning of September 16, Japanese devils sweep into the ravine,
dazed and lost, they grab Erxiao and order him to lead the way.

Erxiao obediently walks in front and leads the devils into our
  ambush,
the enemy know they've been tricked when the sound of gunfire
  rises on all sides.

The devils skewer Erxiao on a bayonet and leave him to die atop
  a big rock,
our thirteen-year-old Wang Erxiao, a pity he's died so brutally.

The Party cadres and fellow villagers are safe, and he sleeps in the
  cold mountains,
but there's a smile on his face, and his blood stains the blue sky
  red.

The autumn wind blows all through this village, and spreads this
  moving tale,
every villager sings with tears in their eyes, singing of Erxiao the
  Cowherd.

Ai Ding couldn't help bursting into tears over life's imper-
manence. He remembered the last few minutes of Erxiao's life,
there'd been no sign of it ending, he was still loudly singing
"Brother Monkey wants to be in the Red Army" to a similar tune
but in a completely opposite style to his brother's . . .

———————————

Ai Ding's torment continued for three days. Now his hair and
beard really looked like Wu Zixu after he'd escaped through
Shaoguan Pass: large patches were graying, and his eyes were red
with bags under them and the corners of his mouth were collaps-
ing downward. He called Director Wang, but nobody answered,
and now, calling his wife, it was their daughter who appeared in
the WeChat video, wearing a mask and raincoat. Inside the raincoat, she looked as if she'd wrapped herself in an iron bucket. Ai
Ding said, "You, why are you dressed like this?" With tears in her
eyes, his daughter replied, "Mama made me do this and told me to
eat by myself, too. I'm not allowed to come out of my room unless

I've got a good reason." Ai Ding asked, "What's happening now?" She responded, "Mama's having trouble breathing and she says Baba will be back in a little while."

The video broke off. Ai Ding was not sure what to do. A car horn sounded several times outside the apartment, and before he could react, Erda opened the door and shouted, "Coming! Coming!" The sun was setting. An off-road vehicle with "No. 111 Special Police Pass" pasted on the window was parked by the door. By the time Ai Ding had put on his coat and gone out, Erda had already put his backpack in the trunk. The two of them embraced, sobbing. Three police officers in orange protective clothing stood behind them, asking: "Are you Mr. Ai Ding?" He didn't hear them at first, until one of them shouted: "Please show us your ID card!" He trembled at this and turned around.

He verified his identity, put on a mask, was pushed into the back seat of the police car by the officers, and they left. He had wanted to wave goodbye to Erda again but didn't have the opportunity. Each seat was separated by bulletproof glass, and the curtains on both sides of him were also closed tight. Through the front window, Ai Ding saw what looked like clouds of flames growing thicker and engulfing all the city's buildings. He couldn't help but think of when he had just returned to China, landing in Beijing and then transferring to Changsha. He'd seen similar sights from the windows of the airplanes: the forty or so days seemed to have passed in a flash, as if it were just yesterday.

They left Bull Town and crossed the provincial border, only briefly stopping at both sides. The expressway was still closed, so the police car used the national highway. On the way, the deputy driver raised his cell phone and Ai Ding heard Director Wang's voice through the gap at the top of the partition: "Ah, Mr. Ai, I never imagined it'd take you so long to get home. I'm sorry. As for Wang Erxiao, that was just an accident. No one wanted this, right? Now Hunan and Hubei are fully coordinated, we're sending you back to deal with your problems at home first. Everything else we can deal with after the epidemic, when society returns to normal, okay? Thank you for your understanding and cooperation."

Then there was a long period of silence. Over the nearly three-hour journey, the four of them said not a word to each other. As night fell, the car lights pierced the darkness before them as they passed through a dozen village checkpoints along the way. Ai Ding had already had the misfortune of fully experiencing the difficulties of passing through these small, lightly populated separatist states. But this time, with a police car clearing the way, they were invulnerable. It wasn't yet ten o'clock at night when they arrived in Wuhan.

He didn't get out of the car at his community's main gate. This was the first time in his life he was enjoying such privileges, as the police car delivered him directly to the bottom of his apartment building. The driver got out first, walked around to the right of the car and opened the door. Ai Ding got out, took his backpack and computer out of the trunk, and entered the stairwell without even a backward glance.

He hesitated for a few seconds at the elevator entrance, and after remembering his wife got sick because of it, he decided to climb the stairs. After only two floors, he was gasping for breath. So he took out a pair of sterilized gloves, grabbed hold of the handrail, and stopped every three steps or so as he spiraled upward.

Home was on the twentieth floor. But Ai Ding, who had now finally made it home, felt his legs wobbling and panic rising. He was racking his brain, panting, thinking about what to do and say when he entered the door. His wife's life was hanging by a thread, and hugging her would be impossible, but he could smile, blow a kiss, and make an exaggerated hugging gesture from 2 meters away. His daughter would be fully armored against the virus, and at most would yell out "Baba!" Any further communication would be done by gestures. Following on, he'd take a shower, cook a hot meal for mother and daughter, then thoroughly clean and disinfect the kitchen, the bathroom, and the other three rooms. He'd not seen them for over a year and wanted to make up for being away so long . . .

Twenty minutes later, Ai Ding climbed the last step, pushed open the corridor door, and turned the corner to apartment 2016. He

broke into a trot. There was no need to ring the doorbell, however, as the door was wide open. His daughter stood in the doorway, staring at him blankly. Her mask was soaked through by
water, or so it seemed.

"Baba!"

"Dandan!"

In spite of everything, she rushed forward and he hugged her
in the same spirit; she pulled down his mask, pinched his nose and
mouth; then she pulled down her mask and pressed her face up
against his cheek.

"Mama?"

She started to cry but didn't make a sound. She was so thin,
like a monkey.

"Your mom?"

"Gone!"

"What?!"

"She's just gone, two uncles came and carried her away!"

He put her down, rushed to the window and looked around,
seeing thousands of streetlights like stars sinking into an abyss.
His wife was one of them. Time and space were insignificant, this
world a blur. They had met, fallen in love, shared a bed for many
years, yet now he didn't know which star was hers.

Life and death are like a relay race. His wife goes, Ai Ding arrives,
and their daughter is rescued from death's door. This is life, and
everyone must accept that this is one of the countless, miniature
human histories that have existed since time immemorial.

After his shower, Ai Ding wanted more than anything just
to lie down, but instead braced himself and told his daughter to
take off her protective clothing and go to the bathroom to take
a bath and disinfect herself, and to call out when she was done.
He started to clean everything, blending disinfectants and spraying and wiping all the tables and chairs, doors and windows, the
floor, the beds, the stove, and then soaked all the pots and pans in
two buckets. Finally, he took off his mask, opened the windows to
air everything out for ten minutes, then closed the windows and
turned on the air conditioner and the air purifier.

"Okay," he said to himself.

His daughter came out and put on a full set of new clothes her dad had brought back from Germany. Then she sat like a princess on the newly refreshed sofa in the living room, eating snacks, and waiting for him to cook.

There were pork sausages and instant noodles in the kitchen and the ginger and garlic were sprouting. Ai Ding cooked two packs of instant noodles, added some pork sausage cut into thin strips, and sprinkled the sprouts of ginger and garlic onto it all. He brought it out and, before she had eaten anything, his daughter said cheerfully, "It smells delicious," seemingly forgetting her mother had just died.

Dandan said she wanted more after eating what he'd brought her. Ai Ding said it wouldn't be so delicious if she ate the same again, but after a bit more of this, he dug a German chocolate bar as big as his palm out of a pocket and gave it to her. She snatched it excitedly out of his hand and ate it slowly, piece by piece, till she was satisfied.

Every few days, WeChat administrators released news that Wuhan and the whole country were about to be opened up again, stimulating everyone's hopes and desires. After first discussing freedom of movement, people started to talk about what they most wanted to eat and to do. Of course, the people of Wuhan wanted to eat hot dry noodles, people in Chongqing wanted their traditional spicy hot-pot, Beijingers wanted hot-pot mutton, and Chengdu people wanted to eat more than anybody, ranging from double-cooked fatty pork, to stir-fried bean curd in chili sauce, to Mom's Rabbit Head, and so on.

Ai Ding was a conscientious dad and couldn't wait to order Dandan's favorite spicy chicken drumsticks online. Three days later, WeChat notified him it was ready for pick-up. He woke up his daughter in the middle of the night, picked up her roller-skates, and then quietly led her downstairs. The two of them dodged the night guards and entered the underpass leading to the parking lot. Ai Ding turned on a flashlight and asked his daughter to put on her skates. As they moved along, his daughter was nervous and excited, asking: "Can we really do this, Baba? We'll get arrested!"

"Who says?"

"Mama says. Mama says we'll be arrested if we go out."

"But nobody knows."

"There's someone in front of us."

"Ghosts, but don't be afraid of ghosts. Baba's here."

"Yes, yes, Baba's here, what am I afraid of? Baba's a foreigner."

"Baba's someone who's returned from a foreign country."

"So, a foreigner." His daughter laughed as she skated, dancing in the light of his flashlight, constantly spinning, "I never knew it was so fun here! Baba, it's my birthday in three days. Could you bring me here again?"

"Ah! Baba almost forgot. No problem, Dandan, if you're not afraid of the dark."

"Mama's afraid of the dark. But you're Baba."

They went through nearly all of the 1,000-square-meter garage until they came up to a gate in the security fence, and, as earlier agreed with the courier, Ai Ding reached through and picked up the "postal express" delivery. Then they eagerly and stealthily went back the way they'd come, cut open the big bag, revealing four small bags inside, each holding eight big drumsticks. Father and daughter ate two each, grinning from ear to ear, greatly enjoying themselves.

After a while, his daughter fell asleep. Ai Ding leaned back against the bed board, thinking of his wife, but also trying to force himself to forget her. So he went into the living room, poured a glass of spirits, dipped a fingertip in, and flicked some into the air. Then, talking to himself, he turned on the computer and called Zhuangzi Gui in Berlin: "Hey, I haven't seen you for a few days. The world here is the same, but people have changed." He sighed but didn't mention his wife's death.

"First, congratulations on returning home." Zhuangzi Gui raised his glass, "Your wife and daughter are asleep, right?"

"Asleep," Ai Ding replied ambiguously. "They won't be waking up for a long while."

"That's good." Zhuangzi Gui didn't catch his drift. "Let's drink till we're drunk."

They drank while talking on all manner of subjects until Zhuangzi Gui suddenly said: "Kcriss has been released."

"That post-90-generation media guy who was hunted down because he ventured near the P4 lab?"

"Yeah, the police chased him and he fled for his life, returning to his apartment, where he turned on his computer and broadcast live for nearly four hours in the dark. Then he opened the door to them and was apprehended. I was one of the melon-eating mob of onlookers. It's surprising he's reappeared so soon. And he made a public confession on YouTube to clarify various conjectures about him at home and abroad."

"And the result?"

"As a result, the speculation has grown even more turbulent. Even I've become suspicious. Initially, he completely avoided talking about the P4, but two months ago, he live broadcasted that SOS for help, and everyone could clearly see he was being chased near the P4. Second, the security organization arresting him changed from the National Security Bureau to the Public Security Bureau, which means the charges changed from 'spying on state secrets' to 'disturbing public order.' He also revealed that 'all equipment was confiscated.' After being isolated in Wuhan, he was sent back to his hometown of Pingxiang in Jiangxi Province by special car to be isolated there where he could watch CCTV's news broadcasts every day."

"What does the government say?"

"Nothing. The BBC called to verify the 'Badajia Police Station' mentioned by Kcriss, and they responded: 'There's no such person, no such thing.' The BBC then called the Wuhan Public Security Bureau, but whoever answered didn't respond to the question."

"They want to cover it up!"

"Of Fang Bin, Chen Qiushi, and Kcriss, the three most influential civilian epidemic reporters, only Kcriss got close to the P4. When people think of him, they remember the circumstances of his arrest . . ."

"The circumstances of his arrest? It's best to say nothing. Otherwise . . ."

"At the end of his YouTube broadcast, Kcriss actually quoted from the "Counsels of the Great Yu" to describe his own situation: 'The mind of man is restless, prone to error; its affinity to what is right is small. Be discriminating, be uniform in the pursuit of what is right, that you may sincerely hold fast the Mean.'* This is quite profound and open to many interpretations. My literal translation is: 'The human heart is the most dangerous and the heart of heaven and earth is the most subtle; faith must be single-minded and never forsaken.'"

14

The Republic of
Disappeared People
A Hitchcock Mystery

The day had finally come. The writer Fang Fang had finished the sixtieth chapter of her *Wuhan Diary: Dispatches from a Quarantined City.* She quoted the second epistle of St. Paul to Timothy from the Bible, verse 4:7: "I have fought a good fight, I have finished *my* course, I have kept the faith." Followed by: "Henceforth there is laid up for me a crown of righteousness."*

Zhuangzi Gui congratulated Ai Ding. Speaking of Fang Fang, Zhuangzi Gui said he had been taking a walk to the outskirts of what was once West Berlin yesterday, when he was suddenly inspired, taking out a ballpoint pen and writing:

The last days of winter linger, the woods are as desolate as a horde of old men at death's door. Suddenly, the cries of birds fill the air as two flocks of wild geese flying south pass through a dark cloud the shape of a warhorse. One flock is in one long line, like the character for "one" in written Chinese, and the other flock is in the V-shape that resembles the character for "person."

As if in a trance, his gaze follows the "one person" as it gradually disappears on the horizon, traveling thousands of miles away, into the depths of time. Now that "one person" has emerged, and her name is Fang Fang. In a story from the 1980s, she portrayed an amnesiac who could clearly remember things far in the past, but nothing that had occurred recently. The character immediately forgets what happens in the present, only to remember it years later . . .

Ai Ding asked what followed, but Old Zhuangzi wasn't able to answer. He had to reread Fang Fang's novel so his own novel would have clues to follow, but he couldn't find it on the Internet, so he had to set it aside for the time being.

Ai Ding was at sixes and sevens. He wanted to say, for you it's all about waiting, but what about me?

Somebody knocked at the door. His daughter jumped up first and Ai Ding followed. "Why didn't they ring the doorbell?" he muttered to himself, as he unthinkingly opened the door. It was his wife's younger brother!

"Uncle!" Dandan rushed forward as her uncle reached out and grabbed her by her arms. He stammered: "I've come from Shanghai . . ."

Ai Ding thought he'd come to deal with his wife's funeral arrangements, because once the epidemic was over, he would have to pick up numbers in advance, line up overnight, and do whatever necessary to collect her ashes and buy a cemetery plot, all of which would take ten days to two weeks if he was lucky. Unexpectedly, at this very moment, several police officers wearing protective clothing materialized from around a corner.

"Looking for you . . ." her uncle stammered again.

The leader of the police quickly stepped in: "Are you Ai Ding?"

"What do you want?!"

"We're from the Wuhan National Security Bureau. My name is Wang, and this is my Police ID."

Ai Ding instinctively retreated. The police followed him into the apartment, pushing aside Dandan and her uncle, and surrounding him: "Please come with us."

"What do you want?!"

"We'd like to clarify some issues. Considering your underage daughter is present, we won't go into details here."

His daughter yelled "Baba!" hysterically. She struggled to get to him, but her uncle had a firm hold on her: "I'll look after Dandan, don't worry."

And so, a confused Ai Ding was taken away again. This time it was not to be quarantined, as, on "suspicion of spreading rumors," he was placed under "surveillance at a designated residence," that is, he was "disappeared" – a unique situation under national terrorism regulations. Previously, residential surveillance was carried out at home, with family; now, under residential surveillance, the time and place are all selected by the police. It can be anywhere. You can be detained in different places or go directly to prison without conviction. What's worse even than going to prison is that you and your relatives don't know where and for how long you're being detained. Numerous suspects have been tortured during their period of "disappearance." It happens all the time these days in China. The famous lawyer Gao Zhisheng worked in Beijing but was placed under residential surveillance in Xinjiang and Shaanxi, where he was burned by cigarette butts during interrogation. On July 9, 2015, over 150 human rights lawyers were arrested overnight, most of whom were given drugs and beaten, and then secretly and repeatedly relocated to various surveilled residences, resulting in severe psychological trauma for some of them. The Swedish human rights activist Peter Jesper Dahlin was also among those "disappeared." After making a perilous escape, he has strongly recommended that people read Michael Caster's book *The People's Republic of the Disappeared* to understand how the Chinese authorities terrorize innocent people by disappearing them: "There are oral accounts by many people who experienced it in the book," Dahlin says. "It's an important source for understanding the surveillance system at designated residences."*

Dong Guangping, a civil rights activist, recalled:

> I finally walked out the prison door . . . [but] my three years and eight months of life in prison still often come to mind. The most

difficult thing was the five-month surveillance at designated residences. To force me to acquiesce, National Security agents in Chongqing put me in handcuffs twenty-four hours a day and two special police officers watched me twenty-four hours a day. They didn't allow me to do anything except sleep, and they sat by my bed the whole time. There was no window in the room, no sunrise or sunset, no day or night, no knowing the season or the time. Even worse was they never let me eat enough or sleep well. This continued up until they were finally convinced I would not confess my sins and repent, at which point they let me eat and sleep normally. . . . But when I was finally sentenced, every two days was only counted as one day, so the seventy-five days I was detained weren't included in the prison sentence. Fucking hell. Even if one day was the equivalent of ten days, I still wouldn't have wanted that treatment. It's truly hard to imagine how you can get through that kind of thing. Even the special police who watched over me said: "If I were you, I'd have gone crazy long ago."

Now it was Ai Ding's turn, who knew nothing about any of this. He was taken down and out of the building in which he lived, stuffed into a police car, and his mask and goggles were removed and replaced with handcuffs and a black hood. After experiencing the ups and downs of the abyss for a long while, just as he was about to fall asleep, he was dragged out of the car and heard a loud rumbling sound as he seemed to rise up into the night sky. After a pause, his handcuffs and black hood were removed once they'd entered what seemed to be a sealed compartment, but was in fact an interrogation room. He was ordered to sit on the floor. The three police officers who would interrogate him sat behind a table. They immediately commenced taking turns interrogating him for three days and nights. Early one morning, the table lamp still shining straight into his eyes, he asked permission to wash his face with hot water, but the police officers were noncommittal, instead once again reading the February 16 statement of the Wuhan Institute of Virology:

Recently, false information has spread on the Internet, claiming that our graduate Huang Yanling is the so-called Patient Zero, the first to be infected with the novel coronavirus. Upon verification, our institute solemnly declares as follows:

Classmate Huang Yanling graduated from our institute in 2015 with a Master's degree. During her studies, she researched the function and antibacterial broad spectrum of phage lyase. Since graduation, she has been living and working in other provinces and has never returned to Wuhan. She has not been infected by the 2019 novel coronavirus and is in good health.

At this critical moment in the fight against the epidemic, related rumors have greatly interfered with the scientific research work of our institute. We reserve the right to pursue legal liability according to law. We sincerely thank all sectors of society for their concern, support and help!

Ai Ding was puzzled: "I forwarded this statement. Is there a problem?"

"How many times did you forward it?"

"I don't clearly remember."

"You only forwarded it?"

"I added a few comments to make it easier for people to understand."

"What comments?"

"I thought Huang Yanling should have made her own statement, not the virus institute. If they hadn't seen her in the past five years, how could they be sure she wasn't infected and is healthy? It's like if the two of us met five years ago and now lots of people say you're dead: could I issue a statement that you're not dead? You have to make an appearance to prove you're not dead."

"It doesn't matter if nobody died at the P3 or the P4 laboratories of the Institute of Virology. Researcher Shi Zhengli of the institute said in an interview: 'At first glance, this was obviously fake news. Not one person at the institute has been infected by the virus, our institute has zero infections.'"

"I also quoted this sentence in my comments."

"But you went on to quote another rumor. An anonymous whistle-blower states: as early as December 2019, a biological sample leakage accident occurred in the Wuhan P3 laboratory, leading to a female surnamed Huang to become infected and die. The laboratory was immediately disinfected and ran laboratory tests on the corpse. The alveolar lavage test showed a positive result, and this was COVID-19's Patient Zero. However, they did not report this to higher authorities and sent the corpse to a crematorium for destruction without authorization. As a result, the funeral workers who handled the corpse were also infected . . ."

"I've quoted both pros and cons. Isn't it good to be impartial?"

"This is a pre-trial investigation, not a court trial. We are not here to argue."

"If you're out to condemn me, you can always trump up a charge . . ."

"Okay, the next topic is the South China Seafood Wholesale Market. This is what you forwarded: 'On February 2, Shi Zhengli posted a message to a circle of friends, saying that the novel coronavirus is nature's punishment of our uncivilized living habits, and will shut the mouths of those who doubt her. To put it bluntly, the Wuhan pneumonia was caused by people in Wuhan eating bats (even though there are no bats there in winter). Just as in 2003 some said the SARS epidemic was caused by Guangdong people eating civet cats.'"

"I reposted it. Is there a problem?"

"Following this, you also forwarded a special report on the fourth page of *China Science Daily* on January 8, 2018. I'll read it:

Since the SARS outbreak, researcher Shi Zhengli and researcher Zhang Shuyi from the Institute of Zoology of the Chinese Academy of Sciences cooperated in detecting a coronavirus nucleic acid similar to SARS coronavirus in bats and found that bats are a natural host of SARS-like coronaviruses. Their research paper was published in 2005 in the internationally renowned academic publication *Science* magazine.*

In 2013, Shi Zhengli's team isolated a SARS-like coronavirus that is highly homologous to the SARS virus, naming it WIV1, based on the English abbreviation of Wuhan Institute of Virology, which confirmed that the Chinese Rhinolophus bat is the source of the SARS virus. The results were published in the internationally renowned academic journal *Nature** and their report was recommended as a highlight article.

Shi Zhengli led a research team to locate a cave in the wilderness of Yunnan Province and has carried out long-term monitoring of the chrysanthemum bat population for SARS-like coronavirus and has obtained bat feces and anal swab samples for several years now. In sixty-four samples, they detected SARS-like coronavirus RNA. The analysis results show that SARS-like coronaviruses that are highly homologous to SARS virus are all present in bats in the cave.

Through further analysis, the researchers found evidence of frequent recombination at multiple sites, and speculated that the direct ancestor of SARS coronavirus may have been produced by a series of recombination events between the ancestor strains of these bat SARS-like coronaviruses.

In late November 2017, the research results were published online in the authoritative journal *PLoS Pathogens,*** and were listed as one of the recommended articles for that week. On December 1st, *Nature News**** also reported and commented on the paper, which led to relatively large reactions at home and abroad.

This unflagging research has revealed that bats in our country carry different strains of SARS-like coronaviruses that have the possibility of spreading across species to people, providing an important basis for the prevention of related diseases . . .

Ai Ding was about to fall asleep amid all the nonsense, until he heard: "After forwarding these two items, your comment was: 'This is evidence of the manufacture of biochemical weapons!' Why?"

This frightened him awake. He jumped up and frantically tried to argue with them, but in the end, he was like a monkey in a laboratory, easily subdued. A square table with shackles and handcuffs attached was brought in. He was stuffed into the round hole in the middle. The chief interrogator sighed, "I'm sorry, Mr. Ai Ding, I still have to ask, why is this evidence of the manufacture of bio-chemical weapons?"

Ai Ding felt overwhelmed. He wanted to say: "Bats have carried viruses for fifty million years and I've never heard of them infecting humans. There is a precious Chinese medicine called 'Dawn Sand' that cures eye diseases. Put plainly, it is batshit. Many Chinese people have never eaten bat meat, but they've eaten bat feces! But has bat feces poisoned people? But then Shi Zhengli herself confessed: 'If the ACE2 receptor in the S protein of the bat is turned on, the virus can be transmitted to humans immediately.'"

But he couldn't say it. If he said it, he'd be finished.

The interrogation was at a stalemate. Ai Ding remained silent for nearly an hour, and the agents were silent with him. He was enveloped by glaring lights, and the agents sat in the dark staring at him as if he were rehearsing a stage play. They had been taking turns interrogating him for three days and nights, and while he was very drowsy at first, now he couldn't sleep at all. Eventually, he began his monologue again by admitting he had been talking nonsense.

They expressed no opinion, and the interrogation came to an end like this. They allowed him to drink and eat. He said he wanted to lie down for a while, so they unlocked his shackles, opened the door, and took him outside for a breath of air. It turned out they were at the top of a thirty-story building. Although the sun was shining brightly, a cold howling wind struck him like a slap to the face, so hard he saw stars. The chief interrogator smiled and said: "Sorry, Mr. Ai Ding, we're still working." Ai Ding said, "Understood." The chief interrogator said: "Look, straight ahead is Hankou's old foreign concession area, the riverbank district." Ai Ding said, "Thanks." Then, the chief interrogator took out a large-screen mobile phone and let him watch an old video from last year. It showed a stiff corpse thrown from a window amidst Hong Kong's skyscrapers, then deflected off a lower floor, before hitting the ground with a loud thud, like a concrete pile. "The Hong Kong police actually declared it a suicide." He tut-tutted, "Ridiculous."

Ai Ding shivered. The officers tucked their hands into their sleeves and looked at him sympathetically. The chief interrogator suddenly said, "This situation and the backdrop reminds me of a poem by Gu Cheng from the 1980s: 'You / Sometimes look at me / Sometimes look at the clouds. / I feel / When you look at me you are far away / When you look at the clouds you are very near.'"*

"He also killed himself. Not by jumping off a building, but by hanging himself on Waiheke Island in New Zealand," Ai Ding said with a forced smile.

"He used to be my idol."

For an instant, they seemed to draw closer together. Meanwhile, the wind was getting ever stronger, so they all went back into the building. The chief interrogator casually asked: "Mr. Ai Ding, do you want to rest?"

"Of course, I haven't slept for three days."

"Then relax."

They took the elevator from the top floor to the eleventh floor and entered an empty corridor. Ai Ding was dragging his feet, so the two police officers, one on each side, held him up, and as they walked, he snored loudly. He was taken into the cell, was fed a pill, then went limp in a reclining chair while wires were connected to his temples, chest, and wrists. Machines lined the four walls, and a pulse-rate lie detector was above his head.

A hypnotist rolled back his eyelids, checked his pupils with a small flashlight, and then nodded to the chief interrogator. The hypnotic inducement began, and life receded step by step. Ai Ding muttered to himself, and the chief interrogator listened, occasionally interjecting a sentence or two. Ai Ding's father appeared, and then a bat, hovering over his father, and it was so dark his father's face was invisible. This scene was reminiscent of the classic 1963 Alfred Hitchcock film *The Birds*. In this horror-thriller, the murderers were seagulls, other waterfowl, and crows that rose up into the sky and then dove down to attack people on land. Thirty-one years earlier, when Ai Ding was about to set off on a long journey to university, he had watched *The Birds* for the first time in his birthplace of Shennongjia in Hubei. It was a village surrounded by mountains. A county government caravan carrying the projector and film arrived at sunset, and they raised a white sheet like a ship's sail between two wooden stakes at the radio broadcast station by the village entrance. The villagers rushed out, over six hundred people, men, women, and children, all bringing their own small stools, gathering together. This was an annual feast of entertainment. After a brief news bulletin, two domestic films and one foreign film would be shown. So when it came time for *The Birds*, it was already late at night.

The exoticism of a foreign land, in addition to the love entanglement between the hero and the heroine, quickly enthralled everyone. Even Ai Ding's sixty-year-old father raised his head from his doze and opened his toothless mouth in a smile. First, Mitch gives Melanie a pair of caged lovebirds. Then there's the gathering of birds, like terrorists croaking their thoughts of death, followed by repeated attacks on people in streets, houses, and schools. Windowpanes are smashed, roofs are pecked open, adults and children clasp their heads and run wildly, as if running off the screen, eliciting screams among the audience . . . a wind blows and thunder and lightning seem to roll over them, but the moon still shimmers in the sky. Everyone knew that it was the bats that had come out of the Tortoise Snake Cave, tens of thousands of them . . . bats are color-blind and have a habit of coming out at night. The cave was 500 meters away and was tens of kilometers deep; it was the bats' base camp and also the water source of the whole village . . . At this moment, the open-air cinema was enveloped by the bat army, the screams and strikes inside and outside the movie were indistinguishable, and the people inside and outside the film were all on the ground holding their heads. Illusion and reality were intertwined, and bats, seagulls, and crows clung to people's shoulders. However, Ai Ding's fellow-villagers knew the bats were not Hitchcock's killer birds. They were blind flying squirrels, and if they collided with you, their claws would involuntarily dig in, leaving spotty bruises. And that would be all.

Ai Ding muttered from his trance: "The worlds of birds, bats, and human beings were originally parallel and do not disturb each other, but the birdcage links the two. At the end of *The Birds*, people are trapped in a house and don't dare come out."

"Did Hitchcock predict the 2020 lockdown of Wuhan in 1963?" the chief interrogator asked.

"Possibly. The P3 and P4 laboratories are bird cages. Shi Zhengli and the others stayed in the caves of Yunnan for several years, capturing countless bats and taking them back."

"Including the bat at the South China Seafood Wholesale Market? The earliest novel coronavirus came from there, and the disease entered orally, no?"

"The disease entered orally?" For people in Ai Ding's hometown, these words are quite unfamiliar, so he didn't answer the question. He continued to travel through the depths of his dreams. The screen showing the *The Birds* splits open and he steps through it to the Turtle Snake Cave, the entrance of which is over 10 meters high. He walks more than 10 meters into it until he reaches Turtle Snake Pool. The water is deep, but so clear he can see the bottom. He lies down like a turtle among the pebbles, and after drinking for a long time, he still feels thirsty. His father swims over, he floats past, the sun's shadow dragging behind him like a tail. Then he sees bats, densely packed, like jet-black nipples, hanging upside down off stalactites. The cavern is much larger than the movie venue in the village, big enough to hold two thousand people without any difficulty, and its dome is all bats. They begin to scrape the batshit off the ground, as it's the precious Chinese medicine "Dawn Sand." Finally, his father raises a flintlock musket and shoots down a few stalactites. "These are covered with bat saliva," says his father. "It's a special medicine for clearing the lungs and relieving coughing, too."

When they return to the village, time is like water, they're drifting back and forth, and without realizing it, he's already finished his PhD, stayed on to teach at university, and returned as an exchange scholar to Germany. He's a historian, but from the mouth of a scientist from his hometown he's learned that bats are the kings of viruses. They hunt for food at night and have no fear of eating any poisonous insects they find. Because the body temperature of bats can go as high as 40 degrees Celsius or more, their ability to inhibit viruses is unique. This doesn't make sense to his father, because our village ancestors have been in close contact with the dung and urine of bats for generations, and no one has ever been poisoned to death. Moreover, an unusual number of people live into their nineties in the village. During SARS in 2003, the scientist from his hometown used equipment to test the water quality of Turtle Snake Pool, which he termed a "pit of bat droppings," and the conductivity index was less than 100, while the conductivity index of French drinking water standards is between 80 and 110 . . .

"Do you mean to say, it's impossible to get sick orally?" the chief interrogator asked.

"If the bat virus is extracted by the P4 laboratory, cooled, and then implanted in an 'intermediary host' at close to human body temperature, the ancient lock of Nature that isolates and prevents the mutual infection of species will be opened by this evil man-made key . . ."

"Where is this key? Who opened the lock?"

"Hitchcock knows."

"What?"

Ai Ding fell asleep. He didn't dream this time. The police officers whispered together to one side. Then the hypnotist said: "Take him up first. The analytical report won't be available until tomorrow."

At some point, Ai Ding began to dream again. He remembered he was now in a scene from the 1970s Japanese chase movie *Manhunt*, and he'd become the protagonist, the actor Ken Takakura. Standing on top of a tall building, a doctor behind him said: "Go ahead, don't look back, don't stop, jump, you'll merge into the blue sky and white clouds . . ."

Epilogue
Wuhan Elegy

Many things and many people will merge into the blue sky and white clouds. But God also has emotions, if just for an instant, such as the moment when Wuhan officially had its quarantine lifted, when millions of people, like prisoners, spewed out of the buildings rolling through the city like mountains, filling the streets and alleys, and the blue sky and white clouds suddenly darkened, and there was a burst of thunder on the plain, followed by a downpour of rain. One child shouted, "God is crying!" Another child also yelled out, but it turned out he'd seen a person falling from the top of a building and hitting the concrete a little over 20 meters away. That person's head exploded like an overripe melon on impact, so nobody could recognize who he had been.

So the drenched people ran back to their homes, like newly released prisoners returning to their cages. Some people opened their windows, some closed their windows; some wanted to vent their emotions, some wanted to remember. The thunder and lightning continued, and Ai Ding's daughter suddenly shouted out the window: "Baba! Come back soon!"

Next, her uncle yelled: "Dandan's dad! I'm sorry, I'm bad, I'm depressed, I've let you down! You've come home from Germany, experienced many hardships, all to reunite with a wife who's now gone, and now you yourself have disappeared . . ."

Just as it turned noon, as the world was as pitch black as the bottom of an old pot, a flash of lightning split the clouds, which then closed again like lips. There was a loud banging sound from afar, one couldn't tell whether it was made by a gong or a wash-basin, but then more gongs, drums, barrels, pots, and pans began sounding everywhere. In response to this human–divine sym-phony, somebody led the others in first hollering:

> The person who can't get to the hospital and can only sit on a balcony and bang a gong to announce they're sick . . .

He was followed by another who shouted:

> The person who chases a hearse in the middle of the night scream-ing "Mama!" . . .

And another:

> The person who read Francis Fukuyama's *The Origins of Political Order* in a quarantine center where a thousand people shared one bathroom . . .

The shouts came one after another, reverberating through the three towns of Wuhan and the entire Jianghan Plain, converg-ing into a "Wuhan Elegy" under the name of "Marilyn Dream Six":

> *The person who drove a truck wandering destitute and homeless on the highway.*
> *The person who died where they sat, hugged by their family, as they waited for a hearse.*
> *The person who starved to death in isolation at home.*
> *The person who was pregnant, spent 200,000 Yuan, but was eventually denied treatment because they had no money left.*
> *The person who, afraid of infecting their family, dug a grave for them-selves, and secretly hanged themselves.*
> *The person who, having nowhere to seek medical treatment and was afraid of infecting their wife and children, jumped off a bridge and ended their life.*

The ninety-year-old person who lined up for a bed for their sixty-year-old son and spent five days and five nights watching over him in a hospital.

The person who commented on a Weibo message pleading for a bed in a hospital: "One of my family has just passed away, freeing up a bed. I hope that can help you."

The person who first swore at someone howling for help, saying they ruined their mood, but then was forced to plead for help in the same way.

The person who learned to use Weibo to ask for help and only ever sent a message saying Hello.

The person who covered their mouth with a scarf during interrogation and cried in shame because they couldn't buy a mask.

The person who used an orange peel as a mask.

The person whose whole family died: father, mother, grandparents, leaving them alone to report the deaths to the Civil Affairs Bureau.

The person who spent all their wages on masks and donated them.

The person who wrote "Pass on with peace of mind" and "It's time to sacrifice yourself."

The person who wrote "able, understand"* and had it printed on a red handprint, and died twice.

The person who returned to his village after working without rest to build the Huoshenshan Hospital but was seen as a plague spirit by their fellow villagers.

The person who suffered from leukemia and needed to go to Beijing for a bone marrow transplant, but had no way out of the city, and who was in such pain they wanted to be euthanized.

The person in a death shroud who unsuccessfully phoned for a bed, then collapsed and died.

The person who couldn't get hemodialysis due to the epidemic, begged without success at the gate of their community, and jumped off a building, and whose body was finally taken away six hours after the suicide.

The person who was forced by the police to write "You must wear a mask when you go out" a hundred times as punishment.

The person who was slapped bloody for not wearing a mask.

The person who shouted, "I'm hungry! I'm going to die of starvation, my wife and children are starving at home, but I think your stomachs must be full."

The person who lived by beekeeping and committed suicide because they couldn't be transitioned due to the epidemic.

The person who left the province to earn a living, traveled for thirteen days, walked more than 700 kilometers, slept in bridge archways and grass huts, and worked in coal mines.

The person who had nowhere to be treated, feared infecting their wife and children, wrote a suicide note pledging their body to scientific research, hoped that the people of the world would no longer suffer from illness, then left home without their keys and mobile phone, and finally died on the road to their hometown.

The person who wrote, "Can I donate my body to the country and my wife after I die?"

The person who walked around for three hours with their mother on their back looking for treatment because of the lockdown and the ban on driving.

The person who entrusted a newborn child to the hospital and wrote, "Childbirth cost all my savings and I've no choice and nowhere to go."

The person who climbed down from the tenth floor to go out to buy meat.

The young person who guarded their grandfather's body for five days and covered him with a quilt.

The person who returned home after being cured, found the family had all died, and hanged themselves off the roof.

The person in his sixties who was solely responsible for shopping, washing vegetables, cooking, washing dishes, and cleaning the kitchen in a police station with over sixty officers, who was finally so tired he cried alone in a corridor.

The person who wandered the streets of Wuhan for over twenty days whose hair turned half-white.

The person who didn't have the money to buy a mobile phone to attend online lessons and swallowed all their mother's medication for mental illness at one go.

The twenty-five-year-old person who resigned from CCTV, went to live broadcast in Wuhan at the most dangerous time, faced up to police who were about to take them away, and recited that the country is strong when its youth are strong, the country is weak when its youth are weak.

The person who shouted "Fake! Fake! It's all fake!!!" from a building during an inspection by Party leaders.

The person who wept after pulling out the corpses of three children from the collapsed Quanzhou Hotel.

The person who wrote sixty diary entries about the closure of the city, whose online account was closed several times, and was beaten and abused by hoodlums.

The young person, only seven or eight years old, confusedly following adults in their ways, who collected ashes for his parents.

The well-meaning reasonable person who phoned a government official to say the virus must be prevented and people must eat, before finally sighing softly.

The person who was loved by patients but was reprimanded by a hospital for wearing a mask, and then died of the virus.

The person who said, "I knew this day would come. I don't care if I'm criticized or not. I'll say it everywhere."

Today is February 22, 2021. The front page of *The New York Times* is covered in black dots, five hundred thousand of them, each black dot representing an American who has been killed by the "Wuhan virus."

And at this moment, I happen to learn that the author of the "Wuhan Elegy" has been arrested and sentenced. This is not a fiction. What follows is an excerpt from the "Criminal Judgment of the People's Court of Sanhe City, Hebei Province":

Defendant Zhang Wenfang, female, born on July 26, 1980 in Yantai City, Shandong Province. . . . Prior to arrest, she lived in the Yanjiao Development Zone, Sanhe City. On April 7, 2020, she was detained by the Sanhe Public Security Bureau for ten days for severely disrupting public order. On April 17, 2020, she was criminally detained by the Sanhe City Public Security Bureau on suspicion of provoking quarrels. She was arrested on April 29 of the same year and is currently detained in the Sanhe City Detention Center. . . .

. . . After the trial, it was found that at one o'clock on April 4, 2020, while the whole country deeply mourned the sacrifice of martyrs and deceased compatriots in the fight against the novel coronavirus epidemic, the defendant Zhang Wenfang was at home and through her Sina Weibo account under the name of "Marilyn Dream Six" published a long Weibo message. The contents of this included information such as one thousand people in Wuhan Fangcai Hospital shared one bathroom; that some people starved to death in quarantined homes; that some people secretly dug their own graves and killed themselves for fear of infecting their families; that some committed suicide because they couldn't get an appointment to see a doctor and were afraid of infecting their family members; that some people's remains were not removed until six hours after their suicide; that some people climbed down from the tenth floor to buy meat; that some people were punished by the police by writing "You must wear a mask when you go out" one hundred times; and that some people returned home after recovering from severe illness to find that all their family members had died and then hanged themselves, etc. Some of the above content has previously been refuted by the government as false. The defendant Zhang Wenfang made the above remarks without verifying their veracity, and the Weibo post has been reposted and read in large numbers, having a negative social impact. . . . At 10:09 that night, the Yanshun Road Police Station of the Sanhe City Public Security Bureau received a forwarded netizen report about Weibo user "Marilyn Dream Six" spreading rumors in a lengthy Weibo message, and it said that the suspect was located at 42-1-1003, Shangcheng Sanji Community, in the Yanjiao Development Zone. The police rushed to the location and summoned Zhang Wenfang/"Marilyn Dream Six" to the police station for investigation. Her administrative detention was announced three days later. . . .

. . . in accordance with Article 293, Paragraph 1, Item 4 of the Criminal Law of the People's Republic of China, the Supreme People's Court and the Supreme People's Procuratorate

"Interpretation on Several Issues Concerning the Application of Law in the Handling of Criminal Cases Using Information Networks for Defamation" . . . The verdict is as follows:

The defendant Zhang Wenfang is found guilty of the crime of creating disturbances and is sentenced to six months in prison.

Dear reader, do you remember the beginning of this book? Kcriss was being hunted down by the National Security Bureau after he'd fled from the area of the P4 virus laboratory and had returned to his residence. He used his computer to broadcast live for nearly four hours before being taken away. At the time I wrote, I could not have imagined that all the characters depicted in this book would be taken away . . .

––––––––––––

It's late at night, September 2, 2021, and I'm still poring over an email from my agent in New York. Last year in September, a succession of US publishing houses, nearly ten in total, refused to publish the initial manuscript of *Virus*, which led me to make the connection between this experience and a similar serial rejection of Elie Wiesel's *Night*, his memoir of experiences as a prisoner in the Auschwitz and Buchenwald concentration camps during World War II – Wiesel later explained it was because the Holocaust was still recent and people were not yet willing to pull the scab off a wound that had just healed.

Just as I was muttering under my breath "How can such an old wound be ripped open again?" a new email arrived in my inbox, this from the human rights worker Wang Jianhong. She'd written: "Today is Zhang Zhan's thirty-eighth birthday. Could you please write a little something for her?"

She repeatedly pleaded with me until I couldn't help but accede to her request. Then I clicked on an attached YouTube video of Zhang Zhan's. It was shot on the morning of April 27, 2020, as she arrived at the perimeter wall of the P4 lab in Wuhan. She cut straight to the chase, declaring: "This P4, I have been here three times this year. The path before me is newly made. Over the wall beside it is the P4 . . ."

My old story of a year ago has come full circle: Kcriss, the original intruder, was monitored, hunted down, then abruptly vanished; a month and a half later, a second intruder, Zhang Zhan, arrived at the same form of paradise.

Yes, from start to finish, all of the characters in this book have been taken away, and, ultimately, they'll all be forgotten. And I'm nothing but an insignificant narrator of events, a useless thing with a heart that is always aching.

But there's nothing else I can do aside from responding to Wang Jianhong by writing:

Nietzsche says: "God is dead."

No matter what I write it does no good.

This planet sees an endless string of tragedies every single day.

Recently at Kabul Airport in Afghanistan, people desperately climbed onto planes to escape. After take-off, one fell from the plane's landing gear.

My God, that man's yearning for freedom was so very great, greater than life itself, that he smashed himself into a mess of flesh and bone!

Next, an Islamic State suicide bombing at the airport instantly killed 184 innocents along with thirteen American soldiers. But the damned Taliban, who controlled airport access, claimed this had nothing to do with them.

So many tragedies! So many tragedies! So many that people can't see an individual tragedy, seemingly shrunken down to ant-size by comparison.

That thinking ant is Zhang Zhan.

On January 23, 2020, the eve of the Spring Festival military lockdown of Wuhan, central China's largest city, because of the uncontrolled outbreak of the "Wuhan virus," Zhang, without authorization, entered the place where that contagion, as dangerous as the Chernobyl nuclear leak, had originated. She was one of four citizen journalists who did so.

The first three citizen journalists were Chen Qiushi, Fang Bin, and Kcriss. Each was made to mysteriously vanish. It was rumored that those three were "placed under residential surveillance at a designated place of residence according to the law." But Chinese law was in fact broken: China's Criminal Procedure Law requires that the detainee's family be notified within twenty-four hours. This was not done.

Zhang Zhan, the fourth citizen journalist, was detained on criminal charges. She was the most determined of them all.

Zhang Zhan first caught my attention when she went alone, without protective equipment, to investigate the alleged break-out point of the "Wuhan virus" – the P4 laboratory at the Wuhan Institute of Virology, Chinese Academy of Sciences. She couldn't get in so she circled around the perimeter wall of the P4 laboratory, explaining as she went along that she was not sure but this building may have been the source of the "Wuhan virus." She was arrested soon thereafter.

In her own mind, she had done nothing wrong. She believed that searching for the truth is every citizen's responsibility and duty. Only by knowing the truth and unmasking lies can we come to a scientific understanding of the virus outbreak, review our past mistakes, and prevent the further spread of the virus around the world. Without realizing it, she became, like the 2010 Nobel Peace Prize winner Liu Xiaobo, who claimed to have "no enemies," the most dangerous enemy of the communist dictatorship. No matter what your political stance, as long as you care about the truth and actually pursue it, you are the most dangerous enemy of the communist dictatorship.

That is why Zhang Zhan was arrested. She paid a high price amidst the human catastrophe caused by the "Wuhan virus." Refusing to confess to any crime, she was abused and tortured during the seven-and-a-half months between her arrest and her trial. Her prolonged hunger strike left her unable to stand. She was sentenced sitting in a wheelchair with her hands tied behind her back. Her mouth was gagged, just as dozens of major Chinese cities in China had been gagged. Yet she persisted – her eloquent facial expressions and body movements testified that she would never give in.

The court sentenced Zhang Zhan to four years of imprisonment. According to PRC law, she has the right to appeal her sentence. Zhang Zhan, however, sees her trial as a fraud from start to finish like something out of Franz Kafka's novel-parable *The Trial*. Therefore, she went on a hunger strike. Two months later, she was sent to a reform through labor (*laogai*) prison enterprise in Shanghai, where she continued her hunger strike. She became emaciated and her life hangs by a thread. Many human rights organizations both inside and outside China have spoken out on her case. They fear that she will die in prison.

Threatening this cold-blooded regime with death can have no effect! Zhang Zhan herself doesn't care if her hunger strike works. What she does care about is that she does not bow her head in submission. Now that all thoughts and actions expressing "civil disobedience" are considered criminal, she can only self-mutilate, hunger strike, and even die to express her natural human desire to pursue truth.

Nature – that is what people called it in ancient China. Westerners today call it "human nature."

Zhang Zhan's bravery and persistence arose from basic human nature. Are you, out of cowardice or fear, turning a blind eye and a deaf ear to the "human nature" of Zhang Zhan? If so, then consider this: you were born a human being. Are you no better than a dog that wails and struggles to the end?

Italy's most famous journalist, Oriana Fallaci, writes in the Preface to her *Interview with History*: "[f]or me the most beautiful monument to human dignity is still the one I saw on a hill in the Peloponnesus. It was not a statue, it was not a flag, but three letters that in Greek signify *No: oxi*."* And as she says in her monumental work *A Man*: "What's the use [of] suffering? Fighting? It helps us to live. . . . A man who gives in doesn't live, he survives."**

Please stand with Zhang Zhan, this very gentle woman. She is the kind of person that Fallaci wrote about: the kind of person willing to pay with her life for her insistence that the truth about "the disaster caused by the Wuhan virus" is no less important than the truth about the Chernobyl nuclear leak. As a poet and writer in exile for ten years, I want all my Western readers to understand that if the pursuit of truth and science is abandoned in favor of the commercial interests of globalization, then we have in our day realized the words of the German philosopher Nietzsche: "God is dead"!!!

"God is dead. God remains dead. And we have killed him. How shall we comfort ourselves, the murderers of all murderers? What was holiest and mightiest of all that the world has yet owned has bled to death under our knives: who will wipe this blood off us? What water is there for us to clean ourselves? What festivals of atonement, what sacred games shall we have to invent? Is not the greatness of this deed too great for us? Must we ourselves not become gods simply to appear worthy of it?"*

At noon on November 14, 2021, the human rights worker Wang Jianhong emailed the "Written application for medical parole release for Zhang Zhan" submitted to the Shanghai Prison Administration by Zhang Zhan's family.

Respected leaders:

I am Zhang Zhan's elder brother, Zhang Ju. Zhang Zhan is currently being held in the Fifth Prison District of the Shanghai Women's Prison; her prison number is 27997. In August 2021, in the reception room of the women's prison we talked by phone with a doctor and Zhang Zhan, who had been sent to a hospital. From this we learned that Zhang Zhan's body was extremely weak and that she weighed less than 40 kg. Zhang Zhan is 1.77 m tall and her normal weight had been 60–5 kg. From when Zhang Zhan was detained in the Pudong Detention Center to when she was transferred to the Women's Prison, her body had deteriorated due to various reasons. I asked the doctor if Zhang Zhan might die. The doctor plainly stated it was very likely.

On October 29, 2021, my mother was notified by the prison to go to the prison for a video meeting with Zhang Zhan. The Zhang Zhan my mother saw was weaker than the person we had heard on the phone in August. Zhang Zhan's weight now is probably less than 40 kg. She needed support from others to walk, and her neck was unable to support her head. Her face and forehead were all skin and bone, appearing bloodless, as if her life was hanging by a thread. In Zhang Zhan's current physical condition, she cannot walk on her own. With the support of others or crutches, she can barely walk a distance of 20–30 m. When my mother heard this terrible news, she was so heartbroken she fell to her knees before the prison staff, pleading with them to give Zhang Zhan humane care.

Prolonged detention and starvation have caused irreversible damage to Zhang Zhan's internal organs and secretory system. According to the relevant provisions of the "Notice of the Supreme People's Court, the Supreme People's Procuratorate, the Ministry of Public Security, the Ministry of Justice, and the National Health and Family Planning Commission on Issuing the 'Provisions for Temporary Serving of a Sentence Outside Prison,'" Zhang Zhan's current physical condition and illness have already met relevant conditions for "treatment on medical parole." Regardless of the relevant laws and regulations or humanitarian principles, we hereby apply for permission to allow Zhang Zhan to seek medical parole. We are well aware that the Zhang Zhan case has a certain degree of sensitivity. From the perspective of our family, we are willing to cooperate with the relevant requirements of the police, prisons, and other relevant departments.

Zhang Ju
November 6, 2021

Over two months ago, I sent the closing paragraphs of my book *God is Dead* to several Westerners, including the former Chairman of the National Endowment for Democracy, Carl Gershman. Carl was deeply moved and forwarded an article from the *Washington Post* to me. Five days previously on November 7, the *Post*'s editorial board had published an opinion piece titled, "She told the truth about Wuhan. Now she is near death in a Chinese prison." This concluded: "Ms. Zhang should be saluted for her intrepid attempts to record the chaos and cataclysm of Wuhan in those early weeks. She was a sentinel of a looming disaster. Her journalism was not a crime. She must not spend another moment behind bars. She must not be allowed to die."*

But my thoughts linger on the words of Zhang Zhan's brother on Twitter: "My sister may not live much longer. In the coming cold winter, if she's unable to persevere, I hope the world will remember her as she was."

Apart from a very few appeals and notations, what else can I do? Beckett's immortal play *Waiting for Godot* has evolved into "Waiting for the God of Death" in this case. There are millions of Chinese netizens following Zhang Zhan. Every one of them knows that Godot or the God of Death will eventually appear, they just don't know where and when: it might be in a prison cell, or it might be like Liu Xiaobo, who, in name only, was "paroled for medical treatment" in accordance with the law, but still died in captivity.

We are awaiting news of her death. We are helpless. In the Bible, the record of the miracle of "resurrection," fictitious or not, like Godot, causes human beings dominated by the World Wide Web to lose patience each passing day. I have been in exile for ten years, far enough away from the time and space of the CCP, yet I am still wrapped up in the shadow of the Wuhan virus, which is even more limitless than the Chernobyl nuclear leak. In a letter to Hans Balmes, the German-language editor of this book, I wrote: "The fictional and non-fictional characters in this book all disappear one by one. Zhang Zhan, the last, is not missing, but waiting to die . . ."

As regards Wuhan, Zhang Zhan produced 122 citizen journalist videos and Kcriss only four. The common denominator with this "intruder" was trying to understand more about the P4 lab. The longest video recorded by Zhang Zhan, 21 minutes and 46 seconds, was made on April 27, 2020. She personally uploaded to YouTube "A Visit to the Mysterious Wuhan Virus Research Institute: Is the Source of the Virus Related to It?" Seventeen days later, the Shanghai police crossed provincial boundaries to arrest her on charges of "picking quarrels and inciting trouble."

I've recorded and compiled Zhang Zhan's intermittent, breathless commentary in the film:

I finally got to sleep sometime after three o'clock last night but was woken up by an alarm at eight o'clock.

This P4, I have been here three times this year. The path before me is newly made. Over the wall beside it is the P4. There's a high-voltage electric wire fence atop the wall. Troops have assumed control, and no one can enter. I'll still walk around it and give it a try. As is known the world over, the most dangerous virus research is undertaken within these two cylindrical and rectangular buildings . . .

The surroundings here are very nice, as the P4's backed by green hills with a small, lush stream in front of it and black birds fly overhead. I don't know what kind of birds they are. If there weren't this high-voltage fence and the workplace behind the wall . . . Last time here I climbed the hills but came across a gorge I couldn't get past. The dense woods also blocked my view. There is a cemetery in the hills that evokes our sad memories of the dead.

Every time I come, I chance upon different sights and things, and each time I get a little deeper than the previous time. We will only be able to trace the truth about the source of the virus through perseverance and patience. Here is the closest we can get to the rear entrance. Before there was any evidence, there was speculation over how the virus moved from bats to humans, over how it passed across the tables of voracious diners, folk rumors, conspiracy theories, and so on, the root causes of which were fear of the regime and the system. Nobody has the power to stop this. Just like today, as we look for the truth from the outside, we can only trust our instincts to find our way.

Okay, I'll go down this pile of rubble. The weeds are thick but there should be no snakes. The oncoming shot is of a big red building under construction. There are four tall chimneys in the distance. The building behind the chimneys is the P4. Every time I come, I can hear the roar of boilers and machines.

The P4 before me is surrounded by iron fences and iron and steel panels. I hope to show the audience more perspectives and more details. But no matter from where you look at it, there are surveillance cameras, even in other places inside the walls that are separate from the P4 . . .

A restricted area within a restricted area . . .

June 8, 2020, finalized in Berlin
Revised on June 15
Revised again on October 19, 2020
Supplemented on February 22, 2021
Rewritten and revised on September 2, 2021
Supplemented and revised again on November 14, 2021

Appendices

How was *Wuhan* Written?

On January 26, 2022, *Wuhan* went on sale all over Germany. This new book had already sparked widespread reader expectations in the German-speaking world, and it all started with the Literature in the Mist festival in Austria in October 2021, where I was the guest of honor. For two days, fellow writers and actors read and discussed my nine books published by Fischer Verlag. At the closing ceremony, Hertha Müller and I came on stage and read "Escape from China."

A very important program at Literature in the Mist was the open dialogue I had with Hans Balmes, Editor-in-Chief of Fischer, about *Wuhan*. We discussed the boundaries between fiction and documentary, the shared fate of the fictional character Ai Ding and the non-fictional characters Kcriss, Zhang Zhan, and Zhang Wenfang, civilian investigative reporters who were arrested by the police, and the more than eight million Wuhan citizens who were forcibly quarantined at home, all of whom were constantly questioning and searching for the source of the "Wuhan virus" . . .

After the festival, I was interviewed by more than twenty media organizations, and the most common question was: you have been in exile for ten years, you are currently living in Berlin, thousands of miles away, and you have lost the "sense of presence" of a writer in China – so, how was *Wuhan* written?

From the start of the lockdown of Wuhan in January 2020, I worked all night every night, frantically downloading hundreds of thousands of words of materials. The sources were mainly the official website of the Wuhan Institute of Virology of the Chinese Academy of Sciences, major domestic websites, local websites, Weibo, WeChat, blogs, and so on, as well as self-produced media on Twitter. The content was varied: (1) the past and present of the "Wuhan virus"; (2) how this "bat virus" infected Wuhan, the whole country, and the world; (3) the overcrowding of hospitals; (4) crematoria busy day and night; (5) the arrest of Wuhan people across the country; (6) spats among specialists over the origins of the virus; (7) related discussions and abuse among ordinary folk; (8) sudden deaths, suicides, jumping out of windows, running away, road closures . . .

Tens of millions of people across the country were forcibly imprisoned in their own homes, overwhelmed by panic and fear. They all crowded onto the Internet, struggling to speak, to distribute photos and videos. The number of Chinese Internet Police was seemingly increased exponentially, but they were still exhausted and too late to delete the rising tide of "prohibited speech" and "rumors." No one dared to go to houses to arrest people. For more than twenty days, the Chinese Internet, with the world's most advanced surveillance systems, actually "lost control" – until one day, my computer was attacked by hackers, the screen suddenly going black, completely frozen. Fortunately, I'd backed up the data on an external hard drive.

I had to wait for a week before Kcriss finally appeared, and I immediately surfaced from the vast sea of downloads, jumped on him, and like a shark "bit" this young former CCTV host. The first report I wrote about Kcriss was published in the *Frankfurter Allgemeine Zeitung*.

Soon after, the record of Kcriss transitioned to the story of Ai Ding – an elegy dedicated to "the missing in Wuhan." Kcriss, Ai Ding, Zhang Wenfang, Zhang Zhan, Fang Bin, Chen Qiushi, Wang Zang, Ai Ding's wife . . . the real and fictional characters in these writings were all arrested, dying of illness, or waiting to die in prison – and all they were doing while being attacked by the virus was trying to figure out where the virus attacking them came from . . .

The Blank-Page Revolution

History Will Remember This Unprecedented Roar of Anger

On November 24, 2022, a fire broke out in a high-rise building in the Jixiangyuan neighborhood of downtown Urumqi, Xinjiang. The city had already been closed for over a hundred days to prevent the spread of the epidemic. Sealing off their building left no way for the people inside to escape. The door of their housing units had been locked from the outside. Outside the building was an epidemic control fence and a metal retaining wall. When firefighters arrived in their fire trucks, they were unable to break through the barrier. According to the Chinese official announcement, ten people were burned alive and nine others were seriously injured. Survivors of that same building confirmed, however, that at least forty people died in the fire.

The last WeChat message of a Uighur victim of the fire named Bahargul read as follows: "There's a serious lack of oxygen right now. The fire is growing bigger and bigger. . . . The apartment unit door is locked from the outside, we can't get out. . . . At this moment, I've no real hopes, I only want to say something here to let more people know what's happened."

Word of this tragic event went viral across the country by way of social networks on the Internet. However, ever since the city of Wuhan was sealed off on January 23, 2020, the "nucleic acid [tests] for all until COVID is zeroed out" model initiated by the great, glorious, and correct emperor of COVID, Xi Jinping, had to be unwaveringly carried through to the end. So, as per usual, the Internet police were whipped into a frenzy deleting messages, sending out warnings, and setting new "sensitive words" to be censored as soon as they caught a glimpse of this content. They tracked down the individual computer and smartphone "health codes" and went door to door to make arrests. But humans are not inert logs, and on November 25, thousands of enraged Urumqi citizens burst through district quarantines and gathered at the gates of the municipal government, demanding an end to the closure of the city and the clearance of COVID. Videos of crowds shouting "Give me liberty or give me death!" captured by countless mobile phones on the scene, like the tragedy that happened the day before, went viral across the country.

Then, on November 26, the day after Urumqi citizens rallied to protest, a female student, Li Kangmeng, dressed in black and wearing a black mask, held up a piece of blank white paper in front of her chest and stood silently before the steps of the Drum Tower at the center of the Nanjing Communication University campus. A cold wind was blowing, but she remained motionless as a statue. After a while, a political counselor ran over and took the blank paper from her hands. A passer-by asked, "Blank paper is no threat. Why take it away?"

Li Kangmeng remained motionless, holding the superfluous "blank paper" in both her hands. Yet everybody present understood its message, and so came others from classrooms, dormitories, corridors, from all directions, knocking down epidemic prevention fences on their way. Of those holding sheets of blank paper in front of their chests, most were female, the males seemingly somewhat slower to respond.

As night fell, there were already countless people holding up blank sheets of paper. A male student came up to Li Kangmeng, bowed deeply, and said loudly: "Thank you for giving me courage! I am from Xinjiang. I was very scared at first, but now I want to fight for my homeland, to speak loudly for my compatriots who died in the epidemic prevention fire. May the dead rest in peace! May the living be free!"

The "illegal gathering" on the campus alarmed the political counselors and the university Chancellor, and they now rushed up to persuade everyone to leave. The Chancellor said, "You will pay a price for what you do today!" which only further fueled the anger. Now, a large troop of armed police arrived at the main university gate. At the same time, however, mobile phone video and text of the scene was spreading all over the country. In more than fifty universities in Shanghai, Xi'an, Chengdu, Guangzhou, Beijing, and so on, countless college students tore down the endless anti-epidemic fences and barricades, broke through the cordon of the white-smocked COVID officers, and "illegally gathered" in the center of their campuses. They all held up blank sheets of paper to commemorate the dead in Urumqi, all clear in their hearts that for the past three years the national policy of "nucleic acid [tests] for all until COVID is zeroed out" was initially tested in countless Uyghur "re-education concentration camps" in Xinjiang. Later, the world-leading "successful experience" of Xinjiang's comprehensive surveillance evolved into an open "health code system" that all Chinese must accept during unending epidemic prevention. Any action of any individual depends on the result of scanning this code – red, yellow, or green – containing basic information about your body and brain, which is immediately seized by the state machine and automatically analyzed and processed. I think if George Orwell were still alive, he would certainly rewrite his novel *1984*.

That's it: the Wuhan virus (COVID-19) has undergone a three-year mutation, and instead of Omicron with which all humankind is to coexist, it is COVID-1984 – a kind of high tech dictatorship never before seen, the monstrous spawn of the Wuhan virus and Internet technologies. The Xi Jinping empire has finally achieved a "communist health code system" within the Great Red Firewall – a system of universal surveillance formed ostensibly for epidemic control. If you reject it, you cannot survive in China.

However, Li Kangmeng, holding a sheet of blank paper in both hands, emerged. Then thousands of people holding sheets of blank paper appeared. Who can "zero out" sheets of blank paper? Even though a large number of shops and companies that sell blank paper received calls from the police and a "patriotic announcement" was published on the Internet to cooperate with the government and not sell blank paper, everyone understands a speechless sheet of blank paper:

> *I know you don't permit me speech*
> *But I want to tell everyone*
> *If you don't permit me speech*
> *I will say*
> *What you do not permit me*

This is a blank-page revolution. Revolution as silent performance art.

When the blank paper arrived in Beijing, at Tsinghua University, hundreds of science students added a physics formula to it, and then they all raised the papers in their hands to protest. This formula is a part of the Friedmann Equation, a dynamic equation for the expanding universe. The omitted last term of the equation is the contribution from dark energy; and the second term, k, is not zero, but rather represents an open universe, implying freedom, openness, no dark forces!

On the evening of November 26, 2022, Shanghai citizens in the east, west, north, and south of the city, holding sheets of blank paper, broke through the heavy police blockades and gathered on Urumqi Middle Road to commemorate their dead compatriots. Thousands of people shouted in unison: "Communist Party step down from power! Xi Jinping step down!"

Communist Party step down from the stage of history. And history will remember this unprecedented roar, a roar from the people of China triggered by a silent sheet of blank paper. Since 1949, millions of people have died tragically due to the communists' tyranny on a scale that had never before occurred in the long history of the culture; and in June 1989, more than three thousand people died tragically in a massacre in Beijing that was similarly unprecedented.

November 28, 2022

Poem

My Sole Weapon is Spit

Translator's editorial note: *Prior to 1989, Liao Yiwu rose to fame and then notoriety in China due to his poetry, especially his long historical surrealistic poems in the years leading up to 1989. Ultimately, he was arrested in early 1990 for writing a long poem, entitled "Massacre," in response to the Tiananmen massacre on the night when the events unfolded, and then arranging for the distribution of the manuscript and a recorded reading of it within China and overseas. During his four years in prison, he turned his hand to fiction and afterwards to documentary-style interviews and other non-fiction endeavors. This poem is reminiscent of this past poetry and also an inspiration for this book, which Liao began writing a few weeks later.*

A crime now being committed wipes out a crime still in process, the illness of Wuhan dims the memory of the carnage in Hong Kong, and as a recorder of these times I feel extremely helpless. I've already written so much, but if I write till I die, I'd probably not be able to keep up with the speed at which they commit their crimes. The significance? Do *Doctor Zhivago, The Gulag Archipelago, The Hunger Angel,* as well as *For a Song and a Hundred Songs* and *Bullets and Opium,** have any significance for the pestilence-plagued multitudes of today?

1. Rumor-mongering

I'm a sick man of Wuhan
but they call me the Wuhan virus
I'm on the run in my own land
and my profession is doctor

I spread rumors online:
A virus, picked out of the body of a bat by a P4 laboratory
a new coronavirus
hovering
by a wild game trading stall
in a seafood market in southern China
Like the Karl Marx of the 1840s spreading rumors in books:
a specter
a ghost of communism
lingering

I predict the virus in its unknown mutations
will lose its shackles
and the whole world will be infected
Just as is written in *The Communist Manifesto*:
In this revolution
the proletariat will cast off its fetters
and obtain the world

2. The trial

Karl Marx was never reprimanded
even though he's the fount of all red calamities
I was, the authorities issued a *Book of Rebuke*
Eight rumor-mongers, eight doctors
like the rats people beat to death in the streets
imprisoned in the same cage
An all-night trial, police pointing to three civet cats
interrogating hundreds of bats, a troop of monkeys
How did these sacrifices to laboratories

slip into wild game markets?

Weren't they eaten by people?
How did they come to be here?

Their ghosts are here, says a cop
Their ghosts wear police uniforms for a time
wear prison jumpsuits for a time, are you and also I

I say are you crazy?
You can't open Pandora's box
and as you've opened it
you must let people know
The cop says are you crazy?
China's not short of people, but of stability
A stable people of China can eat all Pandora's box
An unstable people
can only be eaten by the viruses of civets, monkeys, and bats

I say you're wrong
People test the viruses on bats, civets, and monkeys
It's people who sell and eat the infected beasts
then people are eaten by the viruses on them

The cop says what does this have to do with you?
What business is it of yours if half of China dies
if half the people of the world die?

I say I'll die too
and the cop says but you're not dead yet
I say I'm a doctor, the cop says
I kill your kind of rumor-mongering doctor
I represent the bats, the civets, the monkeys, and the people
I kill your sort of shit-disturber . . .

All I can do is sign, raise my hands in surrender
and wait in a cage

until I admit my crimes on TV and the prison gates open
and beams of winter sun burst in like bullets
We've not been executed, though
Big Brother is hidden in the bullseye of the sun
Comrades, he says, welcome back

3. The closed city

Changeable as clouds and rain, every dog has its day
but I refuse to join the Party on the firing-line*
I accept a surgical mask, gloves, and protective armor
A special train speeds to the front-line hospital
The land barren, people scarce, the city truly is shut
The night before New Year's, a broad plain, the banks of the
    Yangzi
Heavily guarded train stations, intersections, docks
Vanishingly few passers-by
Intercepted by troops wearing gas masks
Temperatures taken, passes checked, filtering
phone messages one by one
one after another rumor-mongers say:
All deleted? Yes yes
Can I forward them? No no
It already seems you're a troublemaker. I, I . . .

Without warning, flipped to the floor
Hands cuffed behind you, stuffed in a prison van
And another rumor-monger who'd fallen
before you, upright
thrown to the curb like a heavily panting stick
A hearse approaches
No, a Party leader beside me says, an ambulance

I want to slap him
like a month before, when he was implicated
and wanted to slap me – then full-court rumor-denial
from local newspapers to the central TV channel

Later, still Spring Festival, people returning home
like a river flowing in all directions, from here
surging everywhere
The virus seizes the opportunity to spread, irretrievable
Only the eight rumor-mongers
are saved by the proliferating virus

4. The hospital

I'm a bird in a cage
Before I've time to flap my wings
transferred to another cage
Outside the window, within the outpatient building
a feverish crowd like an infinite flow of air, from space
brushing by a vast starry sky and the ocean
wave devouring wave
the virus like a shark hiding amid the billows, rams straight in
hunting down our vital organs
The most arduous expedition known to man
from stairs to corridor, from outpatient to a ward
not quite one hundred meters
a trek of several days and nights. Not a few
die on the way, stuffed into body bags and whisked away
no farewells, not even sure of names. Not a few
sleep in the hallways, can't get diagnosis, calling Nurse! Nurse!
    in dreams
A nurse falls apart, beats chest, stamps feet
A twelve-year-old squeezes close
comforts her like a father: don't cry, auntie
four of the five in my family died
nobody cried – could you help me into an orphanage?

Still no beds? An old grannie
muttering to herself, her old fella
quietly passed away in a wheelchair
I know he wanted to lie down, I too
if just for a few moments

As if from another time corpse incinerators, within
easy reach, as I daydream wide-eyed
or close eyes on the nightshift
the entirety of a wall ablaze, mobile sickbeds
also glow, and I become an undertaker
set aside my stethoscope and pick up a shovel to clear remains
I shovel out hundreds of smartphones
like the Nazis emptied the gas chambers of
the glasses, crowns, and other metal objects of Jews

After this, my aides
one drops straight to the ground, one's forever
quarantined, the patient most likely to survive
suddenly rips off his mask, spitting like a machine-gun
This great poet bellows:
My sole weapon is spit
My faith is crawling with flies

I'm rushed into the hospital's police control
Trussed up, mouth sealed by transparent superglue
Somebody asks about food, somebody responds
He can't carry it over tonight, so
no need to eat

5. Returning home

I should rest, a Party leader says
take a break, I've not been home for half a month
the virus long ago changed from an anonymous genetic freak
into a notorious inflammatory goblin
This empire
first sealed the mouths of eight rumor-mongers, then stopped
the mouths of billions of rumor-spreaders, but the mouth of
the virus cannot be sealed. The freedom of speech
of this empire's virus is greater than that of humanity
When the virus rises in opposition
it escapes prison. So cowardly mankind

seals off city after city, and encircles and intercepts
those fleeing the cities

Exhausted, I only think of home, only
think of a return to past ways of life. Hot noodles, warm
    blankets
chatting over wine, aimlessly rambling
not giving a damn about national affairs
so far away, today visiting relatives is
more distant than a trip to the moon, and home is more
a prison than prison
The neighborhood's locked down, apartment buildings
locked too, each home locked from the outside
all keys controlled by the dear Party
My wife uses a spare key to open the door, a neighbor
immediately reports it, and the front door is kicked in
cops stand in the living room, reading aloud from the *Book of*
    Rebuke
We hope you reflect on this well
if you don't mend your ways
you must be punished by law

Understood?
Understood – my wife replies
The infected and dying Li Wenliang also answers this way. If
you answer no, your death will be unexplained
But everybody knows, in a normal society
there cannot be just the one voice

A reunion as the epidemic spreads, a masked
husband and wife under escort of masked police
nodding, entering, locking the door
sealed off by tape once more. God damn
much better treatment than a prisoner on death row
I wash and disinfect, flop on the bed, sleep like a pig
two days and nights, then eat and make love
Scientific researchers all know, even

laboratory mice
make love and eat

Then prowling, from bedroom to kitchen
through the living room, reading books, on the Internet
playing at puzzles with my four-year-old daughter
pondering predecessors aimlessly living out life
in Chinese history books, King Wen of Zhou shut up in a
    cellar
deducing *The Book of Changes*
Hu Feng composing a three-hundred-thousand-word letter to
    Mao Zedong
then being reeducated through labor for over twenty years
Should I also write . . . but, too late
The front door's kicked in again
The cop who'd rebuked me stands in the center, declaring this
    building
has several confirmed cases of the virus, all residents
must immediately isolate

I yell: I've no fever!
But a few are no match for the many. My terrified daughter
like a chick carried off by an eagle
The homebody wife the most stubborn
dives into the kitchen, refusing to leave
Strong men smash the glass door
and wrest away a kitchen knife, as if faced
by a bitch howling at the moon and stars
She screams: I have the right to die in my home!
Closely followed by her lower torso being stripped naked
her pajama pants torn off

Good God!
What a way of doing things
They don't let her cover up, carry her
downstairs bare-bottomed
into a car, jab at her with

electric truncheons, till she faints away
her husband and daughter watching all

6. Isolation

An infestation of corpses, crematoria
all declaring emergencies, so outside crematoria
all offer help to Wuhan, and before they leave, fists clenched
solemnly swearing to the five-star red flag:
To realize communism, burn fast burn many
Burn at the greatest capacity, decades as if a day
Burn hundreds as if just one

This is an invisible war
Armies of the virus topple mountains and overturn seas,
    ceaselessly bursting
spurting, blossoming, charging out at the world
but I move in the other direction
a bat-shaped wind howling
like an unrestrained drunk, stumbling about
Daughter and wife instantly become a memory; I hear they're
in a concentration camp called an "Ark"
no, it's called a "pop-up hospital"
very nearly like the big boat
for the flood in Genesis

But the place I'm going has no name
no trees
no ominous black birds either. There's only
bulletproof glass and brick walls. After
disinfection, I'm naked
like a fish with scales scraped off
sinking into some fish tank
I shout till I'm hoarse
but can't hear my own voice. This is
a nightmare I can't wake from, a doctor before the gate of hell
saving patients, if not very careful

a quilt becomes a body bag
there're three children in one bag
there's an asthmatic woman
pulling off surgical masks, a nurse rushing up, carrying a fire
    extinguisher
she keeps backing away, yelling she's suffocating
then crashes to the ground
truly breathes her last

Losing sleep in a dream
uglier laughing than crying
Do you have a fever? Is your breathing
difficult? No, no, I gasp in reply
Suddenly I can't help but say: Intubate! IV!
Put on an oxygen mask!

A hearse drives through my mind, my soul
clinging to the steering wheel. My soul
runs up for takeoff, like a tightly wound tin frog
The on-duty Party leader arrives, looking distraught
The emperor of today has also come, and I say
I don't want to die here

Where do you want to die
At home
You have no home
So die in the city
This city isn't yours, this fatherland
Also not yours
Whose
The people's
I'm not of the people
If you don't have the virus, you're people
If you've got it, you're not. You know
Chernobyl? You can only die here
Like those poor irradiated devils, the dead may only
Lie inside a lead sarcophagus

My hair stands on end
I leap into the air, like a mechanical spring
The Party leader's chin is hit hard
Alarms go off everywhere, nurses and patients
scream in fear, hurriedly hold me down
inject a double dose of sedative
When I come to again
it's already two days later, in a body bag
like a hard stick of kindling
tossed onto a mountainous pile of firewood

7. The getaway

This is the cruelest season, pregnant with lilacs* . . .
A master of cremation who writes poetry imitating Eliot's
lament in "The Waste Land":
This is the cruelest pathway to heaven
No gatekeeper needed
as the dead cannot run . . .

Before the sound of the words cease, I
sit up from the body bag. The guy
turns pale, calling out he's seen a ghost
in the flickering light of the furnace mouth I answer:
Yes, you've seen a ghost
Then turn and leave

The roads into and out of the city
all blocked off, winding trenches
filled with water, like moats between nations
the sight filling one with fear. I turn around to the south
but a wall is laid across the road
stretching off endlessly, dividing the three
towns of Wuhan into East and West Berlin
Is this the Cold War? Is West Wuhan more democratic
and free than East Wuhan? Are there no Stasi?
Or is novel coronavirus and reported pneumonia

less or spreading more slowly?
I follow along the wall thinking
like a dog of philosophy chasing its own tail
At the moment it stops
two Liberation Army soldiers rush at me
demanding of me a "nighttime password"

I raise both hands: Come on
The people are angry and no longer afraid

I pry off my mask and spit
This is the sole weapon of the people

Like gazelles they dodge away, and like a gazelle
I leap onto the roof of their car, then over the wall
Behind me the sounds of gunshots and sirens – but what else
    could I do
This night everywhere there is quasi
homelessness, people with nowhere to go
diagnosed patients, hearses
ambulances and police cars
shuttling back and forth amidst them all

A little girl chasing a hearse
her mama taken away, yesterday
her papa and grandpa taken too
voice hoarse, she takes a tumble
the hearse is far away, gone, she still chasing it
still yelling: Don't you want me, Mama . . .

On an overpass, I run into
two ghosts thin as skeletons
one's fled the isolation zone, one from his home
they've wandered half the night, hungry and cold
and implore me to film their last wills, put them on the Internet
then they jump over the railing
I use their phones

to inform the police, think about whether
I want to jump too

Almost daybreak, snow falls
The freeway is also closed. A cargo truck
drives back and forth six days, finding no exit
and on the seventh day, God's day of rest
the driver abandons the truck and flees, to the sound of
police yelling:
Stop!
Password!

I see in the distance
he jumps from another overpass
and again I think
about jumping myself

– I'm a sick man of Wuhan
but they call me the Wuhan virus
I'm on the run in my own land
and my profession is doctor –

This is an epitaph I've written beforehand
Even though I know
In this historically unprecedented epidemic
Nobody can leave an epitaph
For those Chinese people buried alive in this empire of lies

February 18, 2020

Addenda

1. Excerpts from a post by Wu Xiaohua, PhD*

Author's note: *This article, one of the most widely circulated science papers on the Internet during the lockdown of Wuhan, was signed with the name "Wu Xiaohua," but there was much speculation at the time over whether this was a real name or a pseudonym, and this remains unverified. The author personally believes that this is a form of smoke screen as self-protection. Assuming that the Chinese police have identified the author, Wu Xiaohua's fate has likely been that of being "mysteriously disappeared" similar to the fate of the fictional protagonist Ai Ding in this novel.*

From January 23, 2020, when the Chinese government dispatched a large number of field troops and police to impose a mandatory lockdown on Wuhan, a city of eight to nine million residents, the "source of the virus" has always been the most sensitive and confusing taboo topic, and this was the first article to break this taboo. It is primarily a response to Shi Zhengli, the head of the P4 research laboratory of the Wuhan Institute of Virology, Chinese Academy of Social Sciences, who had stated that the virus had originated from Wuhan residents' traditional bad habit of eating wild bats, a claim that violated scientific common sense.

It is therefore also possible to believe the name "Wu Xiaohua" may be the collective pseudonym of local scientists with a conscience in Wuhan.

It should be noted that during my doctoral studies and for a period of time thereafter, I was engaged in basic tasks in laboratories such as general drug experiments and vaccine development, and I am therefore familiar with the underlying biology and the work of biological laboratories. Based on this and a conscience rooted in basic research, I became very angry with the WeChat texts of Shi Zhengli.

Facing the infection of tens of thousands of people, the fragmentation of tens of thousands of families, and the lives of hundreds lost, if a researcher openly lies, I could let it go, but to say these people deserve their misfortune as punishment for their uncivilized habits, I have to ask: do you think all these people ate bats? Ridiculous! And furthermore I must also question the silence of you as a scientist, which seems to indicate you've lost the most fundamental aspect of a scientific researcher: seeking truth from facts – in addition to what society considers the "bottom line" for a science researcher: his or her humanity.

When you say this kind of thing, I truly gnash my teeth in anger. So, I will publicly expose your lies. . . .

How did the novel coronavirus jump from bat to human?

This is a model of the SARS virus [diagram not pictured here]. Do you see the beautiful purple mushrooms on its surface? Please take note, they are called spike glycol proteins, or S proteins for short. This protein is very important. It is the key. Whether a virus can be transmitted to people depends on it.

The S protein of a virus on a bat cannot be transmitted to people. If this were not so, one bat could kill hundreds of thousands of people, so the lie about eating bats is basically ridiculous. The so-called key opens this lock.

However, viruses have lived on the earth for over four hundred thousand years. In order to survive, they constantly search for hosts and mutations.

So, moving from bats to humans, the coronavirus must continuously obtain human protein information. If it were only eaten by humans, it would have to be eaten for at least ten thousand years before the "live" virus could obtain human protein information. Moreover, bats are not a human companion animal, so it would be difficult to obtain human protein information from blood and body fluids.

For example, cats also have an HIV virus, commonly known as FIV, but even though they are in close contact with people, FIV is not transmitted to people, as FIV cannot open the code of people.

So what conditions are needed to mutate the coronavirus carried by a bat into the 2019-nCoV coronavirus? There are two possibilities: (1) natural mutation; (2) a laboratory modifies the virus.

1. Natural mutation

Let's talk about natural mutation first. Initially, viruses with bats as hosts should find one or two intermediate hosts in nature, and through these one or two intermediate hosts, gradually find the genetic code of human mutation.

This situation is fundamentally impossible for the 2019-nCoV coronavirus, because if 2019-nCoV is discovered, the first to discover it is the intermediate host. For example, the SARS virus will first seek out the body of a civet, but 2019-nCoV is missing this intermediate host. This intermediate host was later traced directly to the bat by Academician Gao Fu [of the Chinese Academy of Sciences].

Academician Gao Fu is very aware of the lack of this link to 2019-nCoV, but he did not say it, or did not say it clearly enough. He could only say that aside from being a scientist, he also has official status as the Director of the Chinese Center for Disease Control, which makes him unable to speak on the subject.

Therefore, natural mutation may be basically eliminated.

2. Laboratory-modified virus

Next, why does Academician Gao Fu skip over the intermediate host, going directly to the source bat of 2019-nCoV? The only basis for this would be being in possession of a large database of bat viruses.

Here, I finally come to the researcher Shi Zhengli. Look at Shi Zhengli's research results and work over the years. In her database, there are no fewer than fifty kinds of coronaviruses, but there is no database for this bat coronavirus. Academician Gao Fu could not possibly have filtered out the bat as a host so quickly.

Therefore, the original virus of 2019-nCoV must be stored in Shi Zhengli's virus database.

Let's take another look at the small purple mushroom of the coronavirus. Is it difficult to replace it artificially? It's not difficult. If you cannot replace this, you're basically not a student of biology. It can be safely said that 80 percent of the postgraduate students in biology in China are able to do this, and you may randomly select any of the students at the Institute of Biology at Wuhan University to do so, as their advisors are very strong. And this is not to mention the Beijing University School of Life Sciences led by Dr. Rao Yi. Any graduate students studying biology there who are unable to do this won't get a diploma.

There is no need to talk about the process of the operation, as it's just a form of physical activity.

After replacing the small purple mushroom of the coronavirus, what should the laboratory do next? Of course, it's necessary to plant the virus in new hosts, and then record a series of biochemical indicators and the transmission routes to these virus hosts.

What are these hosts? They are laboratory animals, which are really very pitiable, no less so than patients diagnosed with Wuhan pneumonia, and we call these animals SPF [specific-pathogen-free] animals.

I have raised SPF animals. Alas, I feel truly ashamed and deeply regret what I've done as a member of the human race. Even if I were to become a vegetarian for the rest of my life, I won't be able to rid myself of this sense of guilt. What's more, whenever I think of those suffering this wretched disease living in a hot endemic area, I can't help thinking of those living creatures in cages who, like us, also have souls.

Anyway, a virus with modified S protein spreads between the hosts, and these hosts then become selectable SPF animals: mice, rats, and monkeys.

The common modes of virus transmission are: (1) droplet transmission, like the influenza virus; (2) blood transmission, like HIV; and (3) mother-to-child transmission, such as the hepatitis B virus.

So when scientists or laboratory assistants modify the virus, they will select a segment of the protein of the virus and of the host in determining the mode of transmission.

This is when the conscience and interests of scientists are tested. If the mother-to-child transmission method is chosen, even the fastest-breeding mice will have a twenty-two-day gestation cycle during which their pregnancy matures, and chickens will need twenty-one days to hatch. Choosing blood transmission is comparatively dangerous, as contamination is easily possible if not handled properly.

Therefore, in order to produce results as quickly as possible, the fastest transmission method is generally selected: respiratory transmission. The data released by the World Health Organization are as follows:

> 2019-nCoV invades the human body through the ACE2 protein receptors on the respiratory tract and lung cells. At the start, the patient usually has fever, fatigue, and a dry cough as the main indicators, but also nasal congestion, runny nose, etc.

So how did the virus accurately select this human disjunctor? This process is detailed in a 2015 paper published in the renowned *Nature Medicine* electronic journal.* Among the main authors is Shi Zhengli, Professor at the Wuhan Institute of Virology, Chinese Academy of Sciences, and the Institute of Virology, Wuhan University.

The paper states that through their research it was discovered that as long as the ACE2 receptor switch in the S protein of the bat is adjusted, the virus can be transmitted to humans immediately. By way of viral gene recombination technology, the S protein of bats and the SARS virus of mice were recombined. The resulting new virus can be combined with human ACE2, which can effectively infect human respiratory cells with great toxicity. They found that the new virus obviously damaged the lungs of the mice, and all vaccines were useless.

The experiment caused a lot of controversy in the American medical community at that time. Medical expert Declan Butler wrote in *Nature Medicine* that such an experiment is pointless and of high risk.* Due to a lack of technology, Shi Zhengli's team worked with a medical team from North Carolina. In 2014, when the US Centers for Disease Control realized that the virus might become a biochemical weapon, it immediately called a halt to such virus transformation programs and stopped grants for related research.

There is definitely much risk in carrying out this kind of research.

Well, the conflict between researcher Shi Zhengli and me is basically this: her laboratory possesses the original 2019-nCoV bat-hosted virus samples and a coronavirus database, and she has mastered a method to transform it into 2019-nCoV.

And that's all I have to say on this. As to the process itself, I haven't seen it and haven't analyzed it.

This new virus should have been permanently sealed or destroyed in a laboratory of the highest security level, but unfortunately it has escaped, causing tens of thousands of infections and hundreds of deaths. Even though we've observed and captured the chief culprit of this disaster, we have not yet eliminated it. To this end, countless doctors and rescue workers have gone to the frontlines to participate in the rescue effort, which is what researcher Shi Zhengli meant by "to assume responsibility for life."

Finally, there are two things I want to say:

(1) Even given the extraordinary nerve of Shi Zhengli, she still wouldn't have dared to let the virus loose on society. It would be a crime against humanity. Not only would she not dare to do so, but no other scientific worker would do this as it would go against what we have sworn to uphold: undertaking this profession for the health of humankind.

(2) This is not a Chinese conspiracy. This project was funded by the United States in 2014 and its suspension was at the behest of the United States. The most important factor is that there is no group or institution that can profit from this plague as it touches upon the entire human race.

2. On the highly influential "three musketeers of citizen-media" during the lockdown of Wuhan

Kcriss Li, Chen Qiushi, and Fang Bin are the three "citizen reporters" who spontaneously emerged from civil society in Wuhan in the first month or so after the city was sealed off. After they were banned on the social media tools WeChat and Weibo, they all crossed the Internet firewall and went on YouTube to engage in live broadcasts about the epidemic in Wuhan. They gained millions of viewers in the blink of an eye and were immediately named the "three musketeers of citizen-media."

The first local reporter was Fang Bin, fifty-seven years old, a clothing salesman, and a survivor of the Tiananmen massacre in 1989, who soon after returned to his hometown of Wuhan to continue participating in the underground democracy movement. Although he escaped imprisonment, State Security were well aware of his "criminal record." They also knew Fang Bin was usually noncommunicative, and only uttered a few reactionary complaints when he drank to drown his sorrows, and even then, he wouldn't speak clearly, so he seemed a small fish who didn't make any waves. Unexpectedly, however, on February 1, 2020, Fang Bin, who normally would introduce himself as "an ordinary person, a stupid person," suddenly rushed to Wuhan's No. 5 Hospital and caught everybody off-guard when he raised his mobile phone and began filming. The first scene was in a hospital corridor, where patients waiting for the test were lying down or staggering about. He cornered one man and asked, "Are there dead? Where are they?" Then Fang backed away and almost ran into a box-shaped body transporter, its front and back doors open. Fearlessly, he went over, gesticulating and filming, while sighing: "So many deaths . . . one, two, three . . . seven or eight body bags.

In less than five minutes, eight of them have been brought out? What did you say? More yesterday? Ah, so many people dying like this . . ."

Fang Bin is an ordinary citizen, the quality of his mobile phone was poor, and his technique was awkward, so the video uploaded to YouTube was jittery, blurry, and askew. Sometimes it was like he was holding a stick sideways, yet he still achieved a unique and thrilling "field situation" broadcast. As a result, this one video had hundreds of thousands of viewers and was broadcast on all overseas Chinese-language websites. And that very night, a group of extremely angry State Security agents came to pound on his door, which Fang Bin struggled to keep shut while repeatedly saying: "You came so quickly . . . I've not had a fever; I don't need to be isolated . . ." But in the end, the door was broken down and he was taken away.

Due to the uproar and indignation of online public opinion and to stabilize the situation in Wuhan, Fang Bin was released later that night by the authorities. Surprisingly, he was further encouraged by this, and, riding a broken bicycle, continued to bustle about collecting and publicizing "criminal evidence" the government had concealed about the epidemic. Finally, on February 7, he released a video in which he stated:

Dr. Li Wenliang died today, Chen Qiushi is missing, my WeChat has been blocked by them, they pried open my door, and now there are police everywhere outside. I think I can't hold them back anymore, maybe I won't be able to speak anymore, but they won't be able to move me. Instead they'll move every person who speaks the truth! Everyone must be clearheaded; we have no way out! Such tyranny cannot continue! From today, I will escalate the "National Self-Help and Mutual Aid Movement" that I've proposed in the past to a "National Resistance Movement." All the people resist the tyranny of the Communist Party! There's no difference between China's North and South, and it doesn't matter the class, everyone must unite to resist the tyranny of the Communist Party. We demand the publication of the truth about the epidemic and the return of the government to the people . . .

There are so many dead, almost countless, and all caused by their stupidity . . .

On February 9, Fang Bin was secretly arrested. Before this, however, the lawyer Chen Qiushi from the Northeast of China had traveled to Hong Kong to live-broadcast the "Anti-Removal to China" movement. Just as Wuhan was about to be sealed off, he arrived on the last train into Wuchang station. And it was in front of the station that he made the first epidemic video, stating: "As a journalist, if you don't dare rush to the front line at the first opportunity, what kind of reporter are you?" Then he proceeded to interview the family members of a newly declared deceased and also appeared in the scene with one of them. After this, he went to the line-up at a hospital and filmed desperate scenes of people waiting for treatment, one woman losing control of her emotions, screaming like a maniac; he also visited an exhibition center that had been transformed into an isolation encampment.

Chen Qiushi was obviously more professional than Fang Bin, and his thinking and manner of speech were clear and powerful. He said there were probably over a hundred official journalists living in government-designated hotels in Wuhan and waiting for the government to make arrangements before they could go to designated places to conduct pre-screened interviews. Chen, on the other hand, operated like a guerilla unit, but who knew how long that would last.

He also stated his protective equipment was adequate, and often took his own temperature to prevent the government from having an excuse to isolate him. He repeatedly stressed his patriotism and lack of animosity toward the Communist Party, saying he was only interested in talking about what he saw and heard.

Chen Qiushi had millions of viewers, his influence much greater than the openly anti-Communist Party Fang Bin, and many people within the Party system liked Chen for this reason. What his successor Kcriss admired most about him was that Chen never concealed his inner fears – on January 30 stating: "I'm scared. The virus is before me, and the law and administrative power of China are behind."

He also stated that the authorities sought out his parents and enquired about his residence. In order to evade sudden arrest, he changed places frequently.

On February 6, he abruptly ended a video with the message, "I am not even afraid of death. You think I'm afraid of your Communist Party??" After this video, Chen Qiushi went missing. His mother posted "missing person" notices. Eventually, Chen's friend, the mixed martial arts champion Xu Xiaodong. also posted and made it widely known that Chen was "under surveillance in an assigned residence."

3. The most significant political case since the reopening of Wuhan

On May 30 and June 7, 2020, the police in Chuxiong, Yunnan Province, arrested the post-85 generation poets Wang Zang and Wang Liqin, and later prosecuted them for "inciting subversion of state power." The police also arrested Wang Zang's brother and Wang Liqin's sister because they leaked the news that Wang Zang and his wife had been imprisoned. Today, the four young children of Wang Zang and his wife are under long-term house arrest in the care of their poor and ailing grandmother.

This is the most influential political case since Wuhan was reopened. The website of the National Endowment for Democracy reprinted an appeal on Wang Zang and Wang Liqin's behalf that I wrote in exile.* Human rights defenders have supported it. Four domestic lawyers stood up and volunteered to defend Wang Zang. The evidence against him was mainly poems published and circulated on the Internet when Wuhan was closed, including the following:

> I'd like to detain you a little longer
> that little longer gives rise to feelings of home
>
> – "Into Prison"

> As a homicidal maniac
> incessantly killing one self's

the best thing ever
thus dodging severe legal punishment
and the police baton
while still triumphantly
winning a new life

– "A Homicidal Maniac"

I hate the air
The air contains
blades I can't see
I loathe breathing
Each breath of each moment of each day
forever inhaling
invisible blades
carving out wounds
to the heart

– "A Loathing of Breathing"

The Spirits of the Boundless Departed Have Opened and Closed This Book

Thanks to the Friends Who Participated in Creating It

Kcriss

This is a novel based on real events and settings. First of all, I would like to thank Kcriss, a Chinese citizen journalist born in 1995, for inspiring me with his brave deeds. Following him, like a well-trained hunting dog, I started tracking my prey.

I recorded the pursuit of Kcriss across the empty city of Wuhan, and designed Zhuangzi Gui as a fictional character who features throughout the book. In some respects, I am also like Kcriss, trying to get close to the Wuhan P4 laboratory to explore past and present happenings there. I logged on to the official website of the Chinese Academy of Sciences' Wuhan Institute of Virology for several days in order to download relevant materials; I also browsed online platforms in China to extract the confrontations and controversies between Shi Zhengli, who is known as the "Bat Queen," and her colleagues – until, one day, a large number of the materials made public were deleted *en masse* by network administrators. Chinese officials, the WHO, and many virus experts in China and the West also agree that the new coronavirus was not leaked from the P4 laboratory. If anybody even raises this topic, it's considered to be "conspiracy theory" against China, forgetting that the CCP itself is a superpower of conspiracies, having deceived and hoodwinked the international community for more than half a century now.

I began writing this in anger, only gradually transitioning from the real character of Kcriss to the fictional character of Ai Ding. The observer and interlocutor between these two characters is Zhuangzi Gui, who lives far away in Berlin, a character who is also the protagonist in my novel *Love in the Time of Mao.*

Ai Ding

Ai Ding is a historian from Wuhan and a university exchange scholar between Germany and China. On the eve of the Chinese New Year in 2020, he returns home according to the old customs for the New Year, but he does not expect that the plane will be arriving in Beijing just as the novel coronavirus spreads through China and Wuhan has become a closed city. In desperation, he has no choice but to fly to Changsha, Hunan Province, but cannot escape the fate of isolation.

During the compulsory fourteen-day quarantine, Ai Ding frequently talks with his wife and daughter in their home in Wuhan, and also crosses the Internet firewall to communicate with Zhuangzi Gui in far-away Berlin. He, like some doctors, experts, and citizens in the closed city of Wuhan, begins to question the origins of the virus and is also concerned about the struggle in Hong Kong, the military's strategy of "unrestricted warfare," 5G, bats, and the possible leakage of the Wuhan virus, fearing something like the Chernobyl nuclear disaster. Finally, the quarantine period ends, and community epidemic prevention in Changsha approves Ai Ding's request to return home.

No one expects that returning to his home in Wuhan will now be a hundred times more difficult than going abroad. As the whole of China has entered an unprecedented coronavirus era, not only are individuals isolated from each other, but so also are villages, cities, and even sections of highway. Wherever one goes, body temperatures, IDs, and passes must be checked. Ai Ding experiences a series of absurd dramas, and finally arrives home more than two months later when Wuhan is reopened. However, shortly before his return, his wife becomes ill and dies, leaving behind his ten-year-old daughter. Father and daughter are reunited, sorrows and joys are mixed, they begin to enjoy their time together during the epidemic era, but unfortunately the good times do not last long. The National Security Bureau takes Ai Ding away just because of his online remarks . . .

Michael Martin Day

Michael Martin Day, the English-language translator of this book, was the first Westerner I'd met in my life. In the autumn of 1987, he came to me carrying a copy of the underground literary magazine *Bashu Modern Poetry Groups* that I'd edited, which had been given him by Liu Xiaobo. He took a long-distance train from Beijing and a boat upriver from Chongqing for a couple of days and nights before arriving in the hilltop city of Fuling on the Yangtze River. Two years later, when the Tiananmen Square massacre occurred, I recorded the long poem "Massacre." He became my co-conspirator due to his presence, translation, and dissemination of the poem in China, and was ultimately expelled from the country as a "cultural spy" by the Chinese government. Now, thirty-one years later, according to the newly promulgated "Hong Kong National Security Act," we have become "counter-revolutionary accomplices" who deserve to be arrested and taken back to be imprisoned in China from the United States and Germany.

Similar to our discussions on the eve of the Tiananmen Square massacre, we've communicated frequently and debated endlessly about the DNA of the new coronavirus and so on. We have also since been joined by Janice M. Englehart and David W. Novack, who have undertaken to serve as our first English translation readers and critics.

Janice M. Englehart and David W. Novack

Janice and David are the producer and director of a documentary that has been three years in the making and is now approaching completion. In the film, they unremittingly track over 150 human rights lawyers arrested since July 9, 2015 and their resisting family groups. The documentary also addresses the million Muslims held in concentration camps in Xinjiang, and the travails of the imprisoned Uyghur scholar Ilham Tohti and his family, as well as the Tiananmen Square massacre and my own story as an exiled poet. These three historical events intersect and evolve, and the film fully reveals the evil empire of the CCP and its beautiful enemies.

Not long ago, two of those arrested on July 9, the lawyer Wang Quanzhang and his wife, rights activist Li Wenzu, finally returned home and were reunited after five years of seemingly endless life-and-death struggle. At the time, I wrote:

> This is the most moving reunion
> since the Tiananmen massacre
> too poetic for
> any poem to adequately express
>
> All a poet's tricks, all love poems
> are lies
> Oaths of eternal love in the era of COVID-19
> all lies. So
> the love songs of political prisoners also?
> I can't but say most
> are the necessary lies of convicts
>
> Of course, praying to gods
> also a lie
> If you pray till you cry
> do you feel your self is saved?
> It can't actually be so

Janice is full of enthusiasm and has a rare charm. Her first letter was about my long poem "My Sole Weapon Is Spit" (published as an appendix here), which she personally recommended to *The New Yorker* and *The Atlantic Monthly*. It started like this:

Hey, Yiwu and Michael,

At the moment, I am isolating on my boat on the Washington Channel. I was possibly exposed to someone with the virus last Thursday. No test is available to this woman so we don't know. I wait – wondering if the virus will get me too. I feel pressure on my chest. Is that pneumonia finding a home in my lungs or is it the weight of my heart realizing that the China that locked Yiwu up [and] threw Michael out . . . is everywhere.

David's first letter on receiving the manuscript of *Wuhan* was as follows:

Good morning, Yiwu and Michael:

I am very interested, of course, and honored. I love that it references back to Mao and Tiananmen and Chernobyl. I think it needs to. I think it needs to reference back to other things too. . . . Pre-trial detention. Muslim labor camps. Hong Kong then and now. Rising numbers. Europe response. It unfolds. These are the facts that fuel a documentary filmmaker or anyone obsessed with truth. And what's [Ai Ding's] backstory? Why is he obsessed with truth?

But I do have some questions that relate to the documentary nature of the narrative. The novel needs to be protected from accusations that the novel is propaganda. In documentary film how do we do this? Like this . .

The evidence must be real even if we fictionalize the source of the evidence or the way in which the protagonist uncovers it. Opposing views should be represented (and refuted) along with the difficulties in fighting both global propaganda and Chinese soft power. If we are left unsure, then the book needs to be left unsure, but still the weight of the CCP and its web of influence will be clear. That would truly make it a documentary novel.

I believe that even if the answer is not "conclusive," the novel is immeasurably valuable this way and it will make it strong against accusations that the novel is pure propaganda. Of course if the uncovered legitimate evidence is clearly true, that is the climax of the story.

If this protagonist is uncovering evidence as a documentarian, as a journalist, and as a human, with evidence from experts and whistleblowers who exist in the real world (even if we must change their names), then my documentary ethics remain strong and I would very much like to participate in a documentary novel. I would also like to see about a version as a graphic novel.

Warmly,
David

Amy Daunis Bernstein

Later, David and Janice shared a lot of post-reading thoughts, which were very useful to Michael. Michael's about the same age as me, but he's like a child, and needed the encouragement of Janice and David, who have extraordinary energy. Later, Mr. Ross Perlin drafted the publication report. And Amy Daunis Bernstein, a global agent, undertook the editing of the book, to which Michael responded immediately, prompting a new round of discussion.

I would like to express my sincerest gratitude to Michael, Janice, David, Ross, and my unfailing global manager Amy Daunis Bernstein!

Peter Hans Hoffmann and Brigitte Höhenrieder

I finished this work in mid-June [2020], and the English translation was still in progress. I also sent the Chinese manuscript to the Director of the Chinese Department of Johannes Gutenberg-Universität Mainz (FTSK Germersheim), Professor Peter Hans Hoffmann, and Associate Professor Brigitte Höhenrieder. These two are the principal German translators of my works, including *Für ein Lied und Hundert Lieder* (*For a Song and a Hundred Songs*), *Fräulein Hallo und der Bauernkaiser* (*The Corpse Walker*), and *Gott Ist Rot* (*God Is Red*), which were widely praised and have received many honors, including the 2011 Geschwister-Scholl-Preis for *Für ein Lied und Hundert Lieder.* I was also awarded the Peace Prize of the German Book Trade in 2012. I had been nervous before getting their affirmation. Finally, after a month of reading and research, they submitted an outstanding publication report to Fischer Verlag in Frankfurt am Main. Their conclusion was as follows:

> Liao Yiwu's documentary novel provides an exciting, as always brilliantly written insight into life and the handling of the coronavirus in China, conveying much information and detail based on Chinese-language (often short-lived Internet) sources that are generally not accessible to German readers. The multi-perspectival interweaving of different topics makes the presentation lively and vivid. No conspiracy theories are pursued, but questions are asked and clues gathered where satisfactory answers have been lacking. A plea, as always with Liao Yiwu, for humanity and human rights.
>
> An important book for anyone who wants to get an idea of how China is currently acting – an inside perspective from the outside and an outside perspective from the inside.

I sincerely thank Peter and Brigitte! Without you and Fischer Verlag, I would not have such a wide readership among German-speakers! Today, I have married and now have a daughter, and live here in Berlin, which has become a second hometown for me, a descendant of the ancient state of Shu.

Taiwan Yunchen Culture and Liao Zhifeng

Finally, I would like to sincerely thank Liao Zhifeng, the Editor-in-Chief of Taiwan Yunchen Culture books. He has been the publisher of all my native language works since 2009. Many Chinese readers have taken the opportunity to buy these contraband items in Taiwan when there as tourists, taking them back to mainland China for "pirated printing," and thus allowing them to spread in my homeland by way of street stalls throughout the land. This time, due to the unique global circumstances created by the novel coronavirus pandemic, Liao Zhifeng has decided to publish my books *The Escapes of 18 Prisoners and 2 Hong Kongers* and *When the Wuhan Virus Comes* in May and September 2020.

What I find especially praiseworthy is that Liao Zhifeng found so much time in his busy schedule to carefully read and study this new work, suggesting three amendments that I accepted. Looking back at the publication of my first novel *The Reincarnation of Ants* two years ago, he also suggested amendments accepted by me with this same professional editor's demeanor. Not long after, that novel was rated one of the "Top Ten Novels in the Chinese-Language World" of 2018 by Hong Kong's *Asia Weekly*.

Liao Yiwu, August 1–6, 2020, Charlottenburg, Berlin

Notes

Page

viii: *"Who controls the past controls the future."* George Orwell, *Nineteen Eighty-Four*, Harmondsworth: Penguin, 1977: 199.

1: *Kcriss.* The English name used by Li Zehua on YouTube and other social media platforms.

7: *"Massacre."* This poem was also published in English with the alternate title "Slaughter."

15: *Fat Kim the Third.* Kim Jong Un of North Korea.

29: *"How do people get to this clandestine archipelago?"* Aleksandr I. Solzhenitsyn, *The Gulag Archipelago 1918–1956: An Experiment in Literary Investigation*, Vol. 1, trans. Thomas P. Whitney, New York: Harper Perennial, 2007: 3.

38: *Red Cliff.* Also known by its Chinese name, Chibi.

46: *Wu Xiaohua.* See Addenda (pp. 246–52) for excerpts from the article in question that circulated on the Chinese Internet for a time in 2020.

49: *"Ever since the Turkish [cavalry]."* Translated by Stephen Owen in *An Anthology of Chinese Literature: Beginnings to 1911*, New York: W.W. Norton & Co., 1996: 632–3.

56: *"This project helped China build."* https://m.yicai.com/news/10045 2355.html

57: *"China's demands had caused differences."* http://www.rfi.fr/

59: *"Searching and searching."* Translation by Owen in *An Anthology of Chinese Literature*: 581.

59: *Prisoner of Mao.* Originally published in French in 1973, and English in 1976. Republished in Chinese by Reality Publishing House in 1989.

265

59: *"On the afternoon of Friday."* Bao Ruo-wang (Jean Pasqualini) and Rudolph Chelminski, *Prisoner of Mao*, Harmondsworth: Penguin, 1976: 9.

60: *"[T]his ... is the simple and powerful gist."* Bao and Chelminski, *Prisoner of Mao*: 33–4.

61: *"During my fifteen months in the interrogation centre."* Bao and Chelminski, *Prisoner of Mao*: 46–7.

68: *Indian scholars withdrawing their Lancet paper.* See https://asia.nik kei.com/Spotlight/Caixin/Scientists-slam-Indian-study-that-fueled -coronavirus-rumors.

68: *"Wuhan Seafood Market May Not be Source of Novel Virus Spreading Globally."* https://www.sciencemag.org/news/2020/01/wuhan-sea food-market-may-not-be-source-novel-virus-spreading-globally.

69: *also published in the Lancet.* https://www.thelancet.com/journals /lancet/article/PIIS0140-6736(20)30183-5/fulltext.

72: *MapMi test.* A tool for mapping and analysis of micro-RNA sequences.

81: *Liang Shanbo and Zhu Yingtai.* A classical tragic love story known by the names of the two main characters, set during the Eastern Jin Dynasty, 317–420 CE.

84: *Zhuang Zhou.* He was an influential Chinese philosopher who lived around the fourth century BCE during the Warring States period. He is credited with writing a work known by his name, the *Zhuangzi*, which is one of the foundational texts of Daoism.

84: *Ruan Ji.* He was a musician and poet who lived in the late Eastern Han Dynasty and Three Kingdoms period (210–63 CE). He was one of the Seven Sages of the Bamboo Grove.

88: *a Parrot Cay of lush fragrant grass.* An allusion to the poem "The Yellow Crane Tower" by the Tang Dynasty poet Cui Hao (who lived around 704–54 CE). "Across the river in the sun are the trees of Hanyang in rows/ And scented grass on Parrot Island growing thick and lush./ But whereabout is my home village, in the evening light?/ Seeing the misty waves on the river I grow disconsolate." Translated by Peter Harris. The Yellow Crane Tower is probably the most famous landmark in Wuhan.

88: *the beautiful country.* In Chinese, the United States is called the "beautiful country."

91: *the nine orifices.* In traditional Chinese medicine, the nine orifices are the eyes, nostrils, ears, mouth, urethra, and anus.

115: *"Eastward goes the great river."* Translated by Owen in *An Anthology of Chinese Literature*: 579.

116: *"You will laugh at me."* Two lines from the second stanza of the same Su Dongpo poem (580).

116: *Bull.* Also known by its Chinese name Gongniu.

124: *"The number of hospital beds."* https://hk.aboluowang.com/2020/05 03/1445898.html.

131: *"You asked when I was coming back."* A poem by Li Shangyin (813– 58 CE) entitled "Written during the Rain One Night and Sent Back North." Translated by Owen in *An Anthology of Chinese Literature*: 515.

136: *The Emperor of Steamed Buns.* A satirical nickname for Xi Jinping, meaning he's useless for most things but good at eating steamed buns at least.

141: *"Italy has already been completely 'Hubei-ized.'"* Radio France Internationale, March 11, 2020.

143: *"We came to the conclusion."* Both quotes in this paragraph are from https://www.pourquoidocteur.fr/Articles/Question-d-actu/32184 -EXCLUSIF-Pour-Pr-Montagnier-SARS-CoV-2-serait-virus-manip ule-Chinois-l-ADN-de-VIH-podcast.

144: *"The goal of the study."* https://www.rfi.fr/cn/

145: *Voice of America report.* https://www.voachinese.com/a/china-coro navirus-bioweapon-20200221/5298587.html.

145: *"Scientists from multiple countries."* https://www.thelancet.com/jour nals/lancet/article/PIIS0140-6736(20)30418-9/fulltext.

146: *She told the BBC.* https://www.bbc.com/zhongwen/simp/science -52613218.

146: *"Amid Political Disputes."* https://www.bbc.com/zhongwen/simp /science-52613218.

147: *"despite the similarities."* https://www.bbc.com/zhongwen/simp/ science-52613218.

148: *"Although RaTG13 is the closest relative."* https://www.bbc.com/zhong wen/simp/science-52613218.

148: *"The coronavirus is clearly mutating."* https://www.bbc.com/zhongw en/simp/science-52613218.

148: *He told the BBC.* https://www.bbc.com/zhongwen/simp/science -52613218.

149: *Alexander Gorbalenya . . . told the BBC.* https://www.bbc.com/zhong wen/simp/science-52613218.

149: *"Everything has to be based."* https://www.bbc.com/zhongwen/simp/science-52613218.

152: *"The emergence of severe acute respiratory syndrome coronavirus."* https://www.nature.com/articles/nm.3985.

152: *"If the virus escaped."* https://www.nature.com/articles/nature.2015.18787. In response to research at https://www.nature.com/articles/nm.3985.

153: *"How did the viruses of these wild animals."* https://www.youtube.com/watch?v=q9CIKJdcUVk.

153: *"Our institute initially received."* https://www.yicai.com/news/100517870.html. The following quotations from Xiao Genfu are also from this source.

154: *"A SARS-Like Cluster."* https://www.nature.com/articles/nm.3985.

155: *"The Possible Origins of 2019-nCoV Coronavirus."* Now found here: https://chanworld.org/wp-content/uploads/wpforo/default_attachments/1581810860-447056518-Originsof2019-NCoV-XiaoB-Res.pdf.

156: *Le Monde of France.* https://www.lemonde.fr/international/article/2020/04/25/coronavirus-les-laboratoires-de-wuhan-epicentres-de-la-rumeur_6037719_3210.html.

157: *"a clause that calls on parties."* https://www.uscc.gov/sites/default/files/2020-02/U.S.-China%20Trade%20Deal%20Issue%20Brief.pdf (p. 1).

158: *Unrestricted Warfare.* In its English-language edition, published by Pan American Publishing Company in 2002, subtitled: *China's Master Plan to Destroy America.*

159: *In accepting Huawei and 5G.* In July 2020, the UK decided to decouple Huawei from its 5G network by the end of 2027.

163: *Li Hongzhang.* A Qing Dynasty politician, general, and diplomat (1823–1901) who specialized in dealing with Western nations.

172: *"Skynet is magnificent."* An allusion to Laozi's *Book of Changes* (*Tao-te Ching*), chapter 73: "The meshes of the net of Heaven are large; far apart, but letting nothing escape."

179: *Wu Xizu.* Also called Wu Yun (d. 484 BCE), a general and politician of the state of Wu during the Spring and Autumn Period of the Zhou Dynasty.

184: *Guan Gong.* A famous general (160–219 BCE) at the time of the

dissolution of the Han Dynasty, later raised to god-like status in popular folklore.

197: *"The mind of man is restless."* https://ctext.org/shang-shu/counsels
-of-the-great-yu. "Counsels of the Great Yu" is a chapter in the classic Confucian text *The Book of Documents.*

198: *"I have fought a good fight."* Both translated excerpts from the King
James Bible, 2 Timothy.

200: *"There are oral accounts."* https://twitter.com/peterinexile/status
/1110667701603717120.

203: *Science magazine.* https://science.sciencemag.org/content/310/57
48/676.abstract.

204: *Nature.* https://www.nature.com/articles/nature12711?fbclid=I
wAR1oxB4btiYVmSzncbfTPLtCEORxqfdJygsxayF7cklj3my1pUF
1vC-PUnU.

204: *PLos Pathogens.* https://journals.plos.org/plospathogens/article
?id=10.1371/journal.ppat.1006698.

204: *Nature News.* https://www.nature.com/articles/d41586-017-077
66-9.

206: *"You / Sometimes look at me."* Translation from *Renditions: A Chinese–
English Translation Magazine*, No. 19 & 20, Spring & Autumn 1983,
Chinese University of Hong Kong: 211.

212: *"able, understand."* A reference to Li Wenliang. It refers to being
"able" to "obey the police's advice and stop illegal activities at this
point" and "understand" that "continuing to carry out illegal activities will be punished by law."

219: *"[f]or me the most beautiful moment."* Oriana Fallaci, *Interview with
History*, trans. John Shepley, Boston: Houghton Mifflin, 1976: 13.

219: *"What's the use [of] suffering?"* Oriana Fallaci, *A Man*, trans. William
Weaver, London: Bodley Head, 1980: 23.

220: *"God is dead."* Friedrich Nietzsche, *The Gay Science*, trans. Walter
Kaufmann, New York: Vintage, 1974: section 125, 181.

222: *"She told the truth about Wuhan."* https://www.washingtonpost.com
/opinions/2021/11/07/zhang-zhan-prisoner-wuhan-china-covid
-origin/.

233: *Do Doctor Zhivago. Doctor Zhivago* is by Boris Pasternak, *The Gulag
Archipelago* is by Aleksandr Solzhenitsyn, *The Hunger Angel* is by
Herta Müller, and *For a Song and a Hundred Songs* and *Bullets and
Opium* are both by Liao Yiwu.

236: *but I refuse to join the Party on the firing-line.* A reference to Communist Party propaganda showing doctors in Wuhan joining the Communist Party in fits of enthusiasm.

243: *This is the cruelest season.* An allusion to the opening lines of T.S. Eliot's "The Waste Land": "April is the cruellest month, breeding / Lilacs out of the dead land."

246: *Excerpts from a post by Wu Xiaohua, PhD.* https://kantie.org/topics /huaren/2503527.

250: *a 2015 paper was published in the renowned Nature Medicine electronic journal.* https://www.nature.com/articles/nm.3985.

251: *Declan Butler wrote in Nature Medicine.* https://www.nature.com/ news/engineered-bat-virus-stirs-debate-over-risky-research-1.18787.

255: *The website of the National Endowment for Democracy reprinted an appeal.* https://www.demdigest.org/gigantic-empire-vs-tiny-poet -chinas-solzhenitsyn/.